The
Unbroken Harp

David Craig

Whittles Publishing

Published by
Whittles Publishing Limited,
Dunbeath Mains Cottages,
Dunbeath,
Caithness, KW6 6EY,
Scotland, UK
www.whittlespublishing.com

Typeset by
Samantha Barden

ISBN 1-904445-19-5

Printed and bound in Poland, EU

Bu shaillte an duais a thàrr iad
ás na mìltean bharaillean ud,
gaoth na mara geur air an craiceann,
is eallach a' bhochdainn 'nan ciste,
is mara b'e an gàire
shaoileadh tu gu robh an teud briste.

Salt the reward they won
from those thousands of barrels,
the sea-wind sharp on their skins,
and the burden of poverty in their kists,
and were it not for their laughter
you might think the harp-string was broken.

Derick Thomson,
'Clann-Nighean An Sgadain'
('The Herring Girls')

*For Anne the story-teller
with my love*

Chapter 1

After the burial of Allan her father next to Mairi her mother's grave in the loose sand-soil of the dunes, Flo Campbell fled across the island from her burnt-out home. When hunger overtook her she scooped raw meal into her mouth from her bag, and washed it down with burn-water when she choked on the sour, dusty grains. And when it ran out, what would she do?

One desperate night, when her stomach twisted on itself more than she could bear, she crept in among the cows and their calves in one of the new farms along the shore. Crazily she jumped about in the field, stoning them, battering at them with a stick. Her nose filled with the reek of new milk and leathery blood. When the folk rushed out to look after their bellowing, thudding beasts, she was round and in at the back door – snatching the mutton off the plates, and the carrots and potatoes – cramming her mouth as she ran frantically off into the moor between hillocks and lily-lochans – gasping as her throat burned.

Now she might live for another three days. 'Nothing left for me here. Nothing left ... nothing ...' These words writhed in her head, like a fish drowning in air, as she looked back along the coast towards home from the cave on the hill below the old eagle's nest laced with honeysuckle, and later while her finger-ends bled onto the limpets she scarted from the rocks, and then again when crouched on all fours staring down between her arms at the puddle of her vomit, fragments of raw potato coated with phlegm.

Should she have hung on at home after the evictions, after the battle, and built up the ruin with turfs and spars of driftwood? They would only have come wrecking again, that same brigade of bully-boys. Maybe she could have begged a hen-house, an old kiln even, from one of the few neighbours left. And held on till the last of the crofters were driven out. And then strayed south as others had done before, by the hundred, away down to the great harbour at Glaschu and across the ocean with the rest of the beaten ... Ach, it was unbelievable that there should be no life for her here. She looked inside, deep into the last of herself, as though down the shaft of a spent well. She could just make out

– yes – barely – distinctly – a little glistening light. *Not* spent. Her own innermost spirit. She would not curl up into her grave.

Stepping-stones appeared in front of her. Islands. She turned on her side to be sick again and saw them, blae reefs on the stretched white glitter of the Sound – Berneray, Ensay, Killigray, and on and on to the north, each dimmer than the last. She would beg a ride with the ferryman. He knew there was nothing left for them on this coast – nothing left … nothing …

In the morning she put her own island behind her. 'Some mad beggar was scaring the animals,' said the farm folk for days and years to come, 'milking them at dead of night – spiriting the food from the table – opening the kye's veins and supping the blood – rooting up young potatoes like hogs, like polecats.'

Ten miles across the water to the north, Flo Campbell stepped ashore at the harbour of the furthest island. In the port she loitered near a new-built pier to find out what she could. After an hour she had to beat off a drunken east-coast fisherman – suddenly he shoved his hand up between her thighs, she seized him by his yellow hair and he whipped his fingers back out as quick as a rat. His hair was caught behind his head in the stub of a pigtail, his skin looked greased, his eyes swam with drink, he oozed invitation. As he lurched away, she felt herself melting towards – towards something, then closing again like the two halves of a shellfish.

Her head and stomach reeled with emptiness. At the back door of the inn she got a quarter loaf and the information that they were taking on young women and a few men at a new 'mansion' not far away, between Cragorry and Gearraidh. She took the two silver coins out of the purse she wore night and day between the waistbands of her skirts and spent them at a little shop next to the bakehouse on an undyed grey skirt, a woollen jersey, and a pair of leather shoes without holes in them. Then she set off westward along the coastal track.

During the nine miles of the walk her felt herself turn into somebody else. An eyelid closed down over her brain, they would not be able to see into her any more. All they would see would be a crofter girl with a scrubbed brown face, fox-coloured hair nipped in close behind her head, and that look as though hunger and prayer had drawn her mouth down at the corners and made her expect nothing but the next day's troubles. 'Meek' – one of their words. She was one of the meek now, a fatty glaze had come over her, impenetrable, and less deep than her own skin.

Between the gullied heather moor on her right and the rim of haggard rock on the shore, the turf was bitten close already by the droves of the new big sheep from the mainland. Now it had been scarred by the runners of sledges and the wheels of carts, bringing blocks and rubble from the pale wound of a newly opened quarry. After two painful hours, as the unaccustomed shoes scraped her heels raw, she came upon piles of timber in great roped stacks, next to heaps of blue slates. It was like the bits of cities she had seen in pictures, Glaschu or Greenock, where some of her own people would be squatting by now, in cellars or driftwood shanties, waiting for a miracle or a passage to Australia.

In the sultry warmth men with buckets and hammers used her arrival as an excuse to straighten up and look down at her from ladders and scaffolding that clad a huge granite house. They eyed her, openly curious or with cheeky half-smiles. Meek, she told herself, be meek now, and she looked down at the ground and said nothing. By some instinct she made for the back door, not the front door which repulsed her entirely with its lintel carved in the likeness of a rope three inches thick and some sort of a badge above it – deer on their hindlegs holding up a shield. Clearly not a door for the meek. Maybe the smell of cooking had drawn her to the right place at the back, that fine reek of onions stewing and meat roasting. Her head swam, and as she steadied herself with her hand against the post of the open door, a woman in a striped skirt and a white bodice came along a dark passage floored with great square stones. At the sight of Flo she started, and said sharply, 'Nae beggars here.'

'I heard there was work –'

'Wark!' The woman laughed. 'Plenty o' that. Put on your shoon and cover your hair, and you can gang through to the Big Room – there's nobody else waiting – and you can tell your story to herself and Mistress Kilgour. Say naething unless they speak, mind, or they micht – they micht *send you to the Colonies!*' She laughed again and led the way down the passage into a kitchen as big as a church, past smaller rooms with shelves and no doors hung on their jambs yet, down various passageways where the new, unvarnished doors were closed.

Flo felt trapped in a dream, it urged her forward with a pressure like a sea-current, turning her will and her muscles into nothing. She walked and walked until the square stones turned into polished wood and the walls were covered with smooth yellow stuff like fine cloth. Pictures were hanging on them, each as big as four windows put together, of half-naked women filling jars with water beside a broken building, a man in a blue coat pulling on the reins of a rearing horse and waving a sword.

The woman left her there. A girl her own age was coming out through the double doors of reddish-brown wood as shiny-smooth as ice. In each of her cheeks a blot of bright-red blush flared. As she pulled the door shut, she took as much care in turning and releasing the handle as though there was a person dying inside there, or a corpse in its coffin. Flo wanted to speak. The girl hurried past her with her head down. Then the white china handle was cool in her hand as she stepped into the unknown.

Beneath the soles of her shoes the floor was as slippery as frosted rocks. In a bay of the room, against a flaring and flooding of gold light from a huge window with glass in it, two ladies were black shapes on the far side of a glossy brown table as long as a boat. Slowly she saw them better. One was long-faced, long-necked, with waterfalls of dark hair caught in loops and pinned into a velvet ribbon the same colour as her grey silk dress. The other was dumpy, her shoulders rounded under a check shawl, her hair a floury loaf beneath a crimped white cap, her bosom a lumpier loaf inside a whitish bodice like a cloth for making cheese. This one turned to the long one with a dipping motion of her head, then fixed her eyes on Flo again, little pale-blue eyes like very old buckies that had been grazed and bleached colourless by years and years in the sea.

'I am Lady Admair, who *may* employ you,' the long one said, in an English voice, with a strange effect of talking about herself as though she was somebody else. 'And this is Mrs Kilgour, who governs the staff on our behalf.'

The pause that followed seemed expectant. Flo could think of nothing, nothing at all. She smelled the salt of her own fresh sweat. She heard hammering from some other room, above her head.

'And who are you?'

They had spoken, so she could speak. 'Flora,' she said. 'Flora – Cameron. From Benbecula.' As she heard her own voice, giving out its white lies as though from a foot outside her skull, she felt suddenly comfortable inside this story she was weaving. So she was 'Cameron' now – she had sloughed off 'Campbell'. Why not? Her father had transformed himself in his time, shedding 'Cameron' to stay alive when the courts were after him. Round her the silence hummed.

'How many years of age?' The lady was questioning her.

'Twenty.' Would this do? What did they want?

'And your character? We must see your character.'

'The minister wrote it for me. Then – we lost everything. In a fire.'
This at least was true.

'And who, may one ask, was he – your minister?'

'Finlay Macrae.' A blunder. The name from her own parish had come too quickly on her tongue. The lady seemed not to have noticed.

'The Reverend Finlay Macrae – we have his sermons here – they are liberal, and clear. Very well. Now, what can you do?'

This was large. Where should she start? 'Och – I can milk. And churn the butter, and –'

The loaf woman was holding her finger up like a teacher. 'The dairymaids will see to that. It is inside that your work would be, Cameron – if we engaged you.'

Cameron. She was being called that. She had become that name, from her father's old other life before the Rising, in a desert of black moors, or maybe it had been a paradise of green oaks and pines, in that mainland country of his stories called 'Loch Aber'. 'Flora' had been pecked away by these ravens perched there against the light, turning their beaks to each other, turning them on her ... She must fix her mind – some word had just been spoken that had soothed her, soothed her hunger and her worries like dipping chapped feet into warmed water and woundwort. Inside – she was to work inside.

'I will do anything inside,' she said eagerly. Too eagerly. Not meekly enough.

'You will do what you are told to do.' The loaf woman was nodding vigorously, agreeing with herself. 'Which will comprise, under supervision of the butler, the washing, drying and arranging in their places in the cupboards the tableware, one hundred and twelve pieces –'

'One hundred and –'

'One hundred and twelve pieces of each kind, plates for soup, with side plates, and for the *entree*, for the roast, for puddings, and for dessert, with cups and saucers for tea and coffee both, and the smallest size of plate for *petits fours*; with glasses for red wine and for white, for drams of whisky and for brandy, champagne, and port, to be finished with freshly laundered cloths; and the silver for each course, soup spoons, and knives and forks for the *entree* and for the joint itself, spoons for puddings and knives for dessert and for the cheeses, spoons for tea and for coffee, to be kept distinct – the silverware to be washed daily and polished weekly with powder; and in addition all the cutlery for particular purposes, the ladles, the knives and forks to carve with and the steels, and the larger and smaller spoons for serving; along with the necessaries for the presentation of each meal, tureens, ashets, porringers, covered dishes and chafing dishes, egg-cups with their plates, butter dishes and butter knives, salvers, cruets, claret jugs and decanters, coasters, pots for the tea and the coffee, with their milk-jugs, cream-jugs, and sugar-bowls with tongs …'

Such was the music which for years to come would tinkle and rattle behind her life. She saw her lean brown fingers ingrained with black dirt in every line turn plump and supple as they plunged in and out of the suds. She saw her forearms round out, and her breast, and realised how famine and working like a beast on the Committee Road had nearly taken away her sex.

Chapter 2

They all of them ate together in the room next to the kitchen. The ceiling was so high that it looked like part of another world, wintry and dim. It was linked to the lower part where they lived by the ropes and wheels of the pulleys where they hung the dish-towels to dry off. When she shined the glassware with them, a ghostly smell of venison stew reached her nose, or baked salmon or soused herrings. On her worst days, if she was on her own for a rare moment, she bunched up a towel and buried her face in it, breathed through her nose as hard as she could, and sucked the tastes into her head, the toasted fats, the brown juices.

Three weeks after she started at the Castle, as the Ardmairs liked to call it, during the lull after lunch-hour, when Mrs Kilgour had gone upstairs for her 'forty winks' and most of the others were dangling about outside the back door, smoking their pipes or gossiping or jeering at the workmen, she stood still beside the long table and listened. Footsteps clopped off down the passage, echoing, growing less. Inside the range coals clicked down through the bars of the grate. She felt dizzy – she had been holding her breath.

She went through to the main store, light-footed as a cat, made for the bread-bins, lifted a lid, and took out a quarter loaf – listened – no more footsteps, just a drowsy silence all around, pressing through the rooms. She put the stoneware lid back on the bin, gasped at the clink it made – listened – still safe. In the big butter-tub balls of the fresh yellow fat were floating, criss-crossed with the patterns of the bats. She scooped out a handful, dropped them into a cabbage leaf from the scuttles, folded it, and tucked it into the breast of her black dress beside the bread. Then two cold sausages from the meat-safe. An orange from the fruit cupboard. Enough – any more and she would give herself away.

She ran from the room as fast as her bumping, jostling load would let her and stopped at the stair-foot, listening. A curlew from somewhere far outside. The back door thumped shut. She was upstairs in a second, at the end of Mrs Kilgour's landing. Up the final stairs and into the women's attic. Under her own iron bedstead at the far end, in her own little wooden kist – her one neuk of privacy – she stowed the food in a sleeve from her old woollen jersey and was back downstairs, yawning and rubbing her eyes in a show of awakening after a doze, just as the others came in to fill the big kettles and lift them onto the range.

By the end of the week she had made four caches and was starting to feel more secure. Whatever happened now she would never starve, not even if … not even … As she tried to see forwards, her thoughts dimmed and darkened, strings and wires were tightening in her head … One cache was under a floorboard that still smelt of fresh pine resin. Another in a cranny outside a fancy window like an arrow-slit which the workmen had left unglazed in their hurry to get finished before the Lord arrived. She would put the fourth into her kist with the other. She knelt down beside it. As soon as she opened it she knew her stupidity. A rancid reek arose, an evil taint from the sausage. Of course she should have stored bread only. How could she have been such a fool? As she agonised over her next move, the air in the room changed – had the light been dimmed, or the sounds been hushed? There were no sounds. Slowly she looked round. At the head of the stairway, where it came up through the floor, James Meikle the under-butler was standing, watching.

He had no business at this end of the attics. She hated his eyeing and staring from their first meeting, when he took her through the polishing of the cutlery. Hated his needless touching of her hands, her forearms. Get out – the words rose in her throat. Had he seen into the kist? He came forward several paces, snuffing, his face wrinkling like a dog's. When he saw the scraps of food, he laughed through his nose.

'Hungry, are we?' She knelt there, dumbstruck. 'Doesn't Mother Kilgour give you enough, then?' She let the lid of the kist drop and stared down at the scars on it, scraped across the grain. 'Maybe we had better fatten you up, like a Berneray calf.'

Her stubborn silence had brought an irk into his voice. She *must* not fire up at him. The kist grew dark with his shadow. She smelled his trousers, soup, tobacco smoke, urine. She felt his fingers on her shoulder before they touched it. 'Well, Cameron – I will not tell on you so long as …' His grip was sore, bruising. The strings in her head tightened into a pain. She fell sideways, pretending to faint. His breath came warm on the side of her face (tobacco, onions), then cooled again. Light footsteps. Through her lashes she saw the back of his black waistcoat as he went quickly to the stairwell and disappeared down it.

Chapter 3

For two days guests had been arriving. It was to be the first grand dinner of the season – a 'banquet', Mrs Kilgour had been calling it for weeks, with an expansive English emphasis on the 'ban-'. The last dozens of cut-glass goblets had been taken from their straw and washed and polished till they sparkled – no less and no more, in the girls' opinion, than they had done in the first place. James Meikle had broken open case after case of wine with brutal jerks of his jemmy and arrayed the green bottles, like foreign soldiers, in the stone alcoves of the cellar. Outside, behind the louvres of the game larder, the carcases of deer hung from hooks like felons, their heads sawn off, their bellies split from throat to crotch.

And now, with forty guests and eight family to be catered for, to be fed and waited upon, the table staff was laid low. Rachel from Cragorry and two of the Lowland women were running high temperatures and lay silently suffering in their beds beneath the slope of the roof. Mrs Kilgour was coldly furious at being surrounded by mutinous disease. She had lined up all the available womenfolk to select substitutes. As she passed up and down the line with James Meikle at her side, her head kept nodding sharply upwards, like a bird of prey shredding catch to feed her young. She fixed her freezing blue stare on each downcast face as though to draw out the secret weakness that would disqualify this one or that from being allowed within yards of 'the company'.

'Strachan!' she rapped out at last. 'You will do. Go to the laundry this minute and iron one best cap and one linen bodice.' Charlotte Strachan collapsed at one knee in a kind of curtsey and left the room, blushing fierily. Now the Kilgour was opposite Flo. On impulse she raised her chin and met the blue stare straight on. The housekeeper drew her head back like a tortoise, then leant it a little to one side as Meikle whispered something in her ear.

'Cameron – you will help Strachan with the vegetables. Dress yourself in best maids' linen and see me here at six on the clock precisely.'

Flo felt Mairi MacLeod twitch next to her and just caught her whisper: 'You lucky fox.'

Now she was standing with her back to the wall through which double doors opened into the servery. In front of her the ladies and gentlemen bent their heads to their soup spoons, raised them and turned to each other with a flirt of ringlets and a glisten of brilliantine. Their voices were merging already in a kind of rattling surf. The gleam from shoulders and heads, crystal and silverware, the laughs and murmurs, the light clinks and clashes from glassware and cutlery, were reaching her through a luminous haze that made her giddy, as though her feet and hands were linked to her brains by long and scarcely controllable elastic. Nevertheless she stepped forward smoothly when she had to, and reached between shoulders of flesh and cloth; removed the emptied plates – always from the diner's left side, never from the right – as though she had been doing it all her life; carried them through the doors with a thrust of her haunch against the mahogany, turning sideways like a dancer if Charlotte was coming past; brought through the steaming tureens of mashed parsnips and green peas and new potatoes oily with butter. She could have retched at the site of them, remembering the evil mush of their own potatoes years before. But the savoury peas! The parsnips, golden and tender! She could have buried her face in them and gorged on them like an animal.

So she stepped neatly down the rows of backs and shoulders, paused for a break in the conversation between the lady and gentleman, then insinuated the bowl between shoulder and shoulder, watching intently as hand after hand plied spoons and forks, filling the massive plates with their wine-coloured wreathing round the rim and in the centre the Ardmair crest, the two stags on their hindlegs, sinking beneath a brown pool of venison gravy, chestnut stuffing, and claret jelly which shone darkly red like congealing blood.

The men's heads were neatly cropped on the whole and smelt of tobacco or bay rum or the burnt-wool taint of singeing. The women's coiffures were elaborate, massed into coils or festooned in ringlets. Odours of violets and lavender and unnameable sickly flowers shimmered like an iridescent bloom on the gamey undercurrent of red meats and gravies. Saliva brimmed up her gums and she had to swallow and swallow again as she bent forward, proffered dishes, looked down the fleshy gullies of powdered breasts inside their nests of silk, heard starched fronts crackle as the men laughed or leaned attentively sideways in little shows of gallantry.

Words were reaching her now. The two men on either side of the nearest woman had given up the pretence of conversing with their partners to left and right and were aiming remarks at each other past a head of lavishly upswept auburn hair caught behind in a jewelled comb. She could catch whole sentences if she tuned her ears to those two voices only, one English and one Lowland, both of them gravelly and baritone.

'... damn good fellow with the glass,' the Englishman was saying. 'There we were, up to our b–, up to our middles in man-eating heather, tormented by those damn flies, and I had not killed a deer for a week. This MacArthur fellow, cool as you like, hands me the glass and says, "Therre's yourr head, sirr – brrow, bay, trray, and thrree on top. If ye get him, sirr, he will grrace yourr walls forrever."' His rolling of the r's had made him splutter and he turned to the auburn head to apologise, his shoulders heaving.

'MacArthur is all right,' said the Scotsman. 'An elder of the kirk, and he has sent two sons to the army. Local, you know. Ardmair did well to take him on.'

The Englishman seemed nonplussed. 'I should have thought they were all local. We use nothing else in Shropshire.'

'I am sure you do. You must remember there has been trouble out here. I believe several men from MacArthur's village were sent to prison for deforcing the Sheriff's officers when Ardmair removed some tenants and re-let his sheep-runs.'

'Scoundrels! They live like pigs in those hovels of theirs, they are as backward as Zulus and as lazy as Irishmen, and they think that the good Lord owes them a living!'

'The good Lord – or the landlord,' said the Scotsman, putting down his knife and fork together on his plate with the air of one who has made a decisive point.

The Englishman's shoulders were heaving again. As Flo came forward and slid her bowl between the broad black back and the auburn head, she suddenly imagined ramming it down onto the man's gleaming hair with its perfect white track of a parting – plastering that scalp with scalding vegetables – screwing the vessel onto it like a lid and making him roar for mercy ... He was dismissing her with a flick of his white hand covered with black hairs and a flash of gold cufflinks.

'Lady Rutland,' he was saying, 'I do apologise. I have broken my own rule – no politics in front of the ladies. Did you walk today?'

'Do you wish me to be raped?' The auburn lady's glassy voice carried clearly above the general surf, with a strange little giggle on the final word. For a moment the surf lulled. The Englishman reached for his wine and swirled it round the glass before draining it.

'I assure you, dear lady, that the island is quite quiet now. Ardmair told me so himself. And if there is mobbing again, or any more mutilation of stock, well then, the telegraph is to hand these days, and there are gunboats on the Clyde. Isn't that so, Ardmair?'

At the head of the table words came from behind Ardmair's covert of moustache. 'What is the question, Soames?'

'I thought you might join me, sir, in assuring Lady Rutland that Scotland is not the Punjab and our own savages are perfectly under control.'

General laughter. Flo found herself kneading her apron between clenched hands. She saw James Meikle's eyes on her and smoothed out the linen with sweating palms. Before the moustache could utter again, Lady Ardmair had interrupted in her breathy, swooping voice.

'Good and bad – there are good and bad in every country, and I must say – I must say that our own island folk are as industrious and God-fearing as any in the land.'

Her husband heard her out expressionlessly and with a nod to Mr Meikle Senior signalled that the table should be cleared for the puddings.

Chapter 4

One morning in late spring as Flo stood in the washhouse with a double handful of her own dirty smalls, the reek of yellow soap and boiling cotton from the bank of coppers rose through her like nausea. The ribbed graining of the wooden sinks, the grey film of steam blinding the view out into the kitchen gardens, the sopping flags of the floor – each piece of what surrounded her was horrible, ugly, no longer new and spacious – a prison now, and it would last forever.

Barely knowing what she was doing, she swung round and strode out of the sheds, out through the gate in the wall, out, out, out … The sunlight sang with bees and flies. The loch was a blue glow on her right, more light than water. A fragrance of bog myrtle reached her on the breath of the breeze. She knew of a good place in the burn. A black pool deepened, then brimmed out over boulders with flat tops, smooth but grainy. There she could wash her clothes through, then beat them on the rock till they smelt of nothing but fresh water.

First she must brave her way through the cleared village at Cragorry. Could she stand that? Here it was – the shells of houses with rounded corners, torn down to the last two courses of big stones. One place where they had failed to pull the cabers out of the roof in time and the wood had burnt after the thatch went up in sparks. Scorched bars still angling upwards with the brilliant sky between them, their charcoal polished by the wind to a glossy black. Would she find the embers of a loom in there if she sieved through the litter? Morsels of burnt yarn still sticking to the frame? Nothing. Birds would have been rummaging for nesting stuff, scoundrels or tinkers scrounging for an old pot. The place was as empty as though nobody had lived in it for a hundred years.

Did their home on the Island look like this by now?

She had taken her shoes off as soon as she left the castle grounds. Now her feet were pencilled over with the black charcoal. As soon as she reached the Allt Eaval she walked straight out into its flow, took the shock of its coldness, stepped out on the far side, flung her smalls on the turf, and began to steep them one by one in the pool.

No blood on her underwear yet. And it was time. Her months had not settled after the turmoil of the flight and the winter's starving. It would be all right. She bent and rinsed, bent and rinsed. The kitchen smells of fat and soap and broth were leaving her. It was all grass and peat here and at times she stopped to snuff it up into her head. A deep draught of the air spread out behind her eyes like a broad tide – the tide at home filling over the strand that nearly connected the shore and the little island. Her hands stopped moving as a verse came back to her. As the words rose, she sang them out –

'My love the lovely island
Where the corn was growing,
If I could get my wish
My life and death would be there …'

She hummed, losing phrases, keeping up the tune –

'… and the girls
With their high singing,
Going out with the kegs and the tethers …'

Was that the same song? She hummed – the happiness was fading – she must not lose it, must not lose the image of Morag, big tall Morag, her cheeks flushed up ready for a joke or a fight.

A rattle of hooves from downstream. A man in a tweed suit and cap was sitting in a trap with the reins of the horse in his hands. He had been there for a while, watching and – she was sure he had – he must have twitched the reins just now to make the horse stir, so that she would look up and … His face was expressionless – broad cheekbones under prominent eyes with clear whites, their centres like burnt holes, a bush of a moustache that blanked out mouth and upper lip and nostrils, cancelling all sign of feeling, of age even – was he forty or sixty? He was as strange as a Chinese warrior in a picture. Now his eyes flared slightly, as though with a pang of shame, or some other secret thought. One gloved hand lifted an inch, momentarily. Then he flicked the reins, rattled through the ford, and drove on towards the Castle.

He was the man in the picture on the drawing-room wall with the candelabra on either side of it – the Lord himself, unseen by her since the banquet. Or his father, the first of them, at the end of the room. Or the heir, whose picture had recently gone up between two of the windows on the seaward wall. Who could tell? They were all the same in different clothes. Pink silk coat with fancy lace at the throat. Black coat with a white stock at the neck. Olive-green tweeds and a cravat with a pearl pin. And above this finery the broad-boned face with the eyes like holes and the dark bristle of the impenetrable moustache.

Did they grow the hair on their faces to save themselves the trouble of smiling, or learning words like 'Hullo' or 'Good-morning'? It had never been like that before. On the Island, if someone looked through you, saying nothing, you knew they were blind drunk, or mad. You still said 'Hullo' to them. In the Castle there were walls of silence you could not pass through. They suddenly went up. One moment Mrs Kilgour would be forgetting herself and speaking to you with an awkward sort of decency – 'And is there any word of your father, Florence?' – the next moment she was blank as a piece of plaster and you knew that one of the gentry had appeared at the far end of the landing, or in a doorway, and a mere maid no longer existed.

She came to herself leaning on her hands with her forearms up to the elbows in water. The ends of her hair, which she could let down when she was not in the Castle, had wetted themselves. She shook them back, straightened up, and took the soaking clothes to the boulders.

The sun had dimmed behind a greyness in the west. An itching round her hairline told her the midges were coming out of the peat. Suddenly they were unbearable, like pepper on the skin. She beat the clothes on the rock, swung them round her head to rout the flies and then gave up and gathered herself for the walk back.

On the track ahead two men were silhouetted against the yellowing pallor of the sky. When she got near them, they were boys, grown boys, with shadows of moustache on their upper lips. There were always some of them about – waifs made homeless by the clearing of Cragorry or some other clachan, who had been herding on the hill when the 'Fire Brigade' came round burning and had stayed in the heather when their families went off, for fear of being made to sign on for the ships. Hungry wolves, with nothing to do but beg for broken meat or a few days' work beating grouse when the Lord's friends were out with their guns.

She walked towards them. They had stopped. One had his two front teeth sticking forward, keeping his lips apart. The other had no teeth, just brown stumps. They were barefoot. For some reason this made her stop and put her shoes on.

'Look at that!' said Teeth. 'Isn't she the grand one now?'

'Grand?' jeered Stumps. 'I thought she was only a Castle hoor!'

What to do? She would walk straight past them. If she said nothing she would be no better than a cold lady. When she was within a foot of them and could smell them, like a mixture of cheese and smoke, words came into her head.

'You look grand yourselves, lads. But are you fit for the hoors?'

How on earth had she thought of that? Teeth seemed frightened. Stumps was looking dangerous. In a moment she was past them, her wet bundle had jostled Teeth, knocking him against his friend. As she left herself in through the gate in the wall, she realised with shame that it felt safe, like home.

Chapter 5

In the sleepy, sunken hour between drying the luncheon dishes and arranging the bread and cakes for tea, Flo and Mairi MacLeod slipped out of the back door and walked off behind the rowan grove on a path to the shore where the Cragorry folk had used to come and gather limpets for bait – and, said Mairi, for their own food in the year the potatoes rotted. On a flat rock they paused to take off their shoes.

'Who needs shoes, on this good grass?'

'Kilgour needs them, to save her bunions.'

'Meikle needs them, to save his skin from getting pricked.'

'To save his prick from getting skint!'

Laughter seized them and shook them, they had to cup their hands over their mouths in case their giggles reached the Castle – servants were forbidden to go to the shore for one mile on either side of the river-mouth, just in case some desperate poacher among them might spear a salmon and smuggle it through to any of his family who were left alive between here and Glasgow.

So Mairi and Flo slunk along at a trot in the cover of little outcrops, and rowan and hazel clumps, until they could stand it no longer and rushed towards a stretch of turf above the high-tide mark. They flung themselves down and began to whoop and laugh and whoop again in an ecstasy of release from all the Meikles and Kilgours, all the tight buggers who dogged every move with their stony looks and their unending lists of faults and commandments.

Their thoughts were turning in the same directions, back to the Castle, over the water to the mainland or the Americas, back to the Castle.

'Do you not fancy Meikle the Prickle?' said Mairi, looking sideways at Flo and down again at the eyebrights in the grass beside her toes.

'He fancies me – ever since the day he caught me at my kist. He's never tried me – yet.'

'He fancies anything with breasts. But do you fancy him?'

'Och, he's too hairy. You can see the hairs in his nose.'

'They're all hairy, the brutes. And smelly – they smell like meat.'

Mairi was wrinkling her nose so that the tip-tilt of it rose up still further. Her cheeks were so rosy with blood, they looked as if they would run red if you passed a straw down them. Her eyebrows ended above her nose in little extra hairs like tufts on a caterpillar. She seemed to be ripening in the sun and Flo felt suddenly that there would be enough happiness in the world if this moment could be held, like this, laughing and sunning, joking and confiding, relishing each other's looks and voices as though they were on some other island, or a cloud.

'You aren't hairy,' she said, running her fingers down Mairi's white calf, letting them rest there. 'Look at mine – and my arms – like a fox.'

'That is not hair, it is down – and anyway, I like it,' said Mairi, stroking in her turn, and the two of them played a delicious game for a minute, running hands up each other's legs to the knee, behind the knee on the soft underside of the thigh where the skin was as silken as a horse's lips. Then they drew back and looked at each other solemnly, their eyes widened and darkened. They hugged each other almost violently, and as they stayed embraced, Mairi's ends of black hair against Flo's mouth, Flo heard her voice, whispering although nobody could possibly be listening: 'My mother said to – to do – to do nothing animal, was what she said. She said never ever to do anything like that unless your month had come, and then the man would dislike the mess, and leave you alone. She had eleven of us by then, I was the seventh, and she was as tired as the old cow.'

'I thought, because you are pretty, you would have been with plenty of men already.'

'Pretty? You are pretty, with your long hair and your brown, brown skin.'

'Like a tinker. I could go with tinkers – if I didn't have to have their babies. What are we going to do Mairi? I don't want to go back to breaking stones and eating seaweed, and I don't want a baby tearing me open every other year. What should we do?'

'Well,' said Mairi, pulling away and sitting straight up, 'we could take their money like auld Kilgour, and sit in comfort in our own wee room. Where is he, then – where is her Mister?'

'Maybe she poisoned him – slowly. She put powders in his broth, and he died in dreadful agonies, and nobody knew because they had no friends and they were both orphans, and she kept him under the stairs, in a massive pickle jar, like eggs in waterglass, and nobody suspected a thing, only her cat.'

'She is a witch. Maybe she keeps toads in her armpits, under that bodice of hers.'

They were laughing again, in spurts and peals, stopping for want of breath and looking at each other to stir up still more laughing, letting the thrill of it take them over like bubbles seething in their blood. Tears glistened and ran down Mairi's face. Flo reached out and wiped each wet cheek with the heels of her hands. She kissed her on the eyelids and the lips and felt the mouth cling to her own. Then she sat back and said, 'The auld witch will be rising now, and she will be peering through her seer's stone and seeing that we are here. We had better go back.'

They walked slowly hand in hand and were still side by side as they went through the lobby and past the door of the butlers' pantry. Pipe tobacco mixed with the smell of baking from the kitchen and soda from the laundry. They gasped simultaneously as fingers gripped their necks. It was agony, cutting into their breaths. They shook their heads like dogs, the gripping tightened cruelly, and Young Meikle's voice was saying, 'Aren't you the lovely pair? Well that's all right, I can manage both of you – I can manage you fine.'

Mairi twisted violently free, lunged round, and faced the man between the dark-brown walls of the lobby. She raised her hand in a fury. Meikle gripped her by the wrist and flung her against the wall like of sheaf of corn.

'If you fight me,' he said, and he was breathing heavily now, 'I'll break you like a horse. Because, you see, I know where your soft spots are, and you know I know. Isn't that right, Mairi? Flora, isn't that right?'

They said nothing. Mairi was leaning against the wall, sobbing with dry catches of her breath. Flo was staring at Meikle. She was seeing every pore of his sallow, healthy skin, every glossy hair of his moustache, which was a replica of Ardmair's. He returned her look with the open appraisal of a cattle dealer, settled his black jacket on his shoulders, and dusted down his lapels. With a final look at each one of them in turn he went back into the pantry.

Chapter 6

On a day of thickening bluish haze, when she had some time to herself and Mairi had set off early to walk the seven miles south to Bealista 'to see if her grandfather had come home from Aberdeenshire', Flo went walking up the burn above her favourite pool. The mountains were featureless in this light. Insects with trailing legs hung mid-air, like tiny hawks, then wavered off sideways above the fading russet of the heather. It must be good to have a grandfather, even if he spent most of his life working on mainland farms that might as well have been in Germany. She tried to imagine her mother's parents – names from stories told in the evenings fifteen years before or up at the shielings in the summer. Sorley, drowned with five others as they struggled back from Heisker against a nor'easterly. Kirsty, the merest ghost, endowed in her imagination with a white skin and eyes green as the marram, who had died four days after Flo's mother had been born. And as for her father's father and his wife, had they stayed in Loch Aber? Or had they been tortured to death when the soldiers went through the country after Culloden like wolves and pigs?

She knelt down on the turf bank above an upper pool and as she tried to see her own face distinctly in the trembling gaze of the water, tried to separate the human image from the greenish and brownish mottling of the stones on the bed of the burn, she saw that the tremor on the surface was wavering upwards from a long, slim, blackish shadow down there. A good-sized trout. Food-getting roused up inside her – make sure of it while you can. She eased back a little from the brink, stretched out on her stomach, and slid her fingers into the water inch by inch. The shadow did not move, except for a slight paddling of its tail. Working along its body from that end, she curled her fingers round beneath the belly, stirring them delicately in the water. The creature hung there, the olive sides below the black back had come into focus, she could even make out its rosy spots.

Still she tickled the water, switching her thoughts off, feeling nothing but her hand fingering down there in the cold. She plunged it down and round, gripping, scooping. As she rolled onto her side she flung the fish up and out. It arched itself among the bents. Its spasms were urging it towards the water. She seized it with both hands and hit its head on a stone, once, twice. It lay inert, sagging out of her grip. As she laid it on the grass, a boy came from behind a thicket of saughs. Stumps – his mouth was unmistakable.

'Who learned you to do that?'

'Anybody can do that.' Her whole instinct was to taunt him, to play the haughty adult.

'I could if I had to.' He could not keep his eyes off the fish. His mouth was open and his tongue came out between his rotten teeth and licked his lips.

'Where's your friend?' She was talking to gain time now. She could not forget the menace that had come reeking off them at that first meeting.

'Archie? Och, he's away on a ploy with some of the lads.' He was fidgeting, unable to look her in the eyes.

'And what ploys do the lads have?'

'It is not for the likes of you.'

At least she had forced him to refuse her. 'The likes of me? Who am I, then – a lady? Do you think I am rich?' A sulky silence. 'What is your name? Eh? What is your name?'

'Neil. What is yours?'

'I am Flora. Did you live here?' She nodded her head along the coast towards the burnt clachan.

'Oh aye, we all did. We are mostly at the Port now. They say there will be a ship in the new year. None of the lads will go.'

'The half of ours said that. But they went right enough, when the lord paid the passage money.' At once she regretted this confidence and wished herself back in the Castle, walled in by its routines, by the incessant work, wrapped round by the flow of meals and the clean sheet once a fortnight. That smell was coming off Neil again, cheesy and smoky. His skin had the look of a dirty nut, browned and patchy, and his arms through holes in his sleeves flared red with the bites of vermin.

He was looking at her now with a more open, less suspicious face. 'Why did you stay?'

Had she anything to gain by hiding, by always denying her own past and her own people? Towards the end of his life Allan her father had said he regretted just that. With her eyes not on the lad but on the tapering length and dulling skin of the trout, she said slowly, thinking intently as she brought out each phrase, 'If I went to America, or Australia, I might starve there. They say there is free land in Nova Scotia. It may be lies. Where are the people who were living there before? I liked our place – if only they had let us off some rent, or given us more time. And I *will* live there again, whoever has it now.'

He seemed to have stopped listening, to have thoughts only for the fish.

'Take it,' she said impulsively. 'If that is what you want.' Of course it was. She was trying to sting him now because he would be the eater of the beautiful flesh. She must be mad. Was she trying to buy his friendship?

'All right.' He had snatched up a reed already and was threading it through one gill and out at the mouth. He stood for a moment, looking at her breast and away again, working his toes into the grass until mud oozed up between them. 'Can you get out again?'

'Look at me.' She laughed. 'I am not a prisoner.'

'At night, though?'

'Tomorrow, when I have done the silver, I can.' The phrase meant nothing to him and she felt a fool, or a fraud, for dropping it in so easily.

'In the Prince's Cave, between here and the Port, a few of us –' He stopped, uncertain. What did he mean? Then a sense of the old togetherness, almost of family, rose up in her and drove her on past all perplexities.

'Can I bring a friend?' she asked him.

'Mairi MacLeod?' How had he guessed? 'I know Mairi. Aye, she is all right.'

He was off, running easily down the burnside. When he reached the track, she saw him crouch, look both ways quickly, then dart across and disappear among the wilderness of outcrops near the shore.

When she seized a private moment to tell Mairi that they were expected at the cave on the following night, she seemed to know everything already. They talked as they folded dried sheets into bundles and sprinkled them with water ready to be ironed. A row of irons stood heating on the range. Flo felt her hatred of them rise in her – their stony weight, their blackish, bruising surfaces – as though they were fettered to her arms with chains.

'Wee Neil – oh aye. It is big Neil you want to watch – he has a wicked eye. They have a ploy on, the bunch of them.'

'You never said.' With a douche she felt a stranger. Would she have to marry here to be accepted? Even that might make little difference. Allan had remained to one side of the life in the clachan even after twenty years and more on the Island.

Mairi was giving a little shrug and a pout. 'Och, they are only boys – though big Neil has plenty of manhood under his trousers.' She giggled, and Flo felt a stoun of jealousy. 'Mind you, the clearance made men of all of them – more men than their fathers.' Her forehead crumpled, as though she was going to cry. 'If they make up their minds to do anything at the cave, it will be the first time since the burnings.'

The night was moonless – damp and mild like a web pressed over nose and mouth. Between the burn and the cave they heard the smack of an otter's tail on the sea, and the urgent piping of an oyster-catcher. The repeated hushing of waves along the shingle was like the hiss of indrawn breaths. It was so gloomy that they only knew they were walking on deserted croftland when they felt under their feet the tender give of land that had once been tilled. Presently a low sound separated itself from the sea-noise, grumbling beneath it, and they knew there was a gathering in the cave. Flo smelt seal-oil. A yellowish shimmer was glowing from a cruisie hanging on the rock wall inside the opening in the cliff. She could make out Archie of the teeth, Neil of the stumps, two girls she had never seen before, and a tall lad who looked full into their faces as though reading their credentials. His own eyes glistened like wet rocks black with iodine, above cheeks sharply dented inwards.

'A strong contingent from the Castle,' he said, and nodded as though some prediction had been confirmed. 'So – did you bring the keys to the gun-room?'

'Only the head keeper has a key, besides Ardmair himself,' said Flo. She had deflated his joke but she could see he had taken in her information.

'That keeper is a tough swine. If he was a sergeant in the Army, he would do the flogging himself. We will get him yet. Now, what can you do?'

'What needs to be done?' said Flo. Mairi was already sitting comfortably on a reef and drawing arcs in the sand with her toe. This lad with the 'wicked eye' was talking like a factor, or an elder from the township planning the souming of sheep. Yet these were outcasts – the remnant of a people whose goods were gone, shipped off, their families scattered on foreign winds.

'Well, are we all agreed – we have to make this place ungovernable. I was hearing that in England, far down to the south and the east, they burned the big hay-stacks that they have, and they broke down toll-gates across the roads.'

'What happened then?'

'What happened?' Big Neil's face tensed in a mask of obstinacy. 'They lost their way, that is what happened. Lost their way because they lost their nerve. Maybe they were too near to London, with its garrisons and its parliaments. Now, up here…' He paused meaningly.

'Up here we can drive them out, island by island,' said wee Neil, his words spluttering between the gaps in his teeth.

'And how do we do that?' Clearly this was their catechism.

'We slit the hocks of their black cattle.' Archie opened the responses.

'And the throats of the great sheep.' Neil had bared his stumps in a weird smile and was sawing at his own neck with the side of his hand.

'Half cut through the timbers of the new bridges between the Port and the Castle, and when the gentlemen come riding across …'

Flo was listening bemused, half her mind reeling off into the blood-stained fantasy of it as though spirits were fuming through her brains, the other half coldly constructing the future with its failures and disasters. She set herself to spell these out.

'You must have thought – they will bring in constables to scour the countryside and who will they be hunting but the remains of those who suffered most at the burnings? And the families of the men who went to the gaol at Inverness?' The battle on the Island was flaring and stinging in her head now. She felt sick as she recalled the muscle-bound rage that had paralysed even the strongest of them between the first fight and the final one.

'I thought you might be a Jeremiah.' Big Neil seemed to relish her opposition.

'Jeremiah? I want to *see* what happens next.' Her look had locked onto his and she knew she was seeing a mirror image of her own intensity in the crazy zeal that was enlarging his eyes in their sockets.

'And what do you see?' he challenged her.

'I see –' she started, then felt ridiculous, as though she was being turned into a prophet. But she would tell them, she would stand her ground. 'I see the last of the houses being broken open, whatever we do. And the roofs thrown down and the looms burnt with the tweeds in them. And the lord's men carting our folk off to the prisons if they will not go to the ships. Och …' She felt her voice failing in her mouth, and behind that in her brain. 'They have powers unlimited' – only she knew she was echoing Allan her father now – 'and we must grapple with them and struggle it through to the end, and we must know that at the end we are just broken timbers on the beach.'

He was eyeing her with real hatred now. Abruptly he turned his shoulder against her and spoke to the others. 'So, we cannot count on her.'

'Count on me right enough' – she was speaking to his back – 'but count on nothing else.'

'We have done our counting' – even in his enmity he could not help following her language – 'and we make it that nineteen families between the Port and Bealista are ready to go into the hill when the law men come. Or the womenfolk are at least. No more fist-fighting, like mad folk from the little isles. Live on the moor – come out only at night – drive off the new flocks, to destruction in the sea, whatever we cannot eat – tear up the tracks, in the darkness, and in the morning they will not be able to drive a cart along them, or a sledge even.'

His voice hammered – was he using his force to teach them or to convince himself? One of the girls spoke up when he paused.

'My mother was going to come out, with the little ones. But now she has a pain in her side …' She was broad-faced, with large exposed eyes. In the glimmer from the lamp her cheeks and forehead had a sheen of yellowed white. Maybe she was ill too. And others hereabouts. Clachans full of ill folk trying to stand up to the gentry with their meals of beef and bacon and root-vegetables fresh brought by steamboat from the mainland … The other girl was speaking.

'Your mother has been ill before. And she will be worse off if she has to thole the ship to Greenock. Or to Quebec.' She laughed, one grating noise, as though struck afresh by the sheer impossibility of it all. She had the same colouring as her friend. Perhaps they were cousins. Or maybe everybody from the south end looked like that. They smelt the same – fire-smoke with a tang of some foreign wood, a lucky haul of jetsam, it might be, which they were using for their wee stills in the caves.

She was gauging them like a visitor – a visitor from another walk of life entirely. In the bleak realisation of this she put out her hand for Mairi's, under cover of the shadow, and Mairi responded warmly enough.

Big Neil had turned his back towards them. Either he did not see their intimacy or he disregarded it as a womanish whim. He seemed to be waiting for some words from them. When nothing came, he said in a remote voice, 'Of course this is a deathly secret between all here. A deathly secret.' He paused again. 'You will do what you like, because you came from somewhere else. And They' – emphasised as though it was a title – 'have given you work. But not in the gun-room.' He grinned without opening his lips. 'One thing – if you hear that They have sent any word to London, about coming troubles here, you had better tell us.' He made the request sound like a threat.

The darkness of the walk back to the Castle might have been a secret room in which they could be close enough to talk through this killing dilemma. They could not well hold back from the rising. They could not take part in it without dropping themselves into a miserable mire. If it succeeded – how could it? If it failed, and they had to watch the lasting ruining of the Bealista crofters from a distance, they would be seen as spies and Judases, by whoever was left living in these parts once the shepherds had been installed. And on and on – there was no end to the happenings that sprang into sight once your thoughts were in a fever.

'Mairi, *you* did not come from somewhere else. So what do you think they can do?'

'Who?'

'Big Neil and his friends, of course.'

'Och, I was thinking of something else.' Mairi's voice was careless, dying away.

'What were you thinking of, Mairi?' Flo was trying to be warm and companionable. She should not have asked.

'I was thinking of a boy – not long ago – he looked like that white-faced pair, but strong. The milk-white bull-calf of Bealista, they called him. We all would have liked to lie with him. And he had eyes only for me. I might find him yet, in Nova Scotia, if I …' She let her voice trail off into a sigh.

'In Nova Scotia?' Flo felt wounded to the marrow – the nearly physical pang amazed her. Of course Mairi might go oversea. If she did, what difference would it make? She was just a soft skin, and a healthy skin with blood in it, after the times when there had been nothing in her life but hunger-pains and eyes too stunned by worries to look out at you. Now she felt again the halves of herself closing tight shut. Best to be invisible. Someone in a boat out there on the loch would have no idea that there were two people alive in the black nothingness under the moor. They would be able to see the shapes of the mountains as a lack of stars in the lower sky. Between that and the twilit stretches of the sea there might as well be no life at all – no womenfolk bruising their feet against unseen boulders, no gutted carcases of houses, no ridges striping the slopes where potatoes had grown, and rotted. Between the yellow lights of the Port and the tall silhouette of the Castle with its fancy edges there was nothing but no-colour, no-noise, no-movement – the deep, sheltering nothingness where for the time being she felt most at home.

Chapter 7

Big black birds were flying north – north – their beaks were full of dangling strings, or wires. They had stolen them from harps. High in the sky they disappeared, they flew into nothingness, one after another … She woke up so suddenly, it was like being kicked in the temples. A stone hit the little useless window tucked below the eaves, which did not open, and let no air and precious little light into their attic. She half sat up and looked along the row of truckle beds. None of the girls was stirring. A light snore was coming from Mairi, in the bed next to hers. Flo rose to her feet in one quick movement, roused Mairi, and each of them put on two skirts above their shifts, a cotton blouse, and a shawl round head and shoulders. With their shoes in their hands they ran down all the stairs and out at the kitchen door, easing back the well-greased bolts without a sound.

In the lane between the house and the kitchen garden an astonishing number of the group were waiting. Their faces were as black as Africans, smeared with peat and soot. Big Neil was there and wee Neil, Rachel and Ailidh, and three others she had never seen before. Their eyes stared in the moonlight, white as peeled eggs. Perhaps to strangers they would be unrecognisable – like savages. Rachel was giving her something, like muck from the bog, so she took it and wiped it over her own face with both hands, smelling chimneys in it. How would she wash it off before morning? At a stooping trot they were leaving the Castle behind them, skirting the kitchen garden – it was still giving off the heat of the day – and picking their way down the river. Ahead the falls roared and the white water leaped out of deep shadow into moon-glare. Without it they could have seen nothing. Under it they were surely too exposed – naked – visible to any of the keepers lurking to catch what they called 'poachers' or to any servant coming back late from family or courtship.

They plunged on, half-falling, picking themselves up, urged as though by a strong wind following them. She felt excitement swell in her chest, in her throat. Her foot dived into a soft place, stopping her dead. Wee Neil cannoned into her, gasped as the wind blurted out of his lungs, then gripped her hands and hauled. Her foot came out with a loud suck, she smelt a gust of his sweat, then they were half staggering, half trotting after the others, making for the toothed skyline of the headland called Camus Airidh.

In the shadow of an outcrop they stopped in a huddle, breathing heavily. Archie and Ailidh seemed the most spent, they were stooping with their hands on their knees. Big Neil was looking from one to the other as though checking their fitness. When the tearing breaths and pounding pulses had calmed, he said, in an ordinary voice, 'Come and have a look.'

They crouched at the end of the crag and saw the bay in front of them, opening out into the breadth of the Minch. A long black creature lay athwart the dazzle of the moon's path over the wrinkled water. Between its foremast and its mainmast two blunt pieces stuck up, with a feather of smoke at one of them. Slowly it swung on its anchor – the tide was on the turn – and as its starboard was lit by the moon, they saw a row of holes between gunwale and water, like square eyes, each with the black pupil of a cannon.

'A monster,' said a voice – Archie's, by its hoarseness.

'A warship – they have brought a warship.'

'An ironclad. I have heard of them – they cannot be sunk and they are as fast as – as a shoal of mackerel.'

'Can they do this?' Rachel was saying in her fearful way.

'Och, they can do what they like.' Big Neil knew – he always knew. 'Ardmair has plenty of friends in London. He has a house there, not far from the Parliament, and they will all be coming to his banquets, and his secret councils.'

'I thought they would be sending the soldiers.'

'The ship will be full of soldiers, and sailors who are drilled as well as soldiers, with stones in their skulls instead of brains.'

'They must turn them into stones, then,' said Mairi sharply. 'There were five from Bealista went for soldiers, and they were not fools when they were at home.'

'They were fools to enlist,' said wee Neil, contemptuous and dogmatic.

Big Neil looked at him with a straight stare. 'I would have taken the shilling myself if I could have tricked them into thinking I had got rid of the tuberculosis.' He turned brusquely away and looked seaward at the black snake with eyes in its side. It was solid and it was spectral. It looked as though it had always been there and as though it would vanish if you blinked. Government had never looked so real, or so much of a bad dream.

Kilgour smelt of peppermints and broth, mutton with barley and shallots in it, and now that Flo knew her better her eyes smacked of the same thing, not blue at all, no freshness of the sea but the discoloured greenish-grey of stock made from the scrag-ends of sheep. And Margaret Coutts the second cook – who had been friendly that first day, when the Lady took her into service – she smelt of fresh bread, or sponge-cake, there was flour on the strong rounds of her forearms, butter in the rich, shining skin of her cheeks and neck. Young Meikle would stink forever now, after that fright in the attic, of tobacco-smoke and urine. And his father, Old James the butler, slouching out his time among the red wine and brandy in his pantry – he had been sent north, it was said, from the even smarter and bigger place where the Ardmairs also lorded it, far down into England – what was that foreign reek he had? The piss of animals, like his son, but something else as well – dusty spice – he had that in common with the Lord's father, on whom she had waited three times now. It was that snuff they took, stuffing their nostrils with the sooty grains from the wee silver boxes in their waistcoats …

And Mairi? Her smell was like the cool perfume in the heart of a rose. This was the lovely surface. Below that, inside that, must be the saltiness of her hidden self, like her own, like the juice from a scallop …

She was drowsing in the privacy of her attic, between tea-time and the dinner hour. No more knives to scour, or porcelain to dry till it gleamed. She let her thoughts slide down the slopes of the sunbeams through the westward-facing windows at her end. She might as well stay here for good – for good and ill – if they did not get sucked into the battle at Bealista. Would anywhere else be better? They said, Margaret said and the Lowland maids said, that there were comfier houses, in Dee-side inland from Aberdeen, in Ayrshire where grandees from Glasgow and Paisley had built their country villas – they gave you money there, and there were more lads from the farms to pick and choose from, if that was what you were after. But not a place, they said, could beat this for the food and the drink, the salmon fresh or kippered, and the venison, even if it was only the salted that they got below stairs most of the time. The Meikles between them had set up such a household economy, independent of cooks and employers (who were down south half the time in any case), that you could live on it all as happily as a pig in a field …

Pink, fat flakes of flesh from the middle of the fish – the colour of it suffused her sight, tinting the old gold of the sunbeams … She drowsed – it was in the roseate films of her eyelids. She smelt herself, that sea-smell of her sweat, her juice. Turning onto her back she reached her hand down her stomach and … That pressure in the room, which she had felt before – she rolled back onto her side and looked down the attic. James Meikle, between the lines of beds, half-smiling. He looked shorter. He was in his stocking-soles. He had been stalking her. Now he came onto her, spread-eagling her arms, kneeling on them near the armpit so that she yelped with pain as their sockets were strained downwards. He had locked his fingers into hers and as he saw her pain he crucified her still more widely and made her yelp again. He smiled broadly with his lips closed, then he pursed them and whistle out a long 'Sssssh' as though calming a startled beast.

'No noise, you wee darling. We wouldn't want them knowing down there. Just you and me, you darling. Eh? Eh?' He dug into her with a jerk of his knees on each 'Eh'. Her eyes turned hot and liquid, tears poured out of them. He seemed to like that and stared full into her, naked in his fascination. The catty smell from his crutch grew suddenly stronger. A creak of wood from the other end. Both turned their heads and a saw a face like a turnip-goblin resting on the floorboard where the staircase entered the attic. Nostrils like brown caves, a tonsure of white stubble, a yellow papery forehead wrinkled upwards in some sort of glee – Old Meikle, come to watch.

His son turned back to Flo, let loose one of her hands, tore open his flies, and pulled out his cock. Its gland pushed forward, a bulge of ham. He was shoving it at her mouth. She bit him, crunched her teeth on the thing, wrenched her head to one side as it lathered her pillow with a mixture of blood and spunk.

He howled, sheer pain at first, roughening into a growl of rage. He rolled off the bed and knelt on the floor, clutching himself, swabbing with a handkerchief, fastening his breeches, all the time growling the same repeated noise like a word from some savage language.

What would he do to her now? And the old man? Torture her together? They would not dare. She would scream. Why had they thought she would not scream as he raped her? Young Meikle's growls had turned into sobbing breaths. The three of them were locked in a hot, wordless, stinking space. It might have been a slaughterhouse after a kill.

'I – will – get – you,' he said at last. 'And – your – wee – black – bitch. I'll – get – her – first.' He was ludicrous as he knelt there, and horrifying, as though he had been sawn off at the knees. He was levering himself up by the side of her bed, forcing a look full into her eyes so deadly he must be trying to mesmerise her, put a curse on her. She lay paralysed. If he came at her again … His face was white and moist with pain.

'Come awa noo, Jamesie – come awa noo.' The old man's voice was pleading, almost cooing, and she retched at that. Lie still. Do nothing. Stay stealthy as though she was guddling for a trout. The goblin mask was lowering into the hole of the stairway. Young Meikle was straddling awkwardly down the room, keeping his clothes off his wound. Then his face was disappearing too, cursing her with a last vicious stare.

She should have told Mairi all about it – the attack, the old man's complicity, Meikle's threat. By the time she realised that, it was too late. It had happened on the Sabbath. Monday was his half-day off. (Of the others only Kilgour and the cooks, and of course Old Meikle, had this privilege.) It was his day for haggling business at the Port, and very likely more personal dealings with some of the herring-girls.

When Mairi wrinkled her nose and looked a question – about her sick look? or her stripped bed? – she only made a face and mouthed with her lips, 'My month has come.' They were topping and tailing fresh gooseberries at Margaret's table. She craved to be hugged, to cry herself out inside the cook's plump arms. Her own arms and hands felt stone-heavy. She could hardly lift her legs upstairs to bed that night and the air between her face and the slope of the roof pressed down unbearably, burying her alive. Next morning, feeling Mairi's gaze on her, she arranged a cotton cloth between her legs. Secrecy was poisoning her like an illness, as though the guilt was hers.

She must tell Mairi now – she was in danger too, she deserved to be warned. In the middle of Tuesday morning, as she watched desperately for an opportunity to speak to her privately, Young Meikle came down from the housekeeper's room, where he had been closeted since breakfast, and went past the three women at the table without a look or a word.

'Cameron!' Kilgour had appeared in the doorway, looking hot about the cheeks. 'Cameron? I have told you before. The larder work is none of your business. Come with me at once!'

Margaret was looking straight at Kilgour in her independent way, Mairi straight down at her bowl of plump green fruit. Meek, now, be meek – be 'properly ashamed'.

She followed the housekeeper's dumpy, swaddled form along corridors into the carpeted region, up one stair, and into Her Room. It was like stepping under-water. Much-used air closed round her, peppermints and lavender and ironed bed-clothes, with some under-smell of bodies, all fogged with the gassy stench of coals from the fire. On the mantelpiece a clock of shiny metal kept time under a bell of glass. At 11 o'clock on a bonny enough morning the place was in dusk, the sky and sea outside were hardly to be seen past screens and curtains and a buff blind drawn halfway down. The furniture gloomed like weedy reefs below the water. Two chests of drawers, two upright chairs. A kist like her own but polished with a padded top, all in a red-brown wood that reminded her of the one choice piece her father had ever made, a small book-case crafted in timber from a ship that had foundered out on Heisker. On the uppermost shelf of a cabinet made to display china an array of books stood guard: four Bibles, the newest looking bound in a limp black imitation leather; an Apocrypha; the fat block of Cruden's *Concordance* and book after book called *The Good House-Keeper and Gentlewoman's Companion,* all bound in a faded olive with gold lettering on the spine.

On a square of tartan carpet a bulging armchair squatted like a fat man who could not get up, muffled in a print cover whose frill reached the floor. Kilgour must sit there, on her throne, to pass judgement on real or imaginary sinners. She did not sit down now but stood beside it with one hand on its back, bolt upright as though she was trying to be two feet taller, while Flo stood in front of her with her hands linked and her eyes turned down.

'If it was just the *disobedience,*' she heard the Lowland voice saying with its sarcastic twang, 'the disobedience, *and* the disorder in *my* kitchen. If that had been *all,* then I *might* have been able to keep it from Her Ladyship.' Still Flo looked at the carpet. 'But no. *Oh* no.' The note was rising, the twang cutting ever more sharply. 'No, it has come to my ears that there has been *shame*lessness. Under this *roof.*'

She had to look up now. Kilgour's cheeks were burning hotter still, her eyes were sparkling and blinking.

'*Indecency,* if I may use the word.' Her voice was a squeak. 'So, Cameron – what have you to say for yourself?'

Indecency? What did the woman know? She must not stare back, or look ashamed. Or 'shameless'. She must look innocent – which she was.

'Mistress Kilgour,' she began. 'I am sure I have only done my work –'

'Your work is not in question. You are not to fence with me, Cameron. And how long before the work does suffer, when there is *behaviour* between the staff?'

What had the brute said? Nothing against himself. Against whom, then? Against women – against Mairi and herself. Her friend's face rose up in front of her, black-browed and lightly flushing, as though she had stepped into the space between Flo and her tormentor. She would not utter – Kilgour must speak it out. But silence was not meek. Silence was mutiny.

'Very well. You are defying me.' The woman seemed pleased, if anything. 'You are a bad girl. And MacLeod is worse, she is the elder and she is from these parts.' She shuddered slightly at the thought of the locals with their barbarous vices. 'The Reverend Macrae has vouched for you – we are told. Little can he have anticipated *abominations* – little can he have imagined that *females*' – she paused to draw breath – 'that *females* would use each other like those who dwelt in the cities of the plain.'

This was gibberish. Its point was clear though.

'Mairi MacLeod has been a true friend –'

'Friend! Friend!' The squeak was rising to a choked scream.

'But – I will – if you say nothing to the Lady – I will – have nothing to do with her again. She has done nothing. But – I *will* keep to myself. If the Lady is not told.'

Surely this was meek. The words were coming out through her mouth as though some wily being possessed her, an older, seasoned person who could bargain, and pretend, and think like them.

When she made herself look up, she saw that Kilgour was glittering with triumph.

'You admit the blame. So be it. What *I* will say to her Ladyship when she returns is up to *me*.' The smell of mints and body odour was suddenly stronger. 'I will make the case plain and she shall judge it. Go, Cameron. You will be needed downstairs. It is nearly noon.'

Chapter 8

Mairi had gone. And said nothing to Flo. She had gone, and nobody was speaking about her, as though she had never been. Her bed next to Flo's, so near that they had been able to feel each other's hands in the dark, was a bare truckle, stripped of its clothes. Only the faintest smell of the white soap she had liked to use still flavoured the air.

When Flo pulled open a drawer in the pantry to take out coffee spoons and cake-knives, the morning after the day of judgement with Kilgour, it was upside down – silverware showered out in shoals and she heard Meikle sniggering as she went down on her knees to retrieve them. She had barely finished when Kilgour came in, held one spoon two inches from Flo's nose, and said 'What is that?' in her most vengeful tone. Silently Flo washed and re-polished every piece.

That night her pillow had hen's dung on it. As she tried to sleep, she smelt rancid butter. When she reached down below and put her fingers cautiously into her kist, they sank into a slippery mess of old food. She herself had long since given up storing, and she had found a better place for the occasional irresistible pickings of smoked meat or biscuits, in the jam pantry behind two pitchers of rhubarb that nobody seemed to want.

One of her best shoes for waiting at table went missing from beneath her bed, and she used her worn moccasins instead, Kilgour took her aside at the end of the evening and hissed at her 'You are a *sight*, Cameron – disgracing me before the company. This will be counted against you when next the wage is paid.'

These were the plagues of the job. They stung and bruised her skin and left her heart intact. She could have opened herself to Margaret Coutts, who looked at her from time to time, her black eyes solemn with pity, then looked away as one or the other Meikle came spying around the door. No, there were no real allies here – just bad strangers and good strangers. Only Mairi had been anything more.

One afternoon, she set off, without permission, to walk the whole way down to Bealista. Surely Mairi would be there. And then? And then at least they could cuddle behind the dyke somewhere, and she could find out why her best friend had left without a word of goodbye. It might hurt to hear the reason. But she must know.

The whole place was in a lull. The word was that the Lord was staying in the south 'to conclude some business in the Parliament before the Recess' – Kilgour and the Meikles loved to mouth the gentry lingo as if they knew what it meant. At this time of year no shooters were in residence, and would not be till The Twelfth, when the grouse became permitted targets for their guns. Across the island an easterly was gusting, great flauchts of it that blew more violently day by day, polishing the sky and the grasses, flighting over from far places she knew only by name – Loch-Aber of Allan's people, Peter-Head where Mairi had spent a season at the herrings and there had been 'plenty of boys'.

She trudged for miles, feeling friendless, and free as a tinker. She was outside everything now, light as a skiff before the wind, light as the empty limpets they had set floating on the rock-pools to see which one would reach the far side first and win the race. That had been with her mother and father, and then with Roddy, Roddy MacPhail her lost sweetheart, with his thick eyebrows (like Mairi's) and his smell of fresh blood. If she had stayed on the Island after the Battle – if she had … surely he would never have slunk off with the others, after they came back from gaol in Inverness, down to the black moor on the east side, and rotted there, and let himself be shipped at last to Australia like cheap goods, like slaves. Yes, he might – it had always been his way to leave as abruptly as a gypsy, for Sgiach or the mainland, on some ploy or other. And how could she have waited through that bitter, soaking autumn – how could she have lived, without work or a family, a boat or a roof?

She had thought all this a thousand times, chewing and chewing at it to make it lose its poison and turn it into a tasteless cud. If the past was still a wound, then it had nearly stopped weeping now and a scab was starting to grow. She felt the ground near the shore turn soft under her feet – she had reached Kilbride without knowing it and the huge strand was curving off towards Scarabost where a steep brown headland hid Bealista. As she shed her shoes and set off barefoot down the last miles of machair, she felt almost happy.

What she had not been ready for was the eerie vacancy of the townland. Nobody was raking hay, or herding animals outside the ring-dyke. It was as though the women and children had deserted the place. The potato crop looked fair enough, its white and pink flowers ruffling in the wind – she had heard that after several dry summers the rot had gone but nobody dared to believe it till they lifted the first plants. No black cattle on the hill, nobody at the boats on the shore. A few people huddled on a rock down there – bait-gathering, perhaps. As she came down the last few yards of turf, where hens would usually have been scratching, she saw a man come stooping out of one of the first houses. He stood still when he saw her, then went back inside. No smoke coming from his roof. In the haven a few wee black boats were rocking at their floats and a three-master was being warped in on long hawsers passed through rings on the limbs of rock that enclosed the harbour. The men who were busying themselves looked to be sailors, not crofters.

One of the few kelp-mounds on the shore was smouldering, grey smoke oozing from the brown mass of weed, hovering about it, then fanning over the sea in furious tendrils. The woman working at it, raking round its edges, was familiar – plump and brisk. Mairi, unmistakable even with a plaid over her head. Flo walked down towards her between the dykes of the inbye and waved as she came nearer. Mairi stopped working, and looked, then went on raking. It was Mairi, surely? She gasped as the shingle hurt the arches of her feet and sat down on a rock to put on her shoes.

The woman – Mairi, right enough – spoke up and said in a flat, incurious voice, 'Why are you here?'

'Mairi? I said nothing to Kilgour – nothing at all – not a word.'

'There was nothing to say. Of course you said nothing. And of course I lost my place, and now I am back here with my own folk.'

The words shut her out utterly. She wanted to turn and run for miles, the whole way back to the Castle and its miserable security. She took the final steps towards her friend and put her hand on her arm.

'Mairi – don't be an enemy. *We* are not enemies. Are we?'

Suddenly Mairi was laughing, her voice husky with smoke from the kelp. But she took her arm away. 'Enemies? There are enough of those. Look at the place.' Together they stared round the huddles of thatched stonework, the maze of dykes, the whole honeycomb that should have been busy and peopled. 'Look there.' She was pointing out to sea, and now that Flo could see beyond the headland, past which the schooner had now been worked, she saw the black snake they had first set eyes on a week before, the ironclad, with its sails furled and its funnels smokeless, looking terribly ready.

'What is happening?'

'The sheriff came back with his papers – he has papers to clear every croft. We beat them back the first time – like your folk. Tomorrow, they say, or next week at the latest, they will be back, with the bully-boys no doubt, and the constables.'

'What will you do then?'

'The women and the men are together this time. Not like your place. You said only the women gathered the stones and flung them, till they were beat. Not here. Not if Big Neil's plan works out.' She giggled, and looked up below her eyebrows as though she was flirting. 'He is quite the man, and he has talked us all into a desperate state of war.'

'But where is everybody? Where is the stock?'

'You think the place is empty? They are busy inside, bundling every tool and every stick of furniture, ready to move. They are taking the looms apart. We have every kettle and basin filled with sea-water, to soak the thatch and prevent the torching. We have the beasts in caves, where the old stills were, with mangers of hay and as much eggs and meal and saltfish as we can store, in case they put us to a siege. And we have three guns.'

'Guns …' Flo felt the fire die out in herself. While Mairi was telling her about the plan, she had let herself be roused. Now that one word, 'guns', had broken over and drenched her like a wave. In a vision she saw the battlefield near Inverness – Culloden – as Allan had told it to her near the end of his life. The line of redcoats firing in one broad volley together. The crackle of it, like dry wood breaking into flame. The war-cries turning into screams. The deadly row kneeling down as one man, pouring in fresh powder and ball-shot, while the row behind presented their gun-muzzles. Flames stabbing from each one. The screams coming louder and louder from the clansmen. The front line of the redcoats rising again, firing again. The clans falling in bunches, as though the ground was collapsing under their feet.

'Guns, Mairi? What guns?'

'Father has a fowling-piece – he will load it up with nails and bits of iron from the smithy. And Ailidh Campbell – you saw her at the cave that night – her father has a musket he kept back when he left his regiment, and he has taken the weights from his loom and melted them and moulded some ball-shot. Wee Neil has the auld piece he uses to get swans and herons.' She giggled again. 'So we might kill a few. And Big Neil says, if they hang him, his lungs are ruined anyway, so what has he to lose?'

Flo was gasping. Her head felt darkened, blinded. They were blundering towards a massacre. A bubble of hysteria broke through her horror and she tried a silly joke 'But Mairi – your guns – they will never shoot that far.' She waved towards the ironclad.

'Of course they will not!' Then Mairi saw it and looked disgusted. 'Och, you are no help. The news you were to bring us from the Castle – what have you heard? What is Ardmair up to?'

Had she forgotten already? Forgotten the partitions between the servants and the masters, both solid and invisible? The crimson and tartan curtains sealing every access – the barricades of rank between the lords and ladies and the upper servants, between upper servants and skivvies – the different languages, even, in the best rooms and the kitchens. She had no more chance of eavesdropping on the Lord or getting a sight of his letters than she had of calling on the Queen at her court.

'It is no use, Mairi,' she said wretchedly. 'I might as well not be here – or there – or anywhere at all.'

She turned away, then listened, as she walked slowly off between the silent houses, for footsteps coming after her. Nothing. She would not look. As she plodded back northward, she saw that her way was converging with the little group from the shore. One of them, a woman, was sitting side-saddle on a dark-brown garron with a white forehead. The looped hair under the hat and veil was surely familiar – it was the Lady herself. No time to hide – why should she? She would not curtsey. As the Lady joined the path to Kilbride, the others, who looked like crofter women, muttered some kind of thanks, surly and close-faced, and turned back towards Bealista. Their creels were filled with lichens for dyeing tweed.

'Cameron. Have you left us? Or has Mrs Kilgour excused you?'

This sounded not unfriendly. Had the auld bitch said nothing about the trouble? Maybe it was true, that the middling people were the worst and the lords and ladies knew little about what was done in their name. She gathered her wits and contrived a lie.

'If there is nothing to do, no company in the house, I am sometimes free to go away for an hour.'

'I am free myself this afternoon, Cameron.' They were moving side by side now and Flo could feel the hearth-like warmth of the horse's body. 'Those people have interested me. They weave, of course. Do you weave?'

Allan had woven, after Mairi died. His loom had been crushed and burnt with a tweed still in it at the climax of the Battle. 'No, I cannot weave.'

'You must learn, then, Cameron. It is the future for you all. When the shepherds from Northumberland are put in here, if our tenants will not accept passage overseas then they must find another livelihood, and weaving, you know, will suit very well. Not for your own use – for the trade. Sheds can be erected – I shall not call them factories,' she laughed briefly at the absurdity of the notion, 'no, factories are large and expensive, and use *quantities* of people, who are hardly to be found in this – this' – she was gesturing towards they hazy blue bulks of the mountains to the east – 'in this rather *boreal* land. However, if you must live here then you must work here, and I do believe I can help. And now I shall turn off and pursue my enquiries a little nearer to the Port.'

Chapter 9

Four days later Flo began to piece together the clearance of Bealista from excited talks in the kitchens and the attic, especially the attic, from a few terse comments of Kilgour's and Meikle's, and from a copy of a southern newspaper which her only half-friend among the chambermaids found on a gentleman's bedroom floor amongst a litter of pillows, feather-quilts, a smoking-jacket, two stone hot-water bottles, a pipe (which had partly charred the paper), and a nightshirt (somewhat stained).

At sunrise on the Friday the wind had died and the sea horizon was shortened by curtains of mist. The schooner lay silently by the quay, its crew asleep below decks. The houses were as silent, still smokeless – a visitor would have thought that the fires had simply been smoored the night before and not yet kindled again. A few cows bellowed from somewhere along the hill, then abruptly stopped and were not heard again. The mountains looked colossal as they appeared like Titanic semblances through the mists, which were thickening further into a white fog.

Something throbbed out at sea – two things, in semi-unison, like pumps. On the schooner hatches lifted. Two white shapes glimmered over the water as the fog tore into clumps. They were icebergs – gliding icebergs – a pair of steam pinnaces from the ironclad, each holding forty ratings with staves gripped upright in their hands like pikes. An officer sat in the stern of each boat with a revolver in a holster at his belt and a whistle on a lanyard round his neck.

As the reefs at the harbour mouth turned into silhouettes with the thinning fog, their toothed outlines sprouted human figures: a short man with a hunch [Mairi's father, John MacLeod]; a tall haggard man [the father of Ailidh Campbell]; and a stripling with bad teeth [Neil MacAulay – Stumps], who seemed to be insanely active and reeled about like a spinning-top and skirled like a banshee. He then gave out an ululating cry by clapping his hand to his mouth.

People appeared in the doorways of most of the houses, even the most ruinous that could hardly be distinguished from the crags and screes. The schooner's deck was swarming with people, two in stovepipe hats, carrying document cases, most of them in rough wool trousers and long blue guernseys. A number of these looked unsteady and one of them missed his footing as he stepped over on the quay, fell into the water, and was not seen again.

The scene became silent. The pinnaces had shut down their engines and were coasting toward the harbour mouth, becoming so distinct that the crofters could see the shaven and bearded faces of the sailors and could have identified individuals. (The only person named so far was one of the hired men from the schooner – 'an animal, a terrible bastard of a man, a pig with the drink, who had knocked out his wife's eye one Hogmanay along at the Port'.)

Campbell, MacLeod and MacAulay stooped and picked up weapons from the rock – guns. Campbell shouted to the pinnaces in his own language and got no reply. Each of the three then presented his piece and fired, or attempted to. MacLeod's fowling-piece went off and fragments of metal reached the nearest pinnace, splintering part of its port gunwale and drawing blood from a rating's forehead. He slumped, and his stave fell into the water, whence it was retrieved by his nearest companion. Campbell's musket remained silent. MacAulay's antique gun exploded in his hands, the boy's face and chest appeared to turn into one mess of blood, and he fell back onto the reef.

MacLeod tried to re-load, two hired men reached him, one held him from behind, the other threw the gun into the sea and then proceeded to hit him repeatedly about the face and chest. Campbell made as if to swing his musket like a club, then collapsed, coughing helplessly, and was disarmed.

The houses had by now poured forth all their people – approximately forty in all, including children of not less than twelve years of age. Canvases pulled from the middens disclosed heaps of shingle-stones and nearly every person began to hurl them at the oncoming schoonermen – soon joined by the ratings – accompanied by such cries as 'Up the MacDonald!', 'God shall judge you!', and 'The Devil will rain fire down on you for this!' Two hired men fell, bleeding, and one of them was sick. Others of them were carrying fire-pots into which they dipped tarry sticks and applied them to the thatch. It had been well soaked by now and not a single roof caught fire.

A small, active, black-browed woman [Mairi MacLeod] stood up in the middle of the 'street' and cried out apparently to the officers, 'Will you parley now? Or do you want a beating?' Beside her a tall young man [Big Neil MacLean] endeavoured to read from a paper. The only words heard distinctly were 'ancestral right' and 'not surrender our'.

Some of the throwers then stood still for a minute beside their heaps of primitive ammunition (now much depleted). The sailors and the schoonermen drove at them in two tight scrums. Stones rattled again on the staves, which hitherto had acted like a moving roof or fence and kept the fusillade relatively harmless. As soon as the warring parties were at arms' length, staves were swung, and cudgels in the hands of the schoonermen, and the crofters began to fall like corn under a thunder-plump.

One officer was struck by a stone, and reeled, recovered himself, and drew his pistol as though about to shoot. A woman's voice called out, 'Kill me! Kill me!' A pale girl [Rachel Campbell] was seen to run forward at the man, throwing down her shawl from her head and laying her bosom open by dishevelling her clothes. A club then hit her full on the breast-bone, her skin split, and blood poured forth before some women dragged her into the shelter of a doorway.

The foremost sailors seemed to falter now, then rallied and laid about them as before when the other officer waved his revolver and issued an unintelligible command. The small woman and the tall young man [Mairi and Big Neil] staggered as bodies bore them down. The man drew a gutting-knife from his boot, slashed at an assailant, then was hit by a blow that appeared to shatter his hand. Both disappeared beneath boots and flailing staves. Stone-throwers were fleeing inside houses, where they were followed by schoonermen. Screams were heard. Thatch burst and heaved outward as roof after roof was cast down into the ways between the houses until the whole ground was a litter of straw and bents and heather, and stones and broken sticks, and bleeding bodies, male, female and young.

The officers now blew their whistles. A stillness fell upon the place, broken by blood-curdling groans, and gasps and other noises from inside several of the poor ruins.

During the next hour writs of eviction were read aloud and served on the occupants of the roofless houses (in most cases for 'arrears in rent'). The people, most of them now standing or sitting still with stricken mien, were informed that a two-masted ship would shortly be lying at the Port for those who wished to remove. Nobody said a word, or moved a limb. Nor did they move when Big Neil, John MacLeod and

Sorley Campbell were escorted [dragged] to the shore in irons and sent off in a pinnace to the gunboat. Only, when the remains of Neil MacAulay were pronounced dead ('by his own hand') and covered with a canvas from the middens, his mother threw herself onto the ground, and seized up handfuls of grass, and thrust them into her wailing mouth.

Chapter 10

On the fifth anniversary of the Bealista Massacre Flo met the Lord face to face for the first time since that day at the burn years before when she had caught him looking at her and he had rode on past in silence.

Of course there was no such word as 'massacre' in the owner's talk, or such of it as filtered below stairs through the lips of Kilgour and the Meikles. It was known now as 'the re-arrangement of the southern tenancies'.

The anniversary, which was burnt indelibly into Flo as the battle on the Island or her mother's death-day, was also The Twelfth itself. The Castle had been filling up with guests from the Lowlands, England, Ireland even. Extra dozens of wine were taken from their straw jackets. In the gunroom the padlocks were removed from the racks and the rows of shotguns were freshly cleaned and oiled. Carts from the Port had arrived and the keepers' men were unloading boxes of cartridges by the hundred – enough, said the head keeper, to 're-arrange the southern tenancies ten times over'. Was he being ironical, Flo wondered, when Meikle retailed it as a fine joke at the servants' supper table? There was no telling whose side Hamish MacArthur was on. To look at he was the replica of a gentleman, with his suit of tweeds, his boots buffed and greased for the hill, and his moustache above all, that badge of the owners, dense as unburnt heather, bushing over the corners of his mouth, as warlike as the ivory spike through the nose of a Zulu.

This year there had been a great buzz the night before – 'the minister is coming'. A man of God at the Castle? To bless the slaughter and sit down to a good dinner afterwards? Margaret Coutts cackled at Flo's ignorance till she had to be slapped on the back by the tall thin girl from the Port (Mairi's replacement).

'It's nae a man o' the Kirk,' she said at last. 'It's ane o' the Government. He's the *Minister for War.*'

So wild birds were to be found, beaten out of their coverts, shot and sold and plucked and eaten. And any hares that broke cover (they never stooped to rabbits on The Twelfth, and certainly not in the presence of the Minister, whose game was generally larger). It was mankind against the animals on this festal day. The entire economy of the neighbourhood was enlisted, and might even have included crofters if there had been any left. As it was the shepherds' sons joined the ragged band of the beaters, and such half-grown family as the servants had accumulated by this stage in the Castle's history, supplemented by numerous odd-jobbers from the Port: displaced men who hung about the quays in the hope of a job with the ships; would-be emigrants who had missed out on the paid-passage scheme whereby the estate was trying to populate New South Wales; Crimean veterans short of an arm of an eye (and certainly short of a penny).

As they gathered on the slope of the moor behind the Castle, and shuffled themselves sideways into something like a line, MacArthur surveyed what he called 'my regiment' and roared out, 'By the left – *quick* – MARCH!' And with many a glad cry of 'Fuck off yourself' or 'Awa, ye sodger' the beaters strode off through the heather, lashing the vegetation with their cudgels and counting the hours till lunch.

The Lord and his friends had moved up to the butts an hour or so before, the men on foot, strenuously exhibiting their powers of conversing while walking steeply uphill, the ladies (mostly spectators but three or four would shoot) either walking or, if they were on the elderly side, on pony-back. The brown-and-white garron of Her Ladyship was not to be seen. It was one of several profound and growing differences with His Lordship that Her Ladyship was not fond of the shoot. (He was said to have suspected her of a compassionate or sentimental attitude to the crofters.)

Now the rugged emplacements of the butts were all manned, with a shooter, a keeper's man, and a pair of guns inside each one. The tweedy humps of deerstalkers were to be seen above the battlements of turf and the gleaming dark-grey barrels of shotguns angled this way and that as the shooters aimed at imaginary birds and eased themselves into the sporting role.

Culloden made down into a game, thought Flo, as she looked over the scene at lunchtime, then wondered if anyone else on the hill that day would be having so outlandish a vision, or think it anything but absurd if they read it in her mind. All morning the irregular crackle of the guns had been heard down at the Castle, as the staff worked without a break to fill hampers with pies and claret, hay-boxes for the soup, loaves and cold meats and jars of pickled eggs for the great feast as the middle point of the killing. As she trudged uphill in pale-gold filtered sunshine, she felt the fragile happiness that blew through her like an unreasonable wind when she did not expect it. A collie dog that had taken to hanging round the back door – the runt from the head shepherd's litter two years before, who had somehow escaped being drowned in the sack – was a few paces ahead of her. He seemed to like her smell and now trotted beside her everywhere out of doors on his stumpy legs. On the path he stopped suddenly – the black hairs stirred right down his back. He stepped off the path and walked round something before going on. A thick dark-olive body unfroze as Flo came nearer and twisted off into the heather stems and she knew by the black lightning-mark on its back that it was an adder.

'Good lad, Calum.' He looked briefly round at her before leading on up the zig-zags of the stalkers' path.

Snakes and deer, and goats and martens, and fish and frogs and hawks, curlews and woodcocks and the effortless broad-winged eagle itself – the mountain was alive and she was part of it. 'I to the hills will lift mine eyes' came into her mind – tracing it to its source she remembered with aching love how Allan and Mairi had used to speak bits of psalms (never hymns) that they had liked, although they would no more have entered a church than they would have set off swimming to America.

The gunfire had ceased, as the servants came too near for safety, and the beaters had flopped down where they were or edged a little closer to the gentry in the hope of a dram from one of the more generous flasks. The still air smelt of explosions, burnt chemicals, and in this atmosphere a clamour of conversation had broken out as though a door had been thrown open.

'I say, sir – did I see you bag a right and a left with your first gun?'

'Great birds – great birds! Congratulations to the Keeper.'

'Well done, MacArthur – here, fellows, pass that flask.'

'Quite superb. How good it is to be alive!'

On the trodden peaty ground beside the lowest butt the company was thickest, with a tall figure in its midst – a collar with round points and a cravat with a garnet pin just visible inside the lapels of a turquoise Norfolk jacket – moustachioes that did not bush and drop but curled out and up in a swarthy scroll before turning into Dundrearies and joining the wavy head of hair beneath the deerstalker angled rakishly above the eyebrows. Surely the Minister? Two well-built men like keepers, but not keepers, stood nearby, eating, not drinking. The Lord himself was standing close to the grandee, looking down at the litter of spent cartridge-cases in his abstracted way. Flo could hear the grandee's voice, a vibrant baritone used to being pitched: 'Excellent sport, Ardmair. Quite excellent. Rutland must look to his laurels. How *do* you do it?'

'Management, Collingwood. Investment in paths and ditches. Gaol the poachers, and keep the damn cattle where they belong.'

'The crofters, you mean?' The Minister looked round for an audience for this sally and was rewarded with unanimous smiles and little laughs.

'Oh, those. The best tenant is a shepherd – English, if possible.' This too was greeted with a murmur of laughter, although Ardmair had not invited it.

When Flo looked round at the huddles of camp-followers nearby, unable to believe that nobody would have reacted to this exchange, she saw James Meikle watching her intently as a pointer. Then her own dog got up from beside her and showed signs of edging nearer the heaps of slaughtered birds. She brought him to heel with one quick, barked word.

As she passed among the groups, helping Margaret and Ella the new girl to hand round plates and provisions, the mounds of grouse began to bulk larger and larger, oppressing her like asphyxia. She had to look at them. She hated to. Dark copper and soot-black plumage lay on the ground in great curving swathes, seeming to be solid feather until you saw the beaks with beads of blood congealing on them like strange fruits, eyes glassily open or closed by an ashen eyelid, claws clenched in a throe. A breeze stirred the feathers into a flutter of seeming life. The bodies lay still as a draught of fish in the bottom of a boat.

They had been struck dumb. Really the whole hill was dumb now, under the hoot and caw of the grandees and their ladyfolk. 'Go-back – go-back – go-back-back-back-back,' the grouse had been calling urgently as the first humans invaded their moors in the morning. Not a bird was calling now. Thousands must be left, cowering out of sight. The adders would be lurking under boulders. The deer and the goats would have retreated further into the south-facing corries of Beinn Buidhe or beyond the skyline to the north into the empty green lands of Talladale (cleared eleven years before Bealista; still unfenced). On dozens of outcrops hoodie crows had come to perch as soon as the gunfire stopped. At night foxes and wild cats would slink down here, drawn by the scent of blood and innards, and find not one shred of meat left on the ground. The grouse (and the few hares and curlews they had picked off when there was a lull in the frantic over-flying of the coveys – Flo had seen one curlew lying on its side amongst the feather-mounds, its unbelievable curved beak slightly open as though it was about to let fly that limpid, fluting call) – the grouse were being emptied from the moor as though a tornado blowing through was sucking each breathing thing to perdition.

Transfixed by her thoughts, Flo slowly realised that a mask was facing her – black eye-holes, black forelock under greenish deerstalker visor, black hairy bush between nostrils and lips. The Lord. He might have been trying to hypnotise her, or read her thoughts. He might have been lost in his own ones. Did he even recognise her? Just one more of his Scottish staff (of whom there were now nearly fifty). What was another working female to him? If he and the Lady were now man and wife in title only, what did he do for the secret needs of his body? Probably, far off at his other place in Warwickshire, he had an entire Turkish harem at his disposal – ignored by, or unknown to, herself, who never went south any more and seemed buried in her patronage of the weavers, her restoration of ruined churches.

Flo wanted not to be seen at all by this deadly, potent, eerily quiet man. Did he think she had been trying to interest him, or stare him out? She called Calum again, made him lie down with a mutton bone, and went round the party with Margaret, Ella and the others, collecting the remnants of the feast.

Chapter 11

E arly one autumn, when the first flush of the more killing sort of guests had drained back east and south and a blae quietude was stealing over the countryside and into the corridors of the Castle, Kilgour appeared at the back kitchen door on an afternoon when Flo and Margaret were sitting flushed and drowsy beside the range and said, 'You are wanted by her Ladyship.' When the two pretended not to know which of them could possibly be meant, she said in her most commanding tone, 'Cameron!'

To Flo's amazement she seemed to be required not only by the Lady but by the entire family. The way to their sanctum (a minor suite of sitting rooms in which she had never set foot) was through an ante-parlour, very dark, without a window of its own, smelling of bees' wax and peat-smoke. Inky pictures of ancient battles and gatherings of persons in plumes and robes darkened walls. She further sunk into a dream, whether bad or good she could not tell, when she saw that the looming body in one corner was a Shetland pony, stuffed. At the final door Kilgour knocked, then left her with a sigh of pent-up disapproval.

The light in the major room poured in through triple windows of the usual kind, with some jambs, and curved ones in a turret at one corner. On the window seat the Lady sat draped with lengths of tweed. Beside her, balls of marled green and brown and blue wool were piled like cannonballs in a fort. The Lord was leaning on the mantelpiece, the picture of ease, with a cigar between the fingers of the hand that dangled nearest the coal fire. Again that unwavering black look from the other side of some barrier or gulf. Turning her face from it, Flo saw that the young Lord was present too. He was adorning the semi-circular seat in the turret. It must be him. She had glimpsed him just once before when he had been on his holidays from a strange school in the far south, called Eton, where boys went to live and were flogged like sailors.

Now he was lounging, the body of a man with the uncertain, changeable face of a boy. No warrior-moustache as yet, although the first shoots of it made a smudge on his upper lip, above a mouth turned down in a sulk at the corners. His hands were toying with the ears of a pair of majestic stag-hounds with pepper-and-salt coats as coarse as a badger's. He might have been sitting for his portrait – or for the painting on one wall depicting a nearly naked youth, also a boy-man, with that same pout of grievance, studying his own reflection in a pool.

'Ah, Cameron …' Was the Lady more distracted than usual? She turned her head to her husband, 'Lord Ardmair' (she called him *that?*), 'this is Cameron – who is from out there'– she waved at the window – 'from an island.'

The Lord raised his cigar to his lips and made its tip glow red.

'Cameron, as you perceive, one's brains have not been sleeping on the weaving scheme of which we spoke some time ago, if you remember – before the tenancies were …'

'I do remember the occasion, your Ladyship.'

'You do – yes, yes, of course. The cottagers are busying themselves now, you know – they are doing well, quite well …'

'In Bealista?'

'Ah, no. If only we could. On this shore, rather, and especially beyond the Port as far as Borve. Now, Cameron, if your people, your former people – if they were willing, they might share the benefits of the tweed-work. The dealers in Stirling, who have traditionally handled the tartans, and with whom, one may say, one has had an excellent understanding,' and she swept one hand towards the carpet of dark-green Graham tartan and a wall-hanging of the same – 'where was I?'

'The dealers – Stirling,' her husband prompted.

'Yes. They are eager. They are insatiable. If only the people –' She broke off and looked oddly alarmed, her white brow crumpling inwards. In the brief lull a cavernous, throaty voice sounded in a groan – one of the hounds had yawned. As the sun dipped, the sea beyond the window had clarified and a little shoal of islands, beyond which lay her own one, had risen up out of the horizon and come closer. Flo waited. She could stand being talked at, if she did not have to declare herself in any way.

'The people of the lesser islands – they must see the benefits of an assured trade. Steam-boats can call now, and they can carry tweeds, and cured fish, and – whatever produce the city-folk may be persuaded to require. You know them, Cameron, do you not?'

'The city-folk, your Ladyship?' She heard cigar smoke blown out impatiently and the Lady herself looked faintly pained.

'The island people – you know them, Cameron, of course. Now tell me – will they work?'

'They are working, your Ladyship. In Australia and Canada, and the mainland. In the islands –' She broke off, too upset to go on, still looking down rigidly at the carpet. Pictures glared in her mind's eye: Roddy McCuish in handcuffs, his scalp plastered with thick blood; a hired man with one of their hens in each hand, thrashing the birds' heads to red rags against the stone jamb of the door …

'In the islands,' the Lord spoke in his low, withdrawn manner, 'I have acquired an interest – a substantial one. I am hardly MacDonald, or Argyll' (at this his own son snickered from the turret), 'but that may come, m'm? In the case of your former home I was minded until recently to sell – to Her Majesty's Government, for a penal colony. I was advised, however, that the climate and other conditions were too severe to suit. However –'

'The landless men, and their womenfolk,' the Lady took up the tale, 'will surely be persuaded that tweed shall answer?' She seemed determined to exact a response. Cloud like a bank of clay had formed out of the ocean, shrouding the last of the sun and extinguishing the islands. 'And I should like you to advise one, and to give one the names of useful persons.'

'Your Ladyship, it is too far – too far back. I do not think of it now. There may be people left. My father is dead and lying under the sand. Our neighbours are scattered. If you must hear something that pleases you, you had better ask the Minister.'

Oh, she had not been meek. Had her tone betrayed her? The Lady was a silhouette. The Lord was the same, against the ruddy light from the fire. The turret was in deepest gloom. The cigar glowed again and the Lord delivered what sounded like a series of remarks composed some time before.

'You are an uncommon girl, Flora Cameron. I believe you knew the Bealista people, m'm? Too closely for your own comfort, m'm? And I believe that you realised that it would be wise in you to refrain from committing a nonsense when they – went too far, m'm? Such things are purely historical now. Your co-operation in the new way of things would be appreciated, by her Ladyship and by my son.'

'Your what?' In her surprise she must have sounded rude – which the Lady and the Lord considerately ignored.

'The Earl will shortly be taking charge of the weaving side of things in this district,' the Lady was saying, 'and you, I trust, will be taking charge of him.' She laughed lightly. 'He has been too much of a stranger. He has none of the local language – as one has not oneself, but learning becomes less easy when one is …' She trailed off delicately. 'Randolph,' she addressed the gloom of the turret, 'show Cameron out, my darling, and perhaps you can arrange …'

It was so dark in the anti-parlour that the dead pony was visible, also the pictures of ancient conspiracies, if that was what they were. Coarse hair brushed against her forearms, gentle and frightening. There must be a hound on either hand. Where was the young Earl? The dogs smelt of salmon offal. That more acrid taint must be the cigar-smoke on his velveteen jacket. The door had shut behind her – the fire was out – in a few paces she had lost her sense of where the entrance was. As she put out her hands to feel a way ahead, her fingers met lips, and a nose. She recoiled, and heard him giggling. His voice said, 'I say, Cameron, that felt rather rich. Do it again.' She lurched to one side and her hip bumped against a hairy body, not flexible, inert – the pony. As the groped again, her fingers touched the hard coldness of one of its glass eyes.

'Show me to the door,' she half-shouted, not meekly at all, between anger and panic. A catch clicked and a tall oblong of lighted passageway appeared abruptly. She had to turn sideways to get out, withdrawing her breast and midriff to avoid touching the young Earl as he stood there, his mouth and chin suggestively pouting, one knee cocked elegantly forward, flanked by the great dogs.

Chapter 12

Maybe it was not a trap. It felt like one. She would have to get away now, for good. What on earth was she to them to be worth trapping? It was nothing but their pompous way of getting themselves some bits of local knowledge. And a back door out of their gilded prison. And a bit of fun for their lad. Who had not a tithe of the nous or the pitiless purpose that had helped his father to build up his grandiose wee empire. She could see the future now as clearly as through a hole in a seer's stone. Nobody here would be able to work for anyone except the Castle. Nobody any more would work for themselves.

What were they designing her for? A thought sickened her – they were *procuring* her for the young blood. She had read the word in one of Margaret's books, a *Companion Compendium of Tales from Far-off Lands*. Sheikhs did it, and archdukes in Bohemia – peasant girls were *procured*. Och, the vilest rubbish. And what would they want with her, sallow and still skinny as she was? Nothing like their own young females with their soft, tapering fingers and shoulders white as flour. But all he would need in her would be … Her thoughts were shuddering to and fro, beyond her power to guide them. The knife she was scouring for Margaret jerked and cut deeply into her hand. Blood poured and Calum began to lick it off the floor. Kilgour's voice twanged from the doorway 'Remove that cur!' The auld bitch was getting impossible to live with. Flo footed the dog out at the back door, shut it on him, and let Margaret wind a cotton bandage round her hand.

'Aweel,' she said as she tore the end in two and knotted it round Flo's wrist, 'bleedin's aye grand for the health. An' it maun be guid stuff if Calum likes it.' Twice, as they day wore on, bright crimson tinged through the fabric and it had to be renewed.

She had begun to filch food again, whenever the others were out of sight and hearing – whatever could be kept and carried, oatcakes, pickled eggs, kippered venison that would take a while to rot. It had always been a daft habit, she had never used the food, and if Young Meikle tracked it down she would be thrown out onto the road. But still … in the middle of the night, or on a day when her month was coming on, she would see the future, herself on a puddled track, small rain drenching across the moor, ahead a rocking grey sea – nothing on the far shore, not-Australia, not-Manitoba, not-England – nothing. She would have to make a shelter, and live on what she had carried on her back, and when it was finished she would drop down into the nothing under the nothing …

Islands rose in front of her – places to live … The leaking of her blood must have gentled her into a dwaum … The Island of the Trees, sheltering and secret, its long arms embracing the sea-lochs – they had prevented the people there from planting new trees in case they grew attached and fought against more evictions … The Island of Corn – how could there be an island filled with corn? Like a long shallow ship of golden sheaves that grew year in year out. Surely there had been no famines there … The Long Island – like pieces of a backbone. She would never go back there, they had lost their backbone, or else it was scattered into numberless pieces and would not be found until – until …

At the end of the morning some days later, Kilgour was to be seen in the lobby outside the kitchen, then in the kitchen running her finger along surface after surface, even the hottest, inspecting them for sinful dust, then outside the kitchen again, in front of a long mirror at the far end of the passage in which she must have seen her own image, a blush as plump and frosty as a sugared strawberry on each cheek, her eyes shooting out blue icicles, the pursed lines on her upper lip scoring as deep as though cut with a cheese-wire. She had a message, and she was bound to deliver it even if it cost her as much strain as giving birth to a polecat.

'Cameron,' she rapped out at last, barely stopping in her next progress through the kitchen, 'you are to present yourself in the hall – in the *front* hall …', she paused as though disbelieving her own words, 'at 2 o'clock this afternoon precisely. At the bidding of the young Master. To help him – to help him with his business.'

A grandfather clock began to chime as Flo came out through a glazed side door into the strange chamber of bare dressed stone and polished wood. Here, she knew, the gentry gathered in a morning before going up the river or onto the hill or, on a summer Sabbath, along the shore with picnic baskets and wives, little children and nursemaids. In this doldrum of the autumn – still darkened for her by long-imprinted worries about whether the barley and potato harvests would be full – some toys and costumes for use by family or guests hung on stands or leaned in corners. Tweed capes with shoulder-flaps, like clothy ghosts of former owners. Stalkers' crummacks four feet high with polished stag-horn handles. Telescopes in leather cases, and landing nets, and salmon rods whose fine ends tapered almost to the vaulted ceiling twenty feet above her head.

The whole place with its marble floor and varnished doors of pine and oak would have housed two crofting families with their cows. The coir doormat was roughly the size of a kailyard.

Down the steps from the house came the young laird himself, dressed for the part with his own queer additions. His trousers, tight enough to be elegant without making walking a trial, were a gloomy tartan, dark green and raven-black. His Norfolk jacket was decorated down the front with silken loops, his chin was buried in a purple satin scarf, one end of which flung rakishly over his shoulder, and his head was crowned with a sort of Glengarry that sported a blackcock's curling twin tail-feathers.

He appraised her briefly, half-smiled, then went briskly past as though she was not there. Evidently she was supposed to follow.

On the raked shingle of the forecourt a trap stood with his mother's brown garron between the shafts, flanked by the two stag-hounds, which stood nearly as high as the little horse. The young Lord stepped up onto the driving seat, accepted the reins from the groom, and made a circular gesture that included Flo and the seat beside him. In a waking dream now, she climbed up as stiffly as though encased in brittle ice. They clopped off briskly westwards, the dogs loping at half-speed beside them, quickening effortlessly into a gallop as they felt the freshly rammed sand and gravel under their feet.

'Where are we going?'

'You must tell me that. I am in your hands. I should like to get to know all these villages, and of course the villagers. Mother says I must promise to take their stuff for cash – their cloth and so on.'

'I scarcely know this place. It is not home to me.'

'You know their language. Mother says some of them cannot use English, or will not use it. She has found it rather hurtful.'

'You could learn our language.'

'Oh come now, Cameron – it's worse than Greek!'

What poor souls they were, condemned to be strangers in the country they had bought. For a mile or two they went on quietly. The hounds were as silent as phantoms. When one or the other checked to smell at droppings or carrion, the Lord looked round petulantly and called 'Odin!' or 'Freya!' and the animal would look up with docile eyes and resume its lope.

Presently they pulled up where the track re-crossed yet again the old line of the path. The Lord was looking in a puzzled way towards the sea where there was a soft green place littered with big stones surrounding the mouth of a burn.

'How odd. On Father's map there is a place here – Geer-ad – what does one call it?

'Gearraidh – we do not sound the d.' He giggled at her full-mouthed, guttural saying of the name and continued to look puzzled. 'Has the whole thing disappeared?'

How could she bring it out that Gearraidh had been torched? That Morag Johnstone as a baby had been held by her mother with a hand over her mouth, crouched down between the lazybeds of standing barley in case they were seen by the bullyboys set on by the old owner to pull down their home? Probably he could not even see that the stones were the remains of people's houses. She wanted to howl – she wanted to say nothing to this stranger. Half-choking with contrary feelings, she simply said, 'All gone – oversea.'

'Well' – the young Lord looked peeved – 'I jolly well hope that the people in the farthermost places are still there or I shall have put myself about for nothing.'

Flo knew very well that the townships at the end of the peninsula were still alive, hanging onto their places which were too raked by salt-gust to be wanted for larger farms, not mountainous enough to harbour deer. It took them an hour to reach that last tapering treeless end called Mealvaig. Here the houses clustered, each one still roofed, the thatch tied down with heather ropes and weighted with hefty stones from the shore. The huddle of the place was outlandish, each house in any odd relation to its neighbour. The beds of corn, pale gold now and ready for reaping, stretched outwards from the houses wherever the rock allowed. No landlord's factor had been here, rearranging the holdings into neat strips according to his little map.

At the first house the young Lord was looking up at a grey-bearded man who was tying fresh thatch round a barrel set into the roof for a chimney.

'Good-morning!' the Lord called, as though crying into a stiff wind.

'It is a good morning,' said the greybeard, 'and it will be good afternoon as well but a short one.'

'The days are drawing in, to be sure.'

Greybeard considered this and said nothing, apparently finding it beyond dispute. The Lord was looking round at Flo, desperate for conversational reinforcements, his eyes exposed like a startled horse. She kept quiet. The old man was willing to speak English so she was not needed.

'Is your good lady at home?'

'Ach, they are all at home, unless they are somewhere else.'

'I beg your pardon?'

Greybeard slid slowly down the thatch till his boots were lodged on the thickness of the wall and shouted out, 'Mairidh – there is a gentleman here and he is in need of a lady. He says he would like a good one.'

The woman who came stooping out of the doorway was more than two yards tall and she was smoking a pipe upside down. She wore a grey shawl, a black bodice, and a coarse dark skirt streaked with dye-stuffs, the yellows and oranges of egg yolk, the purple of new heather-flowers, the red of cranberries. Her hands were blue. She looked steadfastly at the Lord and after an uncomfortable minute he took off his bonnet, toyed with its feathers, and put it on again.

'I say,' he ventured at last, 'I'm from the Castle, you know.' Silence, while smoke oozed from the pipe, then from the gaps between the woman's few brown teeth. 'And we, Cameron and I – this is Miss Cameron', he gestured over his shoulder, 'we should like to talk to you about your work.'

'You are not from the Excise.'

'Oh good Lord, no. No, no – the Castle. I am Lord Ardmair's son.' Silence again while the woman smoked comfortably and Greybeard was joined on top of the wall by two men from round the back and six or seven girls and boys.

'I take it that you do some weaving – and spinning – and that sort of thing?'

'We are all spinning. And Old Mairidh can still sort and card. There would be more at the weaving if looms were not so dear.'

'Oh well, that's just the thing. Because Mother – because Lady Ardmair expressly wanted me to say that if there were any want of equipment, her agent over on Sgiach' (he pronounced it to rhyme with 'thatch') 'will be happy to supply the need.'

'It will cost, and we are not having any money. None at all.'

'He will supply whatever is required, on credit – on credit against whatever you deliver – in the way of finished cloth.'

'Supposing we agree – how will we be sending the pieces to this place on Sgiach?'

'Well, not by land of course!' Greybeard laughed heartily at this joke. 'No – he will send his boat …' The young Lord faltered to a stop and looked past the houses to the shore as though he expected to see a forest of masts and ropes.

Greybeard and his friends, or family, were talking quickly in Gaelic and Flo caught a few words, 'gentleman' and 'ask him' and 'fortune'. Another man then spoke, youthful-seeming with a lean, humorous face, greying hair, and a scar where his right eye should have been.

'They say there are a few stones to spare at the Castle. Now, will they build a harbour for this place? Will you do that for us, son of Lord Ardmair? Will you ask Himself to build a fine harbour at this end, and then we will be sending him cloth to clothe a regiment, and barrels of oil if he likes, and salted fish more than he can eat or all his children and their children's children and his neighbours as well. We would be sending him good whisky but, you know,' he lowered his voice, 'we had to throw away the black pot when the gaugers were jumping out from behind every stone and frightening the cattle.'

General laughter. The young Lord seemed nonplussed, as though the threads of the conversation had tangled themselves impossibly and might slip out of his fingers altogether. His black eyes were sliding about and Flo revelled in his discomfiture, even as she felt her own redundancy and wished that the youngest man and the pipe woman would stop looking at her so curiously.

'We are in agreement, then,' the young Lord was saying. 'So, when next I come this way, which will not be long, I shall bring papers setting out the terms. And then we shall all do well.'

Would he hold out his arms next and pronounce Benediction?

The pipe woman said in her deep, decided voice, 'When the papers are coming, we will be having a read of them.'

'Jolly good. Odin! Freya!' The great dogs were at bay against the end wall of the house and the township terriers and collies were tormenting them, jumping up to snap at their ears and muzzles, infuriated by their giant calm. At his voice they trotted straight through the pack and stood ready, one at each wheel. He clicked his tongue to the garron. No movement. He clicked again and they moved off with an undignified jerk that nearly shook Flo off her seat and caused the Lord to clutch her by her wounded hand.

'You will not be needing me again,' she said at a late point in their journey back. 'I did nothing there.' She wished anxiously to have this understood. He must see that her part in the business had been foolish and would not be repeated.

'You were marvellous. So composed. I like that, you know. Because I am so uncertain. I may seem calm, but really … And Father hates that. He says I am like her. Like Mother. And that I shall never grow up until … Cameron … This is absurd – you are Florence, are you not? Florence …'

He had turned to face her. His flesh looked as thought it was melting, like fat in a pan, and would slide off him, leaving some helpless creature naked there, a still-birth, a snail become a slug.

'Florence,' he clutched her bad hand. She jumped at the pain, which he mistook for a recoil of dislike. 'Florence – *please*.' His grip was crushing although his flesh was tender.

'You must let go.'

Still he gripped. Her hand was turning numb except for the one pounding pang of the cut.

'Please let me go. This is very sore.'

His face was white with a sweaty shine and the whites of his eyes were suffused pink as salmon flesh. Suddenly he let go of her. She put her hand on the rail for balance, jumped down, and felt herself held fast from behind. The loop of the bandage had caught on the curly hook at the rail-end. Desperately she stirred her hand round in mid-air to free herself. As though at a spellbound pace, this thing was happening. He had seized the loop of the cotton, and unhooked it, and was slowly bringing it towards himself hand over hand, playing her heavily like a pike. His mouth was set in a half-grin. His eyes were fixed on her, unblinking. Furiously she stirred her hand, the last of the bandage unwound, the lint pulled off the wound and tore the scab out as a hook tears the red gill out of a fish. She screamed and ran, clutching her left hand in her right.

A scudding behind her, a panting. The stag-hounds would drag her down. 'Freya! Odin!' The Lord's voice bellowed out and the dogs stopped instantly, leaving her to stagger on towards the Castle.

That night she left the kitchen after the washing up, while the others settled down to their drams and pipes and dregs of wine, and went first to the food cache, then to the attic. In a cloth she made a bundle of whatever could be carried and could not be lived without – a spare shift, a pair of leather moccasins from Ontario left behind by a guest, an old woollen shawl, ragged but she could darn it, a fresh bandage, waxed thread and needles, the pieces of food, her hoarded coins in a cloth purse. Then she put on three skirts and lay down in her bed.

When the others came upstairs she pretended to be asleep. The hours flowed sluggishly past what she judged to be midnight – one o'clock – two o'clock. Her purpose hardened and came to a point. As she stepped past Margaret's bed, the hoarse Aberdeenshire voice said quietly, 'Dinna be feart, Florrie. Gang whaur ye like. An' dinna be feart.'

'Maggie, I will write a letter to you.'

In the black darkness they held hands briefly.

Outside in the yard a body rushed at her. In all her planning she had forgotten Calum. He jumped on her, making her lurch as the pack swung on her shoulder. She unlatched the gate in the wall and he rushed through, then greeted her all over again, leaping and jigging backwards, wild for a stravaig across the moor. How could she travel with a dog? She could walk with him but not get lodging, probably not feed him.

She put down her pack, picked up a stone, and flung it at him. It hit him squarely on the side with a dunt like a sheep falling off a crag. He yelped, sank back on his hindlegs and snarled, them came scampering on. She picked up a spar of driftwood and swung at his head, missed and swung again.

'Go back, you wild thing,' she hissed at him, starting to sob, then steeling herself, feeling her very guts clench.

She flung the spar and it broke on the ground beside him. He crouched dead-still. As she shouldered her pack and walked away eastward, he still crouched, unmoving as a rock. His green eyes stared at her silhouette as it grew smaller and disappeared beyond a rise in the moor.

Chapter 13

On Sgiach she would become Campbell again – the name her father had taken when he had voyaged in the opposite direction, from the mainland to the Island. How queer that 'Cameron', a word born in the dark-green forests of Loch-aber, should have taken on for her, these last many years, the smack of command and intimidation. Still, there was nothing wrong with 'Campbell' – Glencoe was long ago, and she had no plan to let her feet carry her that far south.

She felt so comfortable on the crossing from the Port, while others were groaning and being sick, that she wondered if she should have cut her hair off, bound her breast tight, and gone to sea as a pirate, or a cabin boy or some other rover from an English song. She sat on the deck and jammed her bundle between her and the gunwale and felt free as an otter while the Port withdrew into the grey murk of its own island. Slowly the greater one spread out its wings of headland and mountain, sharpening and sharpening in her sight until each limb stood out brown and clear. On the little luminous green places long since fertilised with dung and seaweed, grey rocks grew larger and turned into buildings. Burnt out or lived in? Many were roofless.

She asked a pale man lying down beside her in a long black sea-cloak and he answered in an unfamiliar accent, 'Some went by force and some by choice.'

'And you?'

He drew his cloak up round his jaws and said nothing more.

Once past the northernmost headland they drew into grey water as calm and sluggish as liquid ice. A rock reared hugely, a devil's-prick of a thing with lesser horns surrounding it. How could folk live here? The coast sank and softened and she could see plenty of small black cattle with their heads down, browsing on good grass. A mouth of a cave opened, black and unknown. Then they were rounding a pier of rock and slackening off the sails as they glided into harbour. The sick passengers sat up and looked round them, yawning and blinking.

Tongues of water ran between the backbones and ribs of two abandoned boats. In the deep-water dock the crowded masts of the fishing fleet made a thicket. Here the heart of the big island sucked all into itself – the ocean's water, mainland money, men from the other islands desperate for cash, girls shopping for jobs, rooms, tickets to Glasgow or Australia. Sgiach had the name of turning its back on the further isles, shamed by their abject need, looking down on the shoals of comers from there as though they were rats from a wreck. Or so her people had fancied. Her years at the Castle would surely have worked on her speech, made it less guttural. Perhaps by now she could pass for a mainlander? I must be cunning – whatever I feel I hide – whatever I was is only a story now. We never screamed battle-cries at the sheriff's men or stoned the factor's bully-boys, or eased the women out of the sea-tangle with blood welling from their hair – all a legend, as though people must have these fierce histories to get a spice and a tingle from others' troubles. (And I never betrayed a friend by doing nothing when Bealista was destroyed.)

She stood at a loss on the cobbles, still feeling the sea's motion rocking in her womb. Strangers jostled past her. The folk were different here – they were jabbering instead of letting the words come out in their own time, and they did not look at you, or not full-face. She saw a moustache, a savage crescent of shiny black hairs, with two eyes above it like pits of gravy. An enormously fat man with a paunch like a full meal-sack and the golden cables of a watch-chain looped across it was sitting on a bollard, talking to himself. A tall, bow-legged man with a tan on his face like brown varnish was standing beside a wicker cage with some kind of crow in it that had yellow wattles. It suddenly said, 'Hurrah matey!', then said it twice again. Nobody gave it a second look. Three girls, young women, with canvas aprons and filthy boots, went past with their arms linked, kicking up their legs in a slowly lurching dance.

She was seeing people that she knew. The drunken seaman with a pigtail who had groped her once. Roddy, with the dark-brown caterpillars of his eyebrows. As they came near, their faces changed and they turned back into strangers, leaving her shuddering.

Things were opening out all round her now – she was washing about naked on a spar – she was marooned on the wrong side of the world. She clutched her bundle and looked hard at things to make sure they were real, the quays, the boats, the skyline of the hill behind the town with shreds of clouds trailing past its broken rocks, the stone-block houses with one row of windows above another. Where a pier was built out into the water, separating the fishing and passenger parts of the harbour, barrels were stacked higher than a house. Beyond this tarry brown wall, at long boards sent on trestles, a gang of women were heading and tailing fish or gutting them, ends into one great wooden bin, entrails into another. With each squelch a torrent of flies boiled up out of the depths, then sank again. The trio of dancers were sashaying to and fro on the stones, showing off to their friends. They finished, bowed low, and one of them staggered, nearly falling. Then they all took up their knives again.

Many of them looked her own age, many were younger, and surely there were grandmothers among them too, grey-haired women, a few of them with hips as broad as the hoops she had seen on the ladies at Castle banquets. None of them gave her a glance as she walked on towards the ragged end of town.

At the end of the good houses with glass in their windows she came to a little row of black houses. She fixed on one whose gate to keep the hens out of the kail was badly mended, part of a creel tied on with twine. No man here – the woman might have room for another and need the shillings. Blue smoke was seeping through the heather thatch, which was sodden, years overdue for replacement. Through the window-hole she saw a movement – somebody would be seeing that there was a person outside, a beggar, or a neighbour wanting to hear news or borrow an egg. The woman of the house appeared, outstared Flo for several moments, then said in an abrupt, hoarse voice, 'Want something?'

'A place to stay.'

'How long?' The woman looked her own age and had no teeth.

'Until – until the herring finish.'

At that the woman looked curiously at her hands and Flo saw her own fingers smooth as a lady's in a painting, only thicker.

'The girls and wifies generally lodge in the bothies in-by there.' The woman nodded back along the quay.

'There will be no peace there. And I am not as young as I was.'

The woman looked at her quizzically. 'We none of us are,' she said with a wee laugh. 'Come in out of the mist.'

Chapter 14

This was home, then. It was a cramped, dark perch. One tussock, quaking but tough, in the wide watery bog she had set out across. Smelling of peats, which was familiar enough, and made her ache for real home, cut by some other, ugly taint, like dirty boilers – coal-oil, was it? Her bit of a room was floored with hand-sawn planks, laid on the joists without nails, and ceiled with thatch. It looked like the rank heather sagging off the ledge of a crag. At least it was not dripping. Not today.

After the Castle this place seemed as small as a garment that she could wrap round herself and pretend its frowstiness was warmth.

She slept. She came up out of sleep as though she had risen from the utter closure and oblivion of the grave. No – there had been a dream – a fire, eyes staring at her through orange flames … When she came to life again, she was shivering as though cold had wakened her.

She ate porridge with the woman – Kirsty – then watched with foreboding as she took the solidified remnant of it out of the pot and put it in the drawer of the table. So here was poverty again. Ach well …

A piece of mirror was hung on a nail between the window and the door. She looked at herself for a minute before she went out. Would she do? Do for what? Her light-brown skin, still smooth enough on her cheeks and forehead, was greenish in this chill. The fire, in a proper grate, had been out overnight and only recent re-kindled. The reddish-brown tresses of her fringe showed beneath the edge of her shawl. Foreign – I look foreign – where do those colours come from? Mairi mother, who were you? She pulled the shawl lower, to her eyebrows, and went out along the quay.

Two older women were sitting on a board across two empty barrels, one with a pipe fuming in her mouth.

'It is not a bad morning,' said the other. 'And it is not a good one either.' She was looking Flo up and down and clearly waiting for a question.

'Who would set me on?' Flo wanted to be friendly and felt utterly a stranger. It was almost eerie that they shared a language.

'Himself. He is in there somewhere, counting his money.'

'Can I speak to him? Will he –'

'Och, he will speak to you right enough, and if he likes the colour of you, he may give you a job.'

'Or a poke,' the other said, taking the pipe out of her mouth and spitting a brown skein onto the stones.

Inside the long shed, which was dusky and smelt of tar and fish-guts, Himself was sitting at a counting-desk with a sloping top and an inkwell. His thick head of hair was bent. As he finished his writing, before he looked up, she had time to recognise him – that look of a scorched pig, swarthy and bristling – the Black Factor – Cooper – the old Lord's manager – the agent of their ruin on the Island. And she had thought she would be dealing with fishermen. Now he looked full at her and she remembered his trick of waiting for you to speak and give yourself away or else lose confidence and say nothing. But Angus, and Morag's father, Alasdair Mhor, had been able to stare him out.

'I was looking for work. At the fish.'

Another space of silence. She thought she could see him faintly remembering her, or wondering if he did – a worm of memory niggling in the underside of his brain. She tightened her shawl a little.

'Work, is it?' he said at last. 'And what were you at before?' His sarcy drawl was saying, And are you good for anything at all? Now the years at the Castle yawned suddenly behind her like a burnt bridge, a gap. She had no written character. She was nobody.

'I was in service for a good many years. On the mainland. I was at the fish before.' Well, she had gutted hundreds, thousands, long ago.

When he spoke again, after another of his pauses, his tone suggested that he had little interest in her blethers, whether they were facts of fictions.

'I have my fill of gutters here,' he said finally, then stopped for long enough to let her spirits plunge. 'There is a glut coming, though – we expect boats by nine – you may take your chance on the dock. Piece-work, mind. Auld Mother MacLeod will keep your tally.' He gave her a last considering look and turned back to his accounts.

Above the harbour the gulls were in a frenzy. Their yelps, their pointy wings cut at the air like scissors. They swooped, reeled upwards in mad fights, dropped like stones for morsels in the water, hovered and sheered off, and all the time their voices cackled and skirled, shredding the air.

They were a gang of foreigners herded into this place by the fisheries. Left to themselves they would have been cruising the strands and inlets of the small islands, roosting at sunset with their beaks to the ocean, brooding their clutches on the turf slopes above the geos. Here they were rude and rampant, and filthy with it – parts of the town, its ridges and gables and the verges of the harbour, were plastered solid with white shite. At least they were scavengers, they got rid of the shambles left by the fish-work – but then, if there had been no shambles in the first place … She walked out into the thick of it, into the jungle of masts and sheds, stacked barrels, tubs and net-baskets, carts laden or empty, and people, people galore, like a hundred tinker camps huddled into one. They were streaming in gaggles out of the wynds, down from the black shanties that clung like a mussel-scalp to the slope behind the older town.

Where should she go? They would never let her in. Within minutes, as she looked on, the little army of women had settled down at the long tables and the brine troughs and were standing in readiness. Two pretty young ones were next to each other at a gutting bench. They had the same brown hair caught up in fulsome bundles behind their heads. They drew their knives as one from the leather holsters at their waists and held them up for a moment as though presenting arms. Then the one waved hers with a cold flash in mid-air while the other flung hers at the coping of the bench. It planted itself with a juicy thud and stuck there, quivering.

They drew Flo to them as though they were sunlight in the midst of frost. From closer to, the knife-thrower was younger than her sister and her skin was a little smoother and a clearer brown. The cheeks of the other were seasoned, and flushed as though from sitting next to a fire. Their aprons were patterned, only dots, no sprigs or flowers, but decorative among the general drab. At their ease, waiting for the boats, they had turned and leant their backs and elbows against the scrubbed wood of the fish-table. At the sight of Flo approaching they neither smiled or glared, they simply waited as though for the next piece of comedy to happen.

'Is there work?' She should have said something friendly or cheery. Her tongue was still half-tied.

'Work? As long as there are fish in the sea –'

'Dinna tease, Peg,' said the elder one. Then to Flo, 'Are you new in? Of course you are. Have you been to see the Swine?'

'Cooper. Yes. He said to come down here.'

'See that, Peg – she can tell a swine.' The two of them giggled. 'Aye well – fit yourself in here.' She gestured along the bench. 'And when Mother MacLeod comes down the line, you can tell her who you are.'

'I am Flora. Flora Campbell.'

'From Argyll?'

'From along the coast.' Maybe she would tell them about herself one day. Maybe she would not.

'The coast?' The sisters looked puzzled, then Maggie said, 'Ach well, I suppose you have been scattered about like the rest of us. Peg, give her a loan of a knife.'

Peg reached round to the table and plucked out the springy blade.

'And what about yourself?'

Peg stooped and pulled another knife from the ankle of her boot. 'I aye keep a spare – well out of sight – in case the Swine gets randy.'

This was too intriguing to ignore. As she opened her mouth to question them, a shout came from the little pier with a beacon on it at the harbour mouth: 'Boats! Boats in!'

A smack with dark-brown sails was rounding the north headland with another close behind, then three more abreast of each other, some of them built on lines she had never seen before, half-decked, with stems as straight as their masts. A race was on, and some of the women were whooping to their favourites while others sat with their backs to the water, waiting dourly for their stint to start.

It was after nine o'clock, the tide was full, and the boats were nearly level with the quay as they swung ashore their dripping baskets. By the time the ebb was half done and the head of the harbour was floored with glistening shingle, Flo's back felt like a board that was splitting down its centre and her hands were moving like single limbs, the fingers almost too stiffened into each other to manage the knife.

Her first fish was a pollack, grey and gaping. Its black eye stared, dulling already. The skip that took in the load for her section of the table had been filled brim-full by a small local boat – Peg and Maggie had fired off rapid, unintelligible banter at its two-man crew. Flo picked out the big fish to give herself room for mistakes. Would she still have her old dexterity? She laid it lengthwise in front of her, head to the left, planted her free hand on its body at the central fin, set the blade into the flesh just above the tail, and eased it along the roughness of the backbone and out again beside the gills.

That had been slow. It had also been right. Her fingers were in no danger. The knife was so sharp she could hardly feel the resistance of the flesh. Almost with a flourish she set the strip of meat to one side, turned the fish over, repeated the cut, and tossed the spine with the head attached towards the dock. A herring-gull swooped and caught it, and flew off chased by five or six others, screaming and veering.

A clapping at her side. Peg the tease was applauding. 'That's fine, Flora – very fine. But we dinna fillet, we just gut. Put the fancy fish in thon basket at the side there and get stuck into the cuddies or the salt-girls will have our guts for garters.'

And then it was gut-gut-gut for two hours without a break. Knife-point into the vent. Slit up the belly. Scrape out the guts, or tear them with the fingers if they stuck. Fling ropes and lobes of innards into the side skip with its swarm of sizzling flies. Drop the emptied fish into her own set of tubs for Mother MacLeod to count before the salt-girls came to get them for the barrels.

The rotting stench from the fishes' innards clung to the work, oiling and dirtying the air, brewing up an invisible fog that the sea-breeze could not shift. She breathed through her mouth till her tongue stuck to her palate, then gave up and let the stink invade her. Do not fight it, swim in it, make it your own – it is only dirt, not poison.

Her hands had clarted up with scales till they looked like fish themselves and she could not swipe off the flies that clung to her gummy forehead and tangled, buzzing, in her hair. This was a pest she knew of old. The trick was to think, it is only a fly, it cannot sting. She shook her head violently, when Peg saw her at it she wiped down her hands and said, 'Let me draw down your kerchief.' The two sisters had swathed their heads by now and when Peg had done the same for her she felt at once part of it all, no longer holding herself separate – immersed in this seething element, not drowning in it.

'Thankyou, Peg. I though I would go mad at the wee buggers.'

'Why not? We are all mad here.'

They laughed and took up their knives again. More wet, dead cargo was dumped into their skip with a slither and a smack. She had been counting fish as they passed under her knife. When she had cleaned a hundred she would look across at the white face of the clock above the National Bank. A half-hour after ten. By eleven on the clock she had done forty more. Could she manage two a minute by noon? Her blade skidded along a codling's slippery, greeny-yellow side. She nicked her left thumb, scoring a red line down it. Racing was useless. Tricks of the mind were useless and tied knots in your head. Be your hands only, and your eyes fixed on the long fat bodies, the sliding skin, the dark-red innards. Be your blade, its first slitting, its ripping up the length from tail to head, its scrape and stutter on the bloodied backbone …

Now her weight was no longer pressing her heels down into the stones. Her forearms had stopped aching and become as strong as oars. The cut on her thumb was gaping and she no longer minded the sting of it. Words for Peg or Maggie had stopped rising into her mouth and died back down into her depths. Time no longer ticked, it flowed silently, unseen. When the two black hands of the clock merged at noon, and there was a clatter of knives put down, and an exhaling relief arose from them all between a sigh and a groan, she came out of her actions as though released from a dream and looked round her, surprised that the town and its harbour were still there.

By gloaming time, when even the gulls were scavenging less greedily, she was so wearied that her brains might as well have been one of the fish the girls were cramming down between layers of salt, curved and soured and dead.

As Mother MacLeod reckoned up her work and chalked it to her credit on her slate, she saw beyond the woman's shoulder, in the doorway of the shed, the Swine himself, in his oatmeal tweeds. He seemed to be pointing at her with his eyes – coaly eyes set in so deep under bossy ridges and eyebrows like scorched bents that they looked burnt out. Was he sizing her up like any master, or trying to place her? Whatever his interest was she did not want it – that look settled on her, binding her, skinning her.

'Where are you staying?' Peg was speaking to her.

'A black house at the far end. The woman is another MacLeod.'

'Kirsty's, is it? Cheap and wet. There has been no man there for years.'

'It will do. At least it will not burn down.'

The sisters looked nonplussed, then laughed, making it a joke. 'Oh aye, there is a lot to be said for a bittie of wet. It keeps the yarn swack. Just take care she doesna cough in your brose.'

Flo pretended to heave and the sisters giggled helplessly. 'Come on,' said Maggie, 'if you are going to bed down in that bog, you had better take a dram to proof yourself.'

'A dram?'

'There is a fine wee howff at the back o' the Wynds. We aye go there at the finish o' the fish.'

'Have they finished? Already?'

'Finished till the morn's morn, for the morn is the Sabbath when no man shall work, not even the wo-man.'

Chapter 15

The moment they stepped into the fuming warmth of the dram-shop, the sisters folded into the arms of their men and Flo was on her own, as though hanging from a hook in her own little upright space amongst gabbling strangers. On a settle by the darkest wall, some room had appeared where Peg's man had jammed in his haunches, hefted himself from side to side to let her in, and hugged her into him so that he could smother her little weather-beaten nose and rose-pink lips under the brown bush of his beard. On the settle's twin across the room Maggie was sitting beside a man in dark clothes with a face as white as curds. Both were sitting still as though carved in wood, their faces turned towards their men with the calm acceptance of someone who wished to be in this situation for five hundred years.

Nobody asked her what she wanted. Nobody paid her any attention at all. She could turn and run, to Kirsty's clammy house – or she could stay and drink. New arrivals were boosting the whole pack towards the trestle table at the back, with bulky barrels set up on wedges behind it and smaller kegs on its top. When she put her hands onto it to save herself from toppling forward, a grey-haired woman with a sweating face held out a little blue-and-white earthenware cup and spoke the one word 'Name?'

'Flora. Flora Campbell.'

The woman turned away and marked a slate. From the pale-brown dram in the cup a reek smoked up into her nose like a sulky peat fire. Autumn was in it, the ground, soaking clothes and tar, and barley starting to parch. She sipped, felt her lips numb, and relished the pang and glow as the whisky slid down her gullet. She gulped it like tea, sucked in the last drops, held out her cup for another, and heard Peg's voice through the buzzing roar.

'Flo!'

She turned with difficulty and saw Peg and Brownbeard, smiling broadly.

'Flo!' Peg called again, then turned back to her man.

For minutes she had been sensing, without knowing it, a pair of voices, a throaty woman's voice with an island accent and a man's, maybe a fisherman from the east side, slow and convinced. The one was all sharp and insistent, swooping and peaking unpredictably like a gull's flight, the other more like oars on the side of a boat, trundling and sawing – each coming in on top of the other's last sentence, having their own say regardless.

'What I saw in the quarry in front of my own nose, day after day,' the man was saying – so he was a mason, not a fisherman – 'it wasna Genesis, or it wasna the Genesis o' the Book. What I saw was that the good Lord must have laboured at his Creation for many a long year, for a million year maybe. And for ages he was making the dumb rock, just, and then he was making the ammonites and the trilobites. And it was many and many a weary year afore he even thocht o' the fishes, let alone –'

'Fishes and tribulites is it!' the woman broke in with a weird, gleeful passion. 'Millions of years is it! And who was counting? On the third day the grass was yielding its seed and the trees were covered with fruits, and only two days more had gone down into the sea before there were birds flying there, of every kind, and cattle all you could wish for, and haddocks and salmon in the waters more than you could get if you went upstairs to Heaven itself, for the Lord our God provideth –'

The woman Flo saw when she turned to look – and a dozen others were looking too, standing with their cups in their hands and listening unashamedly to the tournament of words – had a head of flourishing hair as white as bog-cotton and could not have been more than fifty, with pale blue eyes and an unaging face as smooth as a drum-skin, coloured deep red like sunset on low cloud. The man had a high, overhanging brow with brown hair above it in a thick coarse tussock and a mouth he clenched in an unhappy frown as soon as he was forced to be silent. His hands were out of scale, massive where his limbs were fine, and lay like tools on the lap of his dusty tweed trousers.

'To be sure he provides – that is outwith the present case – I am only concerned to bring home what eyes can see, for if we dinna see with our ain eyes, we are nothing – nothing at all. And if we read the book that is in the rocks, we shall see the Creation with a new vision and a clearer vision – clearer than the ministers have given us to see, because a minister, an *Established* minister' – his emphasis on the word was ferocious – 'is only a laird's lapdog, and he will yap out any magical nonsense to keep us all –'

'Nonsense? Magic?' the woman skirled out on her shrillest note. 'Is it God's own Word you are miscalling now? Ach, He will spit you out surely, for all His mercy, and you will be a poor shabby wanderer all the rest of your days, and a sorry weakling in the battle to come,

When the mouth shall be closed,'

– she was singing now, in a piercing voice with a cry on the last note of each line –

'When the eye shall be shut,
When the breath shall cease to rattle,
When the heart shall cease to beat,
O Jesu, Son of Mary, shield my soul ...'

The audience were divided now. A young man laughed and turned away. Some folk were humming along with the singer's air. The mason kicked the fire with his boot and sent an ember flying, then sat looking angrily into the red coals. From the hubbub behind her Flo distinguished Peg's full-throated laughter.

'Remember me in the mountain,'

– the woman was singing, and the last yelped syllable passed over Flo's brains like the edge of a knife –

'Cover me over with your wing ...'

Her mind was dazzling now, wincing at the nakedness of the song. The roar of talking in the little room was deafening her like storm-surf. She put one of her shillings on the table, made sure the woman saw it, and went straight down a passage at the back of the room and out into blowing damp blackness. Streaks of orange glitter on the harbour water were crossed by black rods of masts and bulks of hulls. Under her swaying head her trunk and legs were carrying her down the quays, down into the place of the smallest lights or no lights at all, with Kirsty's house at the end of it. She fell through the gate and braced herself grimly to enter without embarrassment. Beside a guttering fire Kirsty sat knitting. As she started to look round, Flo gave out the merest word of a greeting. Next minute she was lying on her back in her bed, unable to focus any detail in the vague tangle of the thatch above her, while the woman's song pulsed and died and pulsed again through the feverish thumping of her heart –

> Remember me in the mountain,
> Cover me over with your wing ...
> Remember me ... cover ... remember ...

On the Sabbath, by the time she rose, Kirsty was nowhere to be seen and the house was chill. She chewed cold porridge from the drawer to steady her stomach and went mooning up the street. Maybe Peg of Maggie would have come down from the Wynds for walk – or were they still cuddled up with their men? Where was her own man? When would he come?

The morning service seemed to have come and gone. The whole place was as mute as a field full of tombstones. At the quayside a single being was alive – a whitehaired woman, last night's singer – sitting beside a basket with a long line in it and baiting the hooks with small herrings from a cree at her feet. She looked up and wished Flo a frank good-afternoon.

'You are not indoors like the rest of them?'

'Well, you are not indoors yourself.' The woman laughed, with a touch of her wild high note.

'Will they ban us for it?'

'They can do what they like. I was at Mass while they were still snoring. We never miss a clear afternoon in Mingulay, not while fish are in the bay or the birds on the cliff. Are you from Barra?'

'No, no. North a bit.' She minded as ever to keep her tracks covered even with this candid woman. The candid woman gave her a shrewd look, said nothing, and went on working with flying fingers while her lips let out a croon that gradually singled itself into words –

> 'Columba, tender to all distress,
> Lovely Mary full of grace,
> Steer us to the banks of the fishing,
> Settle the breaking waves ...

And that is my lot – more than enough for a weary Sabbath.' She dropped the tail of the line among the coils of hooks and silvery fish. 'And maybe the old swine will be satisfied for once.'

Old swine? This hardly sounded like a husband. And the woman had been alone in the dram-shop. 'Is your man not owning a boat, then? Or going out with the fleet?'

'My man?' The woman suddenly looked wry, as though at some unspoken joke, 'Och no, my man is not going anywhere at all. Come you back to the house for a drink. My mouth is like glue.'

The tenement, on the second floor of a narrow house at the seaward entry of a wynd, smelt of soot and fish roasted in their own fat. From behind the curtains at the end of the room came plaintive breathings of the wind.

'So you are from north a way?' The woman, who gave her name as Eilidh MacSween, was supping her tea still scalding and narrowing her look at Flo as though she would wheedle the last marrow out of her bones. 'And you were burnt out, when some of the lords were clearing their lands of twenty-shilling tenants and putting some kite of an English drover into your place. And you have been roving about for a year or ten, and where you will ever settle – well, who can foretell the flying of a wild bird, or a spout-fish on the face of the deep sea?'

Flo felt plucked bare. 'Are you a seer?'

Eilidh MacSween laughed in her wild way. 'There was a man on the island was a seer right enough. He used a stone, he looked through it and he saw my life in it, and your life, whatever life he had a mind to, and he saw the coming of the iron ships, and the people in chains, and black men in chains and women too, and he saw the lands with a long fetter round them with hooks in it that would have the blood out of you, and the men all gone away to a filthy bog on the other side of the world and their eyes falling out of their heads, and iron hailstones beating against them, beating them into the bog …'

She was rocking now, nodding and agreeing with herself. Her words were nailing Flo to her chair. 'Can we live here?' she asked the woman. 'On Sgiach? Is there a life for us here?'

'Niall MacInnes would have told you your life. I am only seeing what you are.' Eilidh MacSween drained her tea and sang lines of a song –

'May no ill-doing come to me
Through door-leaf or through bar …'

Her eyes were firing up, looking outward again. 'Supposing the hill men, the crofters down the road here, supposing they would be robbed no longer, and they would have grazing for their beasts, and they would be driving them onto the mountain again … Ach well, supposing the moon turned red, and supposing wine would come pouring out of the well …'

She might as well have been singing a song from Ossian. Where Flo craved solid food of information, she was getting only tunes and lilts, which thrilled and inflamed her and turned her inside into a sick smush.

'Can you not live on Mingulay? she insisted.

'It was a stepping stone, just. They turned us out of Sandray, and Mingulay might have done, or Vatersay, only the want of a harbour made the work very sore, and my Sandy had gone off with the boats from Campbelltown, to see the world, he said, so after a few years he was bringing his father and myself across the water to see the doctors. Well, they could do nothing, and now we are here.'

'You were ill?'

'He was crushed when a boat ran over him on the shore.'

In the silence of her inability to say anything, Flo heard the wind breathing again at the dark end of the room, where the husband of Eilidh MacSween was living out his days and nights in a bed the size of a grave.

Chapter 16

The year that Flo took up with Sandy stayed always with her as one when the season changed from dour to gentle in a single hour, and so it was, it was not a wishful or a sentimental fancy. The air above the harbour was feathered with the dazzling wings of gulls, like the tail-end of a blizzard when the sun shines through. They were all feeling yet again, This is the last hard day – the herrings are moving north now, into Pentland, the haddocks are steering away at the same time – whether or not we must follow them round once more, and far down to the southern ends of England, at least here is a holiday from cutting and gutting.

The sun was celebrating with them as the cloud rose after a week's harsh weather, blue channels appeared in it and single sun-shafts came slanting through, warm on the skin, shifting its spots of light along the coast and brightening each green place where the fields of a township were ripening with new grass – fodder now for the Great Sheep, the Cheviots, not for the goats or the brindled cattle or the little horses whose owners had sold them off to pay their ways to Australia.

One boat was bringing in its own snowstorm of gulls as the five men of its crew cleaned a few fish to take home for their tea. A yellow-haired man six feet tall looked up and waved the shiny blade of his knife to a woman on the quay – Eilidh MacSween, who skirled out, then ran along to a spare berth on the quayside near Flo and Peg's station. When the man, who was in his twenties, jumped with the rope from the gunwale onto the stones, Eilidh wrapped her arms round him and pulled him to her with a kind of desperation. He looked across her shoulder, past her white hair, caught Flo's eye, and smiled brilliantly as though to say, Mothers – what can you do?

He had her sun-flush on his cheeks and forehead, her Arctic blue in his eyes. With his back to the midday sun, he was rimmed in a dazzle, his curly hair glinted pale gold like oats in August, and his forearms round his mother's back were frizzed with hair that made a brazen pelt like the wild boar in the legend.

As they looked at each other and failed to look away, she felt her skin tighten around her breasts and down her thighs in a shudder of warmth. Behind her Peg and Maggie had started a wicked dialogue.

'Sandy-Pandy, God's gift to the lassies.'

'Sandy-Pandy's back again –
Lassies, hide behind yer men!'

'His breeks must be full of money.'

'Full of something.'

Whatever he could hear, he seemed to like what he saw. He winked at the gaggle of them, let his look rest full on Flo, or so she thought, then pushed his mother away and got on with the tying up of the boat, which was a fine two-mastered 'Zulu' with a varnished deckhouse and its name, *Star of Hope*, in yellow letters twined round with crimson roses. For the rest of the day she worked fast, as excitement fed through into her hands, and with such absence of mind, saying nothing unless she was spoken to, that Peg and Maggie looked sideways at her and said little themselves.

She knew he would be in the dram-shop, once the sun had gone down behind the wooded hill, and he was, and so was Eilidh, in full voice –

'Son of the brown-haired lady,
Who never handled basin or cream-bowl,
Who never put her hand in the flour
Or laughed aloud in the cattle-fold …'

MacLeod's Lullaby – she was giving it the sound of a love-song, filled with husky yearning.

Flo got her dram and went to sit against the wall at right angles to Eilidh and Sandy's settle, where she could avoid his full look and see him as well.

'I see your darling coming,
Great with your brood across the Irish Sea,
White as the swan in early May,
Your children's voices sounding in the … in the …'

She was half lost already, turning to her son with a smile that glistened on her face like sweat, her arm linked in his, while he sipped from his cup, and swilled the dram around, and called across to a friend

– they seemed all to be his friends – 'Hector, how are you? Hugh MacMillan' – to Peg's man – 'have you room for another over there? Iain, keep a clear head, now, for later on.'

What happened later on? Some ploy or ceilidh that would shut herself or anybody else from outside their familiar circle …

> 'Darling of the young men
> Strong for the battle,
> Green tree when the sap is rising,
> The women are ready for you …'

Eilidh was staring straight ahead of her now, her face pallid. Did Sandy like it? Was he minding the nudges and looks from a knot of men beside the table who never sat down, whose cups and mugs were always at their mouths? At all events he turned now and held his hand straight out with the cup in it, perfectly confident of being served. His arm was grazing his mother's face and her singing faltered as he said to the shabby man on the other side of her, 'Donald MacDonald, are you very well?'

'I am all right.' The man had a dark face as though a shadow had seeped into it.

'All right, is it? Fighting fit do you mean? Fit for the mountain, eh? Or are you still creeping about the shore?'

Donald MacDonald bent his head a little more and spoke with a whistling noise through a gap in his teeth.

'Never mind the mountain. We have enough ado to be living at the shore at all. Duncan the Balloch was warned out of No. 6 because he went with his dogs across the corner of the Home Farm there. And he has gone to New Zealand. And Alasdair son of Alasdair was docked a half of his half-croft to make room for a ground officer. And Donald Robertson – ach, you do not want to be hearing all this miserable stuff. Had you a good winter yourself?'

'Well, we never died a winter yet.' Sandy laughed at the saying as he uttered it. 'And the Great Storm was nothing but a wee blow when it came by us at Kinsale or we would none of us be here.' He dropped his voice almost below Flo's hearing and she caught only the word 'rents', then 'round a petition' – mutter, mutter – then 'deal with anybody'.

He seemed to be well in the know, for someone who spent his winters hundreds of miles away on the coast of County Cork. His flow of easy speech was rousing her like liquor. She must have leaned forward to drink in his words. As Sandy MacSween turned away for a moment from his crofter friend, he saw her and smiled, and she smiled back, feeling the blood throb behind her eyes.

'How is your drink? Give it here.'

His hand was held out for her cup. Hers rose automatically and their chapped finger-ends rasped together. Eilidh's head swivelled sideways, her eyes looked vacant while her voice said, 'Woman from the north, burnt-out woman from the north, this is my beloved son –'

'In whom you are well pleased.' Sandy MacSween was delighted with himself and said to Flo, 'My mother knows the Book as well as a Presbyterian. The north, eh? You are not from Lewis, surely?'

So he had not his mother's powers of seeing, although he had her eyes. 'Och, no, I am not from anywhere. I am just myself.' How easy it was to flirt, to find a teasing remark, in the lightsomeness which this blond man spread round him. The heads and shoulders of the people on all sides of them had melted into a bright blur.

'Of course you are. Of course you are. And we are not from Sandray, and Donald here is not from Caradal. Nobody is from anywhere any more. And if they are not, then the Lord is not from Tormore – now is that right, Donald, what do you say?'

'He is from England,' said the dark-faced crofter. A roaring laugh went round their end of the room. They must all have been listening. Flo felt nakedly exposed, then drawn again into his bright circle as he spoke to her in a voice quite without his public jeer.

'Northern or not,' he said, ignoring his mother, whose head had slumped onto his shoulder, 'you are Flora from the far end, are you not? Because the lads said there was a fine brown woman living there who works at the fish.'

'My name is Flora right enough.' She wanted to say something else, something clever, or sarcy even to keep him at arms' length, but interested. Words were deserting her. 'And I live at Kirsty MacLeod's and I am going there now.'

Her balance felt doubtful as she crossed the room, her feet felt too far away, not with the whisky – surely she had taken two drams only – but with the charge she felt all through her, the delicious stir. How could she go home now? How could she stay? The night air was sharp, not hostile, refreshing as a draught of water. She turned the other way for once, along the harbour front and the few shops and yards and towards the moorish ground she had never bothered to explore, the fringe where

MacDonalds and Robertsons, Nicolsons and MacLeans were trying to live. The stream of stars flowed above her head, the great white bow that bent among single flashing sparks. Usually they made her feel small and temporary. Now they seemed remote, wee nothing-lights, lifeless stones, and she felt at the living heart of things, on edge with impatience and desirousness.

She was waiting for him, waiting for this man, which was humiliating in a way, and the humiliation was thrilling in itself. Perhaps it was all nonsense. He looked like that at everybody – every woman. And he would have to carry his mother home. She turned back down to the harbour in a swither of nerves. The moment he stepped from the entry to their wynd and seized her arm, she felt as calm as snow. In the middle of her, her blood was throbbing uncomfortably.

'You *are* a bonny woman, yes you are,' he was saying, like a learnt lesson, like something he had said a hundred times before. 'You look it and you feel it.' His left arm was right round her cloak, his fingers on her ribs, and his right hand was snaking inside her blouse, gripping her breast.

'Lovely tit, you have a lovely tit there.' His voice was choked – he was as roused as she was.

'Not – here.' She spoke into his mouth, which had fastened onto her lips.

'Not – in – the street.' He half dragged her, by one hand, into the doorway, towards the stair. 'Your – mother. Where's – your mother?'

'In the howff. Under the table.' He spoke with a laugh in his voice, half jeer half triumph. She felt molten, now ready to give in completely. When they were inside the room she thought with a stoun of horror of the man, Iain MacSween, in his cell behind the curtains. There was his breathing – the hissing sighs like wind. And if they could hear him … He had her against the wall now, in her back she could feel the bristle ends of the hay-swathe they had stuffed into the unglazed window. Hard, he was hard against her belly – hard, hard, hard – his cock had found her, parted her thighs by its own force while his hips drove her back against the wall. As he came into her she screamed sharply and knew by the liquid down there that her blood was mingling with her juice. He spurted into her, and gasped. She had closed her flesh round him and would grip to make this moment last forever, in spite of the hurt, in spite of the mess, in spite of that sighing at the dark end of the room.

'Mind the blood.' As she surfaced out of the daze that held them both, she knew she must be practical.

'Are you a virgin, then?' Was that the triumphant laugh again? 'No harm in that. I like you fine.'

He sounded almost reassuring, and in spite of her pride she was reassured, she was pleased that he was pleased, because she still wanted him, she wanted to keep him sucked into her flesh, to know that he could not help himself, and because something was still missing, she was stranded and only he could float her off.

'I will see you tomorrow.'

That was it, then? He was wiping himself on a cloth. In the firelight it looked clean enough. Awkwardly he held it out to her.

'Bonny woman.' He had still never used her name – if he remembered it at all.

At Kirsty's the window was still glimmering. Kirsty looked round sharply and before Flo could get to the stair she had come over and sniffed at her, at her face and front, like a dog.

'I smell a man on you. Will you be leaving this place now?'

'No.'

'All right then.'

Chapter 17

For a few weeks they worked at the tail-end of the white-fishing, while the days grew longer and folk who had almost given up living in their hunger after the bad, wet autumn and worse winter, scarcely crossing their thresholds, came outside again, holding onto the doorpost, some of them, and looked disbelievingly at the mild sunlight. And in this sunlight, when the day's work ended early and Cooper paid them off to save on wages, Flo sometimes persuaded Sandy to walk with her, up the steep hill above the Wynds, and into the scattering of old birch trees, on mossy ground starred with primroses. Amongst clumps of heather that had never been cut for thatch or burnt, they embraced each other freely. Her periods had continued, in spite of his coming into her again and again, and she felt free of fears. As for him, was there ever a man less set to turn into a father, or a husband?

She still wanted to be sure of him. She still wanted to feel un-tied, and light. Somehow, presently, the mixing feelings would resolve themselves.

'Sandy?' He had fallen into a contented doze and his face was smoothed of all thoughts, and sweet as a boy's.

'Sandy!' She brushed his mouth with hers.

He embraced her as though by instinct. She rolled free a little and said again, 'Sandy – are you taking the *Star* round to Shetland this year? When the rest of us go?'

'Any day now.'

'At once? Why must you go at once?'

'I will be needing the cash. And so will mother.'

'You have your winter's money, surely?'

'We have empty pockets after buying the *Star.*'

'And what are you thinking I will be doing?'

'You wifies will go by train to Aberdeen and steamer up the coast, and we will go through the Canal.' All this in a neutral voice. He was disinclined to stir out of his comfy sleepiness.

'I could come on the *Star.*'

'The lads would have something to say about that.' He opened his eyes and looked at her straight-faced, saw her unhappy annoyance, and closed them again. That night, when he wanted her, in a loft full of nets they had taken to using for the sake of privacy, she held him away and he stormed off home in a furious sulk.

Peg and Maggie seemed to read her like a book. They knew full well why she had been laughing and singing at work these past few months, although she had not found it in herself to confide in them. Now they appeared to know perfectly that the lovers had been quarrelling. Were they going by their own experience, or was this the habitual course when Sandy MacSween took up with a new woman, a blaze and a dazzle followed shortly by some fight or other? The thought of him with some other body – with bodies enough who were maybe still living a few yards away – made her feel ill, and threw her into a dwaum that the others wanted to relieve.

'Are you following him round to Balta?' asked Peggy as they swept up spilt salt and made other wee jobs for themselves on the last morning.

'Him' – leaving him nameless gave her a warm feeling that their coupledness was acknowledged. It also took her for granted.

'Sandy MacSween can do what he likes. Is your Hugh going round this year? And are you going?'

'To be sure I am. I would never let him spend the long summer evenings with the Buchan girls! Maggie has the right way of it – settle down with a crofter and you know where you are.'

Flo thought of Maggie's man, John MacAulay, always pallid although he worked outdoors, as darkly dressed as though for a funeral. Living in a sort of stone shed he had built up between sunset and sunrise in the hope that the estate would let him squat. He still had a few cattle with the fine needle-stripe of blond hair down their backs. They were living on seaweed – what good were they, or any of the herds in the townships cramped along the shore, as long as they were prevented from grazing on the mountain?

'John is a good man,' Maggie suddenly sobbed. 'If I go round to the other side this year, he will maybe kill himself while he is alone. And if he comes over for a job there, and leaves the animals, his family on No. 8 will sell them while our backs are turned.' She suddenly pulled her knife out of the table and held it up in front of her face. 'If Tormore was here, I would put this into his throat.'

'Or his balls.'

'If he has anything between his legs at all.'

'He has nothing, he is a queer hare, everybody says so, and he is only wedded to that Lowland creature because the old Lord wanted to hide the shame of it.'

The talk of the howff that night was more practical and no less vengeful.

'Take a leaf from Ireland,' voices were saying. 'Our own Land League ... Factor Stewart has children of his own ... Rotten with tuberculosis ... We would pay for the mountain ... Pay *us* to keep the bracken down ... Sooner part with his foot than a pound of his money ... His wife's gowns are worth £3000 ... A fine skin on her, what I could see ... Build them a pier at Carradal ... And one at Toskaig ... The government ... Stewart has a bloody sight more say than twenty governments ... Burn his barn ... In Ireland they would torch his house ... A League or a Committee, what is the difference ... Eating nettles and lucky to find them ... Going the way of Uist or Tiree ... Guns – or scythes ... Too far away, and the rents too low ... In Edinburgh, or Glasgow ... Another winter like the last ... Sooner die than serve ... Tried to raise a regiment, so they bleated him down like sheep ... I learned to fight ... In Ireland ... All we ask ... Withhold the rents, and burn ... Whoever does not ... The factor ... The government ... In Ireland ...'

They were talking to no plan, most of them, yet as the currents mingled, arguing and swearing, young bloods and veterans, some tendencies began to prevail, like the twin tides round an island, crossing and fighting each other and the whole sea rising as it headed for the land. Flo felt at ease here now, in this smoky place with its permanent taint of ale and spirits and sweaty bodies. Was it because she had friends here – workmates, anyway? Because she was somebody's woman at long last? Because she had felt for herself, and lived, each one of the pains she was now hearing spoken aloud? It was all of these.

She revelled in Sandy's shining presence, her skin tingled beneath her clothes because he was there. Why would he not catch her eye? And what did he mean when he said loudly, 'The God-fearers along at Bracadale had better try prayer if they trot along to Stewart at Whitsun and pay up like lambs' and exchanged winks with two of his fisher friends from the *Star*? John MacAulay, intense and quiet, had the knack of making himself heard whenever he spoke, although he seemed to have only one thing to say, 'The mountain is ours, and before we pay for it we should all be gaoled in Inverness or hang for it,' which made Maggie cling to his arm all the closer. Hugh the Beard was brimming over with good-fellowship – overriding some heavy heckling, 'Be quiet, Hugh, you are only a carpenter', with ripostes of his own, 'And so was Jesus' – hammering the argument that if they set up their own Committee of Vigilance, and elected every single soul along the coast to serve on it, the women with the men, then if they summonsed them for mobbing or deforcement they would have to arrest the entire parish and how could they do that unless they sent for the Fleet?

'They would do that, too,' put in a massive, iron-haired man. 'On Tiree, now, when they occupied the western crofts again, there was two gunboats came up from the Clyde – two, mind. I saw them myself. My boat was hired that summer to carry peats over from the Ross of Mull – and och, it was no harm, no harm at all – the people there were offering the sailor-boys drinks of milk when they came marching by in a stour of heat …'

Sandy's eyes were snapping as the big man wandered off into anecdote, his blue eyes watering and unfocussed. Of course, it was his uncle – she was seeing Sandy thirty years on, the fitness of his limbs clogged with fat and his brains going soft … Now he was breaking in on his uncle's story in his most fleering vein. 'Never mind Tiree. It is Argyll's island and he is a hard old swine. He has more friends in London than Tormore – and more concubines. Now tell me, Diarmuid, are they as wicked as that in Dublin?'

The man to his right had seemed to have his eye on Flo, or he had his eye on everybody, with the roving, restless look of a younger man, although his hair, which was lank and wavy, had a lock of white among the black – like her father, she suddenly remembered. His hands had never been still all evening, tapping his knee or fingering imaginary flecks of rubbish out of his dram.

'Dublin is the wickedest city in the western world,' he said in his unfamiliar accent. 'We call the rich ones Horse Protestants because they hunt so much they turn into a sort of animal themselves. But now, you see, we are hunting them. There were two of us one night – I'll name no names – they were lying in the middle of a bush waiting for the Lord of Lisnaskea, with pistols in their hands. He had turned their families off for arrears after the Hunger and they were after giving the man a little dose of gunpowder to improve his philosophy. And hours went by, and the moon went down, and no Lord came riding by, and at 3 o'clock in the morning Ryan turns to Murphy and he says, "I hope to God nothing has happened to the poor man." '

The room roared with laughter. Flo found she had a poor taste in her mouth – the man had seemed to be talking to curry favour, not to bring them news. Sandy was delighted and called on all present to raise their glasses in honour of 'the Leaguer from across the water.' A painfully deliberate voice now broke in – she recognised a red-haired man called Archie Gillespie from Ferrinbeag, the township on the other side of Bracadale.

'They had guns, you say. Now tell me – are they better things to have on your side than laws?'

'When the weapons are out, the laws fall silent,' Dublin Diarmuid answered at once, with his air of having a neat thought for all occasions. 'Look, if you play it right, it may not come to shooting. The ben was yours before and it can be yours again. Withhold your rents by as much as Stewart has failed to pay you all these years for the use of your grazings, and sure, if they try and gaol you they will not have a leg to stand on.'

'And neither will our families,' Archie Gillespie answered, 'if we are rotting away in Inverness and there is nobody at home to plough the crofts, or to earn a bit of cash while they are waiting on the harvest.'

'The women can turn the ground,' Flo surprised herself by saying out loud. 'And they can bring in a wage as well. And they cannot gaol us for the rent because it is not our names that are in Stewart's book.'

Sandy was looking at her as though he had never seen her before. A man beside the table called out, 'Fine words, fine words, but they will clear you off just the same, and your children if they were sucking at the breast. Fight them, I say, because hard fists is all they understand.'

'All right, and the women will fight as well.' Peg had come in to her support. 'I believe they did on Uist once, and up at Eriboll long ago. And I heard there were plenty of girls and wifies over at Bealista flinging stones at the bully-boys.'

The familiar names entered into Flo like a dead stroke. She felt cold as though she had gone out naked into the wind. Why was she arguing? She remembered her own words to Big Neil from Bealista as though they were a lesson she had learned by rote: 'They have powers unlimited – we must struggle with them to the end – at the end we are broken timbers on the beach.' When she had thoughts like that she felt a traitor, and when she said what she had said just now she felt like a daft heroine in a ballad.

Dublin Diarmuid must like that kind of thing, he was making calf's eyes at the two of them like a boy who has touched a girl's breast for the first time. And then he was breaking into song, some ballad from his own country –

'We are the boys of Wexford
Who fought with heart and hand
To burst in twain the golden chain
And free our native land.'

She felt half crazed by the words and by the drumming of people's feet on the floorboards as they sang along with the Irishman. She was only brought back down when a grey-haired man next to her, a crofter from Bracadale, said to her in a low, confidential voice, 'You are in the right of it – I know you are. But if I am taken away by policemen, there will only be my sister left on the place and she is eighty-two and very bad with her chest …'.

Chapter 18

When rent day came, it was fine as usual. 'Why does the sun always shine on us when we are ruining ourselves?' a man was saying – a country man with deep furrows trenching his cheeks and a jacket on his back that looked as though he had been sleeping in it for twenty years, and his father before him. Flo and the other fish-wives were sitting on bollards at the quayside, frankly making an audience for whatever show was about to unfold. They must have been worrying inside themselves as she was not. Many of their parents crofted down at Ferrinbeag and had been talking darkly about refusing to pay.

It was only an hour before noon when the first tenants came along the road and stood about outside the door of Stewart's new office. He was agent for the National Bank now, as well as factor to Tormore, and his office was conveniently situated next to the Bank, with a fresh hardwood door and a brass plate proclaiming 'Estate Office' in hammered letters.

Would Sandy appear in support of his uncle, whose croft was at Manish on the edge of the moor behind the town? She had seen too little of him lately to know his mind. He seemed content to stay in a huddle with Dublin Diarmuid and the lads from the *Star*.

Here came Archie Gillespie with his sisters, two widow-women from Bracadale. They looked neither right nor left but went straight in at the office door and came out with their eyes down five minutes later.

'Have you done your duty?' a man called out – it was the man from the dram-shop who had favoured making a fight of it. 'Are they well pleased with you in there?'

The three went silently back the way they had come.

Peg's Hugh arrived next, with a look of suppressed anger that made his forehead swell. He looked over at the women without his usual open smile and went to join the growing group on the stones outside the office. When Peg and Maggie's father arrived from Eilean Neist beyond Bracadale, he went to stand with Hugh and they spoke to each other in undertones. By now so many had gathered that in the buzz of their noise you could hardly make out which words were coming from which mouth.

'... looked me full in the eye,' Flo heard, and 'if there is any grievance' and 'red-faced scoundrel ... food in our mouths ... nothing left, nothing at all ... up the mountain ... Cooper was there in the back ... the winter coming ... go oversea ... the government ... hands on his throat ... cannot make it grow ... a quarter to pay ... the scoundrel ... the government ...'.

Here came Sandy's uncle, Big Alexander, escorted by Sandy to her surprise. When last they had talked, he had sounded as though his family meant no more to him than a toad in a ditch. Sandy saw her, gave her his gleaming blue wink, and the two men disappeared inside. Minutes passed.

'Do you think they are arguing the score?' Maggie asked, as though Flo was an expert in the ways of MacSweens.

'They will pay nothing – not one sovereign.' Would the estate drag money out of people who had arrived from Mingulay like paupers and had a breadwinner lying helplessly in his bed for the rest of his days? She would not have liked to try out this plea on Factor Stewart, or for that matter on Stewart the Banker. A few minutes later the MacSweens came bustling out, flushed and glinting about the eyes.

'They are advising us,' Sandy announced, pitching his voice in a way that gathered people into one crowd, 'no, I am telling it wrong – they are threatening us that whoever does not settle their arrears in full, *on top* of this half-year's money – that any such a one of us will be warned out –'

'No, no,' Big Alexander broke in, 'we will be served with papers and *then* they will –'

'It is all one thing!' Sandy was shouting now. 'They will have us out, in a week or in a month. And if we *league* against the estate – he used that very word – if we get in a league, then there are heavier laws yet to use against us.'

A hush. Voices rose up here and there, questioning and exclaiming – 'What next ... damn their laws ... I will not go in ...' Two women from the shore at Bracadale had arrived. Flo saw Sandy give Hugh and his crew a look. They moved quickly round the outside of the crowd, and when the women got near the office they found themselves blocked by a row of broad backs, which did not budge. One of the women had reddened eyes as they turned away.

From somewhere a rotten potato flew over and burst in a brown smush on the fanlight of the door. Gasps and laughs went up. Almost at once Stewart himself appeared, in his best rent-day tweeds, his bearded cheeks and chin mounted on a deep celluloid collar, 'like the Prince of Wales disguised as a grocer' in Dublin Diarmuid's much-repeated quip. He eyed the crowd for a full half-minute – 'remembering names and faces,' they said afterwards – then turned, studied the fanlight, and knocked the pulpy flesh off it with flicks of his cane. Deliberately he turned his back on the crowd, paused as though defying further bombardments, and went back inside.

By close of business – that is, by the time Stewart had clopped off south to Tormore Castle in his pony and trap – a head count showed, according to the *Star of Hope* and their many friends in the townships south, north, and inland, that four tenants out of five had 'refused to pay until such time as the grazings on the hill were restored wholly and fully into the hands of their rightful possessors.' This was a mouthful, not everybody had it exactly right, but nobody was in any doubt what it meant.

In the net loft that night Sandy was more passionate than ever. He overwhelmed her, driving down onto her so that her backbone felt the floorboards through the layers of twine.

'Great times, eh, Flo?' he said as they lay side by side, looking up at the pale orange afterglow through chinks in the roof. Then, without waiting for a word from her, 'The rest of them will never hold out. A few milksops and unco-guids.'

Flo thought of the women who had walked seven miles to town and returned seven miles without the factors' signature in their books. She was about to speak when he rolled her towards him, kissed her on the lips, and suddenly came into her again.

Back at Kirsty's, her landlady as usual looked up at her wordlessly but this time she swung the kettle over the fire. When Flo hesitated, wanting the comfort of the tea and the company, she said 'Great times, eh?', a weird echo of Sandy half an hour before, and gave her a sombre look from those black eyes, exposed and large in their brownish hollows, that seemed to damn each thing they rested on.

'What do you really think?' Flo had neither the confidence in the woman nor the happy enthusiasm about the rising, if that was what it was, to say anything easy or blithe.

'I think they will be sorry they ever tried to pull their boats against the current.'

This was too like her own darker thoughts to be endurable. The woman was only talking bad luck to everything because she was a damp, unhappy creature without a man. No, this was gross – she had taken her in, for a shilling a month, she had done no harm, and maybe her uncanny distance from the struggle gave her a clear sight of it.

'Drink up your tea,' said Kirsty abruptly. 'And go to your bed and dream about your fisherman. There is money aplenty in Shetland and Peterhead, if there will never be any here.'

During the next weeks news and rumours spread from one excited talker to another. The house of someone who had paid up had had the hay-stuffing in its windows set alight by an unknown hand and 'the sparks came flying into the room like a rocket'. At another such house a lamb had been found with its hindlegs slashed across the tendon. The Ferrinbeag crofters had held a meeting of their own and resolved to withhold payment until the grazings were restored and every tenant given grace to find their arrears. The MacSweens had been seen on horseback coming back from Bracadale 'with soot on their faces.' The *Star* had put to sea after dark one night and taken the word as far up the coast as Caolas and as far down as Eilean Neist. Finlay Nicolson, the teacher, had given the names of the 'chief rebels' to the estate. He was well hated anyway for strapping the hands of the children who spoke their own language in the playground. On the Monday after, the dram-shop was talking about nothing else – he had arrived to find only a handful of girls and boys at the gate and had to close up and go home early – between the school and his house not one soul greeted him or even looked at him as he went by.

How would the summonses arrive? 'On a velvet cushion, with a trumpeter,' one wit suggested. On a morning of white mist a small boat came rowing through the silken levels of a perfectly calm sea.

'Who is that with the brim of his hat down over his eyes?'

'Stewart himself – who else?'

'No, no, it is that pale bastard – Anderson – the sheriff's officer.'

'And ground officer MacKenzie – look at the belly on him.'

'And Cooper's labourer, wee Shaw from Uist – what is he doing in that company?'

The trio came up the iron stair on the harbour wall and walked up the hill road towards Manish, Anderson and MacKenzie carrying their leather cases with all the dignity of butlers, Shaw following, looking nervously behind him from time to time.

At the first house beside the moor, which looked little different from a heap of scree, with peat cladding on its walls and an old barrel for a chimney, MacKenzie read out the tenant's name from a list – Alexander MacSween. The door leaned open on one hinge. Anderson knocked on it with his stick – a crook with a horn head, although he had never been seen to herd a sheep. Three hens flustered off squawking as Sandy's uncle came round the end of the house with three collies close behind him. Anderson's crook was in mid-air ready to knock again. Big Alexander seized it, broke it over his knee, and threw the pieces into the midden. The sheriff's officer started back and found himself bumping into the breasts of the women who had ranged themselves behind him – township women mostly, reinforced by Peg and Maggie, Flo, five more from the neighbouring station at the quay, and Mother MacLeod, who had stunned them all the night before by coming into the howff and singing a new song by Mairi Mhor nan Oran –

We shall see the breaking of the horizon
And the clouds of slavery dispelled ...

Overwhelmed by so much tender womanhood, Anderson flushed up as red as hen's wattles, turned back to Big Alexander, opened his bag, and took out a document.

'You will know what it says here –'

'If I know what it says, then I will not be needing to look at it at all.'

Anderson fired up redder still, laid the document on the sill of the window, put a stone on it, and said to James Shaw, 'Now do you witness that this paper has been served in accordance with the provisions of the Act.'

Shaw nodded, blinked, swallowed, took off his cap and put it on again, and said almost inaudibly, 'I do.'

Female voice – 'The wee bugger is sorry he ever came to the altar.'

As the trio progressed from house to house, and they missed very few, so the crowd behind them grew – the bulk of the people of Manish

Dubh, women, men and children, supplemented by a tail of collie dogs, three pigs, a middle-aged man with no legs who propelled himself on a wheeled cart made out of a half-door, and two pet lambs. They looked to Flo like the most ill-starred army in the world, this straggle of folk with their frayed clothes and ill-coloured faces. Was there any place at all where the people were sonsie with well-being and were always comfortable? A flock of geese were advancing on them from beyond the last house named by MacKenzie. Their heads were pointing as low as snakes and a bony hissing seethed in their necks. Shaw squealed as a goose gripped his ankle in its orange beak. He booted it heartily on the head. At once clods hurtled from the youthful element in the crowd and dirt splattered onto the last summons as Anderson held it out.

Peat-smoke fumed in the air and a blue haze wafted across. The men turned to retreat and saw Big Alexander holding a red-hot turf to a bonfire heaped with papers – the sum total of the writs so far served. Everybody was frankly applauding now – in a minute they would be linking hands and breaking into a dance. As the official party went off down the track, clutching their cases to their chests like shields, one last clod came flying and hit Shaw in his back, a midden clod, which plastered his coat with dark-brown glaur and sent straw flying like shrapnel.

By nightfall the whole neighbourhood had heard how much the same ceremony had been enacted at each township as far down as Eilean Neist. At Ferrinbeag they had heaped up driftwood on the excellent paper kindling supplied by the Government. When the embers had settled into a compact red glow, they had roasted potatoes and herrings and made a feast of it.

The calm weather prevailed. Flo and Sandy could dally as they liked, lying almost naked on mossy ground screened by a covert of saughs until the midges found them and tormented them back into a state of decency. Her flesh was warmed through by his constant attentions. She had never felt so well. Lapped in loving, she would forget or at least cover over her doubts so that they only surfaced when she awoke in the small hours, tormented by fleas or by Kirsty's coughing in the room below.

'What will you do next?' she made herself ask Sandy one evening. She meant, How much longer can you afford to stay away from the fishing?

'Make sure that every one knows what to do when they come to arrest a puckle of us. They will get their teeth into a few – whoever

MacKenzie wants rid of, or whoever is named by that snot who keeps the school.' His head had room for nothing but the Rising, as everyone called it now. It was fuelling him like a tar in a beacon.

'Are you not afraid, Sandy my dear? There is gaol at the end of this, surely.'

'Afraid?' He turned his blue stare onto her. 'I am afraid of nothing. Except fear itself.'

'But if they come with too much force ... a military kind of force ... I think I know what that is like.' It was the nearest she had come so far to talking about her life before. He was as incurious as ever, seeming content to see her as this woman who had blown his way like some passage bird from Norway or Faroe or any distant place.

He was looking past her hair, into the bluish-green ungle of the leaves. 'If they are so military, they will have to come on the steamer, and then we will have warning enough. They will not get up the hill.'

Chapter 19

A child was crying – her son. Her son had bright blue shiny eyes, as naked as the sky in summer, and they never blinked. Nearer he came, nearer, nearer, saying not a word. He was trying to bind her in a charm – she could not move. His bright eyes were not loving, they were poison-blue – he wanted to terrify her. Nearer, nearer – she felt her own face crumple, hot liquid rose behind her eyes – her own voice was wailing …

In the street somebody was wailing, high and thin and monotonous, as though it had settled into a piteousness that could not be staunched.

'Flora! Flora!' Kirsty's hoarse voice, breaking into a cough.

She was down the stair in a trice.

'Look.' The door was standing open. Out in the street, with his bare feet in a gutter of cows' urine from the nearest byre, a boy was crouching – it was wee Calum from three doors along. His mouth stretched wide, showing the gap where the first of his milk-teeth had fallen out, and it was pumping out those wailing cries.

Behind him, across the quays, between the fishing-boat masts, she could see the weekly steamer, the *Marmion*. It was lying slantwise on the reef that rose out of the harbour at the lowest tide and was covered just now. Its regular day was Thursday. Today was Monday. What on earth … The boat looked like bad luck, a black bar of a silhouette blocking the way to the open sea, fine grey fabrics of rain blurring the dark hulk of it.

'What on earth …'

Kirsty looked sharply at her as though to say, Need you ask? 'Calum MacVicar was out fishing from the rocks when he should have been in his bed. He saw the *Marmion* sneaking in and grounding – that Captain Mackie, he is a drunken fool – and Calum was too afraid of his father's belt to come back with the news. They are saying a terrible lot of men came off her in wee boats –'

'What kind of boats? How many?'

'Nobody was counting. Most of you were asleep. There was a great many were in uniforms, with a kind of hard hats on their heads, and there were toffs in tweed hats and capes – och, they have brought an army right enough and it has caught every one of you dozing, for all your fighting words.'

In a minute Flo was dressed and along at Eilidh's door. Sandy had been roused half an hour before and had gone off down the Ferrinbeag road with Sorley and James from the *Star*, on the heels of the police.

'No, he said nothing about you.' Eilidh gave her a quick, fierce gleam from under her brows.

As Flo turned away, feeling betrayed, the wynd was starting into life. Shawled women with their shoes on were coming out of door after door, children in ragged jerseys, men with tangled or combed hair and their braces over their shirts. And here came Maggie, looking triumphant.

'I told you they would be coming!' She had said nothing of the kind. 'Let us have the helmets off them, and the breeks as well, and whip them back to Glasgow.'

'How many are there?'

'Fifty in uniforms, and MacKenzie and Anderson, the two fat pricks, and writers from the papers, would you believe.'

'From the papers? From Inverness, is it?'

'From there, and Glasgow and Dundee, and there are two from London, and one of them has a book for making pictures.'

This was gibberish – rumour was running mad. They had better knit up their wits and be going down the road.

'Are we still meeting at the Pass?'

'Aye, at the Pass, to ambush them coming back. The crowd from Ferrinbeag will be there by then, and Big Alex is bringing down his mob from Manish. Bracadale are useless, but if the bobbies get as far down as Eilean Neist, Mother and Father will give them a fine welcome.'

'We should have chased them.' They were all surging along now, ignoring the rain which was blinding over from the sea on their left hand.

'They were in a couple of wagonettes, the nobs were anyway, and the bobbies were trot-trotting in double time – Mother MacLeod said their boots were beating the road like cattle in a panic.'

'Had they guns? No. They would never send real soldiers – we are not Zulus.'

'They had long clubs, every man of them, and they were holding them like warriors in a picture.' Maggie suddenly pranced on the spot, raising her knees high and holding up her hand in a fist. She laughed with an undernote of hysteria. Her face went still as a corpse's and she said in a hiss, 'If they take John, I will fly at them and bite their throats out.'

The dense rain had turned heavier, big drops pattering on thatch and slates, then on the black pools and myrtle bushes at the roadside. As it struck through their sleeves, Flo rearranged her shawl round her forehead and shuddered with a mixture of chilliness and nerves – not fear – expectancy – as painful as a fever. If John was taken, or Hugh … If Sandy went berserk … She could see him with that look of blazing delight as when he came at her to embrace her … She could no more hold back from the fight now than she could say no to him.

By the time they reached the Pass there were hundreds of them, quite quiet now, soaked almost through, steeled by a purpose that Flo could feel in herself like muscles grown young again – fit as when they spent the warm months up at the shielings, following the herds for miles as they stravaiged freely, being chased by the boys in the long yellow afterglow … Here at the Pass Sgiach changed from the brown northern moorlands, lochans brightened only by water-lilies in summer, rotting crags whose weeds dripped except in the driest drought. To the south the inland drew back in a spread of fair pasture, a green skirt on the mountain rising to the west. Once the townships had been huddles of houses, small and low and comfortable enough, sheltering each other and sheltering their kailyards, in easy reach of the common fields surrounding them. Now the folk of Ferrinbeag, Bracadale, and Eilean Neist – the survivors after the exodus to New South Wales and Nova Scotia – lived along the shore on half crofts, on quarters even, cut off by the new farms from the grazings on Beinn Bhreac. Was that pasture as remote as Canaan now?

The white rains had wiped out the vista southward of the townships, Tormore Castle with its fancy towers, its windows of many panes – they said a single one had cost £500 – its bunches of sycamores and strange evergreens shipped in from Canada and South America. People said it was even grander inside than the Ardmair place on the western island. Flo had kept quiet during this conversation, she would never let out a word of that bad old dream of a life.

The crowd of them were spreading up the slopes on either side of the road as though they had practised it many times. To the west, blackened flakey outcrops reared up twenty foot or more. Heather grew rank between them and rowans deformed as though by rheumatism shook their young green fruit in gusts from the sea. To the east, on shelves of a harder rock, the heath was shorter, broken by tongues of bent-grass and falls of scree that had split off from the scarp. On both sides of the road ammunition was plentiful, fragments sharp as arrowheads on the inland side, shingles like cannonballs on the other.

Threes and fours were coming up from the southern townships now, breathless, some of them weeping. The folk from Manish and the town greeted them with cheers, then calmed down into a rumbling murmur as the news went round that the force had reached Neist already, seized Alasdair MacKinnon, and were on their way back now, still trotting in that steady double-time, 'like cavalry in France' according to a very old man Flo had never seen before.

'They have father?' Peg was crying out unbelievingly. 'Did he not fight?'

'Is he hurt?' asked Maggie.

'He is bleeding from his hair.'

'Who have they taken from Ferrinbeag?'

'Brown Hugh and John MacAulay.'

A scream from Peg, as grating and unearthly as a heron's.

'And a big man with grey hair. We never saw him before. Some kind of hill man.'

Alexander MacSween? Had he cut through the moor and gone straight down to the thick of the battle? Where was Sandy? She saw him now, in the midst of the crowd across the way, his hair soaked brown, still springy. He seemed not to see her. On the fringe of the crowd a few strangers were standing in long coats and capes, looking useless. Only one of them was busy, his hand moving to and fro across a pad of paper under the shelter of an umbrella held by another.

A drumming of boots from the hidden part of the road among birches and saughs, south of the highest point where horses rested in a quarry. Flo ran up the nearest hillock and looked hard at the straggling woods, seeing them eerie – each leaning, dripping tree could turn into an ill-willed stranger, if she looked away for a minute. Hill fog was smoking through the branches, blurring the road. Shadows in the grey became solid bodies – jerking, prancing shapes in dark-blue tunics and dark-blue helmets. Nearer they came and she could make out prisoners in their midst, one sagging, being dragged, the other three still struggling in sudden hefts against the arm-locks that held them trapped. From the two wings of the crowd a roar was gathering, first a surf, then throaty and rising like one massed growl from a dog-pack.

The stones had been piled by now, picked from the scree, pulled out of the rotting crags. A boy flung one when the posse was still a hundred yards away. His friends jeered as it dropped absurdly short. The enemy were so *silent* – how could those fifty or more breathing men come onto them, facing them, with not an oath or a shout? One last jeer went up as the laird's agents were seen in a wagon well to the rear – 'MacKenzie, your father was a *bastard!*' Then the stone flew.

Flo flung a blade with all her force. A constable on the right of the foremost rank flinched, his eyeballs white between crow-black hair and shaved blue stubble. Stones bashed helmets, thumped on shoulders, and the formation faltered, then came on in ranks of four, their serge uniforms dark with wet. As she stooped, tore out more stones, flung them down at heads, trying to avoid the prisoners, her first battle, long ago on the Island, came thickening in her head like a waking nightmare. She felt her hands no more, heard nothing of Peg and Maggie swearing and yelling next to her. Here it came again – the fires seething red and orange through torn holes in the roof – the loom with the tweed in it disappearing under a shower of burning cabers from the roof – Allan her father on his back, charred thatch and turfy litter piling onto his chest and thighs, the drizzle falling into his open eyes while his mouth said, 'Make a ring and never falter –'

She cried out as a stone in the ground held back her thumbnail and tore it right across. She bit it loose and spat it out and plunged both hands into the bank – it was a morass now – wrenched a clod free, stones more than earth, and flung it at the man nearest her with all her force, feeling the muscles tearing down her side. It caught him on the visor of his helmet and knocked it off, baring a pure-white dome like a peeled egg with a frost of stubbly hair round its back and sides. He gasped with shock, flushed up to the white rim of his baldness, and looked furiously up at the slope. She waved at him and scooped out her tongue like a sexual invitation. Maggie was giving him two fingers while Peg sang out, 'Good shooting, Flo,' and skrieghed as though she was spinning in a dance.

The posse had haltered, without any order from the bald sergeant. They were still in rank, less compact now, their lines uneven. As though it was a game the Sgiach folk had stopped too and were staring round them with big eyes, looking flummoxed like driven cattle, some leering in triumph or crazed exhaustion. They could see now that the sagging prisoner was John MacAulay. Thick scarlet stood out on his temple and cheek like blood from a slaughtered pig. Maggie screamed 'John!' She lunged, she would get to him. Flo clasped her from behind and shouted, 'No – no – watch out.' A panic smell was reeking from the woman like fresh meat.

'Peg!' That was Hugh, roaring from the midst of the army. From across the way a singing voice trolled out –

'See you the hosts of armed men
With sword and pike in hand
From farmsteads and from fisher cots
Along the banks of Bann ...'

Diarmuid's favourite song – so he was back again after days away. She knew the next lines too well –

'They have come with vengeance in their eyes,
Too late, too late are they ...'

Why was he putting a spell of failure on them at this moment? He was all pose, even now. She yelled out at the full of her voice, '*Get* them *now. Get* them while they are *stopped.*' In perfect rhythm, as though waulking a tweed, they all stooped and tore and flung. The air was a hail of brown muck once again. The bobbies were fidgeting, turning their faces away from the fusillade. A hand would go up and wipe away a clot of dirt or wrench harder at the prisoners' arms. The bald sergeant had retrieved his helmet and was setting it on his head with a show of punctilio, pulling the point of his visor down between his eyes, stretching the band tightly round his jaw.

'Go for him, Flo,' growled Mother MacLeod from somewhere close behind. 'Go for the coconut, if you hit it you can have it.' She felt hysteria boil, choking her. She took a huge breath, grabbed up a clod and flung it. It was the merest dirt and burst in mid-air. Diarmuid was still carolling –

'There was never a tear in his blue eyes,
All sad and bright they were,
For young Roddy MacCorley goes to die
On the bridge at Toom –'

Oh wasn't he the raving Irish martyr – he should never have come here ... Then they were all surging down the slope, to reach the enemy, to reach their own men. Flo saw moustaches and sideburns – helmets tilted and straight – the bald sergeant, popping eyes and broken veins in his cheeks – Hugh's brown beard draggled red with blood. She smelt a stink of stale beer, fried onions, beef. Wet truncheons glistened as forty arms went up. Beside her Maggie was screaming again, 'Hugh! John! John!' Her eyes felt swelling, her temples drummed and seethed, each enemy face was clouded round in sparkling haze. A scarlet sunburst – lights – exploding lights – green sparks – spinning – swooping – faces, far above – moustaches, bristles, beasts – spinning, swooping –

From the dark underside of the world above, Kirsty's face swam down like a turnip lantern. Her mouth was moving. Deathly quiet. The face grew huge and near, swooned in a blur. The pain-axe cleft her head in two.

A red glow pulsed, flickered – fire-light. Yellow hair in a curly aureole, beneath it Sandy's eyes. Peat-reek on him. Her mouth was wet – her eyes – her cheeks – her breast. Kirsty was pressing hands down onto her shoulders. She raised her head, the pillow rose with it, sticking to it. The axe cleft her head.

'You have been in the wars.' Mother MacLeod was a silhouette in the silvery glare of the doorway. Kirsty was at the fire. The lid of the kettle rattled. 'We have all of us been in the wars.' Spilt water hissed. 'Get well now.' The door was empty.

A black mountain angled steeply upwards, downwards again. Above it a crescent moon hung, a gold blade. The mountain's faces glittered, its armour of rock was sloughing, she was spiralling backwards. The moon was a bright slot, smaller and smaller, a burning eye half-closed. If she did not look away from it she would be here at the bottom of the pit forever. She could not look away.

'Drink up the soup. You are so thin your man will never know you.' Peg was smiling at her, from a lopsided face. One of her eyes was dragged down and half closed by a healing scar.

'And where is her man?' Kirsty, from the fireside.

Flo was propped up on a bundle of bedclothes on the floor. She had felt serene all morning, lapped in this air of broth simmering, made from a fowl – silvery light from the open door – and under it all, the astringent tang of simmering woundwort. She had not smelt it for more than twenty years. Now she looked forward to the moment when Kirsty, or Peg or Mother MacLeod, supported her sitting up and sponged the crown of her head. The pain-axe threatened, then the itch of shaved hair growing again and the deep ache inside her skull were softened for a time, and her thoughts melted in warmth.

Where was her man? 'Where – he?' Her tongue still fumbled between her teeth and Peg made her practise saying sounds clearly, slowly. 'Where – Mag? Where?'

'Where – is – she,' said Peg distinctly. 'She is mending too. Her breast is not so good. Her head has healed, though.'

'Where – he?'

Peg and Kirsty looked at each other. Kirsty said roughly, 'You had better leave things be. You are ill yet.'

'Where is he?' Her head was splitting again.

'They have taken the *Star* up the Canal to the other side,' said Peg in an ordinary voice. 'Now, sup up your soup.'

From that moment Flo bent all her powers to becoming perfectly fit once more. She held onto furniture and stones in the walls as she walked round the room, then went outside and sat on an old chair without a back, getting up every hour to walk fifty paces along to the quayside, then a hundred, then a hundred and fifty. She struggled to ignore the blinding pain in her head and shut her eyes when it peaked until it died down again. Questions churned less bearably than the pain. Why no message? Eilidh – why was she staying away? He would be up at Wick by now, or north as far as Balta – where should she try first? Fares for the steam, for the train – would her wee store of coins be enough?

'Stay here,' said Peg one morning. 'We can maybe get work from the Swine, barking nets or redding up his sheds for the winter.'

'You two are all right,' Flo retorted, petulant with weakness and frustration. 'They have only fined your Hugh. And John will be out of gaol in another month. And they will be staying here. But Sandy – if he has gone, then he does not love me.'

'Love' – she had never spoken it before. It was a word from the songs. It made things worse, setting free feelings like heady perfume from a crushed flower. So that had not been his real hair and real eyes she had seen in the sick-bed. Yet she had smelt him … She was crying now with the helpless misery of a wronged child.

'Do not be envying Maggie. A weakness has come on her chest where they kicked her when she tried to get to John. And word has come from Inverness – John is not good in the gaol, he can keep nothing down –'

'Tell her some good news,' broke in Kirsty in her contrary way.

'You are right. We did some good. They have been talking about us in the Parliament, in London. Those writers have put the truth of it in the papers.'

'Tell her about the valuation,' Kirsty insisted.

'Och – they have been doing their fancy arithmetic. A farmer came over from Aberdeenshire to do the factoring instead of Stewart – the fat prick had gone away to Glasgow – and this new man says the townships can have the mountain grazings for £70. But never mind the rent – the cattle are back on the hill – we just herded them up there through the new farms and nobody as much as came out to swear at us. Father came up last week to sit with Maggie and he is overjoyed. He cannot find the money for his fine but he was singing like a lark about the place. Father singing! He says they are in new heart down at Ferrinbeag and Neist.' Her face stilled and her voice dropped. 'If only it is not a wet winter coming. If only Maggie can get her dander up again.'

She looked at Flo, expecting some words of encouragement, and saw her friend's face turned towards the fire. All she could think of was affording the journey to the mainland and across the country and the sea to the summer fishing grounds where Sandy must be if he was still in her world at all.

Chapter 20

Shredded mists of white steam from the engine trailed off above their shadows, across the light lime-green of the oats, the frosty green of the later-planted crops on the hillsides of Strathmore, the dense gardens of the potato fields. Flo followed the rags of it with her eyes till it became transparent, became air. If her life was as fugitive as that … A weakness of convalescence swam through her, tears poured down her cheeks and into the corners of her mouth until she swallowed the salt liquid. She shook her head at Peg in the seat opposite, beneath a brown photograph of the Auld Kirk at Alloway, and pretended to snap at her, 'What are you looking at?'

'Och …' Peg shrugged. 'It is never as bad as you think.'

For a long minute Flo looked inside herself, searching for some core that was still not cracked – saw it, distinct as a clean, whole stone on the floor of a perfectly clear well – and only when she had this image safe in her head did she dare to speak her thoughts aloud – her one clear thought – 'If only he is there, we will be all right.'

This was ridiculous. There was no 'we' about it. Peg's Hugh had travelled ahead and would be at Baltasound by now – he might even have joked and bullied some curer into keeping a berth for Peg as well as for himself. As for Sandy, maybe owning the *Star* had set him free as a buccaneer, who made is own laws. Saying 'we' was only a desperate wish – no better than a prayer – that all the Sgiach folk would still be a clan in Shetland, in England even if they went south this year, and would win home together at the end of yet another season still close-knit and all one wool, as the weavers said.

Where was home? Sgiach? Or the Island? Or …

In the station at Aberdeen a roof of glass pieces and metal spars made echoes far above their heads. She seemed to be walking beside herself, watching herself move and speak just as she had done some day or hour before. Since her head was hit, this had plagued her – it was like looking on at your own dream, knowing you were unable to step out of it. Then she did see herself. A kind of shop in the station displayed a little rampart of newspapers – more hung on wires above the seller's head – her own face was looking back at her in a dozen pictures, each exactly the same as its neighbour. A drawing in bold black pen – her head with its hair hanging down, blood dropping out of it – her shawl falling off her shoulders – her body limp, cradled in the arms of a big old woman she suddenly recognised, Mother MacLeod, her grey ringlets, her knobby nose, her eyes wide open in a glare of accusation, her mouth widened in an ugly slot of fury and grief. Her own eyelids were closed, corpse-like. The high bridge of her nose, that she had never liked, was exaggerated by the falling-away of her cheeks and hair and blood. It was still unmistakable.

Behind the two women other figures were suggested by curves and hatchings of the artist's pen. Behind them again, a thick grille of black bars angled this way and that – the truncheons of the constables.

Below the drawing were three columns of print, above it a kind of scroll with curly ends and lettering in blue with red initials – GREAT BRITISH PICTORIAL MONTHLY.

The two women had stopped dead at the same moment. A man with a small trunk on his shoulder bumped into them from behind, then shouldered past without a word. They looked at each other, feeling suddenly undressed, betrayed. Peg gave a little gasp through her nose and said gruffly, 'Mercy on us – he has made you look like … like the drowned girl in the song.' Still Flo could not speak. She felt sick now, to be so exposed.

The paper-seller was looking at them with cold assessment, as though they were beggars. Braving this, she stepped nearer to read the title of the story below the picture: 'Wounded Heroine of the Highland Affray', it said. The drawing was signed in clear black script, 'Richard Burley'. Below the name of the paper the price was printed – 'One Shilling'. A whole silver coin for something you could read in an evening! She had forgotten about London prices. They should have been thrifty and gone north and east with the boats. But most of them had left by the time they had recovered. And her head would never have stood the wild churning of the waters in the firth of Pentland.

The stall woman had recognised her now and was calling over her shoulder to somebody at the back.

'Come away from here, Peg. We must find a man to cart our barrels to the lodging.'

The porter took one look at the label on Flo's barrel of belongings and said the name out loud in a voice of triumphant discovery – 'Florence

Campbell! Aweel now, you fairly bested the brutes. Na, na' – looking at the pence they proffered – 'keep your mecks. I wadna tak ocht fae a heroine.'

At their lodging in the Green, on the ground floor of a blackened building that towered up like a cliff, the landlady – recommended by Hugh's mother as 'clean, and religious enough' – recognised her at once and said emphatically, 'There has niver been ony fechting in *this* hoose.' She shut the kitchen door behind her with a clunk.

As they ate their kippered herrings in the evening, the man of the house seemed to regard Flo's picture on the front of an English magazine as a licence to make up to her and said roguishly, 'Tak aff that mutch now, Hielan' Mary, and gie's a peek at the scar,' at which his wife cleared the table with a whisk and a clatter and said decisively, 'We turn aff the gas at *nine* o'clock. And you will find *twa* jugs of *cauld* watter in the room.'

The deck of the boat was laden with people, barrels, animals. As it waited to cast off, the stokers must have been building up the furnaces to their greatest heat. Scarves of black smoke streamed from the funnel, then swooped in a gust of wind blowing down the river and set them gasping and coughing and wiping smuts from their brows. The ship moved under them, the elaborate grey-granite buildings were sliding backwards, from somewhere by the funnel a giant bird screeched, screeched again, and the sound rifled in at Flo's temple and out at the other side. Echoes skirled round the harbour, cannoning off ice-houses, coaling yards, the facades of chandlers and banks and inns and Customs House. When the siren shrieked again, it collided with the yelps of the gulls that had risen in a blizzard from the fish-market docks, the bellowing of terrified black cattle in a pen on the after-deck. The whites of their eyes stared, tails lifted, dung splattered on the boards and a youngish woman next to Flo turned instantly white and sweaty, bent over the rail, and sicked a stream of brown matter into the water.

'I aye dee that afore we're at sea,' she told them, and wiped her mouth with the back of her hand, then looked closely at it as though remembering with interest what she had had for breakfast. 'Aince we hit the real waves, I'm fine. The waur the sea, the better my wame.'

Slowly Flo was getting used again to the new language or languages all around them, the Aberdeenshire speak with its scooping, swallowed sounds, the soft, ingratiating chat of the Irish women who had half filled the train from Glasgow, the mingled, quicker twangs of the women from Fife, Leith, Eyemouth who were making the annual trip north to harvest their money from the herring glut.

There would be a place for themselves – there always was – she would swim or she would sink. She found she had actually shaken her head to rid it of these maudlin thoughts. Peg was looking at her with doubt, and perhaps with impatience.

'Will you stand the sea, now? Maybe we should have left it for another week.'

'And missed our money? No, no – the wind is on the other side of the country, and you heard what he said at the lodging, only the channels by Stroma and Sumburgh should do us any harm at all.'

'Did you trust him? He had a wicked eye. And she would have poisoned the porridge if she could have got away with it.'

'Och, we will never see them again. There are better houses in Aberdeen.'

The *St Sunniva* had trailed its long wash into the outer harbour by now. The waves of it were riding along the inside of the north pier like a line of porpoises with backs of foam. Under the great chalky tower of the lighthouse on the south ness the fringe of their wake boiled suddenly on a flat reef like dough on a griddle. Then they curved northward and were cleaving calmly through a sea as grey as fog. The deck and the rail shuddered rhythmically to the beat of the engines. Otherwise, looking seaward, they might have been becalmed on this never-ending expanse. What life lay on the far side of it – people like themselves? The German Ocean – why German when that country could not even be seen?

To the west the town had ended in benty hillocks and a long pale-brown strand, broken briefly by the river-mouth with its five-arched bridge. Above its parapet she could see the black backs of a line of cattle rippling and dipping as they walked slowly south towards the town. It had always looked to her as foreign as Africa. After the long tract of the sand-dunes red cliffs bulked up with tall caves darkening between them, arching back into unknown innards. On Sgiach they would have been saying, 'The Young Fool was hiding there after the Forty-Five before he got away to Benbecula.' In the middle of the sea a mass of black rock yellowed by lichen and whitened by bird-lime stood up on two legs, with a hole in its centre like a window. The *St Sunniva* gave it a wide berth and steamed north by east. A shape hull-down on the eastern horizon turned slowly into a steamer very much like their own, black-and-white with a trail of coal smoke behind it. Beyond her a further ship was slowly gaining on them.

The sick woman was cheerful now, looking about her and inclined to speak. 'Faur ye gaun, you twa quinies? Are ye Hielant?' Seeing Flo look doubtful, she assumed she was slow-witted and tried speaking in single words as though teaching a child. 'Wick? Balta? Eh? Are ye gaun tae Wick? Or the haill wey up tae Shetland?'

'My man is in Shetland.' Seeing Flo tongue-tied, Peg took over the exchange. 'And maybe hers is too. We will be looking for them there.'

'Looking?' She laughed in a hoarse, smoky voice. 'Aweel, guid luck, an' if ye canna fin' the richt eens, there's aye ithers will feel the same in the dark.'

In the hazy weather the shore had dimmed. The sky brightened again and when the land dipped they could see the huge fields sloping gently, perfect carpets of barley and oats with hardly a poor patch where seed had failed to take – acre after acre, and one field of it would have made crofts for a whole clachan in the west. Flights of gulls were coming out to meet them, from the harbour with its long arms of pier, houses stacked up the hill behind it, and a lumpy, quarried skyline where brown rocks jutted like ruined forts. The steamers were closing in. Maybe they were having a race together. They could make out white-lettered names on the sterns now as their rivals drew slowly ahead – *St Magnus, St Rognvald*. More foreign words. Then everything was happening at a fevered pace as they slid alongside the quay and hawsers were hitting the water, being hauled ashore on thin lines and looped into bollards. Huddles of women were looking up at them, so many faces framed in shawls, rosy or brown but some were pale as cheese. A horse with massive haunches and feathery legs was swung ashore in a net while a gaggle of boys cheered and one pluffed peas from a shooter at the animal's belly, then was chased by a docker in coarse grey trousers and boots like river-stones coated with oil and coal-dust, and cuffed till he cried.

'Will we not get off for a while?' Flo said to Peg.

'And lose our places? They are all a big gang here, you know, and Fraserburgh is worse. They are all mad for money, they will do anything to catch the curer's eye. Will a dram settle us, now, before we get to Pentland?'

She had taken a stone bottle out of the cloth bag she carried and turned her back on the seething deck before taking the stopper out and passing it to Flo. It must have come straight from a still in the maze of rocks north of Sgiach town. It was tasteless, then turned to fiery acid in the throat.

The *St Sunniva* had docked last and was first away. Round the headland, after Fraserburgh, the deck was hardly bearable. They could no longer turn or stretch but had to squat where they were, staring north or west and losing their thoughts in the wide water that made a broad desert for as far as they could see. A sharp pain hammered into her ankle and she looked down to see a hen's indignant eye fixing her from its roost in a woman's straw basket. She pushed its beak away with her foot and the woman took her pipe from her mouth, glared at her, and said angrily, 'Will ye mind thon fowl!'

From somewhere out of sight in the thickets of heads and hats and bodies a man was singing with a chuckle in his voice –

'I can drink and nae get drunk,
I can fecht and nae be slain,
I can kiss anither man's wife
And aye be welcome hame again …'

The last they had seen of the coast was a pulsing red shimmer – the flames of a bonfire reflected from the low-slung, foggy cloud. Old Wicked-eye had been right, the wind could not reach this side, or it had died as the day gloomed into night. They ate a loaf and two cold boiled eggs they had bought for sixpence at the lodgings and their stomachs accepted the dry food without complaint. The whisky helped, and it helped them drowse their way up the dark coast that slid slowly into sight. The moon was high and full in the east and undimmed enough to light the shoulders of a group of rock stacks that rose out of the silvered water like devilish chimneys.

'Duncansby at last,' said Peg. 'Pray for calm now.'

Nothing happened. Then the ship wallowed a little and righted itself again. The hen clucked once. For miles and miles the water had stretched away from them like a whitened blue skin, puckered here and there. Now, ahead, a shadow-line stretched across it like an old turf-dyke on the moor. Beyond it Flo saw sharp lights dancing in a fever, like the sparks in her head when she coughed. Waves flashed, baring their teeth. The *St Sunniva* pitched and rolled at the same moment. A metal ball banged from side to side in her skull. The hen beat its wings against her leg and from the pen a stirk bellowed at the full stretch of its lungs. The funnel and the after-mast were arcing widely to and fro against brilliant stars.

In minutes the sea was uneventful again. From its source in the crowd a song came trolling out –

> 'And across the burn, oot-ower yon lea,
> Safe in a glen whaur nane could see,
> They twa wi' muckle mirth an' glee
> Fae a new cheese cut a whang,'

and a rumble of voices came in the chorus –

> 'La-lalty tow-row-ree.'

Long before they reached Lerwick she felt unreal with exhaustion. Weary discomfort coated her like stale fat. In the grey, numb half-light before sunrise she lurched down steep stairs with metal rims to use the lavatory. In the cramped wash-room smelling of sickness she saw, in a mirror framed in shiny red mahogany, a woman she barely recognised. Gaunt, with a shallow gully showing in each yellowish cheek. Her hair felt clogged. She took off her cap, which had made her look so old, and heard it rasp on the bristles growing in beside her scar. At the front of her hair – the russet brown that Mairi had once liked – a white spray had grown in, as strange and startling among the rest as the bib on an ousel's breast. It was the image of Allan her father – that show of age in his hair which had always been a sign to her of his other life, before the Island.

She was seeing herself with more clarity than she had been able to for years. The bit of a looking-glass in Kirsty's smoky lair of a house had become too mottled brown to show much and she had grown used to making do with a quick look in the window of the Bank, seeing herself like a ghost amongst reflected masts and hulls. She leaned on the rim of the basin and looked into her face as though searching the picture of a forebear. Her mother surfaced – light-brown, uncurved eyebrows over eyes the colour of the browner sort of dulse, a mouth with a thin, tensed lower lip and an upper lip moulded in a surprisingly perfect Cupid's bow. Her eyes looked at bay under the strong bone arches below her brows. Why could she not look out easily and debonairly at things? Sandy would think she was long in the tooth now – he would be itching for some younger flesh …

This thought infested her brain like a fly inside her ear, it hissed and crackled for days while they settled down on Unst and found themselves a space in one of the huts at Hamar on the north shore of Balta Sound. Here they helped a crowd of girls from Northumberland to make it into a home of sorts, papered it with fresh paper sprigged with roses, hung new-washed pale-yellow screens at the windows, frayed but clean and smelling of windy sunlight. A girl called Pearl, from Eyemouth, hung a large piece of mirror on a nail where the light was good and stood in front of it, trying out smiles and winks and demure, flirty looks.

At times Flo felt she had walked through the glass into a sort of cosy dream – coming home at night, while the lustrous northern sunset paled gradually in the north-north-west, her fingers raw again in spite of her gutter's bandages, the women's voices bubbling and whooping in the long space below the rafters.

It was in the hour after sunrise, when everyone was trying not to wake up, that the fly became a wasp, and stung. On the second morning she said to Peggy in the next bunk but one, across the space they had left for Maggie, 'Where are they, then?'

Perfect silence, no sound of breathing, so she must be awake.

'Hugh and Sandy – where are they?'

'I know fine who you mean. Hugh may be out at the wee island – he has worked there before.'

'But you never went over on the boat with the singing lassies at the end of yesterday –'

'Will he want to see me with this eye?' Ever since the battle she had spent hours with her tongs, crimping her hair to veil the side of her face where the cheekbone, as it healed the socket, had given her an almost Chinese cast.

'You are as pretty as ever.'

'You look fine yourself. Your wound is at the back, you lucky lass.'

'My hair is grizzled at the front. And anyway, Sandy is thirteen years younger than me.'

Silence again. Why did Peg always take a minute to speak up when he was mentioned?

Throughout the day they were both on edge, snapping at the young packer who had been set on to make up their crew until Maggie arrived, scolding her when she spilled salt from her scoop, forgetting she was there at all when there was a lull before the next trolley of fish from the unloading berth and the girls expected them to gossip about 'the grand-looking sailors from the steam yachts.' At night they could hardly bear to take the time to wash out their finger-cloths or finish their dish of herrings and potatoes. Then they were both at the mirror, looking and comparing and giving little bursts of hysterical or derisive laughter. Peg pulled her left eye down to make it match the right and tilted her head this way and that in what she supposed was the style of an Oriental dancer. Flo looked sardonically at herself for a long minute and said at last, 'If I have a veil at my wedding, the bristles at the back will come prickling through like a gorbling crow's.'

Then the Eyemouth women were calling impatiently and they went down to the last pier at the seaward end of the huts and squeezed into the rowing boat. The sea had turned hard Prussian blue as the sun sank beyond the end of Unst. Balta across the water lay low like a ship dismasted and becalmed. Chimneys were smoking, coopers' yards and gutting tables were deserted. The life of the place had turned inward to the huts and to the one howff above a sandy bay on the island, where Betty Sandison sold tea (and no drink).

The clap of a single hammer was echoing from the knoll in the middle of the island. A thickset man with hunched shoulders and a full beard was busy at a cluttered yard, stooping and straightening, slipping hoops over staves, hammering home tacks from a supply in his mouth.

'Hugh,' said Flo. Peggy called out 'Hugh-y! Hugh-y!' Her voice rose at the end of the name, giving it the note of a curlew.

He stopped his work, shaded his eyes against the streaming orange sun-rays, then walked quickly down to meet the boat as it beached. In a parody of courtliness he handed the English women ashore, ignoring Peg and Flo. When he had seen them off up to the howff, he took Peg's arms and pulled her to him, saying nothing, and kissed her deeply – held her away again – looked closely at her, reached out his hand, and eased her hair away from the distorted eye. Then he kissed her again before turning to Flo and hugging her till her ribs creaked.

'You are a sight for sore eyes, the pair of you. I have been having wicked dreams.'

'Hugh MacMillan – why must the women always be coming after the men?'

'And how would I be knowing that this was the day of days when the Queen of Sheba herself would be coming sailing up the coast?'

'So you were going to be searching for us in a while, when you were in the mood –'

'Mood? I would like to be rich enough for moods. Look at my hands.'

He held them out. Most of his nails were shattered and some were blue. Two finger-ends on his left hand were flattened lumps. His knuckles were all scabs, some brown, some red.

'It is desperate here now, mad. And I am the worst of the lot. I must pay Father back the fine – he has little enough himself. And if you and I are ever to have a place …'

He looked solemnly at Peg. His beard parted in a smile. She looked ready to swoon into his arms. Flo was forgotten. She said in a low voice, feeling like a beggar, 'Hugh – has Sandy not left word? Or is he hereabouts at all?'

Again she imagined a pause. Then he said, 'The *Star* is as busy as the rest of them. I believe I saw her moored in the wee cove over at Skeo Taing, because the piers were full.' He seemed to be waiting for some other question. Then 'Och – well, it is too dark to work any more, thank God.'

In ten minutes he had gone off with Peg to 'a hut he knew of' a short way along the shore and Flo had sat out the evening in Mother Sandison's howff, then rowed back to the huts with the happy, singing boatload.

The cove at Skeo was not half a mile away, due south across the mouth of the Sound. At four in the morning she could see the *Star* at anchor, a sharp black miniature, mast and deckhouse and curving hull. As the light, which had never wholly died in the northern sky, expanded slowly, gilding the sea too brilliantly to look at, buttering the many pastures and the cleared crofts with their prostrate bones of houses, she walked down to the pier, cast off one of Edmonson's boats, and paddled as quietly as she could across the glassy water.

She could hardly tell whether the pressure at her heart was doomed or expectant. Her throat was parched as though she had drunk too much spirit the night before. When she looked round, the boat was already near. Its hull was as glossy as a raven's back with fresh black paint. She tied onto the anchor chain, let her dinghy rub gently along the side, and pulled herself up onto the deck by the combing below the gunwale.

The fore hatch was closed. She would surprise him. She eased it up and off, laid it down on the deck as gently as an egg, and peered into the semi-darkness. Only one bunk was occupied. Next the hull a woman was sitting bolt upright, her big breasts dropping over her bedclothes. Beside her Sandy was opening his eyes, unfocussed, then furiously, his bluest and most glowing stare. The woman drew the blanket to her throat. Then Flo had jumped down into that den, that nest of heated bodies. The back of her head hit the frame of the hatchway and she screamed, then screamed again as she saw them startle. The woman struggled up, wrapping a cover round her, and Flo seized her, bared her teeth as though to bite her, hefted her like a barrel and boosted her straight up through the hatchway. The heavy woman felt light as a swathe. The hatch clunked down and she was next to Sandy in near darkness, inhaling a reek of fish and old sweat and the starchy smell of semen.

'Who is that?' She grabbed his hair with both hands and hissed at him. 'Who is that?'

'She is just a woman from the south.'

'Just a woman. Nobody at all. And I am nobody at all. I am not your lover. *Am* I your lover?' She tightened her fingers in his hair and he winced but would not struggle.

'We are not married.'

'No. No. But we are wedded. We have wedded time and time again. You animal! You knew her before you came here. Why did you not –'

'I never knew her before. She is nothing at all.'

'I was nothing at all on Sgiach, I suppose. *Was* I nothing?' She was battering his head against the bulkhead behind the pillow. 'Was – I – nothing?'

He wrenched his head away, leaving gold hairs in her fists, gasping at the pain. He grabbed her wrists in one of his hands, in a clench that felt like iron not flesh-and-blood, and seized her under the chin by the other. 'We are not married. Nobody owns me. None of them.'

'None of who? The other women? A wife in every port? They all know – Peg knows – and Hugh. And now I know at last. You should have left me alone.' She was drowning. Her chest could get no air. 'Why?' Words were dying in her. The world was bursting into sparks. 'Why?'

'Yes.' He was managing to look quite scornful now, quite icy. 'I should have left you – untouched. Because I know you will never have a child, although I rammed right up you. No child. Barren. You are a barren cow.'

They had frozen as hard as statues. Silence set round them. They looked into each other's eyes, not blinking. Perhaps he meant to mesmerise her, or strangle her. She would reach him yet. 'Barren,' she said, calmly enough, with a tremor of fear or disgust. 'Barren. I may be barren. And those others up and down the country – have they had children with you?'

He said nothing. Surely, if he could claim that, he would? He still said nothing, only his eyelids blinked and blinked again.

'They have not,' she said in a voice that had less feeling than a judge's. 'So how do you know that you are not the barren one among us?'

Chapter 21

S he was all one bruise, as though each part of her had been tortured. She could not lie in the bunk at night with her face turned to the wall, it buried her alive. When she turned onto her left side yet again, she could hear Peg's breathing catch as she half-sensed Flo's incurable unrest. It went on and on. She lurched into vengefulness that appalled her. He should be keel-hauled, she had heard about this from an old deep-sea man from Barra – *him*, with his fair hair streaming, matted with crushed barnacles, his face raw, red, sodden, half grated off by the wrenching under the hull … Images flapped and cawed in her head, black carrion birds with bloodied beaks, hammering a hole in *his* ribs, tugging between his legs …

She opened her eyes to stop this awful seeing – the darkness hovered above her, lowered and lowered, pressing her nose shut, gagging her. She groaned aloud, then felt Peg's hand grip hers and squeeze it three, four times. A little signal of friendship and consolation. If only she could speak about it …

At last she did, and it came out like an accusation. She sat with Peg and Hugh one Sabbath afternoon in Ma Sanderson's howff, supping tea, saying little, letting the crowd seethe round them, Dutchmen and Swedes and Danes as well as the English and their own folk.

'If you knew,' she said, then stopped. 'If only you –'

From inside Hugh's arm Peg said, patiently enough, 'If we had said "That Sandy is a bit of a ram," what would you have done?' Her measured voice suggested she had said this already, in her head, a hundred times.

'Och – just skelped you with whatever was in my hand.' Flo's forced laugh turned suddenly into a sob that left her breathless.

'A loving woman can never be told. You would have gone at him, and quizzed him, and he would have pooh-poohed you out of it. Like he does.'

'You know him well, then. Better than I did. Have you –' Horrible thoughts were rising in her like nausea.

Peg turned to Hugh and said, 'Is this our Flo?'

'She is famous now,' he said, with the melancholy unction of a preacher embarking on a jeremiad, 'and the truth is not in her. Flo – you have never said – what is it like to be celebrated, with all those fingers pointing you out?' He had seen, as they all had, the six likenesses of her on six covers cut from the *Pictorial News* and pasted in the window of a little office the Land League occupied near the steamer dock in Lerwick.

'If I had had the money I am sure they paid the artist, then I might have got a better surgeon. And Maggie might. Do you think she will come?'

'She can hardly be here before the herring are away to England. Hugh says we should send her a letter, or a postcard with a view on it, and tell her to come to Lowestoft, if she comes at all. But och, she will be slow for a while yet. Maybe next spring will be time enough. When they lifted her down the wynd on a door, I thought she was dead. She was so grey – do you mind the grey that was in her face, Hughie?'

The two of them, in their endless recalling of the struggles on Sgiach and their pleasure in each other's agreements and confirmations, made the worst times seem almost cosy.

Meanwhile, as the summer staled, the steam-yachts swanned in and out of the Sound, and if there was no wind to fill their snow-white sails, their gold-and-black funnels streamed smoke instead, and soot fell out of the sky in flakes on the airing bedclothes of the fisher folk while the parties, French and British, American and Russian, cruised smoothly out past the headlands, a mast or a funnel seeming to ride along the land before it disappeared.

'They are off pleasuring themselves out of sight on the other side of the Ness,' the Eyemouth girls would say, with a thrill of envy. By next day the longest-staying one among them would be there again, painted on the middle reach of the sea as though it had never moved – the *Orient Pearl*, home port Great Yarmouth. Reflections of wavelets trembled in a web of rainbow lights on her sheer white flanks.

By six the sailors had risen, almost as early as the fisher folk, and were drawing up buckets of sea-water to sluice down the decks. By the time the first of the barrels were packed, the tops nailed own, and the brine replaced, all brasses on the *Pearl* had been polished yet again. By the time the fish dock paused to eat their pieces and sup their cold tea from a bottle, the gentlefolk were resting in deck-chairs from their exhausting night's sleep or diving in striped bathing costumes from the after-deck and exchanging loud, self-conscious jokes and dares and mock congratulations.

'The newspaper crowd,' said Hugh one morning, as the menagerie performed. 'New money, and plenty of it.' He was the prince of gossips. By next day he knew a little more. 'The man with the pointed beard – can you seen him? Like the Czar.' As Flo wondered who 'the Czar' was, he amazed her further by saying, 'If you do not know his face, well, he knows yours.' He paused, enjoying his puzzle. 'He was on Sgiach with his pencils, drawing the battle, and he made you famous.'

'I am not famous.'

'What is he doing here, I wonder? There are no wars here, or likely to be, but he is aye scribbling.'

She felt strangely owned. He had come into their life, or to its edge, and plucked out something from it, and then sold it. True, they were still alive and free – unlike the tigers that had begun to sprawl in the drawing-rooms of the Castle before she left, the stretched and gutted skins, stunned heads, and glassy eyes. Yet somehow this artist should have asked them first, before he put them in his freak show even for a day.

As Maggie did not come, and did not come, and as Peg and Hugh behaved more and more like a perfectly wedded couple, Flo's sense of being outside it all spread through her like an illness. At night the two women went over to Balta on one of the boats – this was accustomed, this was homely, and worries and discomforts melted down into the general joking and singing. Someone would be seized by mischief and rock the boat a little – a little more – the rowers on one side would be unable to reach the water with their blades and as the skiff plunged sideways and spun round at the same time, the women would get up a chorus of 'Woop! Woop! Woop!' – a sound of plunging and mounting again and being sick, all rolled together in an orgy of hysteria. Then the bow was grating on shingle, the women were stepping and jumping out, putting on their shoes, and walking up the slope to Ma Sandison's as though this was how they were happy to spend the rest of their lives.

On the way back down, at the end of the evening, as their spirits gathered and rose up gently into the endlessness of the dark-blue sky and the sheer gold lustre of new-born day in the north, nostalgia welled up in them and one voice, then eight or nine, crooned out a yearning song –

'Busk, busk, bonny laddie,
An' come awa' wi' me,
An' I'll tak ye to Glen Isla
Nigh bonny Glen Shee …'

In the meantime Flo spent hours on a bench in the room, and supped tea till the inside of her mouth was as grainy as sand, and stared at the yellow distemper on the walls, turning its flakes and wrinkles into every kind of shape. There was a fish-hook, curved and barbed. There was a baby's head, bald as a bird's egg. There was a whorl like the sooty bruise of St Peter's thumb-print on the flank of a haddock …

The images bored into her, riddling her thoughts, for which she was almost thankful. *He* would have regaled his cronies by now with great stories of how easy it had been to part her legs – how they had gone at it day or night, under a roof or under a tree – how trig and tight she had been beside the slack auld hoors of that port of this. At least he had taken to mooring somewhere else. The black shape of his boat in the bay still stuck to her vision like a weal left on her eyeball by the sun. She heard her own teeth grating and felt a pain in the hinges of her jaws. What would Peg and Hugh be thinking of her? She glanced sideways and saw them snugly touching, happy in the pressure from each other's bodies. Peg saw her look and said, 'A good night, eh, Flo?'

It was the first time her friend had ever seemed to say something out of politeness.

'Yes, it is a grand night.' As her mouth spoke, her mind was asking itself, Why am I here? Who do I only ever perch, like a gull on a rock? In another fortnight we will be following the fish down south. Like gulls again. And if I was mothering children, would I have any more of a place in the world? The Island had been a place. And if Roddy MacPhail with the close brown brows and the sudden, daft, fearless ways had been her man … She should have found some way, after the Battle, to reach him at the gaol in Inverness. It was so long ago, to think of it was like looking at a wee picture. It grew smaller every year – as she must seem to him, if he ever thought of her at all, on the deep sea somewhere, a stoker or a deckhand, if he was not slaving in a mill in Glasgow and drinking his brains to a mush in the bars at night … It was hard to live. There was a great hand that could close round you at any time and finish you off like the runt of the litter, strangling you and throwing you to the bigger dogs.

Did Peg think this? Or Hugh? If they did, they drowned it in giggling and kissing, and romancing on about the croft they would have one day in the broad lands of Aberdeenshire.

Some sailors had come in tonight – to a place that sold only tea, for a wonder – and were laughing and looking round them as freely as though they were full of beer. A white linen cap with a name-band round it lay upside down on the bench beside her and she found herself trying to read its name. S.S. *Orient Pearl.* The pleasure-loving mob. The menagerie. Playground of the pirate with the beard who had taken her face and sold it to a thousand strangers.

The young man next to her must have been looking for an opportunity. 'Nice here,' he said the moment he saw her examining her cap. 'Homey. Pity they don't sell' – he winked – 'something a touch stronger.'

The wink had made his brown face glint with humour. His bare arms were tanned as though smoked and almost hairless. Their smooth skin, and his cheeks and sunburnt neck, asked to be stroked. Slowly she eased her shawl back from her forehead, baring the white stripe in her hair, then drew it right back to her shoulders so that he could see at least in profile the bristle of stubby hair beside her scar. He would surely flinch. As his eyes widened and he blinked quickly, she leaned forward as though to confide in him and said in a low voice, 'Och, there is good stuff on the island, if you knew where to go. But tell me, is there not drink enough on your grand boat?'

He looked mortified. 'Oh, we get our tot. Rough old stuff. The fine liquor, it all goes down the throats of the toffs and their lady-friends.'

'That is a shame. Rich and mean – a terrible mixture. Are the backhanders not up to much?' She was remembering the sovereigns the grandees visiting the Castle had used to hand out at leave taking – to the Meikles and Kilgour, not to 'the girls'.

'Yes, well, some of them give us a bit of brass. If they like the looks of us – know what I mean?' He winked again.

Was this one a 'queer hare'? And he had looked so manly. 'Are they all like that?'

'Who knows? What the eye don't see … That lot, they buy what they like, see, and they drop it when they're finished. Women, boys, horseflesh, yachts. One time, my boss, he sees this actress on the front at Cowes, bust on her like a swan. I don't what he said, made her an offer, know what I mean. Next thing she's cuffed him round the chops, I heard the slap, and he's in the drink. We had to fish him out. Thing is, she wasn't no Drury Lane tart or nothing like it – she was a Duchess! No, he can pay, cash, for whatever he fancies, Derby winners, pictures –'

'Artists?'

'Come again?'

'I suppose he bought that artist?'

The sailor was looking at her with new eyes. 'Haven't I seen you … Yes, I have – that Burley – you're the one he drew! In the paper? Stone the crows! They didn't kill you, then?'

He was running his eyes all over her now, inspecting her as though she was made of wood or plaster.

'You speak English all right,' he was saying with a tone of generous compliment. 'Where d'you pick that up, then?'

'From our masters.' Why was she making an effort? What did he care? Since he had recognised her, he seemed to be seeing her as a curio. 'You see, when they burned our houses, there was nowhere else to work, but they needed our hands, so they offered us a wage, or a passage to the Colonies.'

'I'd have gone overseas if they'd paid me. Or taken to the hills.'

'They also own the hills.'

'Oh well …' He looked confused, inclined to argue, lost for reasons, and the discomfiture made his tanned, overgrown-boy's face drop in a sulk. 'He got your likeness anyway.' He was studying her again, frankly appraising, faintly greedy. 'Made you younger, didn't he? Like they do. Made you a right little Joan of Arc.' He nudged her, then leaned still nearer and pinched her cheek. As she recoiled, he turned away and said to his shipmates, 'Best be off, lads. Stars will be up now. Sounds breezy an' all.'

As the men paid Ma Sandison and filed out, consciously fitting their caps on at snappy angles and flicking crumbs from their white-duck trousers, she saw the boy remarking on her to a friend, who looked back at her, grinning.

When the women opened the door to leave, it blew back against the wall with a slam. They had to walk crouched against the scathing of the wind. The rushing darkness of it was so fierce that they were looking at each other with white eyes, excited and wondering. The boat was knocking against the jetty. On a calm night two of them might have rowed with a pair of oars each. Now it took four of them, each pulling with the whole of their strength.

The tide was still filling, helping them against the blasts of the westerly. Flo measured their headway against two lights on the north shore, a bigger orange one low down, a small yellow one further up. Slowly the lower one moved below the upper, as though sliding out to sea. They were barely halfway back to Hamar when one of the rowers coughed and groaned, 'I'm doing nothing – I can't …' The sea had turned. Now everything was against them. The woman was slumped over her oar, sobbing. Flo balanced along, helped her off the thwart, and grabbed the oar before it swivelled out of the thole-pins and was lost in the invisible sea. She tried to settle into a stroke and felt as though she was lifting a mountain with a straw. She pulled with all her muscle and felt no answering forward thrust.

'Shift, you bloody bitch!' The woman next to her had said that. It was Pearly from Eyemouth, talking to the boat. They were all in the same plight, hauling against impossible forces, hauling so hard that they were half lifted off the thwarts by the pressing of their feet against the cross-battens fixed to the planking.

Too daunting to look sideways at her seamarks to see if they were changing position. She looked. They were staying fixed. No headway. At least the skiff was not being carried back to the island – or out to sea. The rocking, heaving blackness was flooding in on her now, belittling and crushing. She did not know if she wanted the land enough to strive to reach it. Sheer fear was driving her. Those cold depths would drown her face, her throat, her lungs. Thinking of it choked her and her strength was cut off. She grabbed at her stroke, the blade bounced off the water and the haft struck her under the chin, making her gasp. She clenched herself inward after that, closed doors against her brain and let only hands, arms, shoulders work at all. She hauled in time with the others. The crests of the waves were jumping higher, bursting, pelting them with bitter volleys. Her face streamed, her eyes stung, and her hands. They had blistered through, at the base of each finger the skin had torn off in flaps, the liquid running out of her flesh was making her oar too slippery to grip. She hauled on, disregarding everything, feeling the torture grind down her deeper pain till it was too small to see or feel.

She snatched a look at the seamarks. Now the shore light was well to the right of the yellow one above it. They were making headway. They might not drown. They might get back to the hut. She would not look again for a hundred strokes. Rain came on and when she next looked, the lights and all the other scattered glims had been wiped out. A hundred strokes, and a hundred and a hundred. They were being less thrown about. The skiff was jarring along the stones of the pier at Hamar.

As someone tied up to the rings, the others lurched up the steps, as weak as though they were ill. They could hear the gale, now that the sea and the boat no longer possessed them. It was peaking in gusts, in wild screams. In the hut they undressed and dried themselves and got into their bunks with hardly a word, only Pearl said, 'That's better. Nothing like a good blow through. Who's for a picnic on the island?' and laughed at her own sally.

Flo lay down, still shuddering, and at once her troubles stormed in on her with the frenzy of the wind. In the teeth of its shrieking whole pieces of her brain shredded and flew off into the night. The bloodied feathers of the hens smashed up at the eviction – a brown trace whisking in the darkness – gone. Young Meikle's gaping flies, Old Meikle's dirty nostrils – spattering away like shite from the arse-end of a cow. The young Lord's blushing eyeballs, the muzzle-holes of the guns on the ironclad, the war-masks of the Ardmairs, the wet clubs of the constables – all whirling into the currents of the storm, sucked in, sucked down. Sandy's flesh, springy as the muscle of a rope – it held her still – the wind climaxed, an impossible music, past hearing into pain. She could no longer see his face or smell his smell.

Beside her there was a space in the air the length and shape of Peg. Now the gale blasted it into grains that mixed with the other spinning motes, a fever of sparks behind her clenched eyelids, a storm of nothing.

She let them all go, she could not stop them, she could save nothing from all this stramash except her own self, which did still seem to exist. She would let go, and cast off with the fleet next week, if there was anything of it left, and hide herself in England.

In the morning the women were looking at each other with subdued amazement as though saying, How are you here? Are you still the same? When Flo stepped out into the stretched and bared blue morning, she saw the rocks of the shore and stonework of the quay with the same disbelieving eyes. Ramparts of smashed fish-box wood and pulverised sea-tangle snaked along the turf of the coastal pastures, higher up than it had reached for many years. A black boot, its nailed sole lolling free from welt. The corpse of a porpoise, lying on its back, its pale belly already ripped and reddened by the beaks of skuas. Fathoms of hemp rope, frayed and whitened at the end like an old woman's hair.

As though seeing herself from the outside, or repeating an action remembered from a dream, she walked a hundred yards east to a little brown reef upholstered with sea-thrift and looked along the bay. Was that the black, curved shape of the *Star of Hope*? She blinked and there was nothing but green sea chopped into edges and facets by the last of the wind.

The snowy hulls and superstructures of the steam-yachts no longer stood like a mirage on the sea to the east. On the north headland one of them lay sideways like a house on the brink of a landslide, one mainmast gone, the other paralysed at a queer angle to the horizon. From the jetties a dozen small boats were rowing out towards it like starlings flocking. For a moment she wondered if it was the *Orient Pearl*. Then the thought left her, as the bits of memories had done the night before.

Peg and Hugh – had their wee cabin on the island stood up to the gale? There it was, a mere box anchored by wire stays to that spot of land amongst the waters. As she watched, a figure came out, so small in the distance that she could not tell if it was a woman or a man. If one of them was alive then both would have survived. That was the last she saw of them before the journey south swallowed her into its long gut.

Chapter 22

For hours now – hours that had grown into days, then weeks – she had watched her hands work like two strong animals, separated from herself. The fogs that loomed above the Denes had oozed into her head and pressed their webs onto her brain. Seagulls cried harshly out there, invisible. From out there boats appeared on the sluggish flow of the Yare, first like a trick of the light, then turning solid, crewed by shouting men who winched sweel after sweel of herring from deck to quay, swathes and hillocks of fish that never stopped coming. Beyond the nearest wall of barrels, sixty, eighty, a hundred barrels long and four high, a dark upright towered. Its head was a blur in the dense moisture – the Nelson monument, honouring the old sea-hero who was supposed to have been a bairn at a village in the country before he became famous and went off to London with his mistress.

Amongst this wrack of apparitions, women and birds and men, stacks and masts and sheds and gutting tables, their colour drained and their sounds damped by this waterish half-light, she worked by rote, letting her hands and arms go through their practised motions, taking care of her fingers and not much else. They did not mind here if the herrings were packed into the barrels with their bellies torn – anything would do for the Germans and the Russians …

Was she really here in Norfolk once again? They had always called her Florry here – it sounded fancy, flowery, foreign – nothing to do with her. She had never felt herself so estranged from the life all round her. Other people looked as unreal as herself. The fishermen, the draymen with their loads of beer and turnips, the occasional bobby with his black boots and dark-blue uniform – did they really have homes and families in this warren of a town? Or did they vanish like ghosts the moment they turned the corner out of her sight?

It had been like this the first evening she made her way down the Rows, picking her steps on the broken flints, avoiding the central gutter with its trickle of brownish water. She could not bear, after this summer of hurt and shame, to go back to her usual lodging in the Judges'. Every piece of furniture, the smell of scones baking, the Weatherhams' volleys of laughter and their songs and hymns would only remind her of busy, heedless times with Peg and Maggie. A Fife woman on the train had given her an address, No. 45 Salting Row. The alley was so narrow that she had to press up against the door to let some other bodies pass along. A basket caught her in the small of her back and dunted her forwards just as the door opened. Mrs Amy Rising, the householder, held her off, smoothed down the purple bombazine of her dress, and looked at her forbiddingly.

'What can I do for you?'

'Bessy Cockburn from Prestonpans said you had lodgings for the fisher-wifies.'

'I have rooms for the girls, yes. Two to a room, if need arises.'

She still looked unfriendly and Flo wondered if her own worries and confusions were showing in her looks. She was not old but she had that white lock in the front of her hair … She must sound accustomed to the fish-work – where were her mates … Who cared what the woman thought so long as she took her money. Landlady and lodger – the business footing would be the simplest, the least thorny. She would not confide. So she handed over her few shillings' rent on a Friday night, and ate her fish supper in the kitchen-room kept furnace-hot by a cast-iron range with a finish on it like black velvet, and said 'That was nice' before excusing herself and going upstairs.

It would have been more cheerful to stay put. All the surfaces were sleek, lapping her in comfort, the brown velveteen curtains, the glossy yellow linoleum. Even the coals were shiny, and when they heated up the gas bubbled out of them in bright flaming spouts before the whole fire turned into a nest of twisting gold and orange tongues in its frame of black-leaded hearth as juicy black as liquorice.

Had it not been for Mr Rising, No. 45 would have been a burrow that fitted her as snug as an otter under a bank. Mr Samuel Rising. Amy Rising had seemed like a well-dressed widow at first and well suited to her spruce household. No family photographs, no letters behind ornaments on the mantelpiece, no boots or pipe-racks, or smells of brilliantine or tobacco or liquor, to suggest a husband or any other sort of male.

At bedtime, as Flo paused on the second stair, suddenly weary and bereft of upward movement, she felt heat at her back – the air had changed, as though she or someone else was sweating. She turned, and looked straight into two washed-out cod's-eyes with little purses of sallow flesh beneath them, mud-coloured cheeks, a forehead that mounted in bulging furrows to a rampart of beige hair whose ripples were surely not natural. Podgy nose, like a boy's on the scale of a man. Lips also fatty and uncomfortably young and pink. A curiously naked skin where stubble might have been. The woollen pullover inside the man's blue-serge suit was a kind of museum of his meals for weeks past – she could see plainly the samples of gravy, brown sauce, and pale plaques of mashed potato decorating a chest and paunch that made one huge sack of man, as though a prize boar had been dressed in cloth.

'Hul-lo,' said the fatty lips, as cordially as if this meeting was a treat which both of them had been avidly desiring for several months. '*You're* early off to beddy-byes. Tired, my dear?'

'I was on the train all day.'

'From Scotland, too. Oh, I can tell.' He smiled lavishly with a quirk of his mouth, as though he knew some naughty secret. He had moved even nearer in the small dark trough of the lobby with its shimmering yellow aura from one small gas-light. Although his feet were still on the floor and she was still on the second stair, the dirty slope of his torso was quite near her face. She caught a whiff of ageing mutton fat and a broth of peas and onions.

His eyes left her and travelled, quite slowly, down her neck to her breast. 'We shall have to feed you up, my dear. Starve you up there, do they?'

'We have as much fish as we can eat.'

'Fish. Yes. It makes our fortunes, and the Russkies can't get enough of it. In this house, my darling, you shall have fat meat with the best of them. Don't let her,' he gave his quirking smile again with a twist of his head towards the kitchen, 'don't let her stint you, now.'

He had moved his hand to the banister where hers was. Its touch was as gelatinous as new-killed pork and so warm that when she moved hers away it left his with a moist clinging. His other hand hung down in front of his flies, the fingers curved inwards. He saw her notice this and looked pleased. He was surveying her now, like a player in a game of draughts waiting for his opponent to get out of a teasing situation.

She simply turned away, saying nothing, and went up the stairs.

In the weeks that followed, Mr Samuel Rising's movements remained a mystery. He ate with the two women only at weekends. No other fish-wifies had arrived to occupy the empty bed in Flo's room or the two in the other attic room across the landing and the season was too well on now for new people to be expected. The landlady – 'You must call me Amy,' but Flo was still not inclined to – referred occasionally to 'Mr Rising's connections' or 'Mr Rising's time-table', always in such vague and complicated language that he might as well have been a spy or a missionary, a churchwarden or a detective.

'Mr Rising has heard nothing for some time,' she would say after a lull in one of their halting conversations about the ships on the river or the number of holiday-makers in town, 'but as they say, no news is sometimes the best of news, and he has his ear to the ground. He knows what he is doing, so I say nothing.'

Nor did Flo. She had promised herself that the monstrous man would remain absolutely outside the boundary of her life.

In the morning she always made sure that the Risings' door, which led off the lobby opposite the kitchen-room, was shut before she came downstairs past it and slipped out into the close, fish-smelling channel of the Row. Sometimes she heard bedsprings creak noisily, although Mrs Rising had already been up for an hour, kindling the fire and cooking breakfast. Usually the house outside the kitchen-room was filled with the quietude that had made her think Amy Rising was single. On Sundays Mr Rising was always there, carving the fowl or the joint, keeping his plate held out for potatoes and vegetables until a treble helping had been packed onto it, stowing away the entire heap in huge mouthfuls while the others were still pouring the gravy or spooning out the mustard. Then he reached over for a remaining leg or slice with his bare hands and, with his eyes on Flo's or his wife's face, he pressed the piece into his mouth while whole drops of morsels added themselves to the collection caked on the buttons and embedded in the weave of his pullover.

'Oysters and stout, eh, my dears,' he said in a voice clogged with food. 'And beer and cheese. They belong together like man and his mate.' He looked at Flo, chewing busily.

'And the bottle has finished off plenty of souls in this town,' said his wife. 'Although I daresay we shall have port at Christmas.'

'At Christmas, yes,' said Mr Rising, sighing, then winking heavily at Flo with the side of his face away from his wife while a piece of brown chicken-meat fell out of his mouth.

What did Amy Rising think of her husband's habits? What was the meeting between the monster and the smart, self-conscious woman with her stylish and well-laundered blouses? She behaved at table as though all was in order. She scooped up the remnants of meat and pastry that had piled up round his place with flicks of a brush and crumb-tray and, with no expression whatsoever, picked up yet another stained table-cloth by its corners and took it out to the wash-house at the back. Once, when Flo had slept in and came down late, she actually saw Amy tidying up Samuel for his day out and about, firming up the knot of his tie and brushing dandruff off his collar, while he caught sight of Flo over his wife's shoulder and gave her a languorous wink.

So far he had kept his hands off her. All he had done was spoil her peace of mind. If she came back late after drinking at the Mariners' Rest, she found herself easing the door shut and taking off her shoes so that she could cross the lobby silently and reach her room unchallenged. Was he in? Sometimes she heard the kitchen-room door open as she reached the top of the stair and had time to wonder who was standing there, the man or the woman, before she won home securely to her own little place and wrapped herself in the soft, lumpy bed and the darkness smelling of camphor.

Maybe he was all suggestion and no behaviour. How could he ever get a woman to come near him? How could he get near them with a paunch like a bolster glued to his front? Maybe he paid some simple girl to interfere with him along in the shadowy neuks between the Market Hall and the beach, where low laughs could be heard at night and sometimes shouts or screams.

She would have liked there to be just one place where no trouble threatened. Seemingly this was not to be had. Maybe you had to be old, or dead. And old age was ... On the Island you had just been steered into the shadows and left there, to spin or card a bit and rock the baby, and if you were talking to yourself or no longer knew who anybody was, nobody seemed to mind. That was another world and another time. Here, and now, there were so many houses and so many wee families, a new generation in every house – the old people must be inhabiting some crannies in the countryside, like black beetles in old floors ...

She was thinking like an auld granny herself. But she would never be that ... If she could find some comfortable man, in Lerwick or Aberdeen – someone who was not disgusting, and who wanted his bed warmed – then maybe they could keep alive for a while, and grow their own vegetables and potatoes, and she would not finish up lying on a damp mattress and fighting to keep the rats from eating her toes ...

Such thoughts swarmed into her head in the dark silence, hovering through the oblong hole of the skylight, leaking under the door, ghosting from behind the wardrobe with its broken leg propped up, and making her yearn for whisky or for sleep.

Chapter 23

This morning it had looked as though the wet, deep shadow of the fog would lie on them all day, oppressive as the sea itself, the sea come inland and themselves hotching to and fro on the bed of it like crabs. Now the grey was turning silvery, bright glints of blue shone through it, closed over and shone again, and the colours flowed back into things – the raw-meat pink of her fingers, the plum and grape colours of her companions' head-scarves, the flanks of cod, marbled yellow and sea-green.

As the sun came out, so did the folk from the hotels and boarding-houses, the gentry (if that was what they were) and their ladies. By the afternoon, as usual, wee gaggles of the characters were pausing and posing near Nelson's plinth. They were looking up at the names of the battles cut on the lower cornice a few feet above their heads – Trafalgar, Aboukir – then leaning back and screwing up their eyes against the dazzle to make out the ships' names high up, just below Britannia with her four girl-friends and her trident – *Victory, Vanguard, Elephant* – whyever had they called a warship *Elephant*?

The womenfolk were putting up their parasols now against the sun. Some were twirling them, making flowers or fireworks in colours of tangerine and heliotrope. The more conscious of the men were leaning on their sticks, even though most of them were only middle aged – could they not stand up by themselves? It was all play with them – why did they carry gloves on a fine day? Play, and a kind of hunting – that pursey, bearded man with a look of the Prince of Wales was putting on speed now, his wife could barely keep up, as he tried to draw abreast of the prettiest parasol, Nile-green with a pattern of twining curves. How badly he must want to steal, or buy, a chance of whatever bonny face was displayed in its frame of silk …

And so the managers stalked the shop assistants, the young bloods stalked the chorus girls, the sailors stalked the tarts. She felt vulnerable enough herself, or rather not for herself but for her younger mates, as they kept their eyes down on their flickering knives and the never-ending heaps of fish, while menfolk cruised past and gave them a sort of pop-eyed stare and then looked away again, quite bold while it lasted. It was as though they felt excused by the physical frankness of these women, their bared arms, their sallies of loud laughter, their calling out to each other by their first names above the thump and splash and clatter of their work.

'Keep her away from that filth!' Yet another weighty citizen who looked like one of the Royal Family was brandishing his stick, black with a silver head, at a spaniel with a squashed-up nose and brown wet eyes. It was drawing the leash taut, and tugging its mistress with it, as it goggled at a pod of herring roe that had missed the offal butt and landed on the stones.

It's not filth, Flo thought, and heard the woman next to her say to the lady, 'Filth? Do you mind? We scrubs up regular!'

'Here – have a nose of it.' Another of the local women was holding out a fat herring, still whole, impaled on her knife. She waggled it at the couple and their dog, the fish fell off and landed smack beside the animal, which strained and drooled, then yelped like a gull when the lady yanked it back.

'We ain't a *spectacle*,' said the woman who had spoken up first. 'Or if we are, we should charge 'em for it.'

'If there's a call for that kind of thing.'

'Why'd they come here if there ain't? Why does *he* come here? Every day, like.' She pointed her knife at the tall man in a tweed cape who had appeared at the corner of the nearest ice-house and was setting up a tripod of polished brown wood, extending its legs and steadying their brass points in the joints between the cobbles.

'Oh, him – he's harmless. Have you seen him down at the beach? With his little uns? Giving 'em toffees to poke a stick in a pond or cart a sweel about.'

The tweedy man was lowering his camera onto the top of the tripod and delicately engaging the screw. He was talking to somebody with his back to the tables. As he turned, Flo felt herself lurch, her balance give, as when a boat drops into the trough of a wave. It was the artist – Burley the artist – again.

She reached for a herring, slit it up, skited it along the board for her mate to pack, reached for another, slit it. In her head she counted mechanically. Ten fish. Twenty. Thirty. She would not look up for at least three hundred. Five or six minutes would have passed, he would have got bored and strolled off to the pub or the tea-shop. Four hundred, five hundred fish jerked through her hands. She looked quickly over at the corner and saw the photographer with his head buried in the black shroud of his trade. The artist too was busy. He had set up an easel, its legs in the drift of fine-blown yellow sand ten yards away from his friend's tripod. A metal box with trays inside it stood open on a folding stool beside him. She could tell by the movements of his upper arm and the up-and-down looking of his face that his invisible hand was making a shape on the paper pinned up in front of him. Her shape? Could he see her face from there?

'Oh my gawd,' said a woman in the next team, 'Look at that, two of 'em now. Whatever next?'

'Hunting in couples. Like the bobbie. Do they think we're dangerous or what?'

If he did recognise her, well, it was nothing to her. So long as he kept to himself and treated her as nothing but a thing in a picture. Her fluster of anger and mistrust was silly. He was not putting a curse on her, or blazoning her on a Wanted notice like a villain. She felt caught, though, or found out. If he, or anybody, could look at her, as hard as a crofter would look at a horse for sale, and take her likeness away with them to do what they liked with it, they could as well be filching at her own self, finding out a weakness, getting hands on what she felt and what she had lived and – and – *using* it. Manufacturing it. Mixing it up and selling it. Possessing, then getting rid of, *her*.

Queens and kings had always done it, and paid to have it done, and artistes from the halls, and the nobs from this place – Rising the Belly's brother, who wanted to be mayor, and all the other nobs in the world, the Ardmairs most of all, with their killing black eyes and their moustaches stifling their mouths. Well, they *liked* that kind of thing. They put on a new nature before ever they were painted or photographed. They curled their hair and rouged their cheeks and disguised themselves in silks or furs and sat there like gods on clouds, and then the artist could wile away nothing from them except this waxwork, this beauty who was probably a crone, this hero who was probably a thief.

Her mate had nudged her. Her hands had stopped working. She looked across at Burley. He was staring straight at her. His head bent and his arm kept moving. Why her? If it was her he was leeching and not some of the dozens of womenfolk who were here at his mercy … All hands had stopped now. The long wooden farlings were empty and no more fish had arrived for quite a while. She wiped her blade on a piece of oakum, slid it into its sheath and stuck it into the holster at her waist, muttered briefly to the others, and strolled towards the artists' corner. The two of them were looking out over the Fish Quay along the riverside and making remarks about the shipping. She paused beside the easel and stared at the picture of herself and the others – examined it as closely as though she was inspecting her child's scalp for dirt or lice.

Thick black lines like smears of mud had covered the sheet with ogres, kelpies, hulking animals. Yes, there were the women's heads, three of them in a row, humped cowls with hunches on them, like herons fishing. Yes, there were the butts and the farlings, blocks of blackness as though cut from coal. One fish-head gorped upwards from a scribble of furious lines – arched back, sickle-cut of gill – it was wonderful how the fish grew out of the welter. Its eye gaped, a hole of horror in the side of its head. The feet of the women – her feet – could not have been seen behind the gear. In the picture they were twice too large for the heads above them, as though they had lumps of stone tied to their legs for torture.

Out of all this tangle two sharp lines – drawn, surely, with a different thing – cut upwards from one club-like female hand – her hand – and narrowed to a point. The knife. It had just ripped up a fish and the spattering of the blood and shite was a flurry of dots put down with such force that dust powdered the paper surface for inches round and there was a black jag where the pencil or pen had broken.

'It is rough. Not finished, really.' The artist's voice fetched her out of her absorption. She looked up and saw sharp almond-shaped eyes, brownish-green and amused, looking at her above his pointy beard that jutted out over a canvas blouse.

'You can do what you like.' She had meant to say that she did not care what state his work had reached.

'Obliged, I'm sure.' He continued to look amused and also cocked his head as though to provoke her. 'Should we have asked leave? Before we *did* you? You're quite right. Oh blast! Weston!' – to his friend – 'You assured me that everything would be comfortable here, that you had blazed the trail. And now this lady is scolding me. In the politest way. And rightly so. You are right, dear. But – does this help – if you came to the shore beside my studio, when I was working *al fresco*, and you began to do me, I should not be offended in the least.'

He was clever. And he was two-faced. She shook her head as though to rid her hair of a wasp and her scarf fell back. He looked transfixed, then unbelieving. His hand came up as though to touch her cheek and then stopped in mid-air. 'Sgiach. You were in the battle? On Sgiach? You were on Sgiach!' He let out a roar of laughter and shouted to the photographer, 'Weston – my best thing! She was my best thing!'

The other man was looking doubtful, as though he would rather not be there. Burley hugged her, making her gasp, then kissed her forcibly on the cheek. His beard felt like hay and smelt of rum and chocolate.

'You look older, dear. Finer, I mean – finer. Your cheeks have structure now. You still hold up your brow. They thought I was being old-fashioned, that I was sainting you – Richard's Celtic saint – oh, how they sniggered. But the *News* is still paying me, you know – they still sell as many prints as they can make.'

He was standing back, eating her with his eyes, turning to Weston for admiration, ignoring his reluctance, laughing and snorting in an orgy of self-satisfaction. She wanted to rage at him and hardly knew what her grievance was.

'Are we so ugly?' It had come from her mouth like a plea, a flirtation even. How could she get at him?

'He likes them strong.' Weston said this to himself, followed by a little secretive laugh. He was folding away his black bag, looking at the sky as though to gauge the light, glancing sideways at the two of them with similar appraisal.

'Is that hand not strong?' asked the artist pointing at his drawing. 'That leg?' He was prodding her with his questions, and all with a sarcy note in his voice as though it was a bit of sport, this pretending to consult the people whose likeness – likeness? – he had taken without the merest by-your-leave. When he grinned his grin, the middle of his beard just under his lip rose in a pointed tuft, like a trick in a pantomime.

She would not argue. Arguing was one of his ploys.

'We are all strong enough, if we are free of tuberculosis. Did you hear what happened afterwards on Sgiach?'

The change of topic wrong-footed him and he said irritably, 'Sgiach? Tuberculosis?'

'After you went away, with your valuable drawings.' Now she was arguing. 'We won the grazings. And the factor had to leave, with his tail between his legs. The men were gaoled, of course. Did your paper put that in?'

'I think it did. It was even in the *Times*. Perhaps my drawing helped.'

'Helped? A picture?'

'But such a picture! No, seriously, you were mentioned in the Talking Shop. By the Great Pan-jan-drum himself. "Although the behaviour of the islanders was riotous and therefore not to be condoned, nevertheless the suffering in some parts of the kingdom has been undue, not least on the part of the fairer sex – whose likeness has gone into every home," and so on and so forth, in the best flannel style.'

'You never came back to the west.'

'Not easy. Editors must be obeyed.' He pretended to cross himself and the photographer gave his little laugh. 'Wars must be covered – bigger ones than yours, dear, though not so picturesque.'

'He is too modest to say,' put in Weston, 'that he has been to Africa, so now the whole country knows what a Dervish looks like.'

'Picturesque' was still fidgeting in her brain. A word that scuttled like a cockroach. The Trossachs were picturesque. And long-haired, long-horned cattle up to their houghs in a loch like old brown glass. But the pounding truncheons of those constables? The women's split scalps and breastbones? She could almost see the gap between her country and his. From over there, on his bright white island, he had observed her and hers through a telescope with glassy lenses, seen them sharp as sharp, creatures without smell or blood or voices. And yet – this drawing, so black and humped – he had felt their work as she had felt it often enough herself down the years, as a bog of mud that held them by the knees, a creel of wet seaweed as heavy as the world.

She straightened herself, pressing her shoulders back with her hands on her hips, thumbs forward. He was looking at her intently and she felt exposed, as though her breast was uncovered. She drew her scarf round her hair again and gave him a wee bow, as smart as his own mock manners. As she turned away, he said, 'I should like to draw you again. Or better, paint you. My drawings are too cartoon. Even this one.'

She felt boxed in, as though she was on the wrong side of a looking-glass and would need some cunning key to get out again. Outrageous that she, or anybody, was fair game for these hunters. If she said no, he could still get her – do her, as he put it. Suppose she bargained – suppose she named her price and called his bluff ... Some of the other women were going past now, looking curiously at the three of them.

'I am not cheap,' she said to him – feeling as though she was acting in a play, with some queer other sensation, like whisky rising in her head. 'If I lose work here, there is still my board to pay.'

'£5 for the afternoon.' £5 – five times the best money she had ever made, and that had taken her a week. She would do it the once – act out this play – and if he made her into a figure of fun, or put her name on the picture, she would call it off.

'Where should I come? How should I dress?'

'Come as you are, of course. Come to the Mariners'. We can nip up to Swavesey in the trap.'

The photographer laughed again, and when the artist looked quizzically at him he said, 'Studio work – tut, tut. So much for "life *en plein air*, life on the wing".'

'Oh, that was yesterday. Tomorrow, or next week or next year, I shall paint from photographs and do as well as Sickert. The Mariners', then – tomorrow, shall we make it? At noon or thereabouts.'

Chapter 24

She was sitting on a cloud now, a cloud shaped like a throne, in the middle of Burley's studio, surrounded by wooden walls distempered white as clouds, while clouds pale and heavy as geese towered in the space between the flat horizon and the height of the sky and sailed gradually eastward towards the sea. When he showed her it, she had laughed outright at the thing on its dais, covered in a swathe of gold velvet that spiralled down to the uncarpeted floor.

'Fit for a queen,' she scoffed, and laughed again. So he whisked the cloth away and threw it to one side, unveiling a big gawk of a chair nailed clumsily together from timbers four inches square with a tea-chest lid for a seat.

'If you want to be uncomfortable,' he said, as he clipped a primed canvas into the easel.

'I think I am strong enough,' she retorted. He did not respond and took a brush from one of dozens of pots crammed onto the trestle table.

'How will I –' she began and looked at him for instructions. He just stood, staring at her. She stepped up onto the dais and sat down on the monstrous chair. She folded her hands on her lap, then felt like 'a good girl' and put her forearms along the rough wooden arms of the chair. How gracious it felt – she could give out favours from here. Was this what he wanted? He was looking from woman to canvas in a rapid, jerky sequence. His arm was already moving in quick sweeps that looked gentle, as though he was taking a feather brush to the canvas. The whisks of the bristles as they touched it were like short, light breaths in the wintry enclosure of the room. He never seemed to dip into anything but black. Was she being turned into that swarthy ogress again?

His intense activity, whose results she could not even see, was too tantalising. She allowed her head to turn and look for something else. What she saw was herself, again and again, a dozen times or more. That drawing, of course – the 'drowned girl' cradled by Ma MacLeod, arms dangling, hair dropping like black blood and gouts of blood falling like hair – her own hair, tobacco-brown made black by pen-and-ink, and her beak of a nose, she now saw, made into more of a hawk's curve, less bonily bridged, than she believed it to be. Five of these figures, in various sizes, with differences. In two there were no serried flails of truncheons in the background, only a smoky scribble to suggest rain falling through trees. In one her head and neck and bust filled the paper. She leaned her cheek onto her shoulder to see the upside-down head more truly. One eyelid was closed, one open, which gave a hideous look of injury. Had he changed that in the final version for the magazine to make the thing less ugly?

A short, gruff syllable from Burley made her turn her head back. She still looked sidelong, searching for her own looks among the array of visions. There she was again, at bay, or was she charging? Her breast with her shawl pinned across it, the fold of the cloth round her jaw. Both arms thrusting forward, one of them bare to the elbow, with a shading of taut muscle. The palms of her hands displayed, the fingers wide and separate. They could have said she was protecting herself – they could have said she was on the attack. Only the bulky onward surge of her shoulders, the jut of her jaw, made her defiance plain.

Why had he not sent this one to the paper? Why had she had to be the victim?

She heard him grunt angrily again and turned her head right back. Up he looked, down he looked, his arm still busy at the same pace. The colour still, apparently, black. His almond eyes were narrowing and the tightening of them was cutting lines into the smooth, weathered skin of his face. She was passing through those eyes into his head, and through his shoulder into his hand, and had done so many, many times already. If felt suddenly like captivity and she half rose from her chair. He growled yet again, like a threatening dog, and she sank back and set herself to look as hard as she could at him. If he could possess her by eye, well, she could do the same.

His forehead, under a mane of hair as copious and crinkly as his beard, flowed down through his brows into his cheeks in a long, broad, moon-like curve – twice the flesh she had seen on any face before – a Hallowe'en face carved out of one big swede. It was unmoving except for the eyes. She had seen the shadow of her own face as she stitched or polished and knew that her lips worked in time with her hand. His was the opposite – as changeless as a mask – an image of command, as though he made his subject be like what he painted and not the other way about. She looked and looked and saw those cheeks and brow as wood, or stone, or earth in a new furrow moulded in a smooth cake by the ploughshare. It sank into her too much, this face, and when she closed her eyes she saw it still.

'If you fall asleep on me, I shall simply start another picture. Defenceless, instead of haughty.'

To hold her own, she kept her eyes closed as she replied, 'I was not asleep. And I do not think I was haughty. It is the chair. You cannot be easy in such a – such a throne.'

'Lie on the bed if you like. Still more unbuttoned.' His voice was brusque and detached, without the least tone of flirtation.

The bed was in a corner over beside the tall windows that had been made in the north wall of the barn, if that was what it had been. It had an iron hoop back with knobby uprights, painted gold instead of the usual black. Sheets and blankets and a rumpled yellow pillow were just visible under a cover that displayed a peacock made of a great many brilliant silk patches, diamonds and ovals of turquoise and raven black and kingfisher blue.

'Is that where you have them?' Somehow she felt obliged to taunt him.

He laughed. 'You think we're all voracious?' When she said nothing he said 'Greedy', as though translating for a child.

'I know the word. Do you mean men? Or painters?'

'Oh, you know how they look upon us. We do peculiar work, if it is work, and we keep irregular hours, so they imagine we do nothing, really, but drink absinthe all day and consort with whores. Or worse. Ever since Wilde's trial, Weston, poor soul, has had to give up taking photographs of boys.'

'I have seen his pictures, in that window on the Front. Some of the children look too stiff.'

'Not as stiff as the old family portraits, all Sunday-best and aspidistras. It is all art, you know. If he needs to, he slips Rising a fiver to send him a few young characters from Barnardo's and dresses them in guernseys.'

'Why would he need to?'

'To make them look right.'

'If they are alive at all I suppose they look right.'

'You are an idealist.' He smiled without opening his lips and the point of his beard stood out. 'I should like to work until dusk. Then we shall have deserved a glass of wine.'

He had mentioned Mr Rising. Rising and Barnardo's. As his arm resumed its practised movements, she brooded on this news. What did the fat monster do there, in the old converted fever hospital two miles along the muddy north shore of the Yare? The place was supposed to be clean and frugal, so how could they employ such a man? The boys looked decent enough when they came along the quays in little bunches, pinched and white and neatly dressed.

Was Burley a monster? She stared at him again, stared for minutes till a kind of sparkling atmosphere billowed round him and he was a face in the midst of clouds. What was behind his moon-countenance? He spoke to her in such a candid way, which seemed to assume there were no veils or barriers between people – you said what you thought and if folk disliked it, they could always say so and speak up for themselves. It was quite like springtime, this crisp, clean air in which everything was new-made and could be itself.

'You are smiling. Still another picture. Why are you smiling?'

'I like this place. I like those big windows. Even though it is so flat out there. It is a tall sky. Why do you not paint the sky?'

'It is tall because the land is flat. I paint it in summer, on the shore. It needs the human figure, though – bare-legged girls, ladies with parasols. They do well.'

'Better than black women cutting up fish.'

He smiled his pointy smile. 'Look, it is all art. If you like we can dress you in a silk frock and a bonnet and I can paint a meadow round you complete with poppies. Or I can put a shawl and an apron on a duchess, if I can get one, and a knife in her hand, and you will be able to smell the fish-guts on her. Some of them might rather fancy that. Ohhh, *la nostalgie de la boue*.' He kissed his fingertips. 'Let us drink some wine.'

She was not drunk when she got back to the Row that night – tipsy, that was it, a nice warm swimming in her head, thought melting into thought like fish in an aquarium vanishing behind other fish, like dreams she could start and stop and change at will. Orange snakes wriggled towards her across the black satin of the estuary, getting no nearer, each with its tail rooted in a gas-lamp over the Fish Dock shore. The night was an invisible shroud all over – photographer Weston's black bag – the earth of this flat country gathered up into a colossal dome with one side of its circle founded in the sea and the other in the endless acres of cabbages and wheat that spread off into other parts of England where she had never been, never would be …

She did not feel sick. She grued at the thought of food. She let herself into an atmosphere of burnt haddock, then stopped dead as Amy Rising's voice came through the door from the kitchen-room, each word biting into the air like an iron point hammering into soft stone.

'If. You. Touch. Me. Ever. Once. Again. I shall. Cut. Your. Neck. Through.'

Samuel Rising's voice started to say something, possibly 'My dear –'.

'Don't. You. And. If. You. Look. At. *Her*. I will. Cut. You. Through. The. Cock.'

She lay unsleeping in the near dark of her room. She had opened the skylight to let in the sea's sough, the notes of a drunk's singing, the church clock chiming – anything rather than those sounds of hideous hatred. She could see the whetted blade of the kitchen knife riveted into its wooden handle, could feel it slicing into her own skin. Such hatred was no good, it was blighting even to the bystander. Would she have intervened if it had been the man threatening, or attacking, the woman? She knew she would not. It was not the knife only, it was the bottomless, hopeless misery of that much enmity. No way out. They were not chained. If people had reached an end, they had best flee, flee in opposite directions. I did that … three times already … where next … something will happen.

Three days later, when she went to Swavesey again, she refused to start the sitting until Burley showed her what he had done on the first day. She stood obdurately beside the dais. He stood beside his easel glowering at her.

'I do not do that. Your feelings or thoughts are nothing to me. Nothing. At this stage.'

'When will they matter?'

'Oh …' The weathered brown of his face warmed towards plum with fury barely restrained. 'No argument. Argument is killing. If you want to go, I shall gladly pay you off.' He was reaching for his wallet.

Stupid to throw good money away. She turned to the dais – then walked past it to the bed in the corner and lay down. If he was artist enough he could paint her anyhow. She turned onto her side, kicked off her shoes, raised one knee and let her skirt slide down her thigh, and undid her hair so that the fine reddish-brown strands of it flowed over the pillow – all this as though she had been posing for years and years, whether in the studios of Paris or a great lady's chamber.

From the other side of the easel bellows of laughter broke out. Burley's face appeared round the edge of the canvas, brown mask cracking all over, beard pointing, mane of hair a-quiver. 'Florence Cameron,' he shouted, 'you are delicious! But you are not Ophelia. Oh no.' He arm was starting to work. Now he moved his easel round so that he could look at her continually and she noticed that he had begun to build up pats of paint of all colours on a palette, blue and yellow and crimson as well as the black of the time before.

'The knee – higher a little – let that hem *go* – good – yes.' The wildness was dying out of his voice as he settled into the new work. Before, he had seemed to be drawing with his brush. Now he was making many quick small movements, more like a bricklayer trowelling on a thick slice of mortar, correcting the lie of the brick with knocks of his trowel edge, carving off the surplus with flourishes of his blade as though in pleasure at his own handiness.

After a time her elbow grew sore, and she laid her head down comfortably and looked at the white ceiling fifteen feet above her. Would he growl at her? She looked out of the corner of her eye and saw him perfectly absorbed, still the small crafting movements, fast and continual, with no need to consult her face or body. She let herself drowse. Sleep had become so difficult and so fitful in Saltings Row with that festering between the monster and his wife. She had sailed into a harbour here – a white cloud-harbour, an autumn harbour whose high skies seemed brazed wheat-stubble gold …

The bed gave way as another body came onto it. She woke abruptly, scared and confused. Green grapes, translucent fruits with sunlight visible through their flesh. He was offering her a little branch laden with grapes. She reached up her mouth, he raised the fruit higher, she fell back sheepish and annoyed – what was this, a humiliating game?

He popped a grape neatly between her lips, then said with a sigh, 'Tantalus. What brutes the gods were. Or the men who invented the gods. And nothing has changed.'

She looked sideways at his face, all that electric-seeming hair stirring and working as he chewed. The picture was facing towards them. How long had she been asleep? The stretched-out shape of her had become a bird's, a long reclining creature, a peacock or a bird of paradise. Her legs were its tail, plumes no longer than its body, undulating like a python. These were only sketched as yet, a willowy sheaf of pale-blue brush-strokes. The breast was sumptuous already – diamonds of colour like the bedspread, heightened into a fever of carmine and magenta, turquoise and cobalt and mallard-green. And from this plumage her neck and face had begun to form, that hawk-nose again and her brown hair reddened into a fiery crest.

Her knee was being caressed, his hand was cupping its bareness, sliding over it, glossing her skin. She should have worn stockings, what had she been thinking of? Automatically she reached her hand down to thwart him and felt her wrist gripped while his other hand went on stroking. She turned her face sharply towards him and found that he was looking intently at her as though to mesmerise her. In spite of herself she felt roused to her centre. When he let go her hand and reached up to unfasten her blouse, she made no move to block him, then said, 'You must undress too.'

'All right.'

He stood up beside the bed and when he pulled down his trousers she saw that his cock was arched and tense already. His shirt came off with a rush. Her limbs felt swollen, charged. By the time he lay down again she was naked and he at once began to stroke her again, cupping her knees, then her breast, her brow, her shoulders.

'Like birds' eggs,' he was saying, his voice thickened. 'So smooth, so smooth.' He stroked and stroked, until she no longer wanted him there at her side, she must be under him. When she started to move he grasped her between the legs and gasped as he felt her fleece. 'I knew you'd be lovely there, I knew –'

He was lifting her onto him, his arms felt hugely strong, and she was above him, looking down her breasts at his imploring face. Sandy had never done this, her nipples were proud above him and his cock was reaching for them. It was glorious, everything was right, she would prolong and prolong it, she was lowering herself onto him and he came in greedily and suddenly, making her move with him, and they moved and moved and moved until they shuddered, gripped finally as though their hearts would fuse, then fell silently together and lay clutched for a long time, gently smoothing each other's clammy skin.

'I thought tantalus was some drinking thing the rich folks use,' she said at last, as her mind came back to her.

'Where did you see that?'

'In a castle. Long ago.'

'I don't know you at all. That's the beauty of it. A castle – what castle?'

'On one of the islands.'

'Where are you from, then?'

'I am not from anywhere.' She paused, half-longing to swim back into a drowse. 'I came here from Baltasound.'

'From Shetland? I was there this year.'

'I saw you there.' She should not have said that. He would think she had followed him. But with him she could say anything she liked.

He had turned to look at her, still stroking her upper arm and tickling her breast with his beard. 'You really are a most singular lady. But then, I am a rather singular man.'

'A single man?'

'That too.'

'So who sleeps here? Does she sleep here?' One large-eyed face surrounded by glistening ringlets was almost as common on the walls as her own.

'No, no.' His fingers tightened and slackened irritably round her arm. 'She was last year.'

'Why did she go?'

'Why? She went. They come and they go – they go off to Norwich or Northampton, or Beccles or Birmingham or Bermondsey or Bishops Stortford or … Let us eat.'

He served her with cold roast beef and pickles, and promised her baked pike when he 'entertained her next.'

Chapter 25

She was winging northward, amongst the birds, the broad feathers working her shoulders. Far below were miniature towns where field dykes met in stone clusters – a glinting weathervane, the church steeple pointing its spear upwards at her breastbone … She woke at some noise from below, a moaning voice. She felt so contented and complete that her limbs and body seemed without weight. She could have embraced him again this minute, now. If he wanted to … with his self-sufficient ways … and not a word of 'love'.

What would happen next? He had dangled some fruit in front of her. Dangled himself in front of her. What next? Och well, she would take things as they came. Take him when he came. She felt herself bawdy and free to the core, and thought that she would be able to keep this in herself, like a babe in her womb, through whatever dreich days might come to pass.

The dream came back to her, wings, fields, steeple, and she closed her eyes on the blur of the skylight and willed the dream to carry her off again, in a long high flight. Darkness swarmed. Through a welter of images, swimming, the sea, a lighthouse, she surfaced, disturbed by more noises from below. This was an urgency, and some strange male … She put a shawl over her nightie, her feet in her shoes, and went downstairs.

The kitchen-room door was half open and the way in was blocked by a uniformed man, his back towards her. A policeman. As he half-turned she pushed past him and saw – Amy Rising, sitting by the fireside, in her purple bombazine dress, holding up her hands to a man with a waxed moustache, brown overcoat, brown bowler hat with a curved brim. He was putting handcuffs on Amy Rising's wrists. On the other side of the fireplace, in his favourite ornate mahogany easy-chair upholstered in slippery chocolate American cloth, Samuel Rising lay back, motionless. His legs were apart, his crutch and his thighs were one spill of scarlet blood. It had made a thick puddle on the lino, spreading as far as the coal scuttle.

'Mrs Rising – what –'

Amy Rising looked up at her and said from a face as still as a picture, 'No trouble now.' Her eyes were enlarged and unseeing. 'No trouble now.'

Flo wanted to hold her. As she moved, Bowler Hat said to the bobby, 'Cox, see to her.' Irresistibly strong arms manhandled her backwards and half-lifted her into the lobby. She turned to look into high-coloured cheeks and a brush-like blond moustache and said, 'I must – say goodbye.'

'Best stay clear of this. You go to bed. In the morning, now, the guvnor may need a word.'

In the morning she gathered up the little she had – her Canadian moccasins, worn so thin now that the soles of her feet felt every stone, nightie, spare shift, spare shawl in a Shetland stitch that Peg had knitted her at Balta for a treat, waxed thread and needles, and her cloth purse with its coins and three precious notes. She put them in her hessian bag, checked that the room was empty, left her bed unmade, and went out of the house past the closed door into the kitchen-room. From the doorway she picked up a handwritten letter to herself – the first she had ever had.

A close little crowd of shawled women and a few older men were blocking the mouth of the Row. She had to shoulder through them, they seemed to stand their ground, and she heard a woman say, 'That's her.' As she walked off down the quay, she felt their hostility and greedy wondering prodding at her shoulder-blades. Then she was hurrying across the Yare bridge and taking the puddled track to Swavesey.

He stood at the easel, still crafting like a jeweller at the brilliant patchwork of her plumage. In her absence the breast and neck had grown towards completion, the curves were iridescent ultramarine darkening and mounting towards the fierce small head. The flamey crest had green now mingling with its foxy russets. The undulations of the body flowing into the tail had been painted strongly to look much more woman, the hollow in the small of the back, the rounded rump. The tail was still a bluish sketch. The eyes above the hawk nose were larger, unmistakably human.

When she arrived, with muddied legs and a hunted look on her face, he had said little, kissed her hand with a mock show of gallantry, and then her mouth, fulsomely. Again he smelt of rum and chocolate and she let herself be wooed by luxury. She put her bag down in a corner – to him it must have looked like the makings of the merest outing, perhaps a picnic – and lay on the bed in what she now thought of as the peacock pose.

He worked in silence. She saw a mass of bruise-coloured cloud with a prow at its highest corner, passing by in the north, with half a rainbow arching across its front. After half an hour the silence became like a withholding and she said, 'I had to leave.'

He grunted, not quite deterrent, not welcoming either.

'I had to. There had been a – death. A murder. She killed him.'

He threw his brushes onto the table, then came to sit on the bed beside her. 'She slew the monster? Good.'

'Good? They will be hanging her.'

'She must have been provoked. From what you've said, he was probably debauching his boys.'

'The Home will keep that dark. Richard – think. She will die in prison, one way or another. Richard – that place was a pit, I had to leave.'

She wanted his confirmation. He said at once, with an air of dismissing the whole thing, 'Of course you did.' He squeezed her foot, then started to stroke her legs, shaping her shins between thumb and forefinger. She felt roused, not urgently, pleasantly. Surely they must talk about their next moves now? She would stay the night, and then … Already he was giving her feet a last squeeze, kissing her lightly on the mouth, and leaving her to go to the easel.

'No grapes?' she said.

'No grapes,' he said from the other side of the canvas.

She settled a little further into the bedclothes. How easy it was to banter with him. She was bantering with an artist – from London or wherever his home had been – a gentleman with wealthy friends who owned yachts. She imagined a cruise with him, on the *Orient Pearl*, the islands sliding past like blue and green lands from a tale. Or they would sail on some southern sea, between white cliffs and flowering trees, and sleep in a cabin of their own … Some question was throbbing in her head. The letter. Who knew she was here? She fetched it from her bag and opened a white envelope, which had been wetted and dried again.

Hamar in Shetland
September the 12 1895

Dear friend Flo

May this find you it is going down by a coalboat returning with unwanted barrels from this place. A friend from Fraserburgh in Aberdeen will see it into safe hands. – All changes here Hugh will wed me back in Sgiach now the work is all done in this place and I will be having a child born during this winter-time let them talk. – We had word came from Maggie very sorrowful she is in her bed and may not be getting out. – One leg useless. – John will be wedding her anyway what will they do? – The boat you know of with the animal its skipper was done to matchwood on the night of the great wind and himself got ashore and they say he is away across the ocean on a steamer. – You had good riddance of him. – When are you back home to Sgiach. – My longest letter of my life.

Your friend Peg.
X X X X X

Hot liquid rose behind her face and she lay back and let the tears pour and pour. Her friends had become figures in the distance, with others behind them, almost invisible – Mairi Bealista, Margaret Coutts the cook, Morag from the Island, Allan her father and Mairi her mother – wee people standing on the crest of the dunes – too distant to see if they were coming nearer or going further away. She was going further, she had drifted, or voyaged, beyond the rim of her own world. And she was still alive … A reddening suffused her eyelids and when she opened them she saw, at the western end of the windows, the sky washed the colour of crushed brambles. He was sitting away from the easel, on a stool, and looking at the great dying fire in the sky. He looked like a goblin, or a wizard who turned women into birds.

'Am I completely a bird now?' she called across to him.

He said, in a voice as though his mind was somewhere else, 'That is not you, and it is not a bird. It is a new thing.'

She got up and went round to see the picture and he made no move to stop her. It was perfectly beautiful now (except for the still unfinished tail), each lozenge of colour brilliant, each different from the next one, as intensely dyed as stained glass with sun behind it, so that you saw nothing but colour patches at first and then it shaped itself and the bird-woman came bodily out from amongst the lattice-work.

'How do you think of such a thing?'

'They have done it already in Vienna.'

'Oh.' Was this good or bad? 'What about the tail? How will you finish it?'

He seemed not to want to talk. After a minute he said, 'A mermaid? No, too whimsical. A peacock is rather obvious. Shadows – perhaps I shall veil the creature in the deepest shadow. Or burn her – the firebird turning to ashes for a change.'

So you could do anything. With this new sort of magic you would make up your own world, and if people were pleased by it they bought it – they bought your dreams, when they were tired of their own ones. Anybody could dream – *he* could dream onto the canvas or the paper – like some tree that bore fruit of any shape at all.

The redness had ebbed. The day was finished. How did he spend his evenings? She had eaten nothing for twenty-four hours and walked five miles in the morning. Her head hummed with fatigue and hunger, lulling her not unpleasingly.

'Let's go out and eat,' he said, as though she had spoken her thoughts. 'In town. No, not in town,' sensing her aversion. 'Where, I wonder? Lowestoft is too far now. Well – I have kippered herrings in the larder. Kippers? Flat brown smelly things with dead eyes and numerous bones? You must have seen them in your time … '

As they ate them dry-roasted from a blackened pan, with slices of coarse bread 'from the farm', she told him about the year she had worked in a smoke-house along the town wall, in the old Blackfriars Tower. She told him about the stifling smoke and heat in the luves, where the fish were hung high up in the vents of the broad-shouldered chimneys. She told him about the women who hung split herrings on the wooden rails studded with bent nails, called borks, or laid whole fish, for bloaters, along rails with no nails, called spleats, and how the men straddled up the luves and fitted the borks and spleats onto ledges in the blackened sides, and she told him how a man called Charlie Bailey fell right down the height of the luve, towards the end of his stint, smashed his head open like a pumpkin on the flag floor at their feet. And a year later to the day his ghost was seen walking through the smoke-house and the women said it still walked from time to time, you could tell he was coming because the smell of smoke grew suddenly heavy even though there was no fire lit. Of course she had not believed a word of it herself but it had finished her with the smoking and she went back to gutting.

He asked no questions, listening intently, and when she paused he fetched a pad, turned past page after page of sketches and scribbled words, and wrote down the gist of what she had said. As he worked, she looked round the walls by the light of the many candles he had lit as the gloaming thickened and saw that he had taken down every one of the many pictures of the ringlet woman and filled the spaces with charcoal drawings and some watercolour sketches of the fisher women. Shoulders humped up and backs curved as the women bent double to pack the bottom layers in a barrel. A pair of women with scarved heads and their forearms straining forwards as they rolled a barrel with split-hazel loops along the cobbles of the quay – each knobby stone scratched in by the pen to make a blotched black crust that you could almost feel.

In a big picture four women faced the artist, knitting, with hands like fists (he should have drawn their threaded forefingers more exactly) and a wall of barrel-ends behind them like so many white eyes. The faces were as living as Weston's photographs – one anxious, with a line between her eyebrows, one horse-faced and homely, with a front tooth missing (Flo had seen her often, she had a head full of filthy stories and there was always a gaggle round her while they waited for the fish), one handsome with wavy hair slanting across her brow, shapely cheeks, a straight nose, and a look of humorous challenge, and the fourth – she was so like Peg that Flo caught her breath.

'Did you see us at Balta?' she asked over her shoulder. No reply. She turned and repeated the question and saw that he was sketching now, fine lines were intertwining freely round and between the patches of words.

'No no no,' he said at last. 'We saw ants, a great many of them – worker ants. I made some pretty pictures there, that's all – greenish meadows, brownish hills.'

'Did you sell them?'

He looked up from his page and smiled appreciatively at the question. 'As soon as possible. I made them into backgrounds for illustrations to a *Morte d'Arthur*.' Then, 'I should have stayed on Sgiach, shouldn't I?'

She felt pleased to be consulted and irked by his easy freedom. Sail here, sail there – draw this, paint that. 'Only if you had good reason.'

'Ah well, my then editor was rather excited by the notion of revolting peasants. My sailor host, not so.'

From the bed they could see a far-flung web of stars, myriads of frozen points throughout the sky from its height to low down where the river fog was rising. She had loved it that when she started to put on her nightie, he shook his head and smiled and they were naked now between the sheets. She wished she did not feel exposed. The dim orange light in the farmhouse window was barely a hundred yards away. She pulled the bedclothes up to her face and said, 'Somebody might see us.'

'There is no-one there. Only fields and cows.'

'There is always somebody.'

'If you live here you must get used to my windows.'

If you live here … From him this was a question. He would not plead. He would define the case and expect a decision. Will you marry me? The words he had absolutely not spoken hung before her in the near-darkness, looming like one of the pictures. Dizzy freedom possessed her, she was miles above the countryside, without wings, not falling, floating. When she spoke she heard her own voice coming from some point feet away from her face.

'I would like to be living here. It is a good place. And you are all right too.' She squeezed his arm and stroked the hair on his chest.

He lay quietly, waiting for more.

'What would I do? I must do something.' She could do nothing. For the first time in her life. At the thought her whole self let out a breath, as though she had been tired for fifty years and could give in at last. No, not tired always. Not when she went with Sandy. Not when she marched against the squad on the road to Ferrinbeag. Not when she was running about with Roddy on the machair of the Island …

'Here is what you will do – what you "will be doing", as you would say. You will be sitting for me and – no, wait – and be telling me the lives of the fishing folk, and I will be writing out a text of it – by hand, I think – I used to letter for a signwriter. And we shall make this book – Morris's *Chaucer* will pale beside it. We shall do all the life of the coasts, from the west round by Zetland and down through the Moray Firth to Northumberland and Scarborough and Grimsby and East Anglia. All the waters. All the people. Perhaps four hundred pages. *Designed* pages, with texts and illustrations dovetailed together. Some full-length black-and-white – you will look rather superb full-length in black-and-white. And colour illustrations tipped in on coated plates …' He paused and she could feel the heat coming off him. 'Perhaps the woman-bird will have to be a mermaid after all. The goddess of the book.'

'Are we going to make a book?'
'Together. Yes.'

For a winter, and through the springtime, and in the summer when the evenings were sweet and long – though not as long as in the north – and he could still see the paper or the canvas till nearly bedtime, they spun and wove a tapestry of the fishing. She told him how the islanders had lived, when barley or potatoes failed, on cockles scooped out of the strand with kelping hooks. And if the factor wanted to evict them, he sent a team of horses to plough the sand and crush the shellfish. When the mackerel came in a flush, they would be taking them with hand-lines and when the fish came flocking on board, two or three or four on the one darrow, they would still be swimming and darting on the bottom-boards with the hooks in their mouths, a glut of fish that heaped up past their ankles to their knees. When the cuddies came in their shoals, the people got into the sea and herded them into the kyle between two islets and shovelled them ashore with their hands. When storms blew week after week and no fish could be got, they had to scrape limpets from the reefs, where they used to grind them down in holes for ground-bait, and eat them for their meat.

'This sounds like ancient times – like Iceland.'
'It was my life.'
And she told him about the onset of the herring madness. The stone-and-mortar breakwaters grew and grew at the entries to the harbours, fleets of boats came round from the east side early in the summer, crewed by men with throaty speech, strong ale-drinkers who liked the women of the west because they had 'faces white as milk and fine obedient ways'. You could walk a quarter of a mile on the decks of the boats, the sea was just a bottomless horn from which the herring came teeming, and soon they were warping in three-masters from Russia and Poland, and southern Africa even, to carry away the tonnage and feed their own poor.

'That is in books already. Did you *see* it?'
What she had seen was folk on Sgiach flocking into town from clachans on other islands where they had been warned out to make room for the Great Sheep – families on the roads with three children on fire with measles, grandfather in a creel on the father's back, and when they came near the port they would be huddling in a tent and the people who

could still stand up took work on the fish dock and hoped they could turn the shillings into meal and milk before weakness finished them off.

'You were suffering like that yourself?'

'I was single.' She could still say nothing about the Island. So she told him about the long bothies at Baltasound where half the voices were southern and the songs were as likely to come from Scarborough or Newcastle, or from the halls, as from her own land.

'Sing me a song.'

'I never sang.' She still knew the words in screeds, songs from so far back they were like limbs of bog oak half sunk in the peat. Her father's verses about some dead folk or other –

> 'Those who survived the battle
> Lie in the hulks in chains.
> We are called rebels
> And the Whig reigns … '

'The Whig? Florry, this is history.'

'It was my father's life, or his father's. He was more than seventy when they had me.'

And she spoke other verses that came back to her in his voice. They were not all mournful –

> 'My net was in clear water,
> I hauled strongly in
> And landed me a sea-trout
> As lustrous as a swan … '

And songs of the emigrants –

> 'If only I had two suits
> And a pair of shoes
> And the fare in my pocket,
> I would sail for Uist … '

And earliest of all, her first hearing of rhythm and melody, verses which still came back to her with the smell of her mother's milk –

> 'An old man won't get Mairi,
> No, an old man won't get Mairi,

No, an old man won't get Mairi
As he got her mother … '

She did not want to be wound forever back, back, back and down
as though she were drowning in the bottom of a bay. They were on the
doorstep of a new century now, trekking south in the trains to earn good
money wherever the fishing prospered, servicing the steam-powered fleets
with the black smoke belching from their narrow funnels, and if he wanted
to sell his book – their book – to the people in the towns, and not only to
scholars and old gentlemen, then they had better pay attention to the
present day. When she said this to Richard, he was only half-convinced.

'The public is a peculiar animal. They like to dream about the
future and they like to hark back to distant things. As for the present,
they seem to like to get it from the penny papers.'

They talked and wrote mainly in the afternoons and evenings. In the
morning she sat for him and he painted her, in her skirt and shawl and
bodice, in a Nile-green kimono with embroidered scarlet poppies which
he took from behind a curtain draped across a corner of the studio, in
a tartan cloak with a hood – this turned satirical when she said it made
her look like Flora MacDonald so he painted in a bonny boat speeding
over the sea to Skye and said he might try to sell it for the lid of a
shortbread tin.

Soon there would be enough for an exhibition. It would be entirely
women, he said, with the woman-bird in pride of place, and enough
fisher-women to give the public an appetite for the book. He was
confident that he would sell well. In the meantime he had made no foray
into London for over a year and 'his' magazine had commissioned nothing,
as far as she knew. (He always opened his correspondence privately.)

They spun and wove in a sort of hive or treasure-chamber of their
own and let the world hum along on the far side of the marshes and the
river. When Weston visited they all drank too much red wine and bottled
beer and he brought them news of Yarmouth. The boys' home had been
closed for good after a visit by officials and the police. Mrs Amy Rising
had been found unfit to plead at a trial – she had never spoken again after
her arrest that morning and was in an asylum 'somewhere down in Essex'.

'They summoned me to the Station,' the photographer told them
in a voice rich with self-pity, 'and grilled me about my "models". I have

never used "models". I told them plainly that the people in my pictures were exclusively local, every one of them, and they could seek them out, for all I cared, and ask them if I ever laid a finger –'

'Weston,' Richard interrupted, '*get married* and then you can behave as you wish – beat your lady, spread her with honey and lick it off each night, instal a harem of gilded youths in the West Wing – so long as you are a married man, you are *sans rapproche.*'

Weston was quite unable to get into the spirit of this sally, drank off another glass of burgundy, burst into tears, and had to be helped to bed down on the couch.

In the morning Flo saw money pass from him to Richard before he set off back to town on his bicycle – white banknotes in a bundle. Richard put them down at one end of his painting table quite openly, with a sheep's skull for a paperweight, and said not a word to her as she came past to take up her position on the throne.

'Richard – he brought the wine. And the beer. He owes us nothing.'

'It's only money.'

'Only money? What is he paying you for?'

'If it were not for me – for the fact of my existence – he would be dead by now.' He was only half visible behind the canvas. The eye she could see was all hostility, even dislike.

'Why? Why would he be dead by now?'

'Florrie – I can work or I can gossip. I cannot do both.'

'Please yourself. I only asked –'

'I am not pleasing myself. I am paying Beighton's rent. And the bills for materials. And a certain amount of food. The occasional bloater.'

'I should be working. I should find a job.' At this he gave her such a look of rage, the almond shapes of his eyes sharpening like blades, that she said no more and sat motionless for three hours in the green kimono, with her eyes shut, until she heard him say brusquely, 'The eyes – the eyes,' and she stared straight ahead at the back wall where the complete woman-bird hung in its splendour.

Chapter 26

They had been dividing The Book into likely chapters – piling pages of raw text round the edges of the studio beneath appropriate pictures or sketches for pictures. At the east end eight unfinished oils leaned unframed against the wall. He had painted her in to take the place of one of the gutting women in the first Yarmouth sketch of his she had seen, the deadly knife ripping up the fish and its innards splattering. Now the blackish dust had been replaced by red. She had seen him loading a brush with crimson lake and flicking it at the canvas with his fingers, which had finished up gory as a gamekeeper's. The foreground was a welter of oil blacks and dirty browns in which their feet loomed bulky as boulders under water. The stripes and sprigs of their bodices were amazingly pretty in rose madder and sap green – the patches of them that could be seen behind their meat-pink arms. Their faces were yellowish shadowed with Chinese blue and behind them the staring yellow of beach and the cobalt of sky were as blatantly appealing as an advertisement for summer holidays at Skegness or Blackpool.

He did not expect, or demand, her comments. If she volunteered something, he listened. On most mornings she walked round the studio, dyeing her mind in the barbarous or lavish colourings. A few days after Weston's visit she happened to say, as she looked yet again at the gutting picture, 'It almost makes my eyes hurt.'

He looked across, then said, 'Very well – there might be less worry in the air if I painted some winsome girls a-paddling. Like Steer down there at Walberswick, shall we say? Or like Israelis? A nice greeny-yallery sea wishing and washing round their ankles. Nubile fillies with just enough white leg to appetise the elderly connoisseur. Or a tot gazing fondly at her little home-made boat. Shall I do some of those?'

'I do not mind the hurt. It feels true.'

'Oh, "true"!' He was visibly on the point of an angry philosophical tirade but broke off and went back his canvas – the herring fleet sailing into Baltasound overtaking some local sixerns, with the coal-smoke from their funnels smeared across the sky and masts behind like the tugs in Turner's *Temeraire*.

She wished she had never mentioned money. He could have no idea how little she would live on if it came to it. They had ample bed-linen, which she washed, and light and room galore. They had pork and fowls and eggs at less than market price from Mrs Beighton at the farm, and fish dirt-cheap from town. How could she persuade him that she had no worries in the world? (Only the worry that this enchanted life might presently be snuffed out like a candle, by some power she could not put a name to.)

She had nothing to do. He had been absorbed for well over a year now in seascapes. Once or twice he asked her advice on a technical point to do with boats. What she looked forward to now were their evenings – nine or ten candles burning calmly upright in their ridiculous gilt chandeliers he had bought for a song, he said, at Norwich Market, and just the two of them unfolding from their minds the unending vistas of the coasts, the quays, the estuaries and bays, the people.

True, it was work now, as much as it was a confiding and sharing. Good work, and for her happy work. Her memory seemed purged of obsessions. She was no longer racked by visions of roofs burnt through – her father dying under a hail of blazing thatch – the reptile Meikles at the Castle, stalking her – her head splitting under the truncheon … Now the past was more like a sequence of countries, sunlit as well as darkened, peopled by a company whose lives and works she could leaf through like chapters of a story.

But she had nothing to do – from breakfast time to sunset – once she had washed a few clothes or a sheet. In autumn she bottled hedgerow fruit, and baskets of vegetables from the farm. One spring she decided to banish the nettles and thorny canes of bramble and wild raspberry from some spare ground at the seaward end of the converted steading, in order to grow potatoes and perhaps some vegetables. She marvelled at the strangeness of the soil compared with the earth of her childhood. She had grown up with peat that cut like chocolate bread or, nearer their house, a free, light ground that was mealy with shell-sand. Now she drove her spade (Richard's spade) into a black mix alive with red-nebbed worms and centipedes like stinging orange flames. Pigs' teeth and a whole jaw-bone were embedded there, short sections of clay pipe-stem, and (strangest of all) the hand and forearm of a china doll.

Should she plant in this old midden? It did look growthy. She set three drills of potatoes, 'borrowing' seed potatoes from the farm. Then, copying from gardens she had seen all over the south, she put in a long double row of runner beans. As she dibbled along and dropped in the beautiful glossy marbled seeds, words were surfacing from a letter that had passed from hand to hand in the clachan, not long before the clearance. It had been written from Cape Breton by an emigrant called McCuish, and it said, 'We have planted twelve bushels of potatoes, half a bushel of white beans, two of barley, and to look after them coming up is a glory you would not believe.'

Allan and Mairi should have gone with her to Canada in the year of the Famine, as soon as they heard the dogs howling at the smell of rotting fields. But then she would never have come here, never have met Richard, never have changed her life.

Now the young beans were swarming up the feet of the osier wands she had set into the ground and the potatoes had pushed through, their furry dark-green leaves shouldering aside crumbs of the black compost. She had earthed them up. She had weeded the beans. She had set beets and greens. She had trodden a path through the weed jungle near their side door and along to her croft. What should she do now – lie down and watch them grow?

Sitting against the house wall in a drowse, after a night when Richard had seemed bent on wiping away any bad blood between them with an attack of passion, she found herself doing just that. The rows of plants stood out sappy in full sunlight. A pad was on her knees – she had had an idea of drawing up a 'Contents' to keep track of The Book's development so far. Her fingers began using her pencil to outline the first pair of leaves on the nearest bean vine.

From the base of the page she let her hand idle upwards, tracing the double spiral of the twin plants. It was delicious the way the lead-mark appeared on the white. It felt instinctive, as though her own arm was doing the growing. And when the pencil-point paused, stuttering a little, then set off more thinly, sideways, drawing the first leaf-stem, she gloried in the precise life of the result. She held the pad away and appraised it. Just so. Not the automatic, slippery line of the ornaments on some old wardrobe or monument. It sprouted unexpectedly. It changed direction, it thinned and thickened, all in its own style.

It would be better green. How did you draw in colour? She quailed at the thought of a bush with its oozing, splaying end. And the mess of colours on the palette, the dribbling oil. The pencil was moving again, making two firm parallels for the base of the supporting stick, hesitating to take on the delicacies of the leaf. Its edges were easy but how did you suggest surfaces? The graphite ran freely, round the cheek of the heart-shaped leaf, out to its point, cutting back sharply to make the other cheek. Perfect. Should she touch in some veining? She did, and the surface was there, the leaf was no longer flat, it stood up from the paper asking to be touched. And when she did that, lightly smoothing the grey marks with her fingertips, they rendered the bloom on the new leaf. Not paper any more. Leaf. Green leaf – it was hardly believable that the drawing was actually grey.

'A flower piece?' said Richard's voice behind her. 'No – I see. Very neat. The Spanish kings used to commission vegetables in full colour – fruit preferably but sometimes the humble vegetable. Come and see my Yarmouth harbour entrance in a storm.'

She praised it so much – the terrific clashing of hail-rods in mid-air, the storms of whiteness, the Prussian blue of waves smashing backwards against adverse waves above the sand-bars at half-tide – that he continued with sea pieces (always with a presence of ships, struggling crews, a beacon or a lighthouse). Flo felt content to be forgotten and, while a heat-wave tired the leafage of the bean rows into a droop, she sat under the brim of a wide old straw hat and turned her croft into sketch after sketch. With carmine pastel from a whole boxful he had found for her in his store she coloured along the veining on the sprouting beetroot, running it like bloodstreams along the barley-sugar yellow of the leaves. The pink-and-purple phase of summer's blooming had spread across the Broads and she used the same crayon to fashion spires of foxgloves, making bell after bell in mid-air before building in the leaning stalks and the fat leaves at the foot like scaly green animals. The colour threatened to elude her so she stroked white into the carmine, rubbed it with her finger, and saw with delight the harsh pink gentled into the sweet pink of the real flower.

A paradise of play was opening out all round her. Campion, poppy, knapweed. She even took on the tight-bunched head of the red clover in the field beyond her fence, expecting it to end up looking like a striped bull's-eye. She laughed aloud as she saw it bloom on the page with each floret exactly moulded against the next.

When Richard took stock of the growing pile – she had taken to working on good cartridge paper, fixing the pastel, and stacking the sheets between tissues on the sofa at the end of the room away from the easel and the throne – he said to her, 'There is no stopping you. Why don't you make a complete *Flora* of Norfolk?'

Would it sell, she wondered. This time she kept the money specu-
lation to herself. It was enough that he had said something practical about
her drawings – something not unfavourable – unless it had been a joke?

The heat built up huge thunderheads in the west and south, which
split in blinding lightning-cracks and peals of thunder like stone roofs
falling on stone floors. She came indoors and started to draw her own left
hand. Richard needed her again, for the figure of a woman baiting long
lines with mussels – she had recited to him, one evening in bed, a rhyme
she had heard from a Broadsea woman in the bothy at Hamar –

> Fa wad be a fisherman's wife,
> Tae gang wi' the creel, the scrubber, an' the knife?
> A foul fireside an' a raivelled bed
> An' awa tae the mussels in the morn.

Reluctantly she ascended the throne – taking with her a pad and a soft
pencil. As he brushed and muttered on the other side of the canvas,
she followed the outlines of fingers, knuckles, back of hand and heel
of hand. It looked pretty and it looked boneless. That hand would
never have gutted a hundred herring a minute or pulled on an oar. She
pencilled in the exact wrinkles where skin drew over joint, grooved in the
shadow beside each bone from finger to wrist, and the whole limb stood
out structured and looked as though it worked.

Work – was this work? Yes, if you made something and people
wanted it enough to buy it, that was work. Or even if they did not?
You needed it yourself, needed to form it and see that it was good – a
picture, a chair, a gate, a creel, a croft.

The whisking of brushes and faint creaking of the easel had stopped.
She looked up, into Richard's stare, inquisitive as a botanist's.

'Let me see.'

She held up her pad.

'Now do it clenched, from memory. I'm joking. But if you get it
right, I will paint out those knitting fingers you were so severe about and
you can make me more convincing ones.'

He knew she could not paint. His offer was unreal, a tease. How
many times had he said, 'It is one thing to colour in an outline. It is
another to *make the form in paint*.' She knew by now that for him this was
the acme and that drawing was next door to 'journalism' or 'illustration'
or 'cartoon'. It must be his way of putting her in her place. At least he had
not told her off for 'fiddling' while she sat.

Chapter 27

O ne morning in early autumn he had no sooner started in at the easel than he put down his brush and said, 'I can't paint any more just now. I feel blind.' He stretched hugely. 'Come for a walk.'

She put away her pad (she had started to draw whole figures, mostly male and naked) and followed him past her garden, through a stile in the fence, down to the river between thickets of scrub willow and then bulrushes that stood higher than their heads. He walked ahead, broad-shouldered, shaggy, in a brown worsted coat. He looked a stranger, unconnected to her, and the fancy took her that if he turned round she would see an unknown face, a foreigner's.

Tidal water sparkled at the end of the bulrush tunnel. For once the mudbanks were wholly covered. His feet splashed. He said 'Dammit to hell!', then turned round to her with a boy's face of naughty glee. He held out his arms and they embraced.

As they walked back, he seemed far away again. At home in the studio, as they sat drinking German wine (Weston had sent a case), his abstraction resolved itself as a question (one which had occurred to her already).

'What are we to call it?'
'*Three Score and Ten.*'
'Which means?'
'Well, do you like it?'
'I might if I knew what it meant.'
'It means all the fisherfolk. Three score and ten and a thousand thousand more.' She looked straight ahead of her and recited –

'It was three score and ten boys and men
Were lost from Grimsby Town.
From Yarmouth down to Scarboro'
Many hundreds more were drowned.
There were herring craft and trawlers
And fishing smacks as well.
They longed to fight the bitter night
And battle with the swell … '

'What is it – a parlour ballad?'

'Och, I heard it once – more than once – in the bothies, and then in town, in the Mariners'.' Tears came into her eyes, which he looked at curiously and left unmentioned.

'It is rather mournful. Striking in its way. "Three score" – at first I thought it meant fathoms.'

'It is full of the sea, yes. Her voice steadied and she went on –

'I think I see them yet again
Spreading their sails abeam
As down the Humber they do glide
All bound for the Northern Sea.
I think I see them yet again
Setting into the night
With their decks scrubbed down and their yards all set
And their sidelights burning bright.

'And it's three …'

She sobbed and could not say the refrain again.

'Come on, dearest, whatever is it?' He had taken her in his arms. 'Who sang it? Should I be jealous of him?'

'Jealous? Come in to town tonight, to the Mariners', and with luck he might still be there.'

He had been forced to sell off the trap in the winter, when they had to buy feed for the horses, so now they had to walk. In the foggy darkness the distance seemed to glide away behind them. Through the fug of pipe-smoke in the tap-room Weston greeted them, waving a glass of gin to and fro like a guard's lantern. His Inverness cape of dog's-tooth tweed stood out amongst the jerseys and canvas jackets.

'Hullo, my darling strangers! Hullo, hullo! Pints, George. And chasers, seeing it's their birthday, for all I know – sixty glorious years – that's between them, you understand.'

George gravely pushed foaming jars and little glasses across the wet surface of the bar and held Weston's banknote up to the light before putting it into the till.

'So what is happening, dear Rich and dear, dear Florrie? In your teeming hot-bed? Is it finished, The Book? Or is it like Pelenope's web – Penelope, dammit,' he enunciated more carefully and looked at them through his tumbler with one distorted eye.

'We shall finish it next year, Weston,' said Richard in a schoolmaster's reproving voice. 'And then, when the uniformly excellent notices have made their mark in London, we shall embark on the sequel. How are the new enlargements going?'

By the end of the evening Weston's eyes were closing, he was swaying slowly forwards and backwards on his stool, and Flo was thinking they had drawn a blank and had better set out for home. The street door flapped open and her man came in, his red cheeks tight and shiny and his black hair combed straight with water. Fog came with him and he coughed his cough that sounded like dry leaves being crushed. George set him up at once with a pint and he looked round the tap-room, raising his jar to a face or two, including Flo. Would he sing tonight? You could never tell, and you could never quite hope that he would, in case his ruined lungs gave out at last.

If only some of those old salts would put out their bloody pipes … In the middle of his second pint the man (she had never known his name) cleared his throat with that choked crackle and then the voice came from him, the bronze volumes of it, a baritone keening, belling and soaring, prolonged as a pibroch –

'November's night brought such a sight
As was never seen before.
There were masts and yards and broken spars
All washed up on the shore.
There was many a heart to sorrow,
There was many a heart so brave,
There was many a fine and fearless lad
To find a watery grave.

'It was three score and ten … '

It was all unbearable, that he should be forcing air across those shrivelled tissues, that he should be mourning whatever family of his had gone down in the foundering boats. She wept and wept, and Richard wiped her cheeks with his hanky, and Weston, who had wakened up to the great ringing of the song, held up his glass to the singer, raised it to his mouth, tilted his head back, and found it empty.

Chapter 28

She had thought they would be writing together, retracing in unison their many months of conversation about her life and the crowds of other lives along the coasts. But no. He was going to 'edit' his sheaves of notes, he said. He was going to 'digest' the style of them, 'make it flow'. He would 'see how it went', and then perhaps …

By herself again, she found she was wearied of disembodied hands, and vegetables and flowers marooned amid white sheets of paper. Where did they belong, these apparitions? In places. Sprouting from their own hugger-mugger lives, jostling amongst hedges, copses, furniture. Hands should be doing. She had seen a pair of them somewhere recently – taut lines straining from knuckly fingers, arms tugged forwards from high-set shoulders. If only her memory was still in its prime … She looked north across the meadow to the fen and saw them again – there they were – a black scarecrow against the white-gold dazzle of the water, leaning back as though to save himself from a topple and a plunge, legs at an acute angle to the bank. Wally the eel-catcher – on his own and almost too old for the task – bringing in his pod-net crammed (she hoped) with eels.

She began to draw fast, with a thick piece of charcoal, scrape-scrape-scrape to block in the main body of the man, angling and feathering to touch in smaller things, his cap with its ear-flaps, the ragged fringe of his jersey. Now the charcoal was crumbling in her fingers, it was so fickle compared with pencils, and she saw that fine lines were out of place. Extend his clenched hands into the bar of the thicker rope – scribble in one bunched, fleshy, writhing catch of eels at the other end of it …

By the end of the morning her hands were black and she had made a frieze of pollard willows across the background – squat, seamed torsos sprouting wands like goblin hair. She had abandoned perspective and treated each piece of the picture as though it was the same distance from her eyes, making an overall pattern like a screen. Shoulders, jutting through dirty sacks of clothes. The rope-lines, spears piercing into a bleared charcoal maelstrom where one eel arched in agony, back fin dilated in a row of spikes. Old Wally's toothless mouth pursed tightly on a crooked Woodbine.

She had got it – caught it, made it – although the subject had killed and carted away his small catch a bare hour after she had started to draw.

When Richard came out at lunch-time, spanning his brow with thumb and middle finger and groaning that writing was 'more gruelling than swopping drink for drink with Weston,' she was brimming over with it, lusting to show it. Let him light upon it, like finding a nest of eggs.

He saw it at once and stood focussed on it for a full minute, bunching his mouth so that the spike of hair stood out below his lip. 'Well, well,' he said at last, 'that is a picture. One would almost think' (she always bristled when he said 'one') 'that you were laying claim to your own space in The Book.'

'I just saw him. And I thought I could do him.'

'And you did, you did. The arms are impossible, of course. But then, you are a novice. Or an apprentice. Shall we say?'

If only, at lunch or later in the day, he had said one thing further, some gossip about old Wally, even. She *would* not allow that he had brought an acid bite of competition into their work together. If she must not draw fisherfolk – if that was to be his preserve – what figures should she draw? Cupids? Nymphs and heroes? Like the posturing personages in those stagey Turners he had seen so sarcy about himself?

In the afternoon, as he dozed on the bed – worn out with writing, the poor soul – she saw her chance and began to make a picture of him in all his majesty, which she disclosed by folding down the coverlet ever so gently. He sneezed suddenly, did not wake, and there he was, Hercules resting.

The largest paper looked as though it would hem her in. There was nothing else but a primed canvas from the half-dozen in the store. She had never touched those. He had 'drawn' the start of a picture with brush on canvas, she now remembered – the first he ever made of her in the studio. All right, then … It would not do to usurp his easel, so she set up a rickety old one from the store and clipped in a canvas. The wide, bare blank of it was daunting. With a brush just moistened with black she stepped towards the easel, reached out, and made the curve of his uppermost shoulder.

Strange – if you held the brush like a pencil, the strokes came out piddling, uncertain. Putting three fingers above the brush-handle she stroked more boldly. The shoulder bulked sideways into the back. Enough of that. Brush sideways again into the fat round of buttock – outline of thigh – well-muscled calf. She fidgeted the brush to create that limb entirely out of curly hairs, no solid line. The foot looked difficult – too many details – not ready for that yet.

She stood back and stared at her work so far, narrowing her eyes and looking through her lashes to blur out any shortcomings. Recumbent male bulk, all shapely and distinct. All right. Her arm was answering. Details next? Morsels of his body, which still excited her and made her long to touch them. She brushed in his mane of hair and beard, jiggling the brush quite randomly, and the crinkly mass grew and grew, establishing the man. Mask of face – eyebrows, nose, eye-sockets, rudimentary – no effort at a likeness yet. Hair swarming down his chest. Clear spots for the nipples that she loved to lick and suck. Luxuriant hair curling up from the firm hill of belly and then she was brushing in his cock, fat and relaxed, and the one ball that was visible, a rough plum.

She had been afraid, even as she painted, that the figure would end up a mere outline, two-dimensional, no mass. And yet, with no contrivance she had been aware of, here it was, in relief, a solid body that stood out bulkily from the flat surface. How wonderful it must be to sculpt, to feel clay clods shaping in the hollows of your palms. She would do that too – if she took to that, he might feel less threatened … She shuddered in the middle of her self. That had been as hard as gutting for two hours without a break. She should try the bony parts now, the ankles, the toes, the hand. She could think only of how to draw them. The brush of full paint would surely fumble.

Richard stirred. His hand reached down for a covering, found nothing. He shivered and opened his eyes, which pointed straight at Flo. Understanding warmed in them and he got up and came over to her, naked as he was. She dropped the brush and it left a dark smear on his foot. He stared and stared at the picture, stepped nearer to examine the brushwork of the hair, turned back to her and began to shake with laughter. It convulsed him too much to let him speak. After a minute's hysteria, which seemed to be unforced, he drew her to him, clasped her and squeezed her and said into her hair, 'Goddammit it, Florrie! What a blow you have struck for a generation of women debarred from the life class. But the Bodley Head will never accept a nude, not frontal, and most certainly not male. And that canvas cost half a guinea.'

They made love as the paint dried on her picture. 'Shall you do me like this now?' he quizzed her as he grew erect, then led her to the bed. But he rushed it and did not speak as they roused each other, none of his usual delicious compliments. They dozed afterwards, and woke up in the half dark. Surely something had just dodged out of sight beyond the window? In a fluster she pulled on her shift and went to look out. The hedge was shaking beside the stile. There was not the least breeze. Many months before, she had said there was always somebody there and he had flouted her. Some day they would be asked to leave. It was as well the Beightons were not Methodist. Now if they were married … She rarely thought about that now. As for Richard, it seemed to have no place in his code. The law and property were as distant from him as ancient Rome and the only papers he concerned himself about were agreements with galleries and publishers.

Chapter 29

The year the letter came from Peg she had answered it on one of the new postcards. You could get 'views' now. 'Yarmouth Beach' with flags flying from the look-out tower and the sand all footmarks and people waiting to be served at the covered stalls that sold 'Tea-Coffee-Cocoa-English Ices'. The *Yarmouth Belle* getting steam up to sail off for a tour of the Broads, with the Mariners' plain to see at the back of the quay. The *Southend Belle*, her chimney pouring out black smoke and her deck crammed with trippers.

You could not write much on them and that was what she liked. How could she write down, in cold blue script, 'I am a writer now, and a painter too, and I am "living in sin" with an English artist'? Could she even have come out with that by word of mouth, if she was still up there in Sgiach, getting tipsy in the howff and confiding all sorts of badness, mad dreams as well as wicked deeds, as they walked home through the misty darkness?

That was fantasy. She had never confided much. The habit of treating the Island as a place that never was, of keeping it behind shutters and under a slab of stone, had made her secretive long since. When she was feeding Richard material, she always let him think it had all happened on Sgiach or Shetland. The Island itself was hull down in that western ocean now, a blue rim, a grey shallow-curving back of the sea-pig, the voyaging whale. She cherished her vision of it like a fabric whose deep-dyed colours would turn drab in the full light.

So her postcards had become a custom. 'Dear Peg,' she would write two or three times a year, 'Hard work here but regular. I go thinning turnips or making hurdles when the fish are away. No plans to travel north at present. Your friend, Flo.' Or, 'Dear Peg, I cut my finger and it grew poisonous. Hospital for a week. Better now. Your friend, Flo.' Or, 'Dear Peg, Good news that John is working in the lighthouse and Mag no worse. All quiet here. Your friend … '

The lies teemed from her, she could invent a whole life for herself quite effortlessly, it seemed. It was all the fault of the postcards – they had never been meant for anybody except the holiday-makers. Really, she knew, she could as well have written a perfectly private letter years before.

As long as Peg kept it to herself and Hugh. And if she did not? There was no family to be shamed by the story of wandering Flo and her flighty ways. What would folk say on Sgiach if they heard about her? Just 'She was never one of ours.' And so, one morning when the sky was blind white after a week of heat, she went outside as though to lift early potatoes in the croft, sat down on an old three-legged stool on the other side of the runner beans, and wrote.

Swavesey,
by Great Yarmouth.
July the 16th 1904.

Dear Peg,

We are still friends although the years pass and I do not mean to have secrets from you. I may stay here for good or as long as he will let me. He. A man. My husband although we have never been to the church. I would never go there and he would not go. You see how bad I have become! I am living here in the man's house, well he rents it. He is named Richard and we saw him once on a grand boat at Baltasound but that is by the by.

He paints pictures and he makes money by them and he is as old as you or me. Old? Are we old now? Not yet. He has a beard and sharp pointed eyes, useful for his work and for noticing handsome women. I suppose I love him. We have good times and poor times. We both work at painting, drawing and writing down stories. No I am not a bard yet but I tell him how we have all lived and one day there will be a book made of it and you may recognise the places and the people from times past and newer times. Are you frightened now? I am frightened that you will think I have gone mad and make things up. You are in my loving thoughts and Hugh and Maggie and John, you will have children now.

Your friend,
Flo.

He drew my picture for the magazine. In the battle.

As she started to read it through, wondering already whether she should tear it up, she heard a rustling behind her. She turned and saw Richard's face between the stalks of two vines, framed in green leaves, one scarlet blossom peeping between the brown hairs of his beard, a pod nine inches long lodged between his ear and his head.

'You're writing too?' his face said. 'Is it going well? Read it to me.'

As he came round the end of the bean-row, she said, 'It is just a letter. To my friend.'

'Your distant friend?'

'All my friends are distant. I do not mind that.'

'And I would prefer mine distant. Poor Weston.' He had stretched out on the narrow balk of grass between the beans and the potatoes and shut his eyes against the diffused bright glare.

'Rich but poor?'

'Well off, shall we say? Enough for the two of us.'

This seemed a strange phase but she said nothing. She had been sure for some time that Richard drew on Weston as though on a bank. Her father had once said, 'Borrowing makes enemies out of the best friends.' Yet Weston was always perfectly genial, and as fond of her now as he evidently was of Richard.

'He is nice – I feel easy with him.'

'Nice – yes – too nice. When other photographers imitate his shots or his lighting, he does nothing. He gets fleeced.'

'Maybe he should marry.'

He opened his eyes sharply and fully at that and studied her face as though he suspected irony or a joke.

'Oh come, Florrie, don't pretend. You must know it is our flesh that he prefers.'

Our flesh? Did he mean men's? Apparently he did.

'Not that we have helped him to be any less melancholic. People are beastly to him as a matter of course. And I am not being righteous. I am no better than the rest.'

What did he mean? 'What do you mean?'

'Oh don't pester, Florrie. The usual thing. When we were together, I was far from faithful. And when I insisted on separate households, he was in tears, poor dear. He practically dissolved. But as you have seen for yourself, he is incapable of grudge.'

She seemed to be hearing a story far-fetched from some other country or time. Together, faithful, households – the language of love and marriage. She felt sweat start on her skin, then evaporate, making her shiver.

'You loved each other?'

'We enjoyed each other. I suppose he loved me. Then I found I no longer enjoyed him. And so …' He had not even opened his eyes to gauge her reactions.

'That is – horrible. How can you touch me if –'

'You primitive thing!' He looked genuinely shocked at her shock. 'We are all animals together, you know. Lusty animals. And if one of us likes another's smell, is the gender material? Have you never fancied one of your own kind?'

Mairi – Mairi MacLeod – the tender skin of her calves and thighs – the clinging of her mouth – the images were rising, clear as a memory of yesterday, clearer than last month's. He was looking full at her again, the lines sharpening maliciously beside his eyes and his beard stirring as his mouth widened in a self-satisfied grin. He reached his fingers up to touch her leg and she jerked away, saying angrily, 'How do I know that you are faithful to *me*, then?'

'Because you sense it. Probably you smell it. Trust the animal, Florrie. The rest is fancy dress and fiddlesticks.'

He reached for her leg again and she let his fingers stay there. A weird pleasure was worming itself into her, like the surrendering to more whisky when you knew you were already three parts drunk. She would not give in to him entirely. As though accusing him, she said, 'If we can smell love, then we can smell unfaithfulness.'

'And then,' he said, still stroking her ankle and the arch of her foot, 'we know the thing is over.'

It struck her like a threat. Fear and resentment began to mingle chaotically with the heady sense of strange possibilities from a moment ago. A minute later his fingers were slipping from her foot, he was slumping into a doze. She picked up the sheet of letter-paper from her lap and read it through. It was almost tongue-tied compared with what she might have said – even before Richard's revelation. She was not confiding – not really. She was passing on the news, as sketchily as if she was talking about some other person. It would have to do. At least she was keeping hold of the far-stretched cord between here and Sgiach – between two continents, two planets.

Chapter 30

She could not believe it when she counted the pages of the manuscript that had stacked themselves up through autumn and winter, spring and summer since they began the work. Nor had she realised that for many of the days when she had been working outside, in an almost pleasurable simmer of resentment at his monopolisation of the writing, he had been copying out text they had agreed on, and reams more, very likely, that might have come from him alone. The paper was sleek, cream-laid, the penmanship unerring as any work by a clerk or a lawyer. When she said with candid gratitude, 'Richard – you have been slaving – we should have shared such donkey-work,' his face did not relax. 'You have been cultivating your garden,' he said in his definitive way. 'Each to his own. Come and see the cover.'

He had taken a painting from the stacks of them with their faces to the walls and set it up on the easel. A turquoise sea glared from the canvas like hot enamel. Oil-paint like molten butter made a spoonful of light in each hollow between little wave-crests, hundreds, thousands of waves and crests. Each of them must have been brushed in with the patience of a jeweller. A valley between heaped gold of sand-dunes scored with crescent-blades of jade-green marram sucked the eye forwards, downwards, out to sea in a perspective so deep she felt herself swimming along it, gliding outwards across the luscious surface of the impasto. Cutting the horizon of the sea an umber sail jutted and curved like a porpoise fin – only the sail – the hull of the boat was invisible in a fold of the turquoise.

'Beautiful! How beautiful! You have done it beautifully!' She moved nearer, stretched out her fingers to touch the scales and clots of paint, then drew them back and said to him over her shoulder, 'It is not like the earthy shores hereabouts … Maybe it is not a real place?'

'Oh yes. A divine place – to look at, anyway. One of those islands well out to sea beyond your Sgiach – "The Outer Hebrides".' He intoned this in an operatic voice. 'Uist,' they called it. One of those splendid holidays Berkeley used to lay on on the *Pearl*. There was nowhere to land. I had to imagine the view to seaward from those pale-gold beaches. Is the lone sail rather a cliché?'

He had 'imagined' the Island. He could actually have seen, behind the dunes, the little hillock with its tussocks of bent-grass where her mother and her father lay side by side beneath wafers of rough-cut stone with no name, no decoration. She could not breathe, or swallow. A raging grief was blowing through her in a silent wind.

'The sail – what do you think?'

She turned to face him, letting her features paralyse into a mask. 'I daresay they have brown sails there.'

'Oh, the place is neither here nor there. It's the effect. Well, if it is thought to be Romantic, the critics will sniff, but as long as the Great British Public shells out … I have done a title page.'

On the architect's table where he sometimes did design work lay a piece of card on which he had lettered with a broad-nibbed pen:

THREE SCORE AND TEN

Annals of Our Island Race
Told and Pictured by

RICHARD BURLEY

in Collaboration with Florence Cameron

The Bodley Head
MDCCCCVI

Above the title was a pen-and-ink vignette of an inshore smack swinging a cran of fish onto a quay, which balanced a neat imitation of the publisher's well-known label below the date.

'Of course they may not take it. And if they do they may not publish it next year. But I thought they might like my effrontery. I shall show it to them on Friday.'

In every limb and layer of herself feelings were churning too violently to be speakable. She must tell him about the Island. She could not. She could not say, It is *our* book – I thought we were equals in it. She could not say, Can I not come to London with you? As she stared, he said, 'I know you would hate the city – filthy fog. And the creatures one must deal with – parasites in blue velvet jackets, *grandes dames* brandishing lorgnettes. Trust me. I shall bargain like an Arab.'

Through stiff lips she said, 'You cannot carry the painting … '

'Of course not. Weston did me a large print and I hand-coloured it. It will do.'

'When?'

'When?' He looked at her with a crease between his eyebrows. 'Oh, years ago. Years ago.'

On the Friday he left early, before the frost had melted the turf, with their work, his pictures and her words, in a portfolio wrapped in oil-skin broad and bulky under his arm. He kissed her deeply on the mouth and she felt excitement in him – for the raid on London, presumably, not for her. He is going to look for a younger woman – this thought appeared in front of her as distinctly as letters printed on the air.

She turned back indoors and went over to the mirror she had found against the skirting-board among his pictures. Her image looked back at her, set in a mosaic of blue and crimson paintings and parts of paintings, door-frames, capes and hats on hooks, cornices of the old wardrobes in which he stored everything. What age did she look? The feather of white hair was odd but the rest of it still shone freshly enough, the brownish-gold of it was not yet drab like winter grass. She moved closer to the glass. Her brown skin was smooth – the beige of it never paled or tanned much, however she was living. But her eyes – the lashes were much shorter than they had been when she was young, the eyes themselves settling deep into the sockets with a dark groove between the upper lid and the eyebrow, the whites no longer clear as porcelain but faintly yellowed and webbed with little veins. Her nose would do, fine but not too beaky – yet. Vertical lines scored her upper lip now, two on each side of the centre. She pursed her mouth and the lines sharpened, then pouted her lips and licked them quickly – pink enough, not yet drained purple like withered raspberries. She would hate it if her chin grew whiskery. She felt it and it was still smooth as a peeled egg. Richard liked her smooth … He behaved as if he did … He said less now as they lay together, and she had never become easy or expert in flirting speech. I am what I am – if I turned myself into a fashion-plate or a sparkling sort of person, he would despise me as a fraud – it is my plain ways that he likes … She had said this to herself many times, and it was fine and self-justifying. It still left her uneasy and wishing for graces and brilliancies she could never have.

The door was opening. Weston's face appeared in the gap, looking absurd beneath a check tweed deerstalker that sat too high on top of his blond and wiry hair. The flaps and their ties hung loosely beside his smoothly-shaven cheeks. He was like a fine-drawn nervous animal as he came stalking tentatively into the studio on his long tweed legs – a giraffe, or an antelope on its hindlegs that she had seen somewhere flanking a shield on a coat of arms. He was carrying a bottle of wine wrapped in a straw jacket. Had this man really been to bed with Richard, embraced him and shuddered to him?

'What do you want, Weston?'

He sensed the change in her, his smile faded and he looked round the high, bright room, then cocked his head to listen.

'No Richard? He can't have left.'

'Left me? Or left for town? What are you thinking of?'

Silence grew dense and awkward between them.

'I would not have come if – I thought he was going later – next week sometime.'

'He told you about it, then – this trip of his?'

'The other day … I think you were out … '

'Weston, do you still – do you still love him?'

The photographer sat down abruptly on a rush-bottomed chair, which creaked and staggered. His face was so crestfallen that his cheeks seemed to droop like the dewlaps on a bloodhound.

'What did he say? Tell me what he said. Please.'

'He said you were lovers. Until he tired of you.' She enjoyed his flinch, then felt disgusting and cruel. Was he going to cry now? She stared at him, imagining his skin fair beneath his shirt and trousers, his limbs long and well enough muscled, his body-hair golden.

'He put it like that? Ah well – it's all in the past, you know.'

'How far in the past?'

'Nine years at least.' He paused to think. 'Nine years exactly. I threw a small party on my fiftieth birthday. It was quite an occasion. All the painting people came, of course, from down the coast, and the Fine Arts Circle from town – we used to sing Gilbert and Sullivan on winter evenings.'

'Was he living here?'

'Oh yes. We never … I wanted a regular ménage and he said I was "too naïve for this world". He said it would be "much too much for Norfolk". Whenever there was a party, he would leave quite early and then come in by the back door and wait in my studio, in the dark, till the others had gone. I fully expected him to do so that night. But then, when I went through to the studio after midnight – it was as silent and vacant as an abandoned house. I shall never forget that silence – that motionless, evacuated air … I rode over here a few days later – three days later – I was putting it off, because I knew what had happened. The sinking *dreariness* inside me told me what had happened, unmistakably. He was busy working, of course – he was at the climax of his gypsy period – so I sat down meekly, on this very chair, I remember, as one does when Richard is busy working, and watched him at it for what seemed like hours, stalking the canvas, coming at it as powerfully and calmly as a lion-tamer. And after hours and hours, two hours, three hours – it was December and I remember the pitiless blue darkness outside all these windows – he put his things away and stared very hard at his picture and said to me, without looking in my direction at all, "Do you expect a reason, Weston? A reason for the absence of desire? Can you smell desire in me?" He turned that stare of his towards me then – his eyes looked about as emotional as the aperture of a camera. I am sure you have never seen him like that, Flo. Why should you?'

He was yearning towards her now – for help? For confidences equal to his? For the cosiness of reminiscing together about the man they both knew as a lover? The sting was going from her, anger was turning into a kind of weary mortification, and even beyond that into a fatalistic acknowledgement that whatever had happened could no longer be changed and had better be viewed like a spectacle, like a painting or a printed photograph.

He had mentioned Richard's 'gypsy period'. She was not wholly acquainted with Richard's periods but she remembered the large-eyed head with glistening ringlets, and she remembered her decision not to be jealous of whoever had lived here before.

'And when did Miss Raven-locks live here?' She might as well know. Not that she cared.

'Some years ago …' Weston's voice faltered. He was looking pained.

'Some years. Nine years? Were you part of the Gypsy Period?'

'Well – yes – but he has never painted me.'

Poor soul – such disregard he had suffered at the hands of the masterful Richard. She herself had evidently been privileged to be turned by those hands into a multi-coloured bird, into a black ogress splitting black fish in a shower of black blood. And into a noble martyr in a battle. The energy of the man – one lover in an elegant villa at a convenient distance and another on the premises. Ach well, maybe it was a sign of ageing that he now contented himself with just one. (What was he up to in London?)

'I brought you rather a good bottle,' Weston was saying. 'But perhaps you don't want …' He had become incapable of finishing his sentences. His head was drooping, like a thoroughbred horse falling asleep on its feet, and he was staring gloomily at the floor between his boots. 'I feel I owe you an apology, dearest Flo – but I don't, do I? Because, I mean …'

She walked over to him and kissed him on top of his head, on his youthful, wavy, artificial-looking hair (it felt as stiff as crimped fabric), then brought two glasses from the assortment in one of the wardrobes. They drank the evening away, hushed into a sort of chastened friendliness as if they had been together at a funeral.

Not long before midnight the key rattled in the door and Richard came in, bringing with him the smell of winter, nipping and acrid, turnips and cold earth and bonfire smoke. His coat was damp. Unusually for him he had a spot of colour burning on each cheek and from close up he smelt of rum. He gave her that full kiss again and strode into the lit area of the studio, rubbing his hands.

'Sausages. I demand sausages, grilled for choice. Shall we indulge in the homeliness of sausages?'

His hands were empty. 'Where is The Book?'

'They kept it. They kept it.'

'Have you a receipt?'

'Oh Flo!' He was humorously patronising. 'They *kept* it. They like it. Lane enthused – *Lane*!'

'Will they print our book?' She had to put in that word 'our'.

'If the colour-reproduction estimates are not impossible.' He was smiling roguishly at her now – uncle had come home with a present for his favourite niece. 'But – Flo – do not be grateful. Remember that they need us. Without us they are a shop without stock, or a bank without gold. So promise me – no gratitude.'

Perhaps she should also refrain from being grateful that he had said 'us'. And yet she was. She so wanted his jubilation not to exclude her, not to brush her away into the margins of his life. London – she had a vision of endless roofs coldly gleaming like frozen, unmapped reefs. He must know hundreds of people there, people who oozed money and the confidence of power. She no more craved money in the bank than she wanted an army at her command but if his life was really there, amongst offices with brass plates and gilt letters on their frontages, and drawing-rooms with Turkish carpets and French furniture, then it could not also be here (could it?) amongst the broad waters reflecting the sky, and flinty houses with red tiles on their roofs and marrows in their gardens, where she felt safe now – not at home but more or less at peace.

As she came back from the larder with the food to cook, a snore sounded from behind the bed-screen, where Weston had keeled over half an hour before. Richard looked disconcerted, then amused.

'I know that snore. What have you two been up to?'

Not until much later, when she and Richard were snug in that same bed and Weston had been tucked up with rugs and cushions on the half-disembowelled chaise longue in the far corner, did she think again about Richard's remarkably easy-going reaction to the other man's presence and wish that he had at least had the decency to be jealous.

Chapter 31

In the fogs of late autumn and early winter she was more dogged than ever by the feeling of being watched. When the unease of it made her itch, she got up abruptly, rushed over to the uncurtained windows, and looked out for minutes at a time, scanning the spectral hedgerows and reed-beds between the house and the water. Each growing thing looked larger than itself, black apparitions against the grey. No figures, neither animal nor human. Nothing moving into the covert of the bramble canes and the yellowing elm and hawthorn leaves.

Usually Richard said nothing, and when he did speak up at one December dusk as the fog was blackening into night, she understood at once that he had been biting back impatience all along.

'Florrie, whatever is the matter?' He knew very well what it was. 'We are not in the wicked city, you know. No Jack the Rippers here.'

He was right. She had spent years and years in places where there was not even a key in the door – although Kilgour and the Meikles had made a great show of bolting and locking the many doors of the Castle – so why was she bothering now?

'I wish – I wish we had some curtains.'

'Curtains! Curtains twenty feet high and as many yards across? What shall we commission from the furnishers – velvet, with gilt fringes?'

He despised money-grubbing and 'commerce' yet he was always forcing it to be a difficulty between them.

'Hang up sacks if you like. I only want to be at peace in my own home.'

The point in his beard twitched as though he was tickled by her using those words. What he said was, 'You are worried about what They think – those goggling strangers out there. Who cares about them? Now if They were people we could respect for their intelligence and taste, or had to please because they were powerful … How many of those does the world afford? Live for yourself, Florrie, and let the herd moo and slobber on its way.'

'I think I am one of the herd.'

'Would I have chosen you if you were?'

'I thought we chose each other.'

He looked nonplussed, then said vehemently, 'To draw, I meant – chose you to draw.'

'If that is what you meant, well then, I suppose you picked me out the first time because I was bleeding, and might be dying.'

She did not know herself if she was being satirical. He looked pleased, if anything, and said more calmly, 'So we are agreed. A subject is a subject. And They, the gogglers, do not understand that. Women must be beautiful – or abandoned. Courtesans, duchesses, or sluts. Skies must be halcyon. Sunsets must be all aglow. Peasants must be work-worn and devout – or in your case martyred. Stories, that is all the gogglers want. Not compositions or tones or colour-values but the sentimental anecdotes … '

He lectured on. At the word 'peasants' she had stopped listening. So her mother and father had been peasants, and Peg and Maggie, and Mairi and her people, and Alasdair Mor and Morag and Roddie long ago. The herd, and followers of herds. And the Dutch Africans and black Africans he had drawn for his magazines – more of the same. He had sailed past all their coasts, and waved his wand of a pencil or a brush in their direction, and they had been no more to him than tones and compositions. Well – if he had done no good at least he had done no harm – he had not made slaves of them, or burnt them out.

For long months after that, while no word came from the publishers in London, she seemed to diminish in his sight and became more a model than a wife. From his point of view, perhaps, this could have been an enlargement, for which was more fascinating or teemed more with possibilities, a person or a painted image? Perhaps the diminution that seemed to be overtaking them was in her eyes, not his, for certainly these days, as she sat again on the posing throne and looked at him looking at her, he dwindled and dwindled – a bearded man with a broad leathery face and a brick-red smock, distinct and miniature like an image seen through the wrong end of a spyglass. She could do it at will – look and look at him until, with a jump of vision, he transformed into a dwarf, gesticulating soundlessly at the far end of a polished shaft.

One morning she doodled this on one of the last few sheets of paper in a pad. At any moment he would do his gamekeeper's growl or grunt and expect her to freeze again. Nothing happened, and she let her stub of vermilion pastel move freely over the sheet, making the picture out of curly lines that wreathed like a drunken vine round the dwarf at the centre. The stub of the crayon crumbled on her as she tried for detail so she flipped the sheet over and enlarged him with a 4B pencil, bulging out his arms and shoulders, his head, his chubby thighs, drawing a sort of pursey god, a cherub with a beard and a hairy chest, whose hands, three times too large for the rest of him, clutched at the converging metal rays and used them as weapons – spears or thunderbolts. They crumpled in his grasp and he flung them down in a pet of kingly rage where they piled up round his toes like used pipe-cleaners.

Usually he said nothing now at the end of a morning session except the one word 'Lunch'. Then they went to the other end of the studio and ate bread and bloaters washed down with the inevitable hock. This morning she walked round by the easel to see what he was making of her. She had turned into a woman-bird again, not preening, not burning in colours like sun through stained glass but coldly glowing in lozenges of topaz and ice-blue and the greens of Northern Lights in autumn. And she was not roosting, she was hovering, her claws stretched down from brazen-feathered legs towards a sort of nest of squirming prey – a heap of women and men and children, naked and helpless on their backs, some without heads, some without arms.

They ate and drank in silence. After the second glass of wine she felt uncaring and said, 'What is the *story* of your picture?'

He gave her a small smile and said, 'Oh – it is what you please. It is not a fairy-tale, nor is it a portrait.'

'I wonder why the bird is female … '

'So do I. Or rather, I would if she were. The creature is female and male. He, she, is all of us. Preying and preyed upon.'

'Then you will not be needing me to sit for you. There is no likeness in it.'

'No likeness whatsoever.' He paused, then said in an unfathomably neutral voice, 'You do inspire me, though. And the head and neck are incomplete.'

She went over to the throne as though sleepwalking and stooped to pick up a full pad as she sat down. Had he once painted Miss Raven-locks as some monster, some harpy or vampire, when he tired of her? If he had, where were the pictures? She could look for them. She could not. She could not be turning into a grave-robber, scrabbling for carrion of his former women. Or his men …

She was letting her hand move, using a sharpened pencil that could cut spiky details onto the paper. The pursey god became a demon from the bushes, running at the naked buttocks of a woman crouching beside a rock, with a six-pronged fork like a salmon leister at the ready to impale her. No likenesses – the woman was sleeping deeply, her eyes reduced to a pair of down-curved lines, the man moustachioed with a black hook drooping from each half of his upper lip. And a juggler, balancing pointed toes on the back of the same crouching woman and keeping his three clubs spinning in mid-air. And two fishermen bent over the gunwale of their boat, only their upper legs and their backsides visible as they hauled in a net that had trapped a woman-fish, her legs a tail, her head a snout with a staring eye and a gill-slit, only her breast human …

Where were they coming from, these creatures? She had never dreamed them. Why were the females all pursued and caught? A real dream from many years ago swam upwards in her head and she drew it, big black birds flying high, flying northwards, their beaks full of harp-strings, they were flying into nothingness and she drew only the tail and half the body of the foremost bird, its wings and breast and lunging head were already nothing … He would think she was stealing his bird, so she cheated herself, ignored the next surfacing images (an adder twining and jerking in the talons of an eagle, a peacock in a waistcoat with a wineglass in one claw) and set herself to think of something he had never drawn or painted (so far as she knew). A giraffe with three legs, the legs of a camera tripod, stepping out between two trees, the lashes of its eyes absurdly long and the fringe of hair down the back of its neck crimped as though with tongs … I am making evil pictures of my friends, I am amusing myself like a witch in a cave. If I could turn myself into a hare now, and run away off into the wild pastures, the grass and heather of the hills …

It was too gloomy to work. Richard was lighting a lamp, then another, and the yellow lustre was blooming, wavering, steadying inside the shades. He never painted by lamplight, only drew or wrote. He was coming towards her – should she flip the cover over her drawings? Now he was standing between her and the lamplight and she could not see his expression. He must be looking at the last cartoon of Weston. The only sound that came from him was a short laugh like a dog barking in its sleep.

Chapter 32

On what she thought afterwards as the Day of the Letter, the world was charmed and favourable from sunrise on. They had waited for months, for spring and for The Letter, while February dragged by in a bitter, frosty drought. Herons starved for want of frogs – in the morning they could barely flap across from their old nests to the nearest sunlit fringe of woodland and stand hunched till their blood warmed again. In March the gales herded the gulls in from the sea in what Richard called 'barbaric hordes' and forced them to stand in wintry rows, heads to the wind and pale eyes stunned and frozen, on the ridges of the barns and cottages.

Now light was pouring and pouring from its source in the east, waxing more buttery as the sun got up. Yellow of daffodils, yellow of primroses. She picked them in bunches and posies from the half-wild clumps along the copses and was arranging them in tumblers, old teapots and jam jars, in anything that did not leak, when the knocker on the front door rattled, a rare event, and she got there just before Richard. She took the cream-laid envelope from the postman and smiled so warmly at him that he blushed and took off his cap.

She turned and gave Richard the letter – after all, it was addressed to him. He opened it at the meal-table and read it in a charged silence that seemed to last for minutes. She tried to gauge his face and could make nothing of it. At last he handed her the letter and she read through the two pages of immaculate brown typewriting.

The Bodley Head,
April the 9th, 1909

Dear Mr Burley,
I have given your book the most careful and appreciative con-
sideration, reading the manuscript not twice but thrice, which
accounts for this no doubt tantalising delay.
It is an original work, for which a public undoubtedly exists. I
shall comment upon it under three headings.
First, the text, which I gather is collaborative, commands my
admiration in every respect. It is quite wonderful, a phrase you will

not often find me using. It is lucid; it abounds in vivid particulars; it is unquestionably authentic whenever it describes the fisheries, from both a human and a commercial point of view; and I do not doubt that readers in many walks of life would be drawn eagerly from page to page. Many of the songs, in my opinion, have a rough beauty which entitles them to the name of poem.

In a word, the text could be published with a minimum of editing, although we should prefer type to your suggestion of facsimile manuscript.

Secondly, the artistic element, which I shall divide into black-and-white and coloured. The work in black-and-white, which I assume is all your own, is replete with grim power and many of the compositions could work well, if I may hazard the suggestion, in the medium of the woodcut. As they stand, in Indian ink and charcoal, the figures are in general so stylised, so angular in their limbs and so 'Gothic' in their features that a kind of ogreish quality prevails, which may or may not be your intention. In this form they are strong meat indeed, and while they might well strike the taste of some generation as yet unborn, at present they have left a flavour in my mouth which I can only describe as too acrid for comfort.

Thirdly, the colour work. It is very fine, even sumptuous; the landscapes are beautiful in an idyllic way; and the scenes of the fisheries are striking: I would have not thought that a codfish or a skate could be made so ornately handsome. Unfortunately, the cost of making colour plates that would do justice to work so rich is at the present time prohibitive; unless, that is, the book achieved sales which I have to say the drawings are likely to preclude.

May I make a proposal to you? We should be happy to publish the text by itself much as it stands; although there are some bookish turns of phrase which I would rather were substituted by the natural language which I seem to hear behind the written lines.

The paintings and the graphic work are, in this form, not suited to our lists; however, I should be more than happy to recommend the names of more specialised art houses, if you were willing to treat that element as a work in its own right.

Thank you for thinking of us as a home for your book. I look forward to hearing further from you.

With kind regards to your co-author,
I am, Sir,
Yours Sincerely,
John Lane.

After she had finished reading, she kept her eyes fixed on the second page, meaninglessly following the flourishes of the signature.

Pulses were throbbing in her temples and in the balls of her feet. Then she heard Richard say, 'You must be thinking – that you could not have read a letter more to your taste – if you had dictated it yourself.'

'What? He does not want our book!'

'He wants your stories. He does not want my pictures.'

'Richard – we are together – we are not competing with –'

'We are all competing – every greedy member of our greedy species. So let us not pretend – let us bite and slice each other like the predators we are.'

It was the way he said it that chilled her to the backbone. Even fury, fury against even herself, would have left her less lonely than this freezing dislike of everybody and everything.

She turned to him saying, 'Richard – dearest man –'. She had never called him anything like that before.

He detached her hand from his arm as though it had been a leech and walked quickly over to the throne, stood for a moment with his arms stretched rigid at his sides and his hands clenched into fists, then flung himself into the throne with a force that almost toppled it from the plinth and stared straight ahead of him, eyes dilated and face suffused with blood.

'Why, I ask myself, since there is no-one else to turn to – why in the name of God or the Devil did I give up my magazine work for *literature*!' The word came from him with the spluttering force of a match scratched into flame. 'Bad news is what they want. Troubles – the Troubles – "good murders" – dying savages. And I knew that, I could do it all to a T. Drawing in the morning, to pay the rent. My own work at night, in the golden age when my nights were my own and I could please myself. Who else is worth pleasing? A dealer in books? That he should lecture me about woodcuts! I know his kind, pretending to admire Beardsley and what he really likes is soap advertisements, or Alma-Tadema, bosomy nymphs and swags of roses – *pink* pictures, when the world is black-black-black as a collier's spittle, black as the bottom of the sea.'

It was as though he was drawing the whole room to him, the paintings, the furniture, the air itself, sucking them into him, consuming them in his blaze, leaving it gutted. The pollen gold of the atmosphere had paled as the sun moved round onto the windowless south side of the house and the pots of flowers stood about now in a shaded, waterish air, looking unsuitably pretty, decorations for a party that would never happen. The man on his throne, scowling and pouting, slumped back into his resentful thoughts, had shifted abruptly, as though a magic-lantern slide had clicked across, into the likeness of a dangerous stranger – somebody you would leave well alone if you came upon him in a public bar. He had never looked so outside her, so unconnected to her breathing and her touching, since she saw him across the water on the rich man's yacht.

Perhaps an hour passed silently. She broke out of herself as though cracking ice from her limbs and said, 'What should we do?'

'I should leave this fool's paradise. And go up to town. And see whether anyone in Fleet Street or Bouverie Street still recognises me.' The sentences were coming out of him with as little energy as cakes of mud collapsing down a bank.

'You would go and work with people you do not respect? Or like?'

He looked at her, at last, as though she was speaking a foreign language. 'And did you, ever, find yourself in so happy a situation? On your funny islands? Did you?'

Yes, she had, but how could she convince him of that, or of anything? She wanted to plead now – plead for their wedded state, for their home. There felt to be no endearment between them to make a pathway into his mind. As well reason with a justice on his bench when the verdict had gone against you. She would say nothing just now and wait till he had been to London to reclaim their book. If he came back – and he would surely need his equipment – they could maybe start afresh. If he did not … When she got up to fetch bread and fish from the larder, her legs and lower back had as little spring in them as though she had aged ten years in a morning.

Chapter 33

She would have gone mad if it had not been the season when her croft at the east end was crying out to be worked. However much she dug it over, relics of old occupants would keep surfacing. A round glass paperweight, one side chipped off, making a seashell pattern of concentric half-circles. A three-tined table fork, the remnant of its wooden handle gnawed by mice or rats. No stones at all, only this fine black earth as milled and enriched as cake. They lived on the potatoes from it. Each late summer they feasted on the long pods of the beans, boiled then eaten with fried shallots. She had dug in horse manure from the Beightons, season after season, and the tilth swarmed now with wee worms, purplish red, wriggling feverishly as though they were being impaled on hooks.

She had never dug over the whole croft in less than a day before. Now she got through it in a morning. When she paused to wipe her face, the stalemate with Richard came poisoning her mind and she drove and drove with her spade and graip, filling her head with the mushroom odour of the soil, letting her arms swing as continuously as a reaping machine, mashing and subduing the wretched thoughts till they were no longer recognisable.

As April warmed the ground she took her dibber, which she had whittled down from the handle-end of an old spade, made a long double-row of holes, and dropped in seed beans saved from last year's crop. She had marked out plots with pieces of flagstone lifted from the floor of the ruinous granary nearby and set down flat to make walkways across and across the sticky loam. The place was a dark mosaic at the start of the season. By June it would be a green one, and more a tweed than a mosaic.

She set potatoes, and as she pressed them in, feeling them firm as door-knobs in her fingers, she realised that she still blenched momentarily as she handled each one – her fingers still expected, after more than fifty years, the awful pulpy mess they had found when they brought home their crop in the year of the potato-rot, and her inner ear still heard the yowling of the clachan dogs as the stench of the sick food breathed over every croft along the north shore of the Island.

Such memories never withered away entirely, she knew them by heart, yet many happenings and sayings of the past five years blurred or slipped sideways out of sight when she tried to bring them up into her mind's eye. I am in an English paradise here, she was thinking now – no gales to speak of, no salt-gust blighting the harvest, the Beightons hardly see their landlord or his agent between one rent-day and the next. We can be eating our own vegetables by July. And I can wear a skirt and a blouse, just, week after week, from spring till autumn … The garden of Eden, only there was no use looking for a snake to blame – if there was one, it was in their own hearts, like a tape-worm lower down, jealousy and envy and wanting more than they could ever have.

She spaded earth over the potato drills and went back along all she had tilled so far, planting sticks to mark the rows. She would not bother with marrows this year, they grew like piglets but they had no taste. Beets again, yes. Shallotts. The small purplish turnips. Lettuces (although Richard said that salad 'would scarcely keep a rabbit alive'). Cabbages, a few (but white worms ate their roots). Sprouts for the winter … Would she still be here to pick them before woodpigeons flew down and ate the lot …

A picture was forming in her mind's vision. One she could only paint directly, not draw first. The weave of the vegetables. Gnarled bluish-green of savoy leaves, in paint-whorls like swollen roses. Next to that colour-patch, darker sap-green of potatoes in their first month above ground, striped onto the picture like corduroy. In the middle layer, light-green of young bean vines (how did you make that colour, luminous like a glass of lime juice with the sun shining though it?). Colours spun and knotted in her head like the back of a jersey growing from a knitter's needles. She wanted the brushes in her fingers *now*. Impossible, there was just one palette in the studio, and though she could use a piece of plywood for that, there was just the one easel and he was at it, still crafting silently at the taloned bird, making an entire world above and beside it and in the background, many-storeyed buildings with faces and shouting and vomiting and weeping in the windows, dogs hanging onto the backsides of children in the streets below, a winding river on which human heads bobbed amongst drowning horses with bayonets sticking into their backs.

'My masterpiece,' he had said one afternoon, looking at his work and speaking as though she was not there at all. 'My Garden of Earthly Delights. It should be enlarged to cover a wall. But who would give me a wall?'

Well, if he got his wall, would she get a turn at the easel? She made one for herself, a simple frame as though to hold a schoolroom blackboard. Clamps to hold the canvas were beyond her but she soon got used to the shaking. She set it up outdoors whenever she could, and as the crops grew so did one picture after another, fabrics of sheer colour, every green they could mix from their dwindling stock. It was as well he was using mainly reds and browns and blacks, colours of burnt skin and toadstool caps. He scarcely looked up when she came in and went to the paint cupboard. So they worked for weeks on end, and all the time it felt as though they were living in different seasons or different countries. Sadness, relief, she could hardly tell which she felt the more.

As she set up her easel one August morning and turned to lift the canvas leaning against the low wall of the asparagus frame, her mind shook. Something had happened. She wanted to lean on something. She would fall down if she took one step. Her mouth had dried. When she tried to swallow, the muscles in her throat did nothing.

She was in an uncanny airless space, cut off from the ground, the plants, the window with Richard visible through reflections of the hedges and the reedbeds. She put out her hand to the canvas again – she thought of doing it – her arm stayed at her side. She brought her left hand round and used it to lift her right – she had to think hard and do it with the utmost care, as though she was handling a heavy, fragile thing. She tried swallowing again and almost panicked, choking, as her throat worked slowly – slowly like a key turning in rusted lock.

I am losing myself – the world is melting under me – I am alone. Bad dreams were flashing in her head – herself high up in black space, her wings tied to her sides ... She did not dare move her right foot, walking would pitch her into an abyss ... She made herself do it, and it was all right. She reached the low wall and sat down clumsily. She clenched and unclenched her right hand and the fingers did answer, gripping with little power.

Had it been a stroke? Had he seen her? Forget him – what mattered was to step back through the door again into the wholesome world. With her left hand she managed to lift the canvas onto the easel. For the rest of the day, ignoring lunch-time and Richard and the creeping of clay-coloured cloud across the sky, she painted at her picture, her left hand supporting her right, in smaller, lighter strokes than she had been using for the juice and curl of the leaves but still the image spread across the white primer – yellow and blue, nearness and distance, cornfields and an upland beyond.

For weeks to come she measured time not by whether Richard had spoken to her without her speaking to him first, or by the dwindling of the banknotes in the biscuit tin, but by the recovering suppleness and independence of her arm. She tested it by drawing straight lines freehand. For a few days the line stuttered, or it went pale, then dark again. After a week it was as even as she had ever drawn and the only wavering left was in her mind. She completely wanted her body to be well, to be unthinking and fluent as an animal. It always had been. She had been able to do anything, run, row, stand gutting fish for hours on end. Now she could not help listening to herself, as though for the creak or breathing of an intruder somewhere in a silent house. She still looked the same in the mirror, clear brown complexion, eyes unblinking, hair brown-gold except for the one white feather above her brow. Inside this front something had changed, and lost its health, and she could not make herself go to a doctor and find out what it was.

Richard went to London and brought their book back. He went to Weston's and stayed overnight, saying next day, 'I drank too much burgundy to tell a hedge from a ditch on the road back.' The three of them went together to the Mariners' as though nothing had changed between any of them, and heard that the singing man with the ruined lungs had died in the spring. Weston had carried out at last his old plan of opening his own shop, at the north end of Marine Parade. He had installed a pretty young man in it to sell painting and drawing equipment and of course prints of the master's very popular field-workers sowing grain by hand and fishermen in sou'westers leaning on rails at the harbour with their clay pipes turned upside down. The shop was doing 'extraordinarily well' – perhaps this accounted for the thickening of the wad in the tin.

In her own life nothing was flowing forward. She was treading water as the last pods shrivelled on the bean-rows, the hearts of the cabbages grew solid, and the shaws of the potatoes yellowed and sagged. Walking down the slope to the vegetable croft furthest from the house, she saw again her home-land, rows of potatoes on the broad backs of the lazybeds, wealth of pink flowers shaking in the sea-wind. The bere-barley was so thin in the ear, it seemed no more than a greenish mist clinging to the stalks, and she was asking her father, 'Allan Mor, Allan Mor, do you think there will be enough for us all?' and her father was saying, 'I *hope* there will be enough for us all,' making his meaning plain, for neither he nor Mairi her mother kept anything from her … She was surprised when she looked up and saw, not a turf slope ending at a beach of white shell-sand stretching away, Nile-green above sand and cobalt above the seaweed beds, but a dense, high hawthorn hedge bound with canes of bramble, hemming her in and barring out all sight of anything beyond.

Chapter 34

For three years or more no word had come from Peg and her own postcards might as well have been thrown into the sea. Now a letter arrived, crumpled and soiled as thought it was five years old, not five weeks. The blue ink of the address was blotted as though with tear-stains. 'BY HAND', it said above the address – why had she not used the post like everybody else?

> *Candlemaker Row*
> *Sgiach Town*
> *July the 31st 1911*
>
> *Dear Friend Flo*
>
> *I will be sending this by a friend who is still going after the herrings. From Balta down the east side to your part is not so far. – If you were here it would be like old times and not like old times. – We are three again Hugh is strong enough so am I Peggy Beg was taken by the measles the year Hughie Beg was born it was like dying with the wee lass at the worst of her fever then the blow. If you have no children you do not know the sorrow. – Come up here one year dear friend and we will all be ceilidhing again. – The picture postcards were beautiful to see and from them I know where you are. – That animal the ram MacSween is back from America with a fancy woman and set up in a house at the west end his mother died of the drink long since.*
>
> *Your friend Peg*
> *XXXXX*

Flo came out of the letter as though from a deep sleep, like burial in the earth. All this had happened, to people she knew as she would never know Richard or Weston or any other of the queer hares down here, and she had felt not a tremor. It was stupid but she blamed herself for being indifferent and hard.

Minutes later the thought of Sandy began to hurt like an ulcer in her guts. Why was it paining her now? Over the years she had watched that time settling and fixing into a page of history. Now it was flesh again.

Maybe such things went on with you to death – unless your memory failed entirely … She realised she was sniffing in deeply and in her head the whisky smell of peat-smoke was as strong as the real thing, peat and the old-fish smell of a foreshore bared by the ebb, and the blood and acid smells of the cattle and the sheep. Not even the recalling and the telling of it all for *Three Score and Ten* had brought those days and years so keenly back.

During the winter, while Richard was over at Weston's, or in town on some nameless errand, or down at the water's edge studying the jetsam for the latest panel of his hellish 'Garden' – birds' skulls, a fish floating belly up, a tree-stump with torn-up roots like antlers – she began to dismantle their book. It was already grey with dust where it lay on a wardrobe shelf, glasses and jars above it, empty wine-bottles below. She untied the leather thongs from the holes in the vellum sheets, separated the pages of text and picture, and hid the written pages, her pages, between canvases of her own that she had stacked against the east wall. She took care to remove only one page at a time. Probably he could not bear to look at it, and if he did take it into his head to bring it out again and torment himself with what might have been, she could invent some excuse or other.

When she looked round the studio, the gear and furniture standing as motionless as though whoever lived there had fled suddenly from an invading enemy, she realised that her pads and stacks of drawings meant almost as much to her as The Book. Her hand had put them forth like flowers, her first and only flowers. So she interleaved them among the green-tweed paintings and the fantastic landscapes she had painted recently and began to wait for an opportunity.

She would go north again. How did you change your life? Quite easily, it seemed. You upped and went, if there was nothing to keep you – or if whoever was keeping you would as soon you melted off the face of the earth. Richard said little to her now and she said little to him. When she went to bed he was usually at the easel, painting the third panel of his 'Garden' with its vision of the Broads as a paradise for predators – above the water surface, flies with long black dagger-tails pierced their eggs into the fat, lardy bodies of their paralysed hosts, and below the surface, signified by a ruled division between the amber light suffusing the upper third of the picture and the greenish-blue of the lower part, a pike loomed with a hooked lower jaw and the skeleton of a great hawk riding on its back with its claws embedded in the fish's spine. He was growing ever more minute, standing inches from the canvas and painting in exquisite details with a brush that had just one camel-hair left on its end.

Surrounded by the lamps he was a wizard in a cell of light, not of this world at all. Usually she had no idea when he finished working, and when she woke up he was a hunched roll of bedclothes on the chaise longue or already out and poking in the water down by the reed-beds.

Somehow he must be finding rent. She would never ask him. Typed letters came, from London she supposed. He read them silently and stowed them away somewhere amongst his clothes. He must be doing some deal, for illustrations or for work in black-and-white – a shrinking market now that photography prevailed in the daily papers. He would decamp, no doubt, when it suited him. With luck she would be the first to go – no, not with luck, with wiliness and determination. Her plan was poised now, like a brittle vase, and she was as brittle herself – a sentence or two from him and everything would shatter. Days went by and he said nothing to her with the faintest note of intimacy. Her own tongue felt paralysed inside the casing of her skull. The whole tender front of her still longed for him, or for someone, on a balmy afternoon or after she had started awake at night when a dog barked. Her memories of their loving had the feel of dreams now, of feverish happenings in some other country – real enough to make life without them stretch ahead in a narrowing grey perspective like a poor, deserted street.

She went to town, giving no reason and he asked for none. Along the quays she asked about the comings and goings of boats from the north. She made it sound as though she was going for a job up there and was willing to work her passage. Really her plans were nothing but a wide, white blank. They looked at her, most of them, as if she was a lunatic – an elderly *woman* working on *shipboard* – until she met a Banffshire man called Doddy Main, swarthy as a Spaniard with deep-set eyes and a black suit and celluloid collar as stiff and spruce as though he was permanently dressed for church.

'I was wanting to take passage for the north …' She used her usual phrases and let the suggestion hang in the air.

'Aweel,' he said, looking across the river and smiling to himself, 'There's nae big liners gangs up thon wey.' He made a small sound of confirmation by drawing in his breath. 'Na na, nae liners ava.' Another indrawn 'Ay'.

She stood quietly and Doddy Main stood quietly. He did not leer, or ogle her, or look suggestive or contemptuous or cross. The river glittered under sunlight hazed with fog. The skriegh of a thousand gulls cut the air like scissors.

'Na na, nae liners.' He was still relishing his joke. 'There's just the ae wey I ken o', lass, and that's to come wi' me an' ma brithers, fan we gang up tae Nairn wi' oor new drifter. Nae new, no' – said as though correcting her, not himself. 'New enough. Nine year auld. Built at Grimsby and selling for use wi' a' the gear, because the puir man died o' a cancer. Robbie an' Jock are comin' doon by the train the morn's morn an' we'll tak her north on Saturday. There's a wee bunk spare in the stem an' naebody will mind if ye keep yersel tae yersel. Can ye dae that, lassie?'

Well, she was an old hand at that. Would there be room for her luggage? 'Foo muckle is't? Nae a haill housefu', is't?' Twelve flat packages wrapped in oilskin, none of them bigger than half a kitchen table, would be 'nae bother, nae bother ava.' And could she be punctual and ready at the South Denes an hour before slack water on Saturday?

She was going to glide out of Yarmouth with as little friction as ice on ice. She was no longer willing it. It was happening to her, and she let it happen. When she came back into the studio, she thought for a moment she was deaf. Silence held each thing in a transparent glue. No memories came out from the corners to address her or keep her company. If he had gone already, surely he would not have left the panels of the 'Garden', draped loosely in a dust-sheet? She checked the wardrobe – the remains of The Book were piled there as ever. Four fresh bloaters lay under the meat-safe in the larder. The jug of milk was standing in the water-bowl covered by the beaded muslin square. So he would be back by nightfall. She began methodically to stack and pack her pictures, four at a time, faces inwards, well padded with ancient straw from a cubby-hole in the granary, parcelled in oilskin bought in town with silver from her tiny store, farmer's twine from the Beightons, who seemed as always incurious and unconcerned about their peculiar tenants.

A bluebottle fizzed somewhere as she worked. Before, she would have looked at it and killed it. The noise of it deepened the fundamental silence. Towards sunset a wind began to keen drily round the corners of the building. If he came back, she would simply go on with her work and explain herself if he began to interrogate her. And if he used force on her … He did not come back, not that night or the next. On Saturday morning, three hours before slack water according to the tide table, the hired cart and horse were at the door and she was driving off to town under a sky sheer as a dome of pale-yellow china, polished by two days of strong winds off the sea.

Chapter 35

The fish quay slid backwards past her, out of her life – the monument, the walls of barrels, the farlings where the gutting crews were bent as ever over their work. She waved and a woman waved back with her knife in her hand.

The brothers had been late in casting off – some trouble with the delivery of coal for the boiler – and now they were worried about the speed of the ebb with the river-run behind it. Dod was at the wheel, Robbie and Jock at the bow eyeing the approaching bend out into the invisible sea. They swung hard left and the expanse of the open water sloped suddenly up towards the horizon. Along the stonework where the North Pier sprouted from the land, crested waves were running along the wall like backs of dolphins. However could they make headway against such forces? The ebb and the current caught the stern with a massive boost, hefting the *Ocean Foam* at the south wall – the boat felt light as a peanut shell, lighter, no weight at all – there was nothing under them, no solidity, no grip. Dod spun the wheel, the boat steadied and held onto the water like a hand locked onto a snake. They lunged seaward, cleared the pier-end with its squat white beacon, staggered sideways toward the beach as the southerly swell lifted them onto the running hills of water, plunged them, lifted them. Black swirls of coal-smoke poured downwards from the funnel, blinding and choking them. Then they were forging forward and the smoke streamed out sideways.

Above the sand-bar between sea and river the crowded masts bristled like a leafless hedge. The Wellington Pier moved backwards past them, the jetty, the Britannia. Before they came abreast of Weston's shop, Flo turned to look out over the broad blue plain of water where one coal-boat was toiling southward, then went below to finish the stowing of her goods.

In a canvas bag with a leather strap she had brought away her necessaries. Nightie, spare skirt, Maggie's shawl, new moccasins she had cut and stitched to replace the worn-out Canadian pair, thread, needles, a thimble, and her purse, now more patches than the original cloth, with the thin wad of notes she had saved. Not much to show for her time down here. At least she had come away wearing the burgundy woollen coat with a collar of Indian lamb which she suspected had been abandoned by Miss Raven-locks.

The 'wee bunk in the stem' would have curled her up like a babe in the womb if some previous user had not cut pieces out of the bulkheads to make room for head and feet. Would not this have weakened the boat? The worry felt strangely outside of her. She stowed her load of pictures beside the foot of the bunk, jamming it between a lamp-box and some coils of heavy rope that smelt of hemp and oil. At least they were dry. Suppose the gear shifted and grazed the canvases? She should have stiffened the packages with sheets of plywood. Too heavy to carry, and too late to think of it – just another qualm of worry that she could not think about, could not grasp ... A sick drowsiness was brimming up inside her. Was that weakness coming over her again? It was the motion of the sea that was in her, making her eyelids heavy. She gave in to the sickness, letting it quell and crush out the regrets and doubts and fears about the future that were stouning through her like pains.

She slept and dreamed and slept. At gloaming on the second day she put her head above the hatch to get some air that did not reek of oil and old fish and unwashed clothes. She caught sight of a red tower on a low round hill, and heard Jock say to Robbie, 'There's thon thing the auld admiral biggit tae look oot for the Frenchies.'

On the third day she woke up feeling weak and at peace. When she climbed out onto the deck, she saw they were in the midst of a water-desert, wrinkled with waves, a million waves and every one the same but different, mounding to crests, to a ruffle of bubbles that came to nothing and slid back down the shiny slope into the next trough. It did not look liquid, it looked like buckling metal. It was neither blue nor green but some colour without the quiver and radiance of light in it.

Her mood lurched. Hours upon hours rolled on beneath her while her spirit drifted out over the dreich waters. One hour would shine briefly when the sight of another vessel raised her heart for a minute, its sidelights burning green and red as night thickened and wiped out the sea.

'Steam-drifter,' Robbie said to nobody in particular. Or 'Dutchman swipin' oor whitefish.' No conversation followed. It felt like the quietest spell in her entire life. Dod had been so talkative on his own back at the dock. In Jock and Robbie's presence he vied with them in not uttering more than ten words every hundred miles. At mealtimes she lacked the energy and confidence to speak up and the brothers were content to munch in silence their kippers and bloaters and porridge thick as wet cake.

When it was time to stoke the boiler, there was always a little flurry of remarks – maybe they were used to a boy or a paid man doing that. They bickered about whose turn it was and on the fourth day, still out of sigh of land, Robbie amazed her by turning away from the furnace door, his face smeared black with coal-dust and grease, running a finger over his lips so that they stood out red and blubbery, and singing a coon song in a gravelly baritone – 'Massa's in de col', col' groun'.' It was as unexpected as a horse standing up on its hind legs and dancing a reel.

On the fifth day boats were to be seen on all sides like beetles on a stone floor, converging on an inlet into the land where a big town stood out in a rubble of grey blocks and ridges, a fume of smoke-haze like smeared dark pastel, a little mountain behind it, and furthest away, in the bight of the land, three broad black triangles spanning the mouth of the river. A coal-boat chugged past near enough for her to read the name on its stern – '*Thrift*. Granton.' Behind her she heard Jock say, 'The auld *Thrift*. Filthy as iver.' An island was near them on their left, crowned with the chalky pillar of a lighthouse, against the background of a coast low and green. Then for a day and a night the waste of waters prevailed again, destroying her with its sameness.

By the time they had veered so far west that they were steering into the sun's eye at the end of the day, she wanted this time of no work and no decisions to go on forever.

'How far to Nairn now?' she asked Dod as they chugged past a shore of torn green slopes, red cliffs, and villages fitted into the neuks like barnacles.

'A hauf day, ca' it a guid twal' oor gin it disna come on a blaw.'

In half a day she would be homeless again, less rooted than a seal or a gannet. The sky was like a roof torn off and the wind scattering her bones to the four points of the compass.

In the evening she brought her packages up the ladder one at a time and ranged them along the foredeck against the gunwale. Still the brothers did not ask what they were. Houses were huddled round a river's mouth. She thought of the doors, rows and rows of them, all closed to her. She must ask nothing from the brothers – their wives would think she was a hoor. She said to the nearest, Jock, holding out a single banknote, 'Will this do – for my keep?'

'Fine that. Faur ye gaun the noo?'

'I will get on the road and take my chance.'

'It's ower late. Come awa' on tae the toon – there's aye lodgin' in Craigpatrick for fisher quinies.'

Well, she had been that before and might be one again. 'Thank you. Thank you. It will make you late.'

'Nae bother.'

From the busy dockside in Craigpatrick she stood beside her little pile of gear and watched them make off back again for their home. Their sidelights glimmered in the darkening reaches of the firth. The quick toot of their steam-whistle could have been a signal to the harbour master or an incoming drifter. Its echoing round the uplands of the coast stretched out the gloaming into a never-ending waste land, homeless and trackless.

Coming out of the shadows a boy with a shafted cart offered to take her to his mother's place for a penny. For another penny she got a place on the rope where women of all ages, in drab clothes whitened with sweat and sea-salt, were already leaning on the line strung from end to end of an attic smelling of tar. She found a place next the wall, to be close to her gear, and dropped down into a stew of nightmares. Birds flew into her face through a window high above the sea – nails hammered into her temples – her scalp was being torn off – she woke suffocating and smelt the hair of the woman next her who had slumped sideways against her like a heavy sack. Flo pushed her upright and she slumped the other way, mumbling in her sleep, 'Fuckin', fuckin', fuckin' …'

The welter of dreams again – she was sliding down a greased pole set in the shaft of a well – the black sump at the bottom was swallowing up towards her – she tried to grip the sides and felt her arms torn off at the shoulder – woke, and found she had no feeling from the armpits to her finger-ends. This was no rest at all, it was worse than lying down. If they all lay down there would be room for only half the people … She was drowning in sticky fire, struggling to pull the flames off her limbs, tearing her skin off in flaps and shreds … She woke for the last time in sunshine filtering through a skylight painted over with white distemper. One of her packages had gone. In her deep fatigue, surrounded by these strays and beggars, she could not make herself find out for several minutes what she had lost.

The place was an old boatbuilder's shed, it turned out, attached like a wing to the end of a waterside inn called 'The Duke'. More coins went on the right to wash at a pump in the yard, eat salt bacon in the kitchen, and store her goods in an outhouse with a padlock. By the middle of the morning she had been turned away from every gutting station along the shore – they had plenty of girls, they said with emphasis, and a look at the white in her hair. The herring season was nearing its end. The town had more than enough 'casuals'. Maybe she should try 'along the coast'.

She sat on the step of a warehouse whose roof had been burnt out and tried to think. Her head was singing with a high white noise that drowned all useful thoughts. She must get round to the West, where there were people she knew. She must get money. People – money – people – money – the words dinned in her head till they turned into gibberish. She would never again be able to travel five hundred miles for next to nothing – that had been the one lucky turn that could not come again. She stood up and stretched, her coat fell open, and a man who was walking past said, 'How much, darlin'?' He had stopped and was smiling. She saw herself in a posh coat, lingering in a back street, doing no obvious work, and knew that she must grip her life by the scruff – scratch up some money, find out if there was a steamer to the West, down the Great Glen perhaps, and put this sty behind her.

For the first time in her life she was helpless without money. She was naked in the world. Another night like that would carve pieces out of her. A bed of sorts in the inn would melt away her few pounds soon enough and leave her with no means of getting away. She would go on the tramp – no, not with the pictures. They were herself, her life. They were becoming a great boulder of a burden. She had walked automatically up one of the range of steep little wynds that linked the shore to the spine of the town, the same as Lowestoft. Through her panicking, gibbering thoughts a voice was reaching her, a guttural voice saying, 'Pennies, pennies. Pennies for my food. Pennies, lady, pennies …'

As she paused, and gave the beggar hope, the woman's voice went higher, almost tearfully wheedling, 'Pennies, pennies for my food.'

Flo tugged herself clear and walked on, feeling callous and ashamed. A penny was one night's rest. Twelve of them paid for eight square feet of floor in a dusty outhouse. How could you live? You could be brushed aside and left for dead like a lame gull dying on the fringe of the flock.

The voice was grating on behind her, 'Pennies, sir … Pennies, lady …' Impulsively she turned off into the mouth of a close between a butcher's and a chandler's and set herself to study the beggar's tricks.

Chapter 36

The woman was doing some business. After an hour four coins had been put into her hand. (How many hours would that enable her to live?) Mostly they were given by the few folk who came by in tweeds and good coats, but then, the woman used her most piteous voice on them, whining the words as though she was at her last gasp. A minister came past in his black suit, black hat, black boots – surely he would be a soft touch, and he was, not without a few words, inaudible to Flo, which presumably fitted the knitting of his brows and the down-turning of his mouth.

The woman had a fair flock to pick at. Fisher-looking men in jerseys and gum-boots. Housewives in coats and hats with baskets on their arms, who often looked away with blank faces and spoke quickly to each other. From time to time a shabbier kind of person came slowly past, in skirts and shawls or jackets and breeks of worn, no-colour material, speaking quietly to each other in her own old language. She felt herself move out to them as though her breast had been laid open. Then she was scolding herself for silliness – they could have been from anywhere – to them she would be nothing. No, not true – folk from the islands nearly always greeted each other, knew something about each other's home-lands, and soon were speaking like tried acquaintances.

Her head was reeling again, in a swarm of longings. The beggar-woman left the island folk alone – did she see them as beggars like herself? They looked lost, some of them, while she was in her element. That nasal wheedling was a practised trade voice. Her eyes and mouth widened pathetically as she used it on a customer. When the moment had passed, she at once looked perfectly hale again, eyeing the coin as shrewdly as a farmer at the mart before palming it into a fold of her ragged clothes.

As the Town House clock chimed one, Flo could see that this was the perfect spot. The high street narrowed, the slab pavement at the side had barely room for one, and most folk hesitated before stepping out onto the cobbles next to the rattling carts and horses. Then they almost trod on the woman as she sat on a worn stone bollard at the mouth of a close. Maybe their partings with the pence was as much as anything a token of apology for seeming to treat her like a stray dog or a pig at a fair.

If you could lower yourself that far, you must somehow have stepped out of life, passed through a looking-glass and left shame and self-esteem behind you. Could she do that – for the few days it might take to get the money for a steamer fare to the West? Could she undress herself that far?

The beggar woman had spotted her and was giving her sharp sideways looks. If Flo started to hold out her hand for money anywhere near here, the woman would surely come tearing at her with black fingernails. The high street bent out of sight in both directions. Was there room for another beggar at the far ends of it? She sauntered off – deceitful already in the pretended laziness of her pace. The cry of 'Pennies, sir – pennies, lady' was cut off behind her as she entered the southern section of the street.

At one side the throughfare widened into a square towered over by a railway hotel with fancy stonework, stone pineapples on its gable ends and stone flowers on its façade and its name in tall gold letters. Shops and more shops lined the sides. People made for the station, their baggage in their hands or carried by porters in uniform. No shortage of custom here. Behind the plate-glass windows feathered hats were for sale – pipes and cigars and walking-sticks – elaborate cakes on tilted glass shelves – and at the north end a fishmonger's with bunches of grouse hanging outside and the inner walls tiled with pictures of stags at bay and salmon leaping.

Between the two shops a side street curved steeply upwards to a wooded ridge where a big house stood lonely among the funeral darkness of fir-trees with draping tapestries of needles like pictures of Canada. The ornamental battlements and little corner towers like pepperpots gave her a qualm like nausea. The Castle. It was like seeing the Castle again, more dream than memory, as though Ardmairs and Meikles could be giving her the black look from behind the long plush curtains. Only this castle had no curtains, just blinds, and in some of the windows metal rods or closed shutters.

She turned her back on the place and faced the stream of strangers. They had become foreigners, they would not understand a bit of English except the one word 'Pennies'. No other sound could pass between them, no look except the plea on her side and indifference or grudge on theirs. She lowered herself into the freezing river of it, perched herself on an iron stanchion meant to fend off traffic from a statue of the Old Queen, held out her hand as a well-dressed couple came near, and said, 'Pennies, sir, for mercy's sake.'

Where had these words sprung from? A voice had uttered them from inches behind and above her skull. She heard with disgust the hissing of the S's, the ingratiating lilt of it all. The woman tightened her hold on her husband's arm and drew him firmly past, looking fixedly ahead of her. The man gave a little cough and his hand went up for a moment as though he was going to raise his hat.

Flo's jaw had cramped shut, making more words impossible. She held out her hand again. The next passer-by, a man with Dundreary whiskers and a strapped-up suitcase, started sideways, looking red and furious, and strode off towards the station entrance. She snatched her hand back as though from a fire. If she was stung so easily, she would soon be starving. The pressure in her head was unnerving her now, it was making her listen to herself as she had done ever since that turn. She was a useless failure. Failures sank down and died. She should have stayed in Norfolk, in spite of the pretence and the humiliation. She was adrift now – she was *here*, she must live or else give up the ghost.

She made her voice come out of her mouth – 'Pennies, sir. Pennies, lady. Pennies for mercy's sake.' Soon after the chime of three a small coin was dropped into her hand by a hand in a lilac glove – sixpence, and the smell of lavender. She put it into a pocket of her coat and went on begging as the hours sounded. Each quarter lifted her spirits with a feeling of another step taken towards night-time and sleep. It must be a bed this time. That sty with the penny rope was like a door with despair and ruin on the other side of it.

By five o'clock she had been given four coins – one shilling and threepence. By six o'clock some drinkers weaving their way from one public house to another had come to a stop beside her. They picked out their coppers with the care of a jeweller assaying precious stones, made her cup both hands together, and poured into them one shilling and tenpence-halfpenny. She had enough for a bed for the night and some to spare. Fatigue was stunning her as though she had been at the fish for a whole day – stunned and shameless she was, shot through with pangs of acrid hate for the dozens who had given her nothing and wolfish triumph over those who had forked out for her.

Back at the Duke she paid for a room, made sure her packages were still intact, and lay staring for a time by candlelight (one penny) at the whitewashed planks of the ceiling. She smelt her hands – the lick of yellow soap had not got rid of the sour reek of coins. Above her, furniture thumped and gasping voices sounded, making her more solitary than ever. Maybe she was past love now. She scarcely wanted it. To be outside it made her feel as light and castaway as driftwood on the beach.

On the second day she took nearly half a crown and felt harebrained with pleasure. She was beginning to measure happiness in silver.

On the third day she had taken nearly three shillings, she estimated by the weight of her pocket, by the middle of the afternoon when a stout leather glove hovered over her hand and dropped something into it. Her palm stouned as though a nail was driving through it, then went numb. She shook it violently. A heated coin was sticking to her scorched skin. She shook it again and the thing flew off and landed in the gutter. The dirty trickle sizzled briefly. She started to her feet and saw a man in a short blue jacket and a peaked cap running out of sight.

That night she scarcely slept. She had wrapped her hand in buttered cotton. It stung and smouldered as though hot acid was pumping inside her skin with each beat of her heart. Rain was tapping, then beating on the window and she made the weather an excuse to lie in a dwaum all day, eating nothing, gulping water until she had drained the wash-stand jug four times.

On the fifth day she was at her perch again. The weather had turned and the louring skies and the drizzle were forcing people in to themselves and souring their generosity. They brushed past her without expression. A gaggle of fishermen, faces glazed with drink. Two men with heavy overcoats and bulging leather cases – they passed her with knowing grins and an exchange of remarks from which she caught the word 'cunt'. No westland folk at all. A woman with a creelful of shellfish layered in seaweed upon her back – she tried to enter the fishmonger's and was turned away. A small man with tiny eyes and a snub nose who was smiling with the merry, open face of a boy on an outing. A soldier with a red jacket and a kilt who stumbled against her and said in her ear, 'Wull ye dae it for siller, then?' and walked on laughing to himself. Two nuns, shell-white faces beneath starched rims and black hoods, who went past with a breath of camphor, a rasping of gown-material, and small tolerant smiles from yellow teeth.

It was a procession of the mad. Here came a woman more than six feet tall, her short white hair bristling like a sweep's brush. As she walked along, she hit the stone or the glass with her fist, stopped suddenly and looked up at the sky, then nodded quickly and walked on lost in thought.

Her face was as white as a fish's belly, thick-lidded and hollowed under the eyes as though she had been crying for years. As she passed Flo, she looked her full in the eyes from her own eyes which were dark-brown as a lochan and seemed as unaware of themselves as a sleepwalker's. She wore a long grey dress, no jersey although it was chilly, and her hands were empty – big raw-red hands that hung down with a helpless look – male hands with massive knuckles.

She turned up the hill towards the house with the towers, round a sharp bend, and out of sight. And all this had happened before. Flo had never been here and it had happened before – never seen that street with its slabbed pavements the colour of stale meat and it had happened before, the tall woman drumming on the fronts of buildings, the sky like sagging cloths.

Next day it happened again and as the tall woman came down from the house with the towers, carrying a straw bag in each hand, Flo remembered her and knew her – that head of flattened bristly hair, the broken-looking nose with a bump in it – Morag Mor, big Morag, daughter of Alasdair the strong champion, who had been lured away from the houses, on the Day of the Battle, by the promise of free oatmeal to be got at Lochmaddy. She herself was mad now, apparently, so mad that she could not shake off this sense that everything was repeating itself and she was trapped in a loop of time that must come round again, and again and again and again with no way out.

The tall woman was coming up to her and saying with the exposed stare of her eyes, 'Florence Campbell, you have your father's hair on your head now. I knew that white feather when I saw it yesterday and last night it was coming back to me till I could not sleep.'

She had put her bags down and was hugging Flo in a grasp that made her ribs creak. Then she was standing away again and smiling as though the best thing in the world was happening. Her eyes were brimming with tears that magnified them, lightening their darkness, and Flo felt her own cheeks streaming. Sobs were rising through her, stopping her breath. Morag Matheson, the daughter of Alasdair and Flora, the best of neighbours, her own parents' comrades, whom she had forgotten and had never seen for nearly sixty years.

Chapter 37

Flo was speechless for quarter of an hour, half an hour – the metal voice of the clock was calling out from the rim of her mind while she sat there with Morag, on a wooden seat with iron legs moulded to look like branches, on the sunny side of the Station Square. Morag seemed not to mind her silence, spilling her own words out in spurts and gushes, touching Flo continually, patting her arm, her hand, leaning towards her with a warm, close pressure of her shoulder, and every now and again, at a peak of excitement, seizing her hand and raising it into the air with a painful squeeze as she half turned to give Flo a full, devouring look.

'Oh mercy on us, we are not dead yet, for all the troubles and trials. And for years and years and too many years I was knowing you were all in the world but where? When Mother died at Loch Burrival, before ever the *Pict* arrived to take us all away, I thought that everything would break and be gone from us. She broke, you know. She had toiled on that Committee road as hard as any of them although Katrine Beag was still in the cradle. The cradle? I am a liar!' She hammered herself on the breastbone with the face of her fist. 'Katrine was on Mother's back in the shawl while she was breaking stones and before the days were growing again she was orphaned, for all we knew – Father was in Sgiach or Glaschu, or the moon or the other side of the world, and I was warming a drop of cow's milk in my mouth before I drooled it down into her wee thin lips as we lay there on the black floor, in the middle of the black moor, and I was putting a bit of rag across her eyes because there were creatures dropping into them from the foul side of the turfs we had laid on the cabers for a roof.'

The story was streaming out of her, the names and places knocking against each other like river-stones in a spate. Tears poured from her eyes and she was smiling wild-eyed, disbelieving smiles and shaking her head at her own words. How could you live for seventy years? How could you lift a rock as big as yourself and not be crushed? Flo wanted to know everything – did Alasdair Mor come back? What happened when the Four came out of the gaol on the mainland and how did they ever find their families again? Roddy, that boy, that man, with his brown eyebrows meeting above the bridge of his nose – tell me he did not go into the army, or poison with drink in a slum? Morag would know, and what she did not know they would find out now, from some of their people, when they came back from New South Wales or Nova Scotia …

She was realising that she had stored up all their names in a place at the back of her mind, and locked it and left it unvisited, because that banishing of their people, that defeat, aroused more hatred and shame than she could stand. Now, as Morag talked and talked, their story was turning into a proof that at least a person could last as long as the keel of a boat or the handle of a spade. She became so calm that Morag looked almost crestfallen, and peered at her as though suspecting her of not attending, and squeezed her hand in convulsive grips.

'Tell me, Flora Campbell – tell me why you were sitting in the street and asking for pennies. I never did that, and if I had they would have driven me away because I am as big as a man and I would have frightened them. What is your trouble, Flora my dear? Have you nothing at all in your pockets? You could always be getting two shillings from the Broo, because they do not want you to die entirely.'

'They would never give you a shilling, surely, if you still had some of your own?'

'What have you got?'

'£8 in notes.' Flo had bent nearer Morag, lowering her voice to a whisper, and the two of them laughed and laughed as they realised they were playing at conspirators.

'*And* your fine coat.'

'And my fine coat. I thought, when I was on the rope upstairs at the Duke, that some of the desperate creatures there would skin it off my back. But all they got was some pictures.' She should not have said that. Now she would have to explain.

'Are you wicked, Flora? Where did you get the pictures?'

'I – made them. I painted them, or I drew them. I was doing that for a while.' It was days ago and already it had speeded away from her and turned her into a miniature.

'You are an artist, Flora. And I am a fish-wife, and a mad-woman. I can go where I like, you know, as long as I am back at night and I bring the fresh fish for the kitchen. I am their longest-staying patient, Flora.' She was looking proud and pleased with herself.

'Why are you there? Is it up there you are, in the big house with the towers?'

'Firtrees. It is my home. It is bigger than any house you ever saw in the islands. You would not believe the wealth that is in it among the rich folk hereabouts. We do the dirty work and they collect, and so it always was.'

'But – why are you there? If you are mad, then I am mad.'

'Maybe you are.' She laughed, 'Ach well, it was for the best. When my Ranald was taken in the great storm of Eighty-nine, and the twins as well, and I had had the three born dead, well, I did not know where to put myself. I wanted nothing to be left, so I set fire to the boat-shed and the house, and they said I would do myself an injury, and so I might – I would have cut my throat but they had taken all the knives away.'

'Who did that? Who said that?'

'My Ranald's sister and her husband, and he had been to the secondary school in Thurso. Where is your husband, Flora? Have you buried your husband?'

Husbands. And the other words. Children. Family. Home. She had chosen none of those. She had not rejected them. They had failed to come her way, and years had passed and her life had been filled enough. It still was, if she could meet a friend as old as herself and talk by the hour with this heady, bursting happiness of newsing and confiding, and every least thing as fresh as the day it happened.

'How did you get away from Uist? Were you not bound to take a passage on the *Pict*?'

'Och, I ran away into the moor, that night we buried Allan in the dunes and the houses were just a stramash of smoking timbers, ours, the MacPhails', the MacCuishes'. I know you would have kept me but I felt shamed to burden you, and I thought, There is nothing here for me – for anyone – so I got away that night – and I starved for a while – and then I went over the water to the north ...'

She paused, amazed at this life she had lived that was turning into a story. 'I got work there, as a maid, in a castle – they called it that, it was only a new, big, fancy house. It looked like Firtrees. We had enough to eat, and more than enough, but they were – animals.'

'The masters, you mean? And what about our own kind?'

'They were the worst. So I went away at last, to Sgiach, and I worked at the whitefish and the herring. And ...'

How could you pack the whole long stretch of it into words? Morag was greedy for everything she could tell her, leaning forwards with her mouth half open. As Flo stayed silent, she asked 'Did you marry there?'

'There was a man ... Never mind about him. You know those men, like pirates, who catch you and leave you when they please. Ach well ... We had a battle on Sgiach – you must have heard of it, surely. It was harder than our own one – they sent more soldiers at us. I am scarred there yet.' She touched the back of her head. 'We got the grazings back, though. It was not my island, but my friends are there now, they are still there and they are living somehow.'

'Why did you leave them, if they are your friends?'

'A great wind blew me away.' That was foolish. It meant nothing. It had felt like that. 'I followed the herrings from Shetland down to Yarmouth, and this time I stayed. I met a man ... an artist ... He had seen me before, and I had seen him. He is clever ...' That was not what she meant. 'He was mad. Or strange.' She could not find the words. 'We were not suited. Although we loved each other for a time. Maybe he would rather make pictures out of his dreams than care for somebody.'

'He should have cared! He should have cared!' Morag was clenching both fists and raising her voice so much that a soldier going past looked round at them and half-leered at the sight of two old women talking so passionately. 'Oh Flo my darling, what sorrows we have seen, and the good years as well, the good –' She broke off, her dark eyes staring into Flo as though seeing not her but something behind her. 'We will be telling it all, my dear, and if it takes a year to tell a year, it will not be too long.'

The clock was chiming, like a blacksmith hitting a horseshoe, clang after clang until it had sounded noon. Morag stood up and reached for her straw bags. 'We must be going to the market now for some fresh fish – I have to gut and head-and-tail them, and you can help with that. I have an agreement, you know – a stone-and-a-half of wet fish three times a week, and that is my keep, with the pennies I make on a load. And if you help me to bring home more, you can stay there as well, and maybe clear out the rooms for some of the poor souls. The worst of them are in the locked wards but in my end they are all as harmless as doves.'

Chapter 38

Somewhere below, a mad woman was giving out a whine every few minutes, a gulp and a rising note, like a dog on heat. In the three-quarter dark of a little box-room with a sloping ceiling, Flo was tired to the core – had she aged five years in a week? She was contented with it, and warm enough. She was curled up inside this nest of comforts and discomforts she remembered from childhood – surrounded by worries, hedged and walled against them by layers of warm relationship.

Filtered moonlight shone dully on the metal body of a lion with a weather-vane sticking out of its back. It perched on the point of the pepperpot tower next to her skylight with its plumed tail stiffly flaunting. Like one of Richard's cruel imaginings. What was he doing now? If he had stolen himself away from Weston's clinging hands, and come back and found the rifled book, would he tell the police? He would paint himself deeper and deeper into his bog – he would paint her as a harpy with dirty wings and a beak between her thighs. Weird animals beyond the hedge, who could never touch her now …

In the room next door – they were nothing but cubby-holes, with a trestle bed and pegs in the corner with a curtain drawn in front of them – Morag was snoring heartily. Had she snored ever since the factor's bully-boys split her nose in the battle? Big meat-faced men, their cheeks slick in the sifting rain, torches and cudgels in their hands, flinching at the volleys of stones from Flo and Morag's little arsenal on the hillside, standing their ground, coming on and battering at any bared head, leaving twelve women and girls lying on the foreshore with red blood worming in and out of the shingle …

No more battles now – the men went overseas to fight and the women could live at home, or in a crows' nest like this, and let the years pass over them. She would draw the women of this place, if she could get some pencils, and the men too, if they behaved themselves. In the near-darkness she reached her hand below her bed and ran her fingers along the edges of the packaged pictures. Pressed swathes – stores of vegetable food – coloured layers and bunched like fruits in a jar …

She dreamed pure colours – sea-blue, dazzling, in which she hung, weightless … Red, painless fire … In the morning all dreams and pictures vanished under a hailstorm of new sensations. Sculleries and stone-floored corridors smelling of yellow soap and carbolic. Steaming kettles and porridge pots making a wet bloom on the windows, blurring the bars outside. Coarse white plates in clattering piles. A chorus of voices shouting above each other, some of them with an accent from the West, and Morag in the midst of it all, like a queen of the gypsies, her hair an uncombed tussock of iron-grey, the sallow skin of her breast showing between the buttons of her overall, seizing a loaf like a hen she meant to throttle and going at it murderously with a gleaming knife. Then suddenly, 'God help us all!' She had cut the back of her knuckle as the blade skidded off the flowery crust, red blots were spreading like runny jam on the cut slices, and Morag was crowing out, 'Never heed, girls, there was worse things happened at Culloden,' as she tore a strip from a dish-towel and wound it round her hand.

The others seemed hardly to notice Flo as she stirred porridge, lifted pans from the cookers to the sinks, and scraped and washed the dishes that came back from the dining hall. Were there so many waifs here that one more was unremarkable? Who were the patients and who were the staff? That man in the lobby just outside the kitchen – surely he was a patient? He was sitting on a hard chair facing the wall with his knees against it and talking continuously. When the hubbub calmed down from time to time, she could catch the same sentences over and over again, 'Thy will be done on Earth as it is in Heaven. Give us this day our daily bread and forgive us out debts …'

It was not uncomfortable, working away amongst the babble of strangers, and it was not uncomfortable afterwards, eating slices of bread-and-marge plastered with orange marmalade at one end of a table covered with a shiny oilcloth. She could have sat there for hours as though she was invisible. But here was Morag making a ceremony of the occasion.

'Ladies, ladies,' she was almost shouting, 'stop yammering for a wee minute and let me tell you – *let me tell you*, this is my darling sister Flora, from long ago, come back from the dead, you might well say, for she was lost and is found, and I have lain awake all night in the light of the moon just thinking and thinking. I do not know how I thought so many things, far more than I can tell you –'

'Well, that's a mercy, Morag,' said a dumpy woman called Jean, who had dark hairs on her upper lip. 'Drink up your teas now. It is high time we stripped the beds.'

Men in dressing-gowns sat in a yellow-painted corridor, or a long room, or a high hallway with windows down one side – it was hard to say what it was, this place of wrecked chairs with dust-bars of blue sun-ray stretched across it. Oil paintings of well-dressed people hung on the panelled wall – presumably not lunatics but the former owners of the place. A man in greenish tweeds with cheeks like sugar-plums and popping, suspicious eyes, in front of several jagged mountains that looked pieced in from some other picture. A woman in a silvery gown, with bare shoulders and long white gloves, staring past a vase of lilies into the middle distance with a look of wintry disdain that made her look tens of years older than her pretty youthfulness. Steam-yacht people. Visitors. Yet they had once lived here. A piece of her father's knowledge came back to her for the first time in more than fifty years – 'When they were selling Prince Edward Island, the rich men in London played cards for slices of it at the gaming tables.'

Morag was saying to her, 'They never come here now of course, the Forsyths. They have gone to France. Their own son – her son, his grandson – he was mad, he cut himself all over. They kept him upstairs, with a servant all to himself.'

Two women in lose cotton gowns walked past arm in arm, one of them with little eyes like a Chinese and a friendly grin, the other with scanty hair, new and old wounds all over her scalp, and a face so white and soft and seamed it looked as though it had been under water for many hours. A rosy woman of not more than thirty was sitting in a bay window with a pair of knitting needles motionless in her hands, a single row of stitches cast-on on one of them. Her eyes were streaming tears. After they had passed her and started up the stairs, Morag said in a lowered voice, 'When they have lost a baby, some of them, they are put in here. For a rest.'

Outlandish voices were echoing up and down the brown-varnished stairwell. 'O God of Bethel by whose hand,' a woman was singing, perfectly in tune, from some hidey-hole in this hive of many cells. Feet thudded on bare boards. A man's voice roared out in a fury, 'Let me have it! I want it!' – then sank into a piteous whine, 'No, no, no – please, no … '

'They are not cruel, Flo,' said Morag. 'But he thinks they are. We must be kind, Flo – we must all be kind.'

The two long wards they entered first, a female and a male, both smelt of urine. The men's was worse. 'I am often thinking,' said Morag as they dropped rumpled sheets into wicker hampers, 'that if there was no drink in this world, there would be no madness.'

'And no pleasure either, ' said Flo. Surely Morag was not going to thump the tub for temperance?

'Well, that is true, yes, that is very true. But no drink in here, mind. If we want a dram, we must go down the hill in the evening when the poor souls are in their beds.'

Morag herself was not a poor soul, it seemed, not in her own eyes or the staff's, not even in the dark-suited doctor's who conferred with her at some length on diet and listened seriously to her advocacy of 'more fatty fish, doctor, for the sake of the rheumatism, doctor, and because it is very economical.'

Their days trudged by in a homely routine, a sequence of washing and wiping, and boiling and rinsing, drying and ironing, scouring and polishing – a sequence of tea from urns and zinc pots with reeking brown interiors, of beef-and-greens and stew-and-greens and broth-and-greens ladled out dripping from huge pans with double handles. The smell of gravy gave her a blink of the Castle long ago – but whose had been savoury odours, eggy cakes, roast game crisply seared. Here wet vegetables prevailed, heaps of grey potato-mash, a dank undersmell of roots and rain in autumn gardens. How bleak it was going to be here in the winter when rough weather and long nights penned them into this place of moaning and quarrelling and unappetising duties …

As they walked down the hill one Friday with empty creels to fetch their loads of herring and mackerel, the firth spread out to the north-east in reaches blue as mussels and grey as slate. The sky was the same, high mounds and shelves of solemn clouds that looked as though they would never change. They sang to each other, lilting wordlessly at first, then singing whole verses as they got into the way of it.

'My little black one, ho hi ri,'

Flo sang in a low, uncertain voice, still feeling shy.

'My little black one, a ho seo,
My little black one …'

She paused, struggling to remember Mairi of Bealista and her singing in the attic long ago – *she* had been the black calf, glossy and milky. The end of the song came back to her before she had found the start of it –

> 'I will not give you to the fiddler,
> Not at all to the claws of the tailor.
> You will go to the gentlefolk,
> They will milk you on the heights.'

'I know that one,' Morag almost shouted. 'I know it, and when I am singing it to myself I am often thinking, these are the heights, these are the heights!'

Did she mean Firtrees? Did she mean that louring, battlemented house with its cargo of injured and ruined people? Good luck to her if she did – good luck to both of them. Beside her Morag was carolling away at the verses of a song Flo had last heard hummed without words, unexpectedly, as Kirsty MacLeod went about her work in that smouldering wee house at Sgiach harbour –

> 'My sweetheart's hair is curved and folded,
> My darling's hair is coiled in clusters.
> Though lovely it is in the maiden's cap,
> It would look fine in the marriage linen –'

She broke off with a high skirl of a laugh, as though they were spinning in a dance, then hugged Flo to her and said, 'So we are both of us in luck – if you have never married, still, you are not a maiden either, so that is the song for us.'

As they stopped at the side of the street, laughing helplessly, people were giving them curious looks, which roused Morag still further. 'They will think we are witches. They think we are all witches in the West.' She cackled, Flo cackled back, and they were still quivering and simmering with the fun of it when they reached the harbour.

So the first years at Firtrees were an idyll and not an idyll. The drowned voices beseeching from behind a half-shut door – 'Help me – help me, nurse, mummy, doctor – help me, help me' – these were bad enough with their notes of unquenchable, never-ending grief. Much worse was the early evening when she was sent, for once, with a tray of sleeping draughts to the male locked ward. Two nurses took it from her at the outer of two doors. Through the glass behind them she saw a pair of orderlies tightening a buckle on a canvas jacket in which a man lay parcelled. His arms were shrouded in long sleeves tied behind his back. His eyes and facial veins were distended. Patches of mania were blazing red on his forehead.

What else could they do? Was life worth living if this was what some mother's son could come to? It had been worse once (perhaps everything had been worse once). Towards the end of her first year she and a sulky girl from Eriskay called Bridget were sent to air and dust the museum. In the shuttered gloom of what had been the music room, manacles hung from pegs, leg-irons, an old straitjacket whose canvas felt unbending as armour and rough as a shark's skin. Just average cruelties of the bad old days. In the centre – unbearable, straight out of nightmare – the whirling-seat, a wooden platform with crude seats on it, mounted on an axle, and by a cranking handle the doctors, the healers, had spun it faster and faster with the mad folk, their patients, sitting strapped onto it, their eyes staring, their hair flying, their nails drawing blood from their palms, while their ill brains reeled in their skulls and the wrong thoughts flew out of their ears and eyes like bats from a cave on fire.

At the sight of it Bridget crossed herself and Flo heard her mutter.

'Holy Mary Mother of Grace ...'

Flo felt free to say, 'Terrible, eh? How could they?'

'Och, the loonies are too daft to feel a thing. They hurt themselves. They like it, some of them.'

She should have held her tongue. The thing still whirled in her head when she went to see the Superintendent, Dr Harbottle. Matron, Miss Findlayson, was in attendance – standing up, of course, darting at the window-screens to straighten them, or at the pen-tray on the desk, with her little clucks and lisps. She was a tall, mild woman with a complexion as curd-white as a nun's and a squint so bad that her small ginger-green eyes almost disappeared into the bridge of her nose – a bony bridge from which her pince-nez would constantly have fallen if she had not dabbed at them with her strangely knobby forefinger, dropping her keys or her fountain pen if they happened to be in her hand at the time. In Morag's eyes she had 'a heart of gold'. Most of the others called her 'soft as crowdie'. Flo was never quite sure if Matron had realised that she was an orderly, not a patient. Whichever it was, her orders were all made as gentle requests and when she discussed the state of a patient, she lowered her voice as though she was talking about a bereavement.

Dr Harbottle looked at the papers on his desk for a while. Tiring of them, he stared over Flo's head at the wall above the door, then past Miss Findlayson at the window into the garden, while her fidgets and mutterings died away. His eyes now fixed themselves on Flo, large eyes like pieces of blue glass set in a glossy red face that looked not so much shaven as flayed. Presently he set out on a series of remarks that occasionally connected with anything she knew.

'Miss – ah, eh – Miss – Campbell, is it not?' She would accept that name – Morag knew her by it and in its small way it rooted her back into an earlier life. 'Yes, well, Miss Campbell, you seem to have, ah, to have, eh, settled down quite well – quite well. And that is what we prefer in this establishment, that comfortable arrangements embrace us all – embrace us all, not least those who are less well adjusted, whose sense of themselves is insecure and, ah, imperfectly oriented, if that is not too – if that is not too, eh …'

After a time she felt quite soothed. He was not going to challenge her – on the grounds of some secret message or other from below stairs – with having been installed in a job she was no more fitted for than any other ageing woman, and by a patient at that. She was not going to be robbed of her wee brown envelope with ten shillings in it every Friday, on which she now relied. Perhaps Matron could hardly see her through those wobbling glasses, perhaps she thought of her as just another dogsbody like Morag, who had fetched up at Firtrees like driftwood on a beach.

She knew she was on the books now and had watched in awe as 'the Treasurer' (a man with a worn Gladstone bag who never took his coat off) put a tick beside her name in his ledger every week. Had some previous Miss Campbell spirited herself away and had Morag smuggled her friend into the other's shoes by some artful dodge? It came back to her how at the Castle long ago there had been women who came and went, and so long as they slept in an unused cellar and did only the filthiest jobs, even the auld bitch Kilgour had seemed unconcerned that they had not been cross-questioned by her Ladyship.

She came out of her dwaum and asked abruptly, 'Then I can be here for some time?' She should not have interrupted. She should have said nothing at all.

Dr Harbottle's face was glowing with red light. 'We *value* your contribution, Miss, ah, Campbell. We all do. You appear to be mannerly and charitable, and the greatest of these is charity, is it not? In the broadest sense. For although we are a medical establishment, nevertheless there are certain cardinal virtues which, while they are no substitute for modern-minded science and its, eh, its attendant methods, are, ah, of the essence – they are of the essence …'

Was this how the ministers spoke? This must be why folk on Uist who had gone to hear the Reverend Finlay Macrae each Sabbath came bursting out of the kirk with such bright-eyed chattering, like children set free from school.

'We are here to ease and to heal, Miss Campbell – to ease if not invariably, ah, to heal. A modicum of security, of mind and of body – assuredly this is the entitlement of us all.'

He had stopped. What now? He was looking at Miss Findlayson as though for a signal, which roused her into a chirrup of clicks and mutters. Should she stand up and say goodbye? Or perhaps 'Good-morning', since they were all so mannerly. As she rose, Dr Harbottle rose too and gave a fidget forwards which might have been a bow. Maybe he would have tipped his grey Homburg hat to her if it had been on his head and not on the hatstand in the corner.

'I scarcely knew what he meant, half the time,' she said to Morag afterwards.

'He has no idea himself. He is nice enough, and we should count our blessings. The auld one was a brute.'

'What did he do? No, do not be telling me.' The whirling-machine had come back to her, and the awful straitjacket – if they had struggled inside it they would surely have bled.

'He took the worst of us off meat. For years. To "thin the blood". And blankets – we could not have a blanket in case we were "too comfortable". Oh Flo, Flo, the cruelty. If I could live where it was all kind, I would live there for a thousand years, Flo!' Her eyes were big with tears.

Flo felt stunned. Old pain was threatening to rise up and overwhelm them both.

'We are all right now,' Morag was saying. 'This place is a good place, and the wicked may flourish outby, but when the day breaks and the shadows flee away, there shall be no more mourning.'

Her face looked naked, like a piece of ground that had been pelted and scathed by heavy rain. She was daft and she was good, and she made Flo regret that she herself was neither of those.

Chapter 39

Gradually she grew used to them, these human cartoons, through the trampling succession of the seasons. Times of frost when the gardens in the morning were covered with greyish fur and everything had the look of a decaying animal. Summers when the sky, after two days of heat, was extinguished by the white haar that grew out of the sea, breathing a reek of fish-meal from the factory along the coast and saturating the air as though with steam from a kettleful of stewing fish-heads.

She noticed how the people of Firtrees changed with these seasons. During one January gale even some of the more stupefied women and men could turn crazed, their voices shrilling in harsh peaks like gulls, their hands picking at their own clothes or their fellows' in uncontrollable gripes and pinches. During her third winter, Maggie MacEachern, who had been raped at sixteen by a 'young blood' at some castle in the West, was wakened out of her placid brooding and unending knitting. She could still not cast on securely and the scarf she had been making for ten or fifteen years unravelled as fast as it grew at the other end. In the late afternoon a violent westerly was screaming through the crests of the ornamental trees. A banging and a splintering. Staff rushed to the lobby on the first floor and saw a wreckage of needled branches forcing its spines deep into the room. Glass daggers had shredded Maggie's dress and cut her all over. At the sight of a squad of nurses and maids coming towards her, she fled off down the lobby, blood-sodden scarf trailing a red smear along the beige-and-chocolate tiling and herself crying out, 'It wasna me – it wasna me – I wasna here at all …'

Flo disliked herself for seeing the patients as cartoons – had she taken on some of Richard's more withering views of their fellow-humans? Elly Bain, who plaited jute twine year in year out into little twisted bands and wanted you to wear them round your wrist or as a circlet in your hair – was she more demented than a jeweller who destroyed his eyesight turning gold and gemstones into toys for the rich folk? Ugly old Jim Hunter with his ape nose and his sore, streaming eyes, whose hands were always busy under his pyjamas – was he more besotted than some ordinary man out there who mounted his wife night after night in spite of the dozen children they could not keep in clothes or food, and the dozens of miscarriages?

Yes, they were. Jim could never finish a sentence, and Elly had no idea what year it was. These were ruined people. At times, though, she found herself shuddering, physically shuddering, with a fear that there was a writhing under-self in her own depths. She might take another turn and be able only to mouth and drool. The hating side of her might burst out and drive her at the people nearby, accusing them, seizing them by the hair.

If this was in her, it would come out in her pictures, surely, and the climbing flowers she drew did not turn into poison ivy, the strands and crofters' fields she painted did not turn into sepulchres. (She knew that one day she would make a great broad landscape, perhaps eight feet long by three feet high, of the Island with the house roofs going up like torches, the looms falling apart in blackened spars, and flowing through the centre of it the River of Blood where they had washed their wounded scalps in the hours after the Battle.)

When she had some money left over out of her ten shillings, after she had bought a few drams with Morag on one of their outings to the Castle Inn or the back bar at the Station Hotel, she spent it on pads of heavy paper, soft-lead pencils, a few colours (pastel and oil), and a canvas once a month, which she stretched and primed herself. There was a stable for which the hospital had no use, with a cobbled floor and wide doors facing north. From it she could see a corner of the gardens stepping down the hill towards the town in a series of mossy lawns, gravel walkways, and stone seats. The Forsyths must have been blind to colour. The scheme here, and throughout the grounds, ran to the full glossy greens of laurel and rhododendron, the dirty whites and water greys of stone urns, stone balustrades, stone steps, stone walls. 'Cemetery', it all said 'cemetery', and Dr Harbottle and his predecessor had had nothing planted to relieve the funereal dowiness.

Beyond the evergreens the roofs of the town overlapped each other like fish-scales made of blae Ballachulish slate. Beyond again, the firth was blue as new-born eyes or, on days of overcast, grey like old ice. On the far side unknown mountains folded off like billows of an ocean stilled by some slowing down of time. Balta was up there, away up there, and through the glens to the west were Sgiach and beyond it Uist. She would write to Peg and tell her where she was. 'Have you written your letter yet?' Morag asked her again and again, whenever the chat had fallen silent between them, and Flo said, bringing out the words as though to exorcise her fear, 'I will – I will – but what if something has happened?' By which she meant, What if she is dead?

They had one afternoon off in the week, and if the wind was not blowing out of the north-east, and if they were not so wearied that they wanted only to lie down in their rooms and doze, Morag would come to the stable and sit for her. She twisted a tartan plaid round her hair, put on a saintly expression, and said, 'Do me as Flora MacDonald, Flo – I am very loyal and good today.' Or she took her teeth out, hunched herself up and said in a croak, 'Make me terrible and old, old as the hills – make me the Cailleach Bheur and I will be raging because my son has run away with the fair-haired maiden of the springtime.'

Flo used black pencil for these portraits at first, drawing every hair and feature with scrupulous concentration, avoiding the least slur into cartoon, Morag's nose would not be deformed into a crone, her mouth would not be pursed into the grimace of a hag. From this care likeness grew, so that Morag, when she came round to look over Morag's shoulder at the paper, clapped her hands, skirled with laughter, and shouted out, 'You are a genius, Flora – you have me speaking there on the page.' Her face fell. 'You will never sell such things. Because I am ugly. And who would want to be looking at an auld cailleach who had her nose split and her hair burnt off in the troubles long ago.'

'My man' – Flo always called Richard 'my man', with a sarcy reflection, when she mentioned him at all – 'My man liked that kind of thing. Suffering highlanders – peasants up to their elbows in fish-guts – he could sell such pictures. To city folk who like to have a look at the rough end of things, when they are fed up with prettiness.'

Morag knew the story of the magazine picture now (though not yet of The Book) and never tired of saying, 'He should have paid you for it. He took your picture and he should have been giving you something back.' To which Flo replied, if she was in a bitter mood, 'He did, though – all those years of his valuable life.'

On a Wednesday afternoon in spring, when the air was bearable out of the wind, Flo stood at last in front of the broadest piece of primed material she had been able to make – a sheet of plywood nine feet by four which had been meant for panelling a launch. She had cleaned it with sandpaper, then glasspapered it and primed it the matt white of a goose egg. The scene had become so present and detailed in her mind's eye that she only half-knew any longer whether it was a true memory or her umpteenth re-imagining of it. The low stone houses with rounded corners and roofs shaggy with thatch, flowering into petals of flame. Dark, lumpy figures, some with arms working, some shielding their heads. Long-haired people on a hill. Between the hill and the houses, a blurry swarm like big hail – a hail of stones. You could not have seen all this at once, or only from far away. So, if she thought of it as a circle, a circus, an arena, and straightened it out so that a good three-quarters of it was displayed as a continuous strip …

It was so big, it might take years … Trial and error – scrape out faulty areas with a sharp edge of glass and paint them again. Try each part in a drawing first of all … So long as she could finish it before some awful interruption. If she took another turn, would it be worse than before? Would her limbs be stricken useless? (Better dead than that.) Or she would be dismissed – she worked hard enough but she could not help thinking of her position as turning on Miss Findlayson's whim, or Harbottle's cleverness with the moneys. Or Morag's health, never mind her own – if Morag dropped dead, the loneliness would crush her …

The whitened board confronted her. Was its surface slippery ice? Or was it a bed of soil, ready to grow? As she touched in a shoreline with a stick of charcoal, and readied herself to interrupt it with the upright wall of a house, a growling voice in the doorway was saying, 'Mishus Cam'l! Mishus Cam'l!' Chesty, choking laughter. Bertha Kemp had found her out at last. She liked to stalk her, jump out from an alcove and throw a dishcloth over her head, then hug her in her massive, sweating embrace, or whip her dinner away when Flo's back was turned and give it her back with a second helping dumped onto the first, the gravy or the custard splashing onto the table in steaming dollops … She was huge inside her filthy brown overall, her nose was as porous and bumpy as a monstrous strawberry, her upper lip was dark with hairs, she could make no movement without disaster – her spoon missed her lips, slides rained out of her hair and fell into her porridge. One arm was puckered into a twisted valley all down its inside where she had tried to open her foster-mother's window, she said, and her hand 'slipped right froo 'e glash.'

'Mishus Cam'l, guesh wha'?'

'Tell me, Bertha – what?'

'Ish ma buffday, Mishus Cam'l!' She stopped, her eyes spilling with pride, as though waiting for applause.

'That is lovely, Bertha. Does Matron know?'

Bertha looked horrified and fat tears rolled out of her eyes. 'Ish no' ma fau't. Ish no –'

'Bertha, it is all right. I meant – Miss Findlayson would have had you a cake baked.'

'Ish a shecret, Mishus Cam'l'. You an' me.' She came nearer and Flo dreaded the overwhelming hug. She also hated to think of her work laid bare, smeared, talked about. She threw her coat over it and it caught on the easel and hung there innocently.

'Look at this, Bertha. We can make a picture.' She flipped over a page in her sketch pad, picked up a stub of green pastel, and drew the skyline of a round grassy hill.

'Ark, Mishus Cam'l. Do the Ark.'

Flo took brown and drew in a boat with a roof, balanced on the green summit.

'Rainbow, Mishus Cam'l. Look!'

And sure enough, there was a shimmering arc of colour out there above the firth, vermilion melting into yellow into indigo, curving high up towards the zenith with one foot on the Black Isle and the other on the Laigh.

'*Rainbow*,' Bertha was demanding, with a spoilt child's pout. Flo coloured in the rainbow.

'Ish for me? Mishus Cam'l, pleeease.' The tears were ready to flow again. Flo started to tear the sheet from the pad, then thought and said, 'Wait a minute, Bertha. Let me think.'

She took her blackest pencil and lettered in on the white foreground, 'HAPPY BERTHA'S DAY'.

Bertha screamed, rushed at her and administered the terrible hug, seized the paper, crushing it, blurring the rainbow into a kind of feverish sunset, and ran out of the stable holding it to her breast like a dressing on a wound.

Next Wednesday she was back, before Flo had so much as positioned the first house on the shore. She was wearing a remarkably well-laundered overall and she had her hair tied back with some broad pink ribbon.

'Lemme do some cullersh, Mishus Cam'l. Wanna do the cullersh.'

Would this be manageable? It would be a shambles. There seemed to be nothing else for it.

'I know the buffdays, Mishus Cam'l. The gurrlses' buffdays. I asked their buffdays.'

'And you want to make them pictures for their birthdays.'

'Thash ri'. Buffday pickshersh. Pleeease.'

She was holding out her hands. Flo put into them a black pastel, a red one, and a green one. Perhaps she could still be drawing ideas for her painting and it could hide safely on its easel. A clench like heartburn rose in her chest as she realised how much she craved to be alone with her work.

She looked over at the hulking shape of the girl-woman. Bertha had spread a sheet of paper on an old door lying on the cobbles and was kneeling beside it, picking up one colour after another and almost hitting them onto the paper. A face was taking shape, outlines in black, the oval of it filling the sheet. Black mask-eyes with black bull's-eye holes in their centres. Red rims round the eyes, red coals in the middle of each cheek, red lips opened to show green teeth with points. A red club-shape sticking out between red lips – the tongue. Green hair exploding from the scalp in spikes. Red drops like pears falling from the green teeth, the red tongue.

Her fingers were working with uncanny control. The sticks of pastel crumbled in her grasp but she was picking up the pieces and managing to mark the paper as she wanted. Both hands were dyed in the three colours, so were her cheeks and forehead where she had rubbed her eyes, and still the mask-head grew onto the paper, one hideous detail after another.

Now there was not a quarter inch of pastel left uncrushed. Bertha was hunched over in the shadow just inside the door-jamb, her shoulders shaking with sobs like retches. Flo went over, into a smell of soap and face-powder, stroked the great fell of springy hair, and said carefully, 'Who is it, Bertha? Bertha? Who is that?'

Bertha leaned back against her thighs and said in a voice thick with phlegm, 'Ma fagher. Ish ma fagher.'

'What will I do, Morag?' Flo asked her friend that evening as they sat on her bed beneath the skylight. The nights were still wintry and they wore two cardigans under their coats when they were in the arctic upper storey.

'I would rent a room in town, if I was rich. Or get up at 4 o'clock in the morning, if I was young.'

'You are kind, Flo – very kind. Bertha has been a sight for years – nobody could keep her clean. Now she is washing her face in the middle of the day, and combing her hair. You are helping her poor spirit into the world again.'

'Helping her to have nightmares about her father.'

'He was no father, from what I heard. He was worse than a sultan and his woman was the same – they took in wee girls to torment them. No –' She interrupted herself with a howl of grief at unmentionable thoughts, squeezed her hands together as though she was killing some awful possibility, and said, 'You are right. You must make your own picture, and you must help Bertha, and others like her maybe. Why are you stripping beds and peeling potatoes when there is better work for your hands? Ask Findlayson – she is not as doited as she looks.'

Flo did not want to 'ask Findlayson'. She wanted to be alone with her painting, and she wanted to keep herself by the simplest, humblest work that would leave her thoughts free and undisturbed. Was her life splitting? If it had been humdrum all those years, at least it had been whole, whole as a bird or a seashell, whole as a room.

Chapter 40

The following Wednesday she was alone and at peace. Hail-bursts chattered on the roof and swept through the yard in mad swirls and skites – the sky tore clear and a naked wintry blue shone through – the mountainous lands on the far side of the firth had turned white, like sudden ageing. She looked across at them, then down again at her broad board, the paleness of it peopled with shadows now, lightly sketched houses, ghostly people, the line of the foreshore cresting along, dripping where the River of Blood cut through the dunes to the sea, lifting up the topknot of Dun Skellor where her mother and father – where the remains of them lay under the marram and the thyme.

It looked fine in itself, she thought, this gathering of shapes. A house looked more a house when not every stone or stalk of thatch was shown. Would anybody else be able to make anything of it? Did she care? She cared that Morag should recognise it, and be fired by it, and Morag was waiting for it, patiently, with a determination to revere it that made Flo feel sheepish.

For two hours she thought, without lifting her hand, thought about styles that would just brush in the shape of a gable end, the shape of a startled horse, the shape of a woman flinging and screaming her defiance ... She came out of this dwaum with a shiver. The yard and the roofs outside were crusted with white hail. It must be well past time for the tea-urns and the stacks of bread-and-marge.

The Wednesday after that, Bertha appeared again. This time the ribbon in her hair was yellow and she had brought 'the gurrlses' – Ella and Madge and Mary and Lolly and Murdina. They had between them seven hands in working order and about as many legs. Lolly was all over the place, her shins and feet flung out sideways at the knee as though some demonic dance was dancing her, both hands flicking out constantly as though she could never rid them of wetness. Garbled guttural word-sounds growled from her mouth below eyes that shone with humorous understanding. Ella talked continuously to herself – it was said that she knew the Bible by heart and she seemed to be repeating it to herself from one end to the other. Flo could just make out her lisping – 'Then the king sent to call Ahimelech the priest, the son of Ahitub, and all his father's house, the priests that were in Nob; and they came all of them to the king. And Saul said, Hear now, thou son of Ahitub. And he answered, Here I am my lord, And Saul said unto him ...'

Madge said nothing whatsoever. She was less than five feet tall and her arms hung so inertly that on a bad day she had to be fed. When anyone spoke to her, she blushed scarlet from the fringe of her hair to the vee of her overall. No visitor had ever come for her, not since 1873 when she was admitted to the Old Asylum, according to Morag, who had heard it from the oldest veteran on the staff many years before. Murdina looked gormless and lost, with no expression on her broad yellowish pudding-face, except when she was furious and thought that a piece of food had been pinched from her plate. Then she spat out the foulest swearwords with the precise delivery of a schoolteacher. Mary was bald – she had been burnt in a fire, her face was coarsely reddened as though by one huge birthmark, and her ginger wig sat on her skull like a tea-cosy on its pot. She was perfectly sensible in every way – had she perhaps set the fire herself, like Morag, to destroy an unbearable grief?

They appeared in the doorway in a giggling bunch, Madge in the rear, saying nothing. Someone, Murdina possibly, pushed Lolly forward and she half-fell at Flo's feet, manoeuvred herself almost upright, and uttered sounds that Flo could make nothing of, loud swallowing vowel-noises. To hide her own embarrassment Flo gave her a pencil and Lolly gripped it in the curl of her palm like a stirring spatula.

'Aaaouhh,' she said. Was she asking for paper? Flo began to tear out leaves and hand them round, a leaf and a 6B pencil to each outstretched hand. Only Murdina hung back, and sulked. She sat on the ground near the door, looked at the sky, and picked her nose. After half an hour she got up, edged over to the group, snatched paper and pencil, and began to draw.

The old door was their table, set up on a pair of trestles. They sat on stumps of log from the wood-store at the back. Lolly's hand was flicking and flicking in her usual way, touching the paper most of the time. On her sheet the burst of black rays was massing gradually into the shape of a gorilla's head and shoulders, the upper centre of it left blank for the face. Murdina might have been drawing or else she was scribbling – her hand was bent round her work and she looked up angrily at the others from time to time, defying them to steal her idea.

Mary was drawing the simplest flowers – each had its own stem, two leaves on one side and one on the other, and a tousled head of petals. Madge's picture was hard to make out at first. The black cloud at the top was unmistakable. From it bundles seemed to be falling, one, two, three. Cloths trailed from them – skirts? angels' feathers? When she saw Flo looking puzzled, she bent over and drew with hard pressures of her pencil point, her tongue twisting between her lips, and when she had finished the head part of one bundle, Flo saw that it had the chubby nose, scant hair, and closed eyes of a baby asleep.

Ella was working continuously, not drawing, lettering. In block letters that trembled but were perfectly clear she had managed so far, 'IN THE BEGINING GOD CREATED THE HEAVEN AND –'

So they could all do something. And Bertha? Had she exhausted her demons in that first monster-father? Flo blenched to think that she might choke them inside herself again – or unleash still more and shake herself to pieces. She was busy, she had got hold of some pastels without asking, and once again the hitting of her crayon on the paper sounded as loudly as thunder-rain against a window. She was crying steadily, without panic, as she drew a simple house, a door, four windows, chimney-pots. As Flo went slowly past, she was colouring in the second of two flanking trees, each of them blossoming into a red head with green pigtails and green tears like gouts of moss falling out of their eyes.

Flo paused beside her and said, 'That is sad, Bertha. And it is beautiful.'

Bertha looked up. 'Ish shad, Mishus Cam'l – ish shad – ish sho shad.'

She seemed to bear no grudge for being led on to bathe in her own bad dreams, or worse memories. 'Ish afful. An' I will finish it, I will, Mishus Cam'l.'

At the other end of the table Murdina was folding her paper into smaller and smaller squares, kneading it with the heel of her hand as though to shut it up for good. Then everybody seemed to be shrieking or staggering about. Lolly had fallen off her log and was stretching up for the table edge like someone drowning. Her fingers brushed Murdina's package and Murdina snatched it away as though from a snake, stabbing words at her, 'Fuck you – fuck you – fucking cripple.' Mary was clumsily stroking Lolly's hair, which prevented her from getting up. Fresh tears were pouring down the green and scarlet of Bertha's smeared cheeks. At the near end of the table Ella was steadily shaping her letters, 'AND GOD SAW THE LIGHT.'

Flo would have run straight out of the door and left them to it. Instead she saved drawings, soothed ruffled heads, wiped tears, made the women stack away the table and the stools, and led them back in a little shambling file to the house, their crumpled papers in their hands. At supper she could see them being passed round and round the tables (except for Murdina's). For her own part she went to bed early, with only a quick hug and a 'Good-night' for Morag, and lay for a while staring into the flickering darkness, as tired as though she had been pulling an oar in a heavy sea.

Chapter 41

For a month or two, as bunches of green began to unfurl in hedges and flowerbeds and the branches of fruit-trees decorated themselves in white and pink as though for a party (but little changed among the evergreens and stony terraces at Firtrees), the walls of the lobbies began to be papered with the work of Bertha and Madge and Lolly and Mary and Ella and Murdina. Murdina, it turned out, drew stick people who stood about between square houses with square windows surrounded by square gardens with stick fences. She drew these always, with tiny variations. Lolly's animals shaped themselves wondrously from their thickets and bursts of grey lines – a bear, a broody hen, a porcupine. Madge still worked at her babies, their faces mostly, which had grown larger and larger, filling each sheet, eyes and cheeks like moons, circle upon circle spreading their ponds of emptiness over the paper, stark black on wintry white, the saddest pictures Flo had ever seen.

Ella had taken to writing the Bible in a single unending line on sheets cut into strips. She had reached *Genesis* 2, verse 24. The frieze of lettering stretched from the doorway of the main Females room along the lobby and round a corner into the hallway outside the dining-hall. On a sunlit morning Flo, busy clearing up the long tables, saw Ella come through with a hammer and some tacks and begin to pin up her latest instalment – 'AND THE NAME OF THE SECOND RIVER *IS* GIHON: THE SAME *IS* IT THAT COMPASITH THE WHOLE LAND OF ETHIOPIA.'

As the right-hand part of the strip still hung loose, Murdina came out of the dormitory, looked furiously at Ella's handiwork, and said with biting certainty, 'That is not a picture, Ella Duthie. That is stupid.'

She grabbed the streamer. Ella snatched at it and it tore through the word 'GIHON'. Murdina seemed inflamed by the tearing and began shredding her portion into smaller and smaller bits. She flung them triumphantly on the floor. Ella was trying to pick them up as fast as they fell, uttering yelps of pain like a rabbit run to earth by a dog. Flo roused herself and ran towards them, arriving at the same time as Miss Findlayson and Bertha. The big woman gripped Murdina from behind. As the two of them staggered, Miss Findlayson shrieked on a note of panic, 'Bertha! Murdina! What do you mean? What do you mean?'

She batted at them with her knobby fingers. Bertha's shoulder caught her. Her pince-nez fell onto the parquet and were crunched underfoot.

'Calm down, girls,' Flo was saying, quelling her own panic, walking forward into the gust of sweat from the wrestling women and some strange phlegmy tang that seemed the very smell of mania. 'Oh please, calm down.' Where on earth had the nurses got to? She pulled hard on one of Bertha's arms and the woman turned instantly from Murdina, overwhelmed Flo in a hug, and began to cry in racking sobs.

'My spares – Florence – I must have my spares.' Miss Findlayson was almost wailing, clutching the twisted golden frames of her glasses and trying to straighten them with gestures as fearful as if she was handling her own shattered bones.

Murdina turned on her heel and strode out of the hallway, straight into the path of Dr Harbottle on his 'morning round', a thrice-weekly ritual that made no difference anybody had ever noticed to what was done for, or to, the patients. The audience was now complete. Everybody Flo had set eyes on in her time at Firtrees was gawping from doorways or standing round Bertha and Miss Findlayson like bairns at a fight in the playground. Even some nurses had arrived, the new pair who had already been nicknamed Jekyll and Hyde, the one calm and persuasive, the other buxom with a pink baby face and an unpredictable temper.

'Matron,' said Dr Harbottle in a tone of sorrowful reproach, 'what – what, may I ask, is, ah, taking place here? Nurses, cannot you, eh …'

Miss Findlayson looked suddenly nine years old, her glasses dangling from her fingers and one foot in its buttoned brown shoe swivelling on its heel. Bertha was giving great sighs and gulps. She knelt down and began gathering glass and paper into a heap with sweeps of her hands. She gasped as a shard of glass bit into her knee. Helplessness seemed to be settling on everybody like a paralysis. Flo felt like shouting out, 'All right, the fun is over, away off to your work.' It was not her place. Let the superintendent do some superintending for a change, the matron some mothering, the nurses a bit of nursing.

Dr Harbottle was shuffling crabwise round the room. He picked with his fingernail at Ella's first tack and frowned – lifted up her hammer as though it might be stained with murder and carefully put it down again – then tried to read the first broken-off phrase of *Genesis* 2, verse 24, his head tilting ever more to one side.

'That is good, Ella – it is, ah, quite correct. If only you had not, eh …' From the direction of the kitchen a draught blew in, shuffling the tatters of paper and carrying a smell of whitefish. Morag was back from the market.

'Mercy me,' she said from the dining-hall doorway, 'is it a ceilidh I have been missing or is it a funeral? Bertha, dry your face, my darling, you are too big to be weeping.' She had lifted her apron and was wiping the woman's cheeks.

Her energy worked on Harbottle like the twitch of a string on a puppet. 'Miss Findlayson, ah, when you are quite yourself again, I will require your, ah, report. We must all be calm, now – best behaviour, please!' He gave a little laugh as though to apologise for this burst of mastery and left the room at a dignified pace, followed by Miss Findlayson, her white cheeks pink as a rose. Nurse Wyllie began to seize people by the arm and give them short, hard jerks.

'There will be trouble, Morag,' said Flo later in the day. 'There will be trouble and all I wish is for a quiet time of it.'

'Ach, Flo, the quiet folk are the dead. No, no, I know fine what you are saying. First the menfolk come at us, and then the children, and then the factor and his bully-boys, and then the bailiffs arm in arm with the grocers and the merchants. How are we still alive, Flo, eh? Well, well, we must just take our rest in our dwelling-place, like a clear heat upon herbs and like a cloud of dew in the heat of harvest.'

Flo looked at her in wonderment. 'How do you know these things, Morag? How are they in your head?'

Morag sighed, 'We used to go to a chapel, in Ross, when all the three of them had been stillborn. And all the folk there would be drumming on the Bible, in a wee hut with a roof of crinkly tin, and speaking in tongues – there was some of them fell down with white spit at the sides of their mouths. But once our boat was lost, then nothing would do at all, and the godly folk might as well have been throwing their heads up and braying like donkeys. Oh, my grief was wicked, Flora' – she was rocking as she sat and her face was afire and her hair was springing from her head. 'And then I wanted nothing but to be in the middle of a sore red flame. But och' – she seemed to be able to shrug from the very pit of herself – 'it is all long past now and the storms are over and here we are.'

'They will not want me here if they think I am upsetting them by making them draw pictures.'

'You are making them do nothing. They are as well working with you as making rag rugs or bits of baskets. There are big hospitals down south, I was hearing, where they have whole farms rife with vegetables, and the mental folk are lifting tatties and thinning neaps to their hearts' content. Can you see Harbottle and Findlayson managing a farm? He is content with his drams of whisky and she is content with her novels. Stick up for yourself, Flo, and they will be as biddable as calves.'

And so the inevitable interview came and went, and Dr Harbottle interrupted himself at every second word, and Miss Findlayson was speechless behind new spectacles in brown frames that seemed to bring her small eyes onto the surface of the lenses like green peas in a bowl of broth. As Flo waited to hear that she was going to be sent away or ordered to leave the patients to the nurses, she realised that all they wanted was for her to leave the room without a fuss.

The pity of it was that the gurrlses had been frightened off. Ella returned to her whispering monologue, Madge to her speechlessness. Murdina was scowling and taciturn. Lolly lay in the her long chair once again, her hands wavering in the air like seaweed in clear water, ignored by everybody except Morag. Only Mary and Bertha came occasionally to the stable. They seemed content to 'tidy up' or quietly watch Flo as she drew ideas for her picture on sheet after sheet from the biggest pad she could find in the Craigpatrick shops.

She began to draw Mary, that scorched face with its amazed look caused by the effacing of her eyebrows, that bonnet of artificial hair with its appearance of unconscious mockery. She drew Bertha, her hips and bosom swollen like ungainly fruit, her look of a puzzled, wounded girl, her lips open, the whites of her eyes exposed. If she put these women into her picture, she would be ousting the real ones from the Battle, Flora Matheson and Mairi Boyd and Annie MacInnes and … No harm in that, it was not a chronicle she was making, or a photograph, it was her vision of what had been, of what must be happening yet in a hundred islands in America or the Indies.

Would she need such careful likenesses, though? Would she need portraits at all? She had been thinking before (still under the influence of Richard's weird black images) that she would show the people more as postures, or gestures, than as characters. Might this not drain the life from the scene, and make the people into dwarfs or ogres? As she brooded in front of six long sheets she had pinned up edge to edge, the exact size of the board, she let her hand rove into the upper part of the scene and drew in faces like masks hovering around the village, like clouds with human faces, peering through hair like showers of rain. There was Bertha in the top left-hand corner. There was Morag beside her (she knew her features by heart now), looking fiercely at the clachan. There was Mary at the right, half seen over a hill.

They were the old dead of the place, still remembered, and the present people, the unforgiving witnesses of what was being done to them, and they were the newcomers who might live there again … If only she could bring it all into the one oblong, this vision and the actual happening of the Battle … She must trust it to work, she would work on and the thing would compose itself as certainly as a newborn face (her own face as her father had described it, appearing under the ice-grey tissues of the caul) … The picture had begun to seem possible at last and she was not at all worried when Bertha stood giggling at her elbow and blurted out, 'Tha' shilly, Mishus Cam'l – gurrlses up inna shky. No gurrlses inna *shky*!'

Chapter 42

As the women's pictures yellowed and curled up on the walls, or were torn down by one hand or another, Flo found herself wondering, as she walked down a tall, dark-panelled corridor whose woodwork seemed steeped in the smell of urine and mashed potatoes and boiled laundry, how much longer she could stand it. On a day when the drab, unlucky smells corresponded to her own mood, and seemed to have become ingrained in her own blouses and cardigans, she felt herself slowly drowning in all this failure. On other days, often of clear views between the mountain shoulders to north and west, she felt ready as a wild goose in spring, all set to be up and away.

Away to where? To Sgiach? She could only be a visitor there. And that island was nothing to Morag. They should plan together, instead of saying nothing practical year after year. Were they afraid? Or dogged by the same helplessness at lack of money? Well, helplessness was better shared than let stew and ferment inside your own innards.

'What are we doing, Morag?' she asked one night, as they sat in the attic drinking cocoa made with skimmed milk. The gas-lamp hissed just audibly, then bubbled up suddenly brighter into a flare that showed every crack in the plaster of the ceiling.

'We are coorying down for a good night's sleep,' said Morag.

'No – I mean – with the rest of our lives. What are we going to do?' She was looking over at her friend, studying her, seeing her bristly hair more white than grey now, her neck stringy under her jutting chin, her lower eyelids sagging a little to show their scarlet insides.

'I used to think,' said Morag, still looking into her cup – 'no, I was not thinking at all, I was only seeing pictures in a dwaum, and what I saw was myself at the door of the house and it new-thatched with fine yellow straw and glass in the windows front and back, and a range inside, good black iron with steam on it, and – Flo – I could see nobody else in my house because –' She made a noise in her throat between a cough and a sob. 'I was at home and I was not at home. I was trying to see Ranald and the bairns in the house but –'

A silence followed, so complete it was as though nothing was living any more. Flo wished she was better at consoling – wished she was less locked up into herself. From the street outside, the clop of a horse's hooves was drowned out by the chug of a motor-car going uphill. A patient's moaning voice came distinctly from downstairs – they knew it would be Johnny Downie bleating 'Help me, help me.' ('*I'll* help you,' Nurse Wyllie said as she pulled down his trousers in full view of whoever else was there and sat him down with a dunt on a chamber-pot. *I'll* help you nae to mak a sotter o' yersel.')

'The houses,' said Flo at last. 'Will someone else own them now – our old houses? And the crofts – what will have happened to the crofts?'

'I heard once, it was twenty years past or else it was more than that, that when the new man got into the Parliament and he was on our side, he went to Uist and they gave him a grand welcome, they were singing and dancing and waving flags they had made, and he made some promises. So I heard. But I am sure they have taken nothing back from the farmer. How could they?'

'The farmer?' It sounded a foreign word. She might as well have said 'the count' or 'the maharajah'.

'Aye – the way they parcelled the crofts into one big farm, and took the stones of our places while they were still warm from the fires and cast them down as a found for a great new barn. I am sure MacDonald of Balranald was never up to getting in a quarter of the harvest that would fill it.'

MacDonald – Colonel MacDonald who had coveted their places for so long. His tightly-shaven crimson face came up before her now, unchanged after more than fifty years.

'He will be dead, surely.'

'He had sons. They aye have sons, and grandchildren by the score – they say the Auld Queen had more than forty of the creatures …' She sighed heavily. 'Let us not be thinking of the Island, Flo. Make your picture, and we can look at it when we need to be sad.' This sounded like a criticism and she hurried on to say, 'Ach well, there is a time to mourn and there is a time to dance …'

Her voice trailed off and she drank up the cold dregs of her cocoa. Flo was speechless. Had Morag not remembered, as she spoke these Bible words, that the last time they had heard them together was when Morag's own father read them over Flo's mother's grave among the nameless headstones in the dunes?

In the kitchen, late in the summer, a young man was standing up with his back to the window, singing with the wholehearted, unthinking flow of a thrush on a tree.

'… All the vain things that charm me most,
I sacrifice them to His Blood,'

he carolled out in a voice like molten copper. His face was invisible. All Morag and Flo could see against the light was a long head with a bush of hair cut short down the sides and a tall body with high shoulders.

'See from His Head, His Hands, His Feet,
Sorrow and love flow mingling down;
Did e'er such love and sorrow meet,
Or thorns compose so rich a crown?'

The piteousness flowed into you like bitter honey. Beside the stoves where vegetables were bubbling and rattling in the pans, Bertha was giving out a high, unwavering note, as though from some helpless part of herself, and she was beginning to rock to and fro on her stool.

'A' richt, Davey, thon's enough,' said a man's voice from across the room, and Flo saw that he had exactly the same shape as the singer, tall, high-shouldered, with the upstanding hair. His face was gaunt, eyes set deep beneath their brows, black eyes that seemed all pupil, a vertical gully in each cheek, a prow of a chin with a cleft in it.

'Who is it?' Flo whispered to Morag.

'The Leipers from along the coast,' she whispered back. 'Brothers, a year apart and like as twins. Only Davey there is mad with the spirit, and when he is very bad Bob brings him in here. Bob is fine and steady. A good sailor – he has been round the world more times than you would believe.'

Flo could see by the fluttering of some of the women that Bob Leiper was a bit of a hero. Bridget from Eriskay was making eyes at him and saying, 'Now are you at home for a while, Bob? Will we be seeing you again?'

'Fine that but nae for lang. There's an awfu' stir doon at the dock, and queer times at sea an a'. We're nae tae use the wireless ony mair, nae in wir ain waters, like.'

Nobody knew what to make of this. Bertha was still crooning and rocking and Flo felt like going over to comfort her, as though she was ill.

Bob was speaking awkwardly across to his brother. 'A' richt, then, Davey? I'll awa' doon the brae, then, Davey?' Davey said nothing, just stood there like a ruined tree.

Afterwards Morag was looking as though she was to blame. 'Maybe I should never have put him up to it,' she said in a low-pitched voice. 'Three year before you came, when Bob brought him first, he was shouting, so I cuddled him and asked him could he sing, because I had seen at the Tabernacle that singing was a kind of shouting, only it was easier for the rest of us to bear. And I thought it might get his miseries off his chest. Does anything do that, I wonder?'

'You mind that wet streak of a minister on Uist? Macrae. He did nothing for us but at least he kept quiet about the spirit.' Faces of zealous neighbours from long ago were rising up before her now – young Roddy's parents, their eyes juicy with greed and victory whenever they caught some young folk coupling, or kissing even. Roddy had been true to himself, he had thrown them off and gone his own road, even when it meant beating his father to the ground when he came at him with his belt, for the last time … Roddy – she could still melt at the centre of herself when she thought of his mouth, plump and demanding on hers, and the flavour of him, freshly salty as though she could smell his blood … Morag had been speaking for a while – these days Flo seemed to swim down into herself without any warning, then surface into the present as though she had been away for hours.

'… the wireless – now what did he mean, they must not use the thing? It costs them nothing once they have it on the boat.'

They looked at each other, Morag perplexed and uneasy, Flo still drenched in images from the depths of her memory. They learned a little more about 'the stir down at the dock' when they went into town for fish next Tuesday, expecting it to be thronged with people in their everyday clothes, and saw shut doors at the banks and the grander shops, the public houses out at the doors with crowds of drinkers, men with their jackets off and their shirts laid open to the sun, women in white blouses and wide-brimmed summer hats.

'What is ado?' Morag asked a woman in her thirties who had fallen against her beside the tap-room door of the Duke, then lurched back again to set her glass down safely on the window-sill.

'Ado? Ado? Nothing is ado. The Holiday is going on till Thursday so we can do what we like till the cash runs out!' She laughed at their astonishment and swung round again into the arms of her man.

At the dock the boats were still moored at the quays where they had been the week before. The few men lounging about were passing round half-bottles of Johnnie Walker as they sat on bollards or up-ended barrels and called out to any woman who went past.

'Calum Mackay,' said Morag to an older, bearded man who was mending a net in the shade of a long tarred shed, 'will you tell me why every soul in the place has gone mad today?'

He looked her in the eye, then back at his work. 'Mad is right, Morag Mor. Oh aye, they are all beside themselves because they think there will be a war.'

Odd bits of news were moving into place now. A grandee had been shot on the Continent somewhere. 'The Austrians' were at daggers drawn with 'the Serbs'. 'The Germans' had a colossal army. It had seemed to be like that for years, and the very names of those far-off people made it sound like a battle of ogres in an ancient story.

'Our folk will not be fighting, surely?' It upset Flo to see Morag treating Calum like an oracle, a messenger of a doom that nobody could escape. Calum himself seemed neither proud nor ashamed of his role.

'There is aye fighting in some land or other,' he said in a tone of wearied acceptance. 'There are worse things happening in Ireland, so they tell me.'

'You are right, Calum, let them fight it out across the water.' Morag sounded happy to be excused from worry. 'Now, is there any fresh fish at all?'

When at last they located a box or two of whitings, the price had shot up by ninepence a stone, which wiped out Morag's tiny profit. No saving to be made that week. Her shoulders were stooping, her feet slurring as they toiled back up the hill.

'If this goes on, I will never make the £100. I have set my heart on the £100.'

The sum had become her gleaming golden prize. Once it stood to her name in the Post Office, and Flo could match it, they could buy a place for themselves. Each had found this vision living in their minds, before a word of it had passed between them. A place. A house on a coast – on a wee geo sheltered from the west. No boat – they would soon be too old for that – a kailyard, and a hen-house ... The thing would only take on the lovely fullness of reality – of a picture – if they could hear of some particular neuk that suited, and where the laird was not a czar. There was supposed to be a new law now – once they were in possession, they were secure. She would believe that when it had come about and not before.

She paused before they turned in between the lumpy granite gate-posts that said 'Fir' on one and 'trees' on the other.

'When we leave here,' she began (there, it was out, not if but when), 'we will surely not be going back to Uist ...' Did Morag see it as she did – familiar, every crag and burn and beach of it, and all of them stained with hunger and defeat?

Morag's brow was crumpling in a weird mixture of fear and glee. 'There are plenty places. Sgiach, you know that island, and there is nothing wrong with it now. We will go over on the *Claymore* one fine day and when we are there, well, we might stay there. Only you must be writing a letter to your friend, mind.'

She made it sound like a jaunt. They were singing a lullaby as they went up the driveway, Morag sounding out the words while Flo hummed the tune –

'The nest of the sea-lark
Is on the plain of the shingle.
Sleep, little one,
And the bird will come to you ...'

After breakfast the next day Dr Harbottle made an unexpected appearance, coming into the dining-hall and standing at one end of the long tables, Miss Findlayson at his side. He stayed standing, looking as important as he could and evidently expecting silence. Porridge plates were clattering onto stacks. A burst of hysteria was coming from three women at the sinks. Morag had taken up their song again –

'The nest of the oyster-catcher
Is amongst the smooth shingles.
Sleep, little one ...'

Dr Harbottle coughed, violently, the cough seized him and he harked and barked helplessly until Nurse Wyllie came through and hit him heartily between the shoulder-blades. Miss Findlayson blushed deeply. In a choked and phlegmy voice that gathered strength as he went on, he told them that His Majesty the King had 'convoked the Privy Council in London' the previous evening and it had 'sanctioned the proclamation of a state of war with Germany' if they failed to withdraw from Belgium 'by eleven of the clock'.

'And they did fail so to do,' proclaimed Dr Harbottle, now in full Biblical stride. 'It therefore behoves us all to respond to these grave, ah, events in a manner that, ah, befits our country. We must be – we must be *strong*, although I may say that any danger – any, ah, physical danger appears to me to be, ah –'

Before he could finish his next word, someone had dropped a plate in the sink and it had broken with a single crack. A flapping noise was coming from among the women – Bertha was clapping, one hand half-missing the other from time to time. Ella was talking continuously in her undertone. Dr Harbottle stood for an irresolute moment, then turned and left the room.

Chapter 43

If the stable had faced east instead of north – or if she had still been living down south near Yarmouth – she might have felt no more separated from the warring armies than by the breadth of a river-mouth, one whose far shore could hardly be seen through the blue-grey haars of autumn but the sounds would be echoing across. (What would you hear, the thump and burst of shells? The screams of horses?) As it was, she could settle herself out there on a Wednesday, or for stolen hours on other days, and huddle into her own thoughts. She had ruled squares onto the pinned-up sheets, so that she could more easily carry over her ideas from the paper to the final board. Now she had taken to drawing in Indian ink as she became more confident in her line, on sheets the same size as the squares.

She watched with a sort of anxious satisfaction as her pen-point completed the fore-arm of a woman, burrowing into a bank to drag out a stone to fling, her fingers disappearing into heavy black hatching as though her arm was turning into a tap-root. The detail was as lifelike as a photograph – each woollen end on the fringe of the shawl, each nail on the toes cramped into the ground. She wanted to feel free to work at the other end of the scale – drawing Bertha, Mary and Morag like clouds above the houses had set her thinking of apparitions, demons, sky-creatures. Perhaps she had gone too far – wherever would she find a place in the picture for this head with its parted lips, its eyelids closed, its hair eddying sideways, the tendrils of it streaming and doubling back on themselves like skeins of spume in the sea below a cliff after a storm of wind?

So the style of the thing was still molten. So be it – time enough to fix it once she had discovered in her brains every last thing that had happened in the clearance, every fist, every wince and grimace, every shouting mouth.

When she went down to the harbour with Morag, they found themselves amongst all kinds of news and rumour. Morag was in tears at the price of fresh fish. 'Findlayson will never put up with this,' she exclaimed, distraught. 'I know she wants to feed us on salt ling, she can get it in bulk from the dealers in Peterhead. May I die before I am ruined!'

They watched in amazement as a crowd of youngish women mobbed the train coming in from the north with its carriages full of volunteers from the Highlands. 'Where are you from? And you? And you?' they were shouting up to the bearded faces in the incoming windows, and again as they left for Aberdeen, Dover, Portsmouth.

'Ross-shire,' said more than one of them, their voices half-drowned in the skreigh and hiss of steam.

'Russia? Did he say he had come from Russia? He had a foreign look right enough …'

A few days later there was a hubbub at Firtrees, with Bridget from Eriskay at the heart of it. 'You will never guess what Findlayson has been telling me – there is a hundred thousand Russians got off the boats at Aberdeen and went off south on the railway, off to the war.'

'They never did.'

'It is true, she read it in the *Daily News*.'

When Flo and Morag tried to tell them what they had heard with their own ears at the station, they were laughed down and Bridget's story was in every mouth inside the hour. Only the most disabled were immune, the smitten ones who sat staring into vacancy day after day or who had to put a hand on someone else's shoulder to find their way to the toilet or the gardens.

That night Flo came upon Bertha in a corner of the sitting room, crouched on the floor, weeping. When Flo got down beside her and stroked her shoulder, she gradually calmed and said between gulping sobs, 'Mishus Cam'l, I dinna like the Russhuns, Mishus Cam'l. Feart of the Russhuns, Mishus Cam'l. Guns an' whipses, Mishus Cam'l – they got guns an' whipses.' Her voice was rising and she was starting to shudder.

'We are as safe as houses here, Bertha. The war is far, far away across the sea.' She did not want to be smarming the woman with false comfort – she could not bear to see her collapsing into panic. She felt much less steady herself when news came in the early winter that German warships had bombarded Hartlepool and Scarborough and an airship called a 'Zeppelin' had dropped bombs and killed people down at Yarmouth.

Morag drew in her breath with a gasp as she heard the names of the towns read out from a daily paper by Nurse Goulding – Jekyll. 'Hartlepool? My Ranald bought his last boat at South Hartlepool.' Her hand was over her mouth and nose, her eyes aghast above it.

Flo said nothing. Word of Yarmouth had given her the first pang of tenderness she had felt since she left Burley. Four people were dead – supposing he was among them, or Weston – suppose the Mariners' was a heap of rubble … She had no wish to re-enter that life and yet – if any more of the past was burned away, she would feel as weightless as a cork on a broken net.

As salt ling gradually prevailed, and tripe edged out boiled beef, and the only meat available came out of tins and looked and smelt like shite, Flo found that her enthusiasm for working in the stable was cooling. When she got there on colder afternoons, she sat hunched inside her coat, with layers of wool beneath it, her hands half gloved in mittens Morag had knitted her out of unravelled ends of cast-off jerseys, pretending to Findlayson that they were meant for the troops. She stared at the sheet she had pinned to a drawing-board, made a pass with a piece of charcoal, barely brushing the paper, and waited for the clachan to appear in her mind's eye. Nothing. A wintry blank, like a bandage pressing round her sight. Maybe an hour passed. Soon the clouds would be turning into pink feathers and she would have lost the light.

Her hand had begun to draw a fruit – a full-bottomed pear with dimpled sides. Its body would glisten with juice as the knife sliced through … A black-and-white pear? She wanted it to glow yellow as though lit from inside. She went to get pastels from her old cigar-box and when her fingers found white and purple first, she thought of a different subject. She went quickly round to the kitchen garden. She looked all ways – not a soul in sight among plots that in the shade were still caked and touched white with frost. She wrenched three small snowball turnips from the nearest row and carried them back indoors. She brushed the earth from them and their cheeks shone satin-purple like a dress, their bottoms were pure white as though carved from candle-wax. She only had time to cut off the leafy tops and place them on a stand of piled logs before the light had drained from the sky and humdrum jobs required her to go indoors.

A few days later, when she went across to the stable, the trailing whiskers of the roots had surely grown. She imitated them exactly on a piece of brown paper, letting an ochre pastel waver down the sheet, thinning and thickening again with its own momentum, enjoying the ease of it, giving in to it in a light trance where everything else, the cold, the ugly news from across the water, the smells and noises of the hospital, sloughed away. Next time, when she compared her work with the turnips, she saw the roots had grown a good inch, like legs of dead spiders fingering down the flakey surface of the log. So she altered them on the paper, then brought up the lustre of the purple and the white so that the turnips shone like precious orbs. Am I worshipping them, she wondered. At least they are really there, they can fill your belly as well as your eye. They are good – what else is so purely good?

That winter she drew and painted nothing else but vegetables, leaves from evergreens, budding branches, and nailed the pictures on the walls. On the shortest days she worked by the light of a hurricane lamp, until its reek of paraffin became the odour of being alone and out of time.

Late one afternoon a yelp came from near the door. She could see nothing, not even a silhouette. Gas-lamps were dimmed these days and the windows of the hospital were masked with cheap black material.

'Who is there? Morag? Is that you?'

Her friend stepped forward into the small enclosure of pale yellow light. 'Flo my dear, you will be catching your death. You looked like the risen dead in the eerie light there. How can you see to work at all?'

Flo gestured at the small plywood board on her easel. She had brushed in two swedes, coarse hefty bulks in purplish green like mounds of clay.

'I could eat them,' said Morag. 'If I had the cooking of them for myself.' She shivered at the thought of the kitchen and its heaps of steamy pulp.

The winter's pictures were glimmering round the walls and they walked along them now, holding up the light to each one. A dish of new potatoes – it had cost Flo three weeks' work to catch exactly, in oil-paint, the brownish tatters peeling off them as thin as shreds of sunburnt skin. A savoy cabbage, its bluish-green leaves so sharply crinkled that Morag reached out her fingertips to touch their surfaces. Runner beans dangling in clusters, mature pods with sides ribbed like boats, unripe ones curled under as little and useless as the legs of babies … And the black-and white pear …

'I am hungry just looking at them. If I could make pictures, now …'

'You can. Sit you down and be thinking about – oh, anything that you know.'

'Maybe I could picture a fish – a fine trout from the lochans with a black back and wee red freckles on its sides.'

Obediently she perched on the table where the gurrlses had worked, closed her eyes tightly, and sat silent for some minutes while Flo held her hands round the lantern to gather a little warmth. At last Morag said, 'I have smelt my fish, and I have touched the slithery back of it.'

When Flo offered her the box of pastels, she laughed and pushed it away. 'Too late for that. I will keep my fishie in my head and I will maybe get the taste of it when we are trying to bite through the tripe.'

Chapter 44

A fluster was running through the building. It had no apparent source, it did not seem to have started in the kitchens or the laundry and reached out through the day-rooms or the wards. It was everywhere at once like a breeze that sent windows rattling in their sashes from the entrance to the attics. Bertha was going up to one person after another and asking, 'Whasha matter? Whasha matter? – then turning away with tears in her eyes when somebody looked at her and guffawed, or glowered, saying nothing, or pushed her away with needless force, or imitated her gobbling voice with clownish grimaces.

As Flo hauled a wicker hamper of dirty bed-linen down the passage-way, she came upon Murdina and Nurse Wyllie, who had struck up an unholy partnership recently. Hyde was flushed as though with drink.

'What is ado?'

'We are a' to pack up and –'

'Wheesht!' said Murdina before the nurse could say anymore. Murdina was looking furious, as though she was hell-bent on keeping the secret to herself. Wyllie was equally determined to break the amazing news.

'A' body will ken inside the hour. We are to pack up and gang awa' up the coast to a grand place near Tarbat. So – will you try an' get it into the heids o' some o' the brutes?'

Flo would have asked for more information, for times and reasons, if she had not felt sickened by her dislike for the pair of them. The thing was to find Morag and make sure that the two of them, together, were ready for whatever upheaval was about to happen. She found her cleaning fish in the scullery, a poor catch of coleys, grey flesh and the smell of haddock that was past its best. She took a knife and began to help with the work.

'What is this move we have to make? Will it be because of the war?'

'I think it is, although they have queer minds, the high-ups. Anyway, down at the shore just now they were fencing off another part of the dock with prickly wire, and when I went in-by at the Duke for a dram and news, they said they were expecting a terrible load of wounded.'

'More than ever?'

'More than ever. They were saying Munlochy was full to the brim and there was nowhere left to put the worst of them – the ones with no legs and no jaws and –' She broke off and stared down at the sink full of fish, her hands unmoving.

'But there has been no bad news for years.' They had taken to reading a paper every week and for a long time now the stories of bombardments and 'threatening enemy movements' in places like 'the Marne' had given way to jubilant stories about 'German reverses' and 'strategic gains'. 'Do you think they have been telling us the truth?'

They looked at each other and took up their work again.

'Did you hear it was Tarbat we were going to?'

'Oh aye, it will be the castle at Dunaldie, a great pile of a place with wee towers sticking out all over it like teats on a sow. They say one window to light a staircase cost a thousand pounds.'

'Is the government buying the place?'

'The government can take what it likes. The lord, he is some kind of an Englishman, he had been away for years, making his money. He only ever came to shoot. So maybe the poor of the parish will get some good of it at last.'

'Like you and me, Morag.'

'Like you and me, Flo.'

They had a laugh at that and carried the ashets piled with drab fish through to the kitchen. The flutter of news had turned into a furore.

'Splitting us up … A hundred miles away … The Doctor will be a duke … In a boat, away to the islands in a boat … A dungeon, full of rusty chains …' Wild phrases were jumping from mouth to mouth. Nobody could keep still. Beside the cookers a fight was breaking out. A cook shoved some maids and patients backwards out of her way with a dunt of her backside. The little crowd swayed forward on the rebound, an arm hit a pan-handle and spirks of hot fat sprayed breasts and faces. Dribbles of it caught fire and flared and spat. The meal itself was a shambles, with more rows and spills than usual, and four people left the room to be sick. Surely, in the afternoon, Harbottle and Findlayson would come out of their dens and the man would make one of his speeches and give them all their orders?

When they escaped at last into the lobby, they saw that the green baize notice-boards had been cleared of the old bits and pieces of instructions which nobody had read for years. One big placard, in four copies, now took up the space –

NOTICE OF REMOVAL

Following upon instructions from His Majesty's Government, as transmitted to myself by the County Board, the entire complement of this Institution are to remove forthwith to Dunaldie Castle in the northern part of this County, situated six miles from the London & North-Eastern Railway Station. The staff, under the direction of the Matron, will assist the Patients in packing up their effects.

<u>N.B. One trunk per person.</u>

Removal will commence this day fortnight. I trust that orderly co-operation will be maintained by all concerned.

(Signed) Edward Harbottle, M.B., Ch.B.
(Medical Superintendent)

'He micht hae telt us hissel'.'

'Aye, an' sent us a' to sleep.'

'A castle – we are going to dine off white linen in a castle!'

On a window seat Bertha was sprawling helplessly like a sack and staring in terror at something invisible. Words stammered from her mouth. 'We will d-d-die up there. D-don' wanna go – d-d-don' wanna go!' Her voice was rising, seeming to come from some animal inside her face. Flo sat down beside her, put her arm round her, and held her closely, feeling sobs shake her, until she let her head with its bush of hair sink onto Flo's shoulder, choking her with its reek like stale hay and dripping.

'It will be good up there, Bertha,' she said at last with as much certainty as she could muster. 'It is beside the sea. We are going to live at the seaside.'

How would she ever find again, at this new castle or anywhere else, a place as much her own as this cold, stony stable, with its opening to the north and its back to everything else? On what would be her last Wednesday afternoon there, she left the stramash of half-crated equipment and nearly hysterical people (maids as well as patients) and walked out quickly through the gardens in the naked, yellowing light of a fine May evening. She must write to Peg at last. No word between them for five years at least. It was wrong. It would not start the least crack in their friendship. 'Till death us do part' – you could take the strong meaning from it and be comforted, or you could let the word 'death' in and feel yourself grown cold already … She sat writing at the home-made table. One side of a sheet would surely do.

> *Firtrees Mental Institution,*
> *Craigpatrick,*
> *Inverness-shire*
> *May the 19th, 1917.*

> *Dear friend Peggy,*
> *At last I am writing to you. Not before time. Where have the years gone? This address will look queer! I am not a patient, I am a worker for the small wage and a room under the roof. Morag is here, she is a Matheson from the island where I was born so she was a neighbour long ago but faithful connections make nothing of the years passing.*

She was sounding like a preacher now, or somebody who made up wee thoughts for the calendars. Peg would want her news. She had little enough of that, although if they were together again they would chat till the cows came home.

> *We are going from here to a big place called Dunaldie Castle, by Tarbat in this county. Because this place is needed for the limbless men. I am thankful that your Hughie Beg is too young to be taken for the Army, Hugh is surely safe, they have not got to the older men yet and maybe it will all end soon.*

She had still not written the most important thing.

> *When we have money saved we will be coming over to Sgiach and maybe find a place. We cannot work forever although we both have our strength yet.*

> *Your friend,*
> *Flora.*

She had had to run onto the other side of the sheet and the ink had blurred through the trashy paper, making it hard to read. No time to copy it out, she must be late already for the teas. Inside the back door a silhouette blocked the passage – Hyde herself, wearing her worst look, her chin jutting and her plump cheeks set like lard.

'What kin' o' a time is this, Campbell? You have the brutes to feed and they're a' gane gyte wi' the move. You will hae to do better at the Castle.'

Flo would not speak and she could not get past. Her eyes had locked onto Hyde's – a mistake, for who could now give way? They stared each other out while a low roar mixed with shrieks came through the dining hall. Then Hyde stood to one side. As Flo came past her she gave her shoulder a shove and said in almost a male growl, 'Dinna think you'll be able to malinger wi' the new man.'

Flo passed on, making herself numb. New man? Was Harbottle finished? Was this new castle to be plagued with bullies like that old bad dream of a place? Although Firtrees was nothing to her, had never kindled the least ounce of warm belonging, it had been safe. It had kept out that nakedness to the winds, with the roof torn off, which was always lurking.

That night she took her older paintings out from below her bed, and the pages from *Three Score and Ten,* and checked the wrappings. She undid the packages and smelt inside them. No mildew – it had been too cold most of the time for anything to grow. The Saturday of the move was coming nearer. Late on the last two evenings she worked in a steady frenzy at the stable, leafing newspapers between her many pictures of the gurrlses and the vegetables, storing her sketches for the Island picture in the hearts of the bundles. The long sheet of plywood, still with only the ghost of the skyline wavering along it, could take its chance unwrapped. On the Friday night she laid out her necessaries once again on the counterpane – the canvas bag, with two nighties now; two pretty blouses, one turquoise and one oak-leaf brown; the coat with the fur collar; Maggie's shawl, unworn for years now, with its yellow and rusts still glowing as a reminder of the lichens on the crags of the islands; her moccasins, which Findlayson looked at with discomfiture because they were not black and stiff; needles, thread, and a thimble; and her patched purse, fatter now with its wad of seventeen £5 notes.

Drum-tap of Morag's fingers on the door. 'Mercy me,' she exclaimed at the grand display, 'you are fit to be wedded! You should see that Bridget's fineries all laid out. They would not disgrace a duchess.'

'I wonder has Findlayson got much in her wardrobe – a dozen black skirts, and a dozen brown cardigans –'

'And a dozen white blouses,' they finished in unison and burst out giggling. Their laughter tailed off and they looked at each other with dark eyes. The same boding was on both of them. Maybe they were too old for a change, for the sheer labour of it, the discomfort of a new place, echoing with unfamiliarity. They sat on the edge of the bed for a while, holding hands, hearing an occasional owl-call from Johnny Downie in the ward below.

'Ach well,' said Morag at last, 'we never died a winter yet, as they say in Caithness. The higher the tempest strikes, the closer we must creep to the great rock in the weary land.'

'Whoever said that?'

'Mary of Unnimore, a hundred year since, when they were cleared out of their place in Morvern, and she with a babe at her breast. But she aye had her God.'

'And what was he doing at the time?'

Morag looked startled, then said 'Och, I know, I know. But it must be nice if you can be thinking that you are not entirely alone.'

The heavy goods were to go by the carrier's carts. A long file of them filled the driveway and a good few yards of the street outside. As crates and trunks and scarred, well-used suitcases were hoisted aboard, the horses were standing like statues or tossing their heads, and one raised its tail and let drop a pile of steaming dung. Miss Findlayson glanced automatically at Hyde. She signalled brusquely to a gardener and he solemnly removed the muck on a shovel. Then the two women were walking down the file like officers and inspecting each load of gear before it was lifted onto a tailboard. Flo had stacked her packages of pictures on edge against the hub of a wheel, more than a yard deep. And here of course Hyde stopped, spurned the nearest package with her black brogue, looked round at the waiting crowd, and said, 'Whose is this?'

'Mine,' said Flo with a dry mouth. She swallowed and said more loudly, 'Mine.'

'It's a sight mair than *one trunk*. You canna tak' it. Can she, Matron?'

If she was separated from her pictures and the pages, if they were left behind to rot or be thrown onto some bonfire, it would be like having a piece of her brains sucked out. She raised her chin and said clearly, 'They are going in the cart.' She stepped forward and handed the nearest package up to the carter. He took it from her and winked.

Miss Findlayson was making small sounds of distress, like sparrows under a roof. Hyde's eyes were frozen stones. Johnny Downie was calling plaintively, 'Help me, help me,' and holding out a shaking hand as proof that he was too frail to go down the steps by himself. Flo continued to hand her packages up to the carter. The nurses and maids were making the patients shuffle into a crocodile, the men at the front, the women next, two by two, each holding the hand or arm of their companion.

In the midst of the women Lolly was being pushed along by Mary on a kind of wicker trolley with rubber tyres which had cost fifteen guineas – it had been paid for, according to Morag, by her stepmother, who had last visited from Dundee in 1902. Lolly's hands waved from side to side as though she was conducting gentle music. Mary had to lean back hard to hold the contraption from racing down the hill. Her wig had tilted sideways, held rakishly by the rim of her ear. Ella and Madge were the last pair, immediately in front of Flo and Morag. They could hear the words rustling from Ella's lips, 'And there shall be no night there; and they need no candle, neither light of the sun; for the Lord God giveth them light …'

As they neared the main street where it widened into the station forecourt the pavements began to be lined. Word of their coming must have hurried down the hill. The forecourt itself was so full that Hyde and one of the gardeners had to go on ahead and clear a way through to the booking hall with shouts and policemen's gestures. At the sight of the crowd, many dozens of people frankly staring and grinning, the procession slurred to a halt.

Madge turned on her heel and Flo saw that her face was afire with mortification. Bertha had bumped into the women in front of her, knocked her down, and fallen herself. A man stepped forward to give her a hand up, her weight surprised him, and he fell on top of her. She clutched him and kissed his mouth and several people cheered. Flags left over from the last entraining of a regiment were being waved amongst the crowd. As Lolly's trolley reached the forecourt, a young woman in a smart blue coat and hat darted forward and put a Union Jack on a stick into Lolly's hand. She fluttered it to and fro, smiling like an angel. Johnny Downie, beholding an audience beyond his finest dreams, was wailing 'Help me, help me' in his most piteous falsetto. 'Help me!' a child's voice mimicked him from the crowd and Flo saw a woman yank her boy's arm violently and clout him on the side of his head until he bawled.

The station master had come striding forward with such a show of official importance that Flo wondered if they were supposed to salute or curtsey. Gold braid glistened on his cap and a full set of Dundreary whiskers looped round his cheeks like a Balaclava helmet knitted in grey wool.

'Who is in charge, now? Your tickets are all ready and I must entrust them to whoever is in charge.'

Hyde looked at Findlayson. The matron reluctantly accepted bundles of tickets tied with string and tried to match them to her charges. She dropped a few and started to count again. The crocodile of patients bulged and eddied in all directions, then lost shape altogether as they swarmed past the ticket collector and made a rush for the open doors of the carriages. Grey-green upholstery and varnished mahogany enclosed them (except for Lolly, installed with Mary in the guard's van at the rear). The train hissed and set off with a jerk.

Presently they were trundling over a low iron bridge and Flo and Morag were looking down a shining stretch of the Canal. The direct way to the West. The straight highway of it, the bristle of masts where fishing boats were tied up beyond the lock gates, waiting for a passage through to the North Sea fishing – the sight was enough to melt away all sense of the bulky mountains between them and the western islands, the years of waiting, the lack of money which ate into them like hunger. At Dingwall they would have willed the train to turn left into the glens. It puffed on north by east into an unfamiliar district, past a long firth with mudflats bared by the ebb, past a barracks with kilted sentries at its gate, and past a bay where several long grey ships lay at anchor, their bows turning towards the flow of the tide, towards the war.

Chapter 45

A vast hedge of naked spines faced them as they stepped into the entrance hall. It was as high as a church. Deer antlers, row after row right up to the ceiling, bristled on the unplastered granite to one side and the partition wall above double doors into an emptied, uncarpeted drawing-room. The antlers looked as stark and thorny as the branches of a pine forest killed long ago by fire. Each pair sprouted from a jagged section of the animal's skull. Flo could make out one of the inscriptions lower down, written neatly in ink on the face of the bone –

> Shot by Lady Mary Allason-Formby
> Kildermorie
> November 29
> 1896

A half-familiar air was stealing over her. Walls that loomed and bore down on her … The threat of a power that could squash you between the thumb and forefinger of its gloved hand or rip you open with an upward jerk of its horn … If she could read the writing on every trophy, even the ones high up in the shadowy staircase-well, would she find one that said 'Shot by Lord Ardmair', in 1866, or 1876, or 1886? And if the year was only just past, would it mean that the young lord was somewhere nearby – not young now – his son would be stalking deer by now, and stalking women …

The whole party had crowded in and were standing about like tourists, looking up at the forest of horns, the soaring walls papered in a black and bottle-green tartan like cliff faces dressed in tweed, the branching joists and rafters sleek brown in their glossy varnish. Lolly was excited and her fingers were pointing and splaying at all angles, as though imitating the antlers. Bertha had sat down on the frosty marble floor and was peeking at the bits of skull through her hands, then closing her fingers again to shut out the sight. As a hubbub began to simmer up, Flo caught Ella's muttering from close behind her, '… enter in through the gates into the city. For without are dogs, and sorcerers, and whore-mongers, and murderers …'

The front door, ten foot high and five inches thick, was standing open, letting in an early-summer breath of pine resin and damp undergrowth. A man appeared in the doorway and stood there with a small smile on his well-shaven, rosy face. As people began to notice him, he smiled more widely and waited, perfectly still, with a look of satisfaction. He wore a suit with wide, pointy lapels, made of grey cloth ruled with chalky lines, and his hat was brown with a crown that tapered slightly. He looks new, thought Flo, he looks almost foreign – what on earth has he to do with us?

Miss Findlayson had appeared at one side of him, on the lower doorstep, and Hyde on the other, in a newly pressed blue cape. The various giggles and groans and eager chatterings were dying into a hush. The stranger came forward into the hall and the press of people parted from him as though unwilling to be touched. Findlayson and Hyde were still a pace behind him as he made for the staircase and took up his stance on the third step. The quietness was now complete but he held up his hand as though calming a stir, cocked his head, and grinned at Findlayson, crooking his forefinger and motioning her onto the step below him.

He gave her a nod. She blushed, dabbed her glasses, sniffed, and said, 'Ladies and gentlemen, this is our new – our new – ah –'

'Lord and master,' whispered Morag.

'This is our new Superintendent, Dr Sorley MacQuarrie.' A silent pause. Was that all? She bent at the waist, then the neck, in a gawky bob. The new boss smiled quite broadly at them all and held out his hand again as though for silence. Everyone remained silent.

'Friends,' he said, 'we will all get to know each other in due course, and I look forward very much to that. There will be difficulties, no doubt, as we settle into these grand surroundings' – he glanced appreciatively at the antlers – 'but together we can make light of them, I have no doubt. I am responsible for you but I am also responsible to you, and I trust – I know – that each and every one of you will come freely to see me whenever you feel a need. I want you to, so that I can understand you. I would like to understand you *very well indeed.*' His smile had gone and he looked keenly over the crowd of faces, fixing one person after another for at least five seconds, or so it felt.

When Flo saw his gaze coming her way, she looked down. Why should she want to be understood, let alone 'very well indeed'? In the evening, across in the room she and Morag were to share in the servants' buildings north of the big house, the two of them gave the new man a good thrash through.

'MacQuarrie?' she wondered. 'I never met one of those before.'

'MacQuarries are from Ulva,' said Morag. 'There will be a few enough there now. Some lawyer from the Lowlands bought the place. They say he removed most of the trees to put the cleared folk off from ever coming back.'

'I thought I heard the Gaelic voice under the Glasgow one.'

'Maybe, maybe. He will have put all that well behind him, to be sure. Did you see the clothes on him? He must be going to the best of shops.'

'A fine figure of a man.'

'Oh aye, shaved and shining, and well pleased with himself.'

'And Hyde was pleased with him.'

'Pleased as a cat.'

They looked wickedly at each other, and laughed, and supped the milk they had heated up in the little kitchen below.

'Are we jealous, just, do you think, because she still has nice paps on her and we are a pair of crones?'

'Speak for yourself, Flora Campbell. It is only yesterday that I was thirty years old and any man would be fancying me.'

At night Flo heard surf as she slept and woke and slept again. It sounded like her childhood, like the islands. She tuned her ears more sharply and knew that it was a small wind soughing in the trees that pressed close on the landward side of the place. They were planted woods, pines and larches and some kind of huge trees with drooping sprays of needles and trunks clad in bark like layers of reddish felt. They closed the castle off from the road and the nearest village and turned the whole place eastward where lawns and broad meadows stepped and sloped downhill to the reaches of the firth. To be turned so wholly towards the North Sea and away from where the sun set made it feel like Yarmouth.

In the morning the castle might as well not have been there. The wind had died, the air was drenched in a sea haar so thick that they felt lost as they walked across the granite setts of the yard towards, they hoped, the castle. As it reared up like a spectre, turrets and gables blurring off into the gloom, Hyde caught up with them. Droplets of water glinted like glass beads threaded onto the yellow curls she had arranged outside the edge of her hood.

'I am in the coachman's room,' she said at once. Then, 'We are a' in clover. Even the brutes. Some of them are twa tae a room, would you believe.'

'Who is Bertha with?'

'Kemp is in the attics. Nae favourites.' She looked sharply sideways at Flo, the prettiness drained briefly from her face.

'And Lolly?'

'Special case. Ground floor, south wing. What they ca'd the billiard room. And Dr MacQuarrie is to live in. Wi' his wife – if she comes.'

Flo badly wanted to nudge Morag. She said, 'Is that the last of Harbottle? Has he retired?'

'That or the knackers.' She laughed. 'I suppose he was weel past it afore he was forty.'

Inside the castle, smells of green vegetables boiling and strong tea stewing wove the day into a thousand that had gone before. How many of the poor souls knew that they were in a different place? Elly Bain, already snug in a chair with a back like a basket, plaiting away at her jute. Maggie MacEachern knitting her scarf, uncaring that the scars from her adventure with the window showed all over her forearms and the backs of her hands like strips of glazed ox-tongue. Jim Hunter with his hand approaching the flies of his pyjama trousers in a series of jerks. They could have been anywhere.

Some of the others must have been shocked down into themselves and were not even asking to be taken to the bathroom. They sat like monuments on chairs and window-seats. Johnny Downie was standing in the middle of the hall, saying nothing, like a twin statue of Davey Leiper who was leaning against the marble jamb of the mantelpiece, staring with his burnt-out eyes, his head propped on a green bronze figure of a woman in draperies holding up a star. After two hours he had not stirred. Johnny had disappeared. Later in the day Flo and Morag heard from Jekyll about Johnny's interview with MacQuarrie. It had been his thirty-fourth since nine in the morning.

'So in trails Johnny,' said Nurse Goulding in her calm, ironical way, 'and would you believe it, the Doctor asks him to sit down. "Please be seated," he says – she put on an unctuous voice. "Please be seated, *John*, and tell me all about yourself." So of course Johnny stays as silent as the grave, and I began to take him away again, but the Doctor says, "Nurse, please," as though I had laughed in church, and he tries again. "John," he says, "let us consider why you are here. Cast your mind back, John," he says, "and tell me, John, why do you think you are here?" And Johnny looks at him as though he must be off his head and says, "Because I burnt myself," and the Doctor says, "And how did you burn yourself, John?" And Johnny says, "There was a friend of mine, he was a very good friend, and he was crossed in love and so he jumped off the bridge, so I just jumped after him, to keep him company." And the Doctor says, "You burned yourself by jumping off a bridge?" and Johnny looks furious and says, "No, no, I was in my lodgings, down in the Nethergate, you know, and there was some awful wild lads there, you know, and one night I was sitting reading my paper and they broke down the door and set fire to my breeks with matches." And he began to weep, he was crying out "Help me," of course, so then the Doctor let me take him away.'

'At least he was taking an interest,' said Morag, as they lay in their beds at night with the unfamiliar air dark all round them. 'Harbottle was kind enough in his way, poor soul, but he might as well have not been there at all.'

'I wonder, is MacQuarrie kind?'

'Maybe Hyde will try and find out.'

'Not if the wife turns up …'

They could have gossiped until one or the other fell asleep and failed to answer. Flo had little heart for it. Pain was cutting across her back above her waist – it must have been the extra labour of moving dozens of iron bedsteads into the spaces of empty, echoing rooms and half-lifting patients who were still too stunned to stir themselves. At the end of the day she had gone to sort out her packages from the miscellaneous gear the carters had left in the yard. The long board had gone astray. She could replace it. And the softly brushed-in outline of the shore might well not survive into the final picture. She still felt emptied in the pit of her stomach, as though she was listening to herself and hearing only silence. How fragile her mind was. If she had been building a boat, like her father long ago, and had been stopped halfway, there would still be a keel there and strakes curving up like ribs. Her picture ideas were more like smokes in mid-air, they could flee away in a moment, or turn into something else.

At least she could stow her work in a safe place. There must be plenty of room in the steadings built at right angles to their quarters. They must have housed carts and carriages here before the war, gear and horses and ponies. The next in the row had a new padlock on it. So had the next three. Every door in the buildings apart from the living quarters was shut fast. Whatever was in there – the best furniture, stuffed beasts, pictures of themselves – the Allason-Formbys wanted to make sure they could get their hands on it when they came back.

She walked right round the buildings. Wide spaces of shadow gaped between trees. In the gloaming the avenue leading to the main road looked vacant and eerie. Its twisting length of rammed sand and shingle glimmered pale orange as though it was faintly lit, all ready for the lord and master to come riding up. She could find no extra sheds or huts where she could store the packages. And where could she be alone and work by herself? It was fine to be cosy with Morag but their room was more cramped than the attic at Firtrees, even. At least the weather was looking set fair. She would stack the packages behind the building where nobody went and maybe they would take no harm in their oilskin wrappings. Somewhere or other, in the woods maybe, she would surely find a refuge, a bothy or a ruin with a bit of a roof.

Chapter 46

There was too much room in the castle and there was too little. At Firtrees the old family, the Forsyths, had gone for good and the Board had been able to do what it liked with the building, fitting bars to upper windows, knocking down walls between bedrooms to make wards. These new grandees, the Allason-Formbys, would be coming back one day, no doubt – they had gone off to Liverpool, where they were supposed to own a fleet of ships, so all must be left in order. This was all very well in the attics, which were partitioned with studding to make 'wee coops for the fowls', as dumpy Jean had described the servants' sleeping quarters. Shortly before the patients moved in, the partitions had been knocked out to turn the attics into wards. Still there was too little room for patients who needed to be fully seen and supervised, and the new man was said to be 'in a white rage' that the work had not been done already.

'He is having the bedroom doors taken out of their hinges so that the nurses can walk in and spot the trouble before it starts,' so ran the word. Presently there was an unscrewing and a lifting away of the many fine hardwood doors, which were stored under lock and key in the steadings. At night Hyde and Jekyll and the other nurses moved up and down the corridors, with candles in their hands if the coal ration for the gas furnace had failed to arrive. They spied through the door spaces, and when Hyde saw anyone getting out of bed again, or beginning to thrash about and groan, she stood staring 'with eyes like a Hallowe'en turnip,' according to Jean, 'and then the poor soul fairly held his wheesht, or died for all she cared.'

Flo tried to imagine MacQuarrie 'in a white rage', fitting a mask of anger onto that pleasantly grinning face, and when it worked and she had the image, she knew she would like never to be the object of such a freezing look. She would keep out of his way – of all their ways – and serve her time, and save a bittie more. Surely they would soon have enough. The 70-year-olds' pension had helped Morag when it came, and her own wage had gone up to thirteen shillings and sixpence. But Morag had lost her fish trade with the move and was now officially nothing more than a patient once again. Would MacQuarrie be wanting to know her 'very well indeed'? That would be a sight – she would talk the hindlegs off him and he would try to make her feel a fool, until he had to admit that she was as sane as Solomon.

She was walking over to the outbuildings by herself after finishing in the laundry, her fingers aching with the wet and the tyauving at the mangle. The sough of the wind in the pinetree needles had a keener edge to it – the sound of poor weather blowing across from the West. Her paintings would not be safe for much longer, for that night, even. She went straight round the back and into the woods to the north, determined that there must be some kind of shelter. These big houses had been built, often enough, on the land of a cleared clachan, so where were the old stone shells of cottages? Or had it been the poorest kind of place, with turf walls on stone founds?

It was hard to see, as though an early night had thickened amongst the trunks and branches. Prickly snares of brambles caught on her skirt and scratched her ankles too painfully to bear. She heard water bubbling somewhere ahead and after a few minutes' more struggle she was seeing pale glimmers like stars on the ground at her feet – primroses, later flowering in this shade. Beyond the clumps of them a burn was running fast in a stony, curving bed. The far side of it was surely artificial – it was a parapet built up with rough field stones. Beyond it stood a wall, five feet high, the side of a wee house with rounded corners. Not roofless – somebody had spanned sawn timbers from one gable to the other and laid sheets of crinkly tin from the tops of the walls to the ridge.

She stepped in through the ragged gap in the main wall and looked up. Perfect darkness – no holes in the makeshift roof. The air smelt of toadstools. The floor was matted with brown pine needles and oak leaves, blown in through the doorway. She felt her way round the inside like a blind woman and her palms and fingers came up against nothing but clammy stone. She snuffed deeply, trying for a taint of fire-smoke, or sweat or tobacco or any other human use. Pine resin, just, and mouldy soil and toadstools. If it had been a tinkers' doss, it had fallen out of use long since.

She went back to the steading to tell Morag. Their room was still empty so she carried her things over to the ruin, two at a time, remembering with a wry stoun that she had been able to lift the lot in just a couple of loads when she came north on the boat. On the Wednesday – if MacQuarrie and Findlayson still allowed the half day off – she would unwrap them and make sure they were dry and whole before she sealed them up again. And she would see if this dark hidey-hole was fit to work in, and whether she could stand the smother of the thick woods all around. Maybe it would make it easier to sink into herself and plumb her memory to its very bed.

There was a glimmer of light in their window. From outside the door she heard a sobbing and a muttering. Morag never wept now, just said 'Och' with that deep shrug and sigh from the full of herself. She was sitting on her bed and by the light of the candle Flo saw that her cheeks were shining wet. She went over to her and Morag keeled forward, grasped her round the knees, and spoke into the cloth of her skirt in a flow broken by big breaths in and out.

'Oh Flora my darling, I cannot tell you, I cannot. There was a rough voice coming from one of the new rooms and I thought, that is not right so I went and listened from behind the door-jamb – still that voice – so I peeked in and there was Hyde, at the side of Jim Hunter's bed, the clothes were back and his breeks were down to his ankles and his thing was up and she – and she – and she – her hand was on him, rousing him, and herself saying in that dog's voice she has, "Gin ye like to mess with yourself, James Hunter, let's see – how – you – like – *this*" – he was starting to skreigh with the sore pain of it and trying not to skreigh, near-about choking he was, and – and –'

Flo held her head and said, 'The others – what about the others?'

'Heads under the bedclothes. Most of them. Two-three of the right dafties were giggling. One of them was getting worked up himself. Oh Flo –'

'Did she not stop when she saw you?'

'I fled away. Flo – I was feared. I am no better than the Levite who passed by on the other side when the man was lying in the way.'

'If I had been there, I would have done no better.' Was this too severe? Morag was sitting upright again. She wiped her face with the fold of her sheet, reached out to the candle between the beds, and nipped out the flame. The smell of hot wax flavoured the air briefly as they put on their nighties and got into bed. Gradually the lighter blue-black of the window grew out of the darkness.

Flo said, 'No wonder she got the name Hyde. But this is too much at last. We had best go to Findlayson, or the new man even. Unless Hyde has him in her pocket by now – along with her keys.' She waited for her friend to speak. Only breathing came. 'It is the fault of us all. I mind when Jim was crying once in the toilets, it was a few months before the flitting, and when he saw me he said, "That bitch will get me yet." Do you know what I said, Morag?' She waited for a reply, then answered herself, 'Nothing. I never liked him and because I did not, I let myself believe he was just a man who had lost all his wits except his power of making a fuss.'

She listened again. Morag was breathing, not snoring, and in a minute she blew her nose and said, 'We are not good. We are not bad but we are not good enough. I mind a lesson that we heard in Ross, when the man came to Jesus and asked for his mercy on his son, "for he was lunatic, and sore vexed, for often he fell down into the fire and often into the water, and even the disciples could not cure him".'

'Who needs curing, Morag – Jim Hunter or that beast?'

'Jesus rebuked the devil that was in him and it departed out of him and the child was cured.'

The darkness was beginning to weigh down on Flo like a mattress pressing onto her face. She put back the bedclothes, went over to the window, and leaned her forehead against the coolth of the pane.

'We had better wait for a saviour, Morag? Is that the way of it?'

Silence grew between them. Perhaps their thoughts were moving closer together and perhaps they were not. At the moment she could not think of the words that would carry over the space which separated them.

Chapter 47

The summer had dried out the moisture under the trees, encouraging her to spend time at the bothy. She had stolen the threadbare runner from the lobby outside their kitchen, rolled it up quickly, and carried it off into the woods. Cut into strips it almost covered the floor. A piece of light boarding from the conversion of the attics was easy to filch. She fixed it to the inside wall of the bothy with wooden plugs and nails as a sign to herself that she would work her picture to a finished state while she still had time. No more vegetables and fruit. She would never be more able to paint her vision of Uist than she was now.

At the flitting she had finally made space for two drawing-pads by leaving a skirt out of her bag. Before the afternoon finished she might be able to sketch some other faces for the cloud-masks hovering above the clachan. Who was this handsome face with a head of crinkly hair and a little smile that had no humour in it? Sorley MacQuarrie, and she did not want him there. He was only a quack who liked the sound of his own voice. She turned the page, and when MacQuarrie's likeness appeared again she made him ridiculous, with fat naked shoulders, curly hair on his chest, and a wreath of leaves resting on his ears.

She was fiddling – she would use nothing of this. She eased her aching backside off her fish-box seat and realised she had stayed so long because the place was a home of a kind, and because it was not the castle. The upper storeys and attics, the whole of the rooms where the patients slept, had begun to seem darkened even by day. When duties took her there she found she was listening on edge for sounds of protest or pain.

They must leave. They could not. You were allowed to sail to the other islands only if you had business there or your 'domicile', and that had not been true for sixty years. To think that steel boats with guns and shells were prowling under the waters where her mother's kin had been at home for centuries. Seers had foretold this kind of thing – as Morag liked to remind her. Well, they were bound to be right about something if you waited long enough.

She stepped out through the breach in the wall, reminding herself once again to make a door. It was as well that shooting had finished for the duration of the war or keepers and beaters would have come flailing through the woods and flushed her out. Wood-pigeons left the trees above her head with a clap of their wings, flew south, then sheered off west, avoiding the water. It was so near. One minute you might have been in the wilds of Russia, the next the sunlit water was twinkling between the branches of the sycamores and alders near the shore in gleaming pieces like a screen of gems. She went towards the castle by the edge of the sea, to delay her return as long as possible. In the scullery next the kitchen Morag greeted her with her darkest face.

'Have you read the notice on the board? Two nurses have gone, they are not saying why, and they cannot be replaced because of the war, so we must all work harder, and some of us may have to help during the night.'

They must both be thinking, Hyde has got rid of them because they were too soft, or because they saw something.

'Who will stand up to her? Jean is strong enough. The rest of the maids are little girls, and the nurses are too weary, even Jekyll, although there is some good in her.'

'Flo, I am too weary. Let us go home now.'

'Home?'

'The West. To Sgiach or another place where there is no imprisonment. Nobody was raving on Uist, or if they were they kept them at home and the cruelty did not spread. The foxes have holes and the birds have nests but the Son of Man hath nowhere to lay his head.'

The corridors at night looked three times their usual length. At each end one lamp was left burning on its bracket, pale blue with yellow centre like a crocus bud. The doorways without their doors gaped in a row of oblong caves. The invisible men and women in their beds were creaking and rustling and snoring and sometimes calling out in scraps of speech. Each entrance was the end of a coffin, opened to let out whatever shell of a person lay in there with a tongue still fidgeting in its skull … At once she abhorred this fancy – it was like the worst of Richard, in that last horrible phase of his. Once such a thing appeared in your vision, it clung to you like a tick.

Findlayson had given out instructions to Flo and Jean, along with three of the younger maids. 'You are to do one night each week – that will be quite sufficient' (as though they were begging to do more!). 'So please be on your best behaviour. Simply walk quietly up and down from time to time and see that – that, eh – make sure that everyone is comfortable and, eh –'

'How can we nurse them if they're taken ill?' Jean asked abruptly. 'An' can we gie them a skelp gin they get oot o' hand, like?'

Findlayson blushed and her eyes turned waterish behind the two thick lenses. 'You are all sensible women and you can be trusted, I am sure. A duty nurse will always be on hand downstairs. And there are bell-pulls throughout the building.'

She reddened again. The patients had soon discovered that if you jerked hard on one of the curly handles, it set up a furious jangling in the passage between the kitchen and what had been the butler's pantry. They had been disconnected on MacQuarrie's orders and had hung there silently ever since, like a row of bats. Now they were being brought back to life each night. It looked like a recipe for confusion.

Flo walked down the length of a male corridor, up some stairs and along another. She was trying to be as stealthy as a thief. How silly – if the rowdiest sleepers did not wake each other, nothing would. At a pair of double doors with china handles she turned back – beyond lay the stairs down to the west wing where 'special cases' stayed and that was out of bounds at night.

A cry like a stab of pain sounded from behind her. In dread she hurried back down the corridors. It sounded again. From the second-last door on the right. She put a match to a night-light and made herself go into the dark interior. Six beds, three on each side. In one of the furthest, next the window, Jim Hunter was heaving from side to side. His eyes were shut, his face and his grey hair were like a white cheese draggled with cobwebs. The bedclothes had fallen onto the floor, his trousers were down, and she could see that the side of his thigh was solid bruise from hip to knee, reds and purples mixed like a mash of plums, with yellow of older bruises sprinkled along the top of his leg like blots of lichen.

'Jim, Jim.' She set down the little candle on the window-sill. 'Jim, please.' She was pleading with him – she wanted him not to disturb the others – she wanted him to make whatever noise he liked if it let out his pain. 'Oh Jim …'

She sat down on the edge of his bed and his eyes glared up at her in terror. She tried to hold his head against her breast and he struggled in fierce twitches. Her thoughts reeled in a fever. It must have been an accident – the older ones were always falling. If it had been, it would have

been dressed, or soothed with arnica at least. His spasms were too strong
for her to hold. As she got up to try and lie him down and tidy his bed,
his jacket fell open and she saw that his ribs were striped with long weals,
angry red, beginning to go septic in the sorest places.

Go for the nurse. The duty nurse that night was Hyde. As though
she was looking at a picture in an evil book, she saw the scene in all its
details. Hyde tormenting the man, in a room with a high ceiling, on a
bed with bare springs, while some assistant (this figure was blurred) held
the patient down, and laughed at Hyde's jokes ...

It was all a nightmare, vile dreams, impossible. She held the man
again, he was less agitated now, and half hummed, half sang him a lullaby
she had not heard for seventy years –

'Well I love you,
Smooth you, soft you,
In the morning
White and bright ...'

When he was fairly calm, she buttoned up his pyjamas. Before she did
up his trousers she bent down and snuffed at this scraggy, hairy thigh. No
– no whiff of embrocation whatsoever. When she had re-made the bed
around him, he lay on his back, a low ridge under the blankets, his eyes
shut in a face as mute as a corpse. Was he lying low for fear of further
dangers or was he really asleep?

She left the room and blew out the candle. The house was silent at
this minute except for a purr and a hiccup as one of the lamps struggled
with a fault in the flow of gas. Hyde would be sitting at her desk in the
pantry that had become the nurses' office. She wanted to rush down and
lock her in – challenge her furiously – wake everybody and tell them ...
Fruitless thoughts swarmed through her as she stepped silently downstairs,
breathed deeply, and almost ran past the office. The door was open, the
nurse was at the desk, reading something, with a lamp in its tall glass
beside her. She did not look up.

Flo went straight on to the cloakroom by the front door and spent
the rest of the small hours there, on a wee stool, shuddering cold and
ashamed. She should be doing something. If she took Hyde on face
to face, the younger woman would knock her down, then swear there
had been an accident ... Her ears strained continuously. Once, a door
bumped shut and feet tramped off into silence. Minutes later they came

back, came near, passed on, came back … Presently daylight was white in the frosted window-glass. She straightened her back with a groan. When many voices and footfalls were sounding in the hall, she slipped out and mingled with servers and breakfast-makers. The duty nurses were two young women she scarcely knew.

Her head felt light and empty. Morag was looking at her with her eyebrows raised. When Flo had a chance she went over and whispered to her, 'Later, later.' Findlayson was useless – since the move she was vague and stuttering as though she had taken a shock and aged twenty years in a few months. MacQuarrie was 'available to everyone' at half-past nine. That would be her chance.

When she knocked on the panelled door of his office, his voice called out at once, 'Come in.' A bank of windows faced south across the lush greens of the grassland and the mussel blues of the firth, with the dustier blues of the highlands just in sight beyond the far coast. A smell of unusual cigarettes flavoured the air, fragrant as pipe tobacco. MacQuarrie was sitting behind a broad mahogany desk with a green leather top, looking spruce and well-to-do. He owns us, it struck her – he owns us all. He motioned to a straight-backed chair and when she sat down and was on the point of speaking, he said in a voice that was neither friendly or unfriendly, 'I was expecting you, Miss Campbell. Let us hear your story first, shall we?'

She was stranded, as though on a rock set in deep water. The room had disappeared into a kind of sparkling haze. What had he been told? As she started to speak, her voice was quavering and she cursed herself and tried to be steady.

'When I was at work last night – when I was on duty – in the first corridor – I heard a noise, a noise of distress, so I went into No. 4. And I found that Mr Hunter was disturbed. His bedclothes were in a tangle, and his pyjamas, and I found that his upper leg was bruised – it was very badly bruised – all down one side and some on top. And his chest was worse – his ribs, I mean. He must have been beaten on the ribs.'

The man was listening with no change in his face. Was he smiling, even, or was that just his way? His pad of hair sat neatly on his head, crimped and brassy, not like hair at all. His cheeks shone. She must get through to him.

'His ribs were turning septic, Doctor.'

'That is your diagnosis, is it, Miss Campbell?'

'He had weals on his body. I do not know about the bruises. But they had not been treated.'

'And what precisely do you infer from that, Miss Campbell?' He sounded interested, like somebody discussing a piece of history.

'I smelt his leg.'

'You were smelling patients' legs?'

'This man – Jim Hunter – he is in a sore way. Has he been able for his breakfast?'

He was looking puzzled now, with a crinkle in his forehead. 'Miss Campbell – I am sure that any patients not accounted for in the dining-hall will be attended to in due course. By the trained staff.' His face smoothed out and he clipped his fountain pen into his breast pocket. 'You have come here with a wild tale, and one that I must ask you to keep to yourself if you do not wish to look absurd, or to be in danger of being in breach of your conditions. Which may be the case already.' He looked down briefly at a sheet of thin blue paper. 'According to my information, when you were supposedly on duty last night – an extra duty which had been properly agreed upon and undertaken – you were in fact not to be seen between the hours of 3 a.m. and 6 a.m. Where were you?'

She sat speechless.

'You do not explain yourself. Perhaps you are unable to. I am willing to overlook this lapse, if it is not repeated. You are a maid, and too much should not be expected of you. At your age.' He paused. 'I believe you have a good friend who is not a maid, although you share a room. I wonder if this is appropriate? At all events I will keep the matter under review.'

He looked steadily at her. The room was full of summer light which shone from polished things, the edges of bookshelves, a four-sided book-case on wooden legs, the desk with its square glass inkwell, the varnished yellow window-sills. He was still looking at her, with an enquiring air, his eyebrows raising his forehead into three straight furrows. She could say nothing, and left the room as though she was stepping on smoothed wet rock, as though she was about to slide and fall.

Chapter 48

She must tell Morag. Bringing the words out was harder than getting a great stone out of the ground. Night after night she tried. Each time she felt too weak for it – to face again the filthiness of that night, to tell about her defeat at MacQuarrie's hands, to have it all made worse by Morag's laments – or her bits of Christian consolation. She was forever looking at Flo, as though she wondered if she was ill. The quietness of their early nights, in which they said little, was adding a helplessness, a paralysis to the trouble itself. And they were only at the edge of the thing – they were not being tortured themselves. Who else was Hyde tormenting? Who were her henchmen? At this rate she would be able to look nobody in the face.

She would tell Morag, tell her everything, by the end of the month – a promise to herself, which she broke. The muscles of her neck felt tired with keeping her face ordinary, her tongue under control. In September, with the sunlight filtered through invisible mist and every room in the south and west of the building gentled by its pale gold light, raised voices echoed down the stairwell and were garbled from mouth to mouth – 'He's ill … Matron! Matron! In No. 4. Where's Doctor?'

Bertha had reared her head up like a horse about to bolt and Flo saw her face go pulpy as though it would melt off her bones.

'All right, Bertha,' she just had time to say. Then she was hurrying up the stair. Through the doorway of No. 4 she could see Hyde bending over Jim Hunter's bed. In the entry Murdina was standing like a guard. Flo brushed straight past her as she looked furious and lifted her arm. The man was lying on his back, motionless, his jaw dropped. His face was beaked and thinned in the look that Flo had seen once before, when her mother was laid out for burial. The bedclothes were drawn back, his jacket open and his legs bare. They were unmarked. Hearing the movement behind her, Hyde turned and Flo saw her pink lips part in the merest smile.

'Puir auld bugger,' she said in a comfy voice. 'His time had come.' She was weighing Flo up now, no longer grinning. 'Go you and tell Matron and the Doctor. The sooner he's aff wir hauns the better. Murdina?' She gave the smallest nod and the woman went off at once.

That night the words came out at last. 'They killed Jim Hunter.'

A night-light was glimmering between them. She turned her head after speaking and saw that Morag was regarding her with a very old, ill look, and a concerned look, as though the sorrow was Flo's own.

'You have been worrying yourself to death. Och Flo, you are the best friend in the world and for many a month I have been seeing that I was losing you.'

Flo reached out, clasped her by the hand, and told her all that had happened, the dead man's injuries, her humiliation at MacQuarrie's hands, the threat to themselves he had hinted at.

'We had best be away, then, out and away like birds over the sea.'

She was waiting for agreement, for a wand to be waved. Flo felt peaceful, purged by her confession. It was true that the place was horrible for them now, and dangerous with it. But how could they live without the roof and the meals? She wanted to fall asleep and had no fire in her to start arguing.

In a deadened voice she said, 'Go – yes – we have to go. When we can. We have not the £100 yet –'

'We are reaching our hands out for it, Flo. And och, it was never more than a number. I will be selling fish until my legs are withered away and you will get the pension when you are not working any more. Think of Sgiach, Flo – think of the place, our place. It must be there. Has your Peggy answered your letter yet?'

'No. No, she may be dead, and who would be telling me?'

'Her husband. You said that he was good.'

'Morag, you know we must go over there for a look. And if we go, there will be no getting back in here. Supposing we wanted to. And in any case –'

She had no need to finish. At that moment they had both remembered the war.

Something will happen … Something will happen and it will make us go at last … If only Peg would write … Maybe the boats with the letters are being sunk by the Germans and nobody is letting on …

'I am swithering.' She had said that aloud, as she sat in the bothy looking out into brown needles, dark-green shadows, the lower branches of firs with dead twigs toothed like beetles' legs. Swithering, like kestrels' wings as they hovered. Like the water of the sea beside an island as the tide set two ways round it, ruffling the surface into a fever. She could no longer stop such flights of thought, or the muttering aloud. At least it only happened when she was by herself. So far. Her peace of mind was gone, even a long, sore, uninterrupted brooding was better than this stammer of half-thoughts, of phrases that fizzed round and round like a fly inside your ear ...

She made herself look steadily at her pad, at the point of her soft black pencil touching it, moving across it. She was drawing a beard, dense and prickly. She was drawing Cooper the Swine from Sgiach who had treated the fisher girls like shite, the man who long before that, on Uist, had been the lord's agent in charge of clearing the clachans. So be it. Cooper. A devil who had flourished in the flames of their houses. Welcome, Mr Cooper. You will make a good figure in my picture.

He would be in a suit, on a horse, with a list in one hand and a torch in the other – his arm would end in a torch, a thick rope's-end soaked in oil. The names and the words would be coming out of his beard like muck spurting from a drain – 'MacCuish – notice to clear. MacPhail – go oversea ...'

It need not be a likeness at all, it would be their whole story in one scene, a telling and a showing. In the upper third, the mask-faces in the clouds, which she had recently sketched onto the new board. In the middle ground, the battle – four houses, five at most, and the struggles between them, some silhouettes, some sharply detailed – a loom being carried out of doors, a woman clinging to a door-jamb. In the foreground, figures – her father, Roddy, Cooper, a bully-boy with a head as naked as a stone – and words lettered onto the spaces between and round their heads. 'Go oversea ... Not be moved ... Murder ... A human chain ... The writs ... Hear me ... Save us ...'

Would the picture not have to be square to make room for all this? She looked out of the door to relieve the pressure in her head. Those shadows between the trunks – were they really dark-green or did she just move the colour with her eyes from the leafage of the trees above? A dark shape was blotting the sparkle of the sea beyond the trees, a person carrying a load – Morag with a creel of fish. She had been up the coast to Ardessie, desperate to resume her trade. She must have been lucky, then. How nice it would be to chat. Morag still did not know where she had found her painting refuge and had never asked, during this cool time between them. Now they had more need than ever to be close.

She went out to the edge of the wood and called. Morag startled and turned, the creel lurched, nearly bringing her down. She recovered with a hefty swing of her shoulders and said, 'Dear heart! You were coming out of the trees there like a ghost.'

They sat down together on the broken lip of the turf where roots stuck out over the shingle and talked while the last flies of the year buzzed over the stiffening fish and Morag chased them away with a branch of fern.

'You have found a supply, then. Are they working in spite of the submarines?'

'They fish close in-by and take no harm. Maybe those devils are frightened by the crowds of battleships at Scapa. We might be safe enough after all if we got a wee boat with two pair of oars and rowed ourselves to Sgiach.' She chuckled like a girl.

'I heard there were MacPhails up at Ardessie, and a MacInnes. Are they island folk at all?'

'I was meeting MacKays and MacLeods, mostly, and a fine wifie called Fraser, who must be a hundred year old, near-about, and she was baiting a line as spry as though she was born since the Old Queen died. I think their people mostly came down out of the glens when Sellar's fire-brigade were at it. Did you ever hear tell of him – the man who gutted the clachans for the Black Duke? The young ones just now were chattering in English but I heard the auld folk use the Gaelic to each other once or twice. They would not use it with me, though.'

'Have they lost themselves, then?'

'I think they are happy here. And making a shilling at last. I said to Betty Fraser, "Are you comfortable?" And she just patted her side and said, "I am fine as long as I have a piece of sack to put on the rock." So I let the thing lie, Flo.' She looked into her friend's face, anxious for agreement. 'It is all past and a long while past, Flo – the bad years on the Island. A time to kill and a time to heal, for all go unto one place ...'

They parted quietly. It was dark in the bothy as she took her last look at the picture on the wall. She could barely make out the faces in the sky – Mary, Morag, Bertha. Bertha's fearing look made her suddenly uncomfortable. For weeks she had been backing away from a proper talk with her. It would not be easy. She felt the eyes of Hyde and Murdina on her all the time, whether they were or not. Bertha herself looked cowed, she had grown still heavier and moved about as though she was carrying a crushing load. Throughout suppertime and in the evening, as the whole place slumped towards weariness and sleep, Flo tried to stay alert. Bedtime had moved earlier and earlier. Lolly and company disappeared into the far wing as soon as they had eaten, coaxed by Jekyll and chivvied by Hyde with short, gruff words like a herd to his dog. The bulk of the patients went off up the stair without being told, filing past the wall of antlers with a soughing of groans and heavy breaths like families at a funeral.

As usual Bertha was last. No, Ella was still sitting in a dark corner, speaking distinctly in an undertone, each phrase coming in a little rush – 'And Moses gave unto them, even to the children of Gad, and to the children of Reuben, and unto half the tribe of Manasseh ...' Bertha began to get up from a sofa, heaving fruitlessly for a minute, then letting herself slide off it, rolling onto her haunch, reaching round and raising herself with both hands planted on the seat. As she struggled upright, Flo helped her and said in a whisper, 'Are you all right, Bertha? How are you doing?'

Bertha stayed put for a while, supported on her hands. Her breaths were snoring. Wetness fell on the back of Flo's wrist. 'Mushn't shay, Mishus Cam'l. She sobbed. 'Mushn't shay naething'. Mushn't.'

Flo reached round with her hanky and wiped Bertha's face. 'I am your friend, Bertha. And Morag is your friend. It will be all right, Bertha. You tell me, and we will make it right.' Mothering words were coming from her, welling out of her own helplessness and fear.

'And Beth-nimrah, and Beth-haran, fenced cities: and folds for sheep,' said Ella from her corner.

Footsteps sounded from the kitchen and from the corner of her eye Flo saw Morag come into the room in a hurry.

'Hyde and Murdina are coming down the back stair.'

Between them they got Bertha upright. When they held her by the waist she winced, then said, 'All ri' now, Mishus Cam'l,' and smeared at her face with her hands.

'... and took it, and dispossessed the Amorite that was in it.' Ella's voice was unchanging, the phrases scurrying out of her mouth.

Hyde came in, Murdina just behind her. She never wore her old dull look these days, her eyes flashed all over the place as though looking for a quarrel. She had taken to curling her hair into fat grey rolls.

'That patient's late to bed. Get her oot o' here, Murdie.'

Murdina got hold of Bertha and began boosting her up the stairs as though she was wrestling a sheep onto the shearing floor. Bertha gasped, then started hauling herself up by the banister.

'These are the journeys of the children of Israel,' muttered Ella, 'which went forth out –' Her voice ended in a sudden breath as Hyde whisked her chair from under her and ordered her fiercely, 'Oot o' here – up the stair.' She turned to Flo and Morag. 'Trouble, Campbell?'

'Oh – Bertha is often upset.'

'She'll be worse upset if she disturbs the others. Or gin ye coddle her. Noo, have ye nae beds tae gang til yersels?'

Chapter 49

In the middle of the winter a letter came from Peg.

Candlemaker Row,
Sgiach town
February 11th 1918

Dear friend Flo,
That was good to hear last year that your friend is alive yet and
come into your life. – All safe here we had a scare when the older
men would be called for the War Hugh's youngest brother Hamish is
forty and six, in the end all right. – We have our health no coals and
too few men to be cutting and bringing home the peats. – Hughie
Beg is growing he needs his father's trousers with the ends tacked up.
– You say you are bound for Sgiach one day, good luck, bad luck to
the War. – A Balta woman married here was saying they have laid
mines in the sea from Orkney to Norway how does she know? – We
will all be ceilidhing when this is over.

Your friend,
Peg
X X X

If she told Peg what they were in the midst of at Dunaldie, she
would never believe it. Nobody would. A medical superintendent and a
qualified nurse would cover everything in long words and leave an orderly
and a long-standing inmate looking like mad people. For many months
it had been all creeping about as soundlessly as you could manage, and
listening at half-open doors, and wondering if a sharp cry from down the
corridor was the noise of torment or just the usual bickering.

If only the bruises on Jim Hunter's legs and ribs had still been
showing, there would have been some evidence. If only Bertha would
speak out. They must be harming her – she was moving about like a
stunned beast – she had pained, surely, when they touched her waist?
In this place of badness your horrors began to mingle with the real
happenings. Was this how madness came on? Or the struggles of very old
folk, trying to hear and see and hearing and seeing only their demons?

As she walked down the best corridor – which someone had dubbed the Royal Mile – between the glossy mahogany of MacQuarrie's door, glinting russet like sunlight in peaty water, and a massive mirror with gilt pillars and a carved frame, she heard low voices from the room. She glanced at the mirror, still walking on. Through inches of gap where the door had not been pushed to, she saw Hyde perching on the end of MacQuarrie's desk and leaning towards him. She looked back down the Mile – nobody about. She listened – nothing but the clashing of dishes and cutlery as one o'clock dinner was prepared. She sidled back as near the door as she dared and listened intently.

'... whatever you like,' Hyde was saying in an excited, confiding voice. 'Of course you can and who can stop you? If ony ither body comes interfering, just throw your weight about.' She giggled. 'I ken fine what that feels like.'

MacQuarrie's reply was too low to catch. Hyde laughed again, a throaty chuckle. From his next words Flo caught only '... when *she* comes north.'

'*If* she comes. Never fear – I'll haud my tongue, dearie, gin you haud yours an' we can still hae wir fun wi' the brutes.'

A sound of furniture moving. Flo darted past the doorway, glancing through it. MacQuarrie was rising to his feet behind his desk. Hyde was leaning right across it and running her fingers down his cheek.

So the two of them were at it. And they had baffled some enquiry, maybe the Annual Visitation by the Board. It was the last indecent phrase that made her grue. 'Fun wi' the brutes' – what would Morag make of that? In most of her moods she still refused to believe that when Hyde said 'the brutes' she meant the patients. She knew when Flo was unsleeping, though. That night as they lay in the dark, saying nothing, Morag's voice came whispering – why was she whispering? Hyde's quarters were many rooms away at the far end and anyway she was probably in MacQuarrie's bed by now ... It was like hearing Morag think – 'The poor souls. Suffering worse than if they were thrashed with whins. Flo?'

'Yes?'

'Do you know, Flo –' She stopped, then went on, 'Do you know that when I went to help Bertha with her bath, she would not be letting me see her take off her shift. And she was never shy, the gentle creature that she is. So I said to her, "Bertha dear heart, are you managing, now?" And she just turned away from me and sat herself on the edge of the bath until I had shut the door behind me.'

The darkness was lying on Flo's nose and eyelids like a mask of lead. She opened her eyes as widely as she could to let the bad things escape and leave her be.

'We will get the evidence,' she said at last. 'We will see with our own sight what is going on and when we have the evidence we will go to – we will go to the – the police station up at Tarbat.'

She disbelieved it as she said it. Two old women with tales of torture from an asylum – tales little different from what most folk thought it was like here anyway ... Morag seized on the hope and said in a less unhappy voice, 'Aye, aye, that is the way of it, it is a mercy one of us is clever. We will creep in at night, when you are not supposed to be on duty, and see for ourselves, and ...'

Her ideas failed her then. At least they had the ghost of a resolve now, and at least they were worried at the same time.

Maybe she would never paint again. Or not here. She should have started working with the gurrlses again, she had been beaten too easily. If they had still been together in a wee club inside the hospital, maybe the hard hands and the bitter minds, the Hydes and Murdinas, would have had their will less easily ... In the small hours these supposings stung her until she longed for daybreak. Now they came at her before she had slept at all. Hard dints hit the window – flung stones, rattling down onto the sill. She sat bolt upright. Morag had started out of a snore, she was saying in a thick voice, 'The house is afire! What?'

Out there nothing could be seen – except, in the middle distance, a light in the castle doorway. The building should have been invisible in its black-out.

'Something is going on.' She was putting on a skirt and cardigan over her nightie, pulling shoes onto her bare feet.

'Ach, Flo – '

'Come on. We are needed there.'

They walked up to the castle as fast as they could, shuddering through and through in the unseasonable frost. The heavy door was standing inches open. A single light burned in the hall, making a tangle of spiky shadows among the deer antlers. Somebody moved upstairs and there was a mingling of voices, shrill and grumbling. They mounted into the half-dark, still shaking from the cold. In the corridor with no doors it was as like a graveyard as it had ever been. The voices were speaking from the attics. As they started up the last stair, a scuffling came nearer and nearer, bumping down the steps.

The two of them looked at each other, aghast. Morag dragged Flo into the tower alcove at the bend of the stair. A stink made them gag. Bulky shapes were bustling past them. Bertha was being dragged down, feet first, her head thumping on each carpeted tread. Hyde had her by the ankles, Murdina by the arms. She was heaving and gasping and her voice burst out hoarsely, 'Mishus Wyllie – pleash – I'll niver wet again – I'll niver – '

'Ye're nae just wet, Kemp. Ye're foul.'

The three of them struggled on past and down. Bertha was sagging, limp, as they hauled her into a bathroom (the lord's private bathroom, off the master suite).

'Come on.' Morag was gripping Flo's hand so strongly that she wanted to cry out. They went down to the half-open door of the suite and saw, in the tiled white interior of the bathroom, Bertha half-naked in the bath, her nightie shrouded round her head, her backside dripping. Murdina was running the water. Hyde was standing over them, her back to the door.

As they watched in a numb sickness, Murdina reached down with her hands and began to scour at Bertha's thighs, shoving her, slapping her, feeling into her. Bertha arched up, her voice came in a wild groan, Hyde twisted the cloth more tightly round her face, the woman shuddered and shuddered for long seconds, then went loose and fell down into the bath. Hyde wrenched the nightie further up from Bertha's shoulders. Her white back was striped red with weals. Hyde nodded to Murdina and she took up a long-handled bath-brush … Morag broke forwards through Flo's restraining arms and ran headlong into the room.

'Devils you are – devils – leave her be! Get out!' She wrenched the brush from Murdina, lifted it to hit her, then flung it behind the bath. She knelt down, with Flo beside her now, and the two of them started to raise Bertha out of the mess of clothes and water. She was a dead weight and they laboured helplessly. Flo's head was stabbed with pains and she felt herself dragged backwards by her hair. She was in Hyde's grasp, her gorge swirled with nausea, her mind was starting to faint away. Hyde let her drop against the door. Murdina and Morag had been wrestling, their grey and white hair was hanging in hanks and they were breathing desperately.

Bertha's eyes were opening. She looked across, saw Flo, and let out a long, pitiable wail that rose and died.

'She is hysterical. She may need the jacket. Get the doctor.'

Through the pangs in her scalp Flo would not believe what she was hearing. Surely even MacQuarrie, if he saw the state of Bertha's back … Morag had turned back to the bath and was smoothing down Bertha's nightie and wiping her face with a cloth. Murdina had turned away to a long mirror in a brown frame and was patting her curls into place. Her face was its stolid, sallow self again, except for a flush on her cheekbones.

'Leave the patient,' Hyde said calmly. Then as Morag went on sponging, 'Leave her!' Her voice was like a lash. Bertha put her arms round Morag's neck, pulling her down. As Murdina turned to go at her, Morag straightened up with a great sigh and stood still, on the verge of tears.

Flo seethed with threats and accusations, they were torturers and perverted evildoers, she would tell the others, the saner ones, and they would – they would … They were all as helpless as mice, themselves included. Herself they could sack and send away, and Morag they could break down again until she was as scatterwitted as she must have been in that old worst time.

'Get the doctor, Murdie,' Hyde said again. The woman looked with a dead face into Flo's eyes and went out. 'Mind this noo, the pair o' ye. I'll say it just the once. Ye ken fine who's the boss in this place. An' him an' me's like that.' She held up two fingers. 'It's a guid place, this, we hae few deaths an' the Board thinks we're braw. They're a' clever men an' they will ken what tae mak o' a couple of doitit auld carlines wi' bees in their bonnets. Campbell – you'd be better takin' the pension an' awa' aff tae end yer days in a comfy slum in town, or in a coo-shed in the Hielans wi' yer ain kind. But if ye maun stick wi' yer friend, just – keep – yer – mooth shut.'

She had brought her face to within inches of Flo. She smelt of scented soap and talcum powder, her pink complexion was sleek as the icing on a cake. Flo stared her out and she turned away with a disgusted breath.

'The twa o' ye, while you're here, get Kemp oot o' her soss.'

Bertha shrank back and began to wail again. Hyde took two quick steps towards her and she at once went quiet, bunching up her lips in a child's mime of holding her tongue. Between the three of them they raised her, sat her on the side of the bath, and helped her to step out.

'Bed-time,' said Hyde in a mockery of a mother's voice. Bertha held out her hand to Flo. She squeezed it and Bertha left the room. They heard her feet fall heavily on the stairs.

'She will catch her death in her wet clothes,' Morag protested.

'Wet clothes – her bed is worse. But,' Hyde looked at them with a grin, 'she'll nae dae it again. Noo then, are ye waitin' for the doctor?'

Chapter 50

They would work their hardest – as hard as their joints would let them – and store up their money, and as soon as the seas were safe again, they would be off. This bothy of hers was only a hidey-hole – how daft, how shaming to have ever thought of it as a studio! She had sat here for three hours now, it must be easily that, while the long summer evening shone on behind the trees, and she had done nothing. She felt useless, to be so idle – where had this come from? Allan and Mairi had never schooled her to feel wicked if she mooned about for an hour or two – although there had been little enough time to spare once they were all slaving on the Committee Road …

She could hardly see the big picture any more, the sheets of sketches she had pinned onto their possible places on the board were white glimmers and little more. Cooper the Swine and Flora Matheson, big faces in the foreground, glaring at each other. The cloud-masks at the top. Nothing in between yet. Her arm felt lazy and leaden. She tested it for weakness – worrying about being ill was as bad as the illness itself – no, the muscles tightened as much as they had ever done. A stroke that felled her finally might be a relief … She would never let on to Morag that she had thought such a thing.

'Why sulk here any longer?' She had said that aloud. She sat and listened in a twinge of worry. Madness – no eavesdropper here, how could there be? The cold was stealing up from her feet into her legs. An owl hooted, a musical note, not eerie at all. Then another, nearer, short and fierce, a blade of sound as curved as a claw in the neck of the mouse … She should have sunk herself into work on the picture. Nothing to show for a precious evening's freedom. A decision appeared in her head – pack up all the work once again and make ready to flit. A chance could open up for them at any time – they were saying the fighting would be over and done with long before the year's end (they had said that every year).

Morag should be back from Ardessie by now. She had taken to going every day and always came back with something. 'If I am killing myself, well, I was never meant to be one of the lilies of the field.' Flo took the sheets from the board, put them inside a portfolio, and stowed it in one of the oilskin packages. If she did something practical on each spare day, their departure might begin to happen.

There was Morag with her burden, coming along the shore. As they walked on to the castle, she could sense that Morag was full of some happening earlier in the day.

'They are grand people, just grand,' she said presently. 'It was like being back at home. When Betty speaks, it is Mother living again.' (And Flo had just been looking at Flora Matheson outstaring Cooper in the picture, shoulders hunched and fists on hips.) 'We could live there, Flo. No, no, how could we settle among strangers? But it would be strangers on Sgiach, mostly. Or on Uist. Unless there are a few strays left there yet who never went to Australia.'

'In the West we could use our own tongue once again, daily-day, not just in a corner at night.'

'They were using the Gaelic in the Free Kirk at Ardessie not so long ago.'

'And now?'

Morag said nothing. She was still simmering and soon she said, 'It is a good place, Flo, and you would like it. You could sit above the port and be as pleased as a bird on its nest. And it is full of stories – wherever you go you are just walking over the dead. I came past the Hillock of the Ghosts just now and because Betty had told me the tale of it I knew I must throw a stone into the hollow on its top and good luck would come of it. Our luck will be on the turn this year, Flo – I feel it happening.'

She looked at her friend for confirmation, or an assurance that she had not been blethering, and Flo could do nothing but take her arm as she trudged forward with her hands locked onto each other, bracing her load.

For weeks and weeks they had been wondering, until it deaved at them like heartburn – who had thrown the warning stones at the window on the night of the offence? The patients seemed more than ever locked up and behind their faces – red, inflamed ones, pasty yellow ones as dull as old dough, masks in which every line and quirk was bitten as deep as though with a blacksmith's tool. There was a quietness in the place now, like after a death – unless they were fancying it. If only there had been a matron with some pith in her. Findlayson came out from her room as little as she could and when she did she reeked of sherry and her face was a white, shapeless thing, like raw fish.

Perhaps it was Ella who had thrown the pebbles? She was too besotted with her Bible. Or Madge the unvisited? Inside her was the woman who had drawn the angel-babies falling out of the sky. Now she was mute as ever and even more helpless. On most days she sat waiting to be fed and under the new government of Hyde and Murdina nobody dared to cut up her portion of pressed meat or lift her spoon to her mouth. She sat, staring downwards at her hands in her lap, her old brown cardigan slipping off her shoulders.

Why need it have been one of the gurrlses? Why not any one of the fifty or sixty souls? Not one of the men, that was unlikely, they were the most helpless of the lot. Tam the Strap, who had had his belt taken away when he had tried to hang himself with it a few times and now he shambled about with the front of his shapeless green tweed trousers bunched up into his giant knuckles swollen with rheumatism and chilblains. The Laird – he was supposed to have been a shopkeeper in Tain who had been crazed by ruin – he strutted about, stared out of the long front windows at the lawns between the castle and the shore, and bellowed suddenly, 'Where is Sellar? Where is my man? Clear out the debtors! Clear them out!'

Flo and Morag argued and argued the case, turning their helplessness into reasoning that never reached an end. 'Only the gurrlses would have thought about us as the ones who could do anything … If some other body threw the stones, then they are all looking to us for a lead … No, no, they do not care, most of them – they cannot care, they are past it … Mary is not past it but surely she would have said a word to us by now? Lolly, then, she is as sharp as ourselves … Lolly is special, why mention her? You know full well the others could be in another century for all they understand … They can still be suffering … I never said they could not suffer …'

They were jarring on each other because they were prisoners. And because they wanted to flee and leave the mess behind them. They had no need to say this. Each knew it was what the other had in the very centre of her mind and all through her body, making her itch with indecision.

Flo badly wanted to soothe Bertha, to ease well-being back into that bruised, discomforted body. She should be given a liking for herself again, a desire to be less bulky, less incapable. She must be stealing bread, or eating porridge scrapings from the pots and fat from the dinner plates. Her eyes had curved brown smears under them and she rocked all the time now, when she was not lurching from side to side in her chair, smoothing and smoothing her skirt round her thighs. When Flo briefly stroked her hair as she went past her in the day-room, she flinched violently and looked up with a face of rage that made her jowls swell and her eyes turn bloodshot.

What was happening in the corridors now, during the short summer nights when yellow overspread the firth only a few hours after the west had lost its salmon glow? The watches kept by the maids had been stopped the day after the offences in the bathroom. Rumours crept about that there were noises and scuffles along the corridors after dark. 'It's oot o' hand – fair oot o' hand,' said Jean in a gruff whisper as she stood at the kitchen bins with Flo, scarting uneaten tripe and turnip from the stacks of chipped white plates.

'What –' Flo began to say. Jean nudged her so hard that she was winded and both women felt that Murdina was behind them somewhere, listening, watching.

No more could be said that evening, and no more was said as the watchful, uneasy weeks dragged by. Was Jean an ally? Had she thrown the pebbles? On a night when Flo was too oppressed by an uncanny, balmy smell of autumn warmth to sink easily into sleep, she heard Morag speaking from the other bed and seized greedily at the chance of conversation.

'… worse than ever,' she heard Morag mutter in the thick, lightless atmosphere that smelt of soda from some scouring of the pitch-pine walls. 'Worse than ever – worse than ever.'

'Morag? Tell me, dear, has there been another offence?'

'Awful – awful. The fire will bring the roof down. Father!' Her voice had become a screech. She was raving, confused. Flo struck a match and lit the night-light. As the dim yellow glow spread through the room, she saw her friend roll over and stare at her with enlarged eyes, then roll back and try to throw the bedclothes off. Her white, coarse hair was greyed in streaks with sweat and her face was wet all over. She had had 'a cold in her head' for a day or two and had continued to make the trip to Ardessie for fresh fish. There had been word of an 'epidemic fever in town', repeated by carters and tradesmen who brought supplies to the castle. Chinese 'flu' – the weird foreign phrase had been disquieting – it had been so outlandish that nobody had paid it much attention.

Flo rose from her bed, soaked a towel with water from the jug, and laid it onto Morag's forehead. At the cold touch she shuddered violently, grabbed Flo's forearm, and said in a hoarse voice that seemed to come from some other body, 'Worse than worse – the fire – save the children.' As the towel grew less chill against her skin, she lay back on the pillow and took Flo's hand in a gentler grip. 'Rub my neck, dear. It is hurting me.'

The night passed – the candle burnt out – Morag clutched Flo's hand, and relaxed – woke, and slept. Her breathing was too fast, too chesty. As grey day shone through the window, she seemed to fall deeper asleep out of exhaustion. Flo felt light-headed, her thoughts plunged into dreams and up again in sickening heaves – a rocking sea, its waves jumping straight up into torn-off spouts – a long, long fall, she was struggling to spread wings that would not open …

When she woke finally, she laved her face in water, made sure that Morag was at peace, and walked across to the kitchens. Three of the maids were putting the big kettles on to boil. Bridget looked round with a cross face and said, 'You rose from your bed at last. Are you ill as well?'

'As well as who?'

'Jean. And Wyllie herself, and a terrible lot of patients.'

Flo went through into the hall, and thought for a moment she was deaf. It was too quiet. In the near silence the well of the staircase seemed loftier than ever, the antlers on the wall more bony and more alien in their deadness. The usual groans and garbled voices were few, with vacant intervals between them. 'Bugger off, Jock – bugger off!' That was Johnny Downie, starting the day in his usual helpful spirit. A few heavy steps. 'Dinna hit me! Help me!' Long moments of silence broken by a woman's crowing laugh.

At the head of the stairs Ella appeared, moving as calmly and unseeingly as if she was walking in her sleep. As she came down step by step, Flo could hear her saying, '… wash thy face, that thou appear not unto men to fast, but unto thy Father which is in secret …' Each of her cheeks had a red glow in it. When she reached the hall she collapsed and lay on the coconut matting that had been substituted for the owners' Turkish carpet, her hair winding out from her head like seaweed on a beach.

Perhaps two-thirds of the usual company had gathered by the time breakfast was being doled out. Some of them had red eyes and throaty voices, as the influenza started to fume through their heads and chests.

The remainder looked more at ease than they had done for months. They were not looking over their shoulders for fear Hyde was there, at the ready to shove or slap or scoff. Murdina was slumped and hang-dog, her expressionless yellow face giving out no clue whether she was angry or unhappy or afraid. Some patients were giggling – opening the fronts of their dresses to scratch their armpits – throwing crusts of bread or snatching them from each other's plates. Nurse Goulding appeared briefly, said sharply 'Shush, the lot of you – Doctor MacQuarrie can hear you from his study' – then disappeared again as a painful cry came from somewhere upstairs.

When Flo went to see how her special friends were, she thought she could smell the disease in the air – phlegm, acid skin, polluted cloth. In Bertha's attics the black-out had been left across the skylights. Three of the beds were still occupied. Bertha lay on her side, staring at the doorway. As Flo came near, she looked horrified – unblinking for more than a minute – then, as Flo reached out her hand to her cheek, she squeezed her eyes tight shut and turned away.

From the other beds, gasps of quick breathing. On a bedside locker a glass of water lay on its side, dripping. At one skylight the dark cloth was flapping with the noise of a bird panicking to escape. She looked at Bertha's clump of black hair for a moment, thinking – when she has recovered, she will still be ill. Hyde's spell has turned her nature … She walked out and down the stair in a cramp of grief. She would break the damned rules, go right through into the south wing, and see if Lolly needed help.

On the connecting stair she met Mary coming up, her wig squint above her eyebrows. They stopped as they met and Mary said at once, 'Hyde is real ill. Do ye nae think it's a judgement?' She looked younger than usual, unafraid, and Flo knew it was she who had warned them with the pebbles. 'And d'ye ken whaur she's bedded? In the wee spare room aff MacQuarrie's!' Her eyes were bright with glee. The two women hugged and Flo went on down to the far room.

It was as peaceful as a dovecote – sunlit quietness rippled by murmurs of 'Oh' and 'Oo'. Under her bedclothes Lolly made no more of a heap than a few sticks would have done. Her eyes were open, her fingers above the counterpane were flickering like bleached grasses in the stir of the air. Her lips stretched sideways, her eyes widened more and more

– she was greeting Flo – her 'Oh' sound was grating now like a bird being throttled. Flo wove her fingers into Lolly's and let their hands waver together until the ill woman weakened, the tension went out of her, and she lay back with her eyes shut, breathing quickly and quietly.

For weeks on end the temperature of the whole place rose and fell, as though the walls and furnishings were ill themselves. Nurse Goulding suddenly spoke with a voice as hectoring as Hyde's, then calmed down again into her usual sonsie self. Flo heard her own tongue whipping out orders as she had never done in her life before. 'Sheets – get me *six* clean sheets. Clean *up* that mess.'

The bedrooms, the kitchens, even the corridors looked at the end of each day like the scene of a back-street fight. Brooms and carpet sweepers lay about like surrendered weapons, swathes of soiled laundry heaped up in corners like uniforms stripped from casualties. It was as well the first-floor rooms lacked their doors – the fever of four or five or six ill people, the shut windows and closed curtains, bred up a sick heat that made her sweat when she went in to sponge and clean and tidy the bedclothes round huddled bodies. Surely MacQuarrie would give orders soon to move people down out of the sweltering lairs of the attics …

She hated everything she had to touch – sticky glass tumblers, damp sheets, badly scoured pans with scabs of food on their sides. So many staff were in their beds that the whole habit of the place was shaking apart. She no longer knew whether she herself was a maid or a nurse – although she knew that what she had better not do was venture near, let alone cross, MacQuarrie's threshold to smell out what was brewing there.

When she went back to the steading to see how Morag was, the ill woman lifted her arm an inch or two, if she felt better, or just lay there if she had relapsed. 'The shoulders,' she groaned once. 'Oh, oh, the shoulders. No! Do not touch me, dearie – I cannot bear –'

If they went on sharing a room, she would come down with the flu herself. There was nothing else for it – the disease was everywhere.

Goulding had taken charge now and flew round the castle eighteen hours a day, keeping tabs on the supplies of fresh food, inspecting the toilets and getting disinfectant herself from the store if she found anything foul. Early one evening Flo smelled tobacco at the back door and was amazed to find the nurse sitting on a stone trough that had held flowers and smoking a cigarette.

'Sit you down,' she said when she saw Flo hesitating in the doorway. 'The fresh air is a boon – fresh air and a puff of this.' She held up her cigarette and looked at it with affection, then blew three rings of smoke that gradually lost their shape in the moist gloaming. 'You're looking younger, Flora – that brown skin of yours would become a woman half your age. Nothing like work, eh? Plenty of work and not too much money.' She laughed, a short, tight laugh. 'No, if nobody spoils you, you can keep your own character. Whatever that may be. Take this lot here. How many of them were born sweet and then ruined before they could walk? Although, mind you, if the skull can come out the wrong shape, so can the brain.'

'Is that where the cruelty begins?'

The nurse's face lost all expression. Then she let out a stream of smoke with a dry hiss of her lips. 'Oh, that. There is a lot of it about. If it comes your way, all you can do is keep your head below the parapet. As the boys would say.'

Her voice had gone jaunty and Flo saw her green eyes and lightly-freckled milk-white face glimmer as though with a remembrance of sexual pleasure. It made her look harder, not softer. And her words had been a warning, more or less. No doubt she was nursing her colleague Hyde in the boss's quarters. Maybe MacQuarrie kept both of them in his tender toils, like a sultan.

Chapter 51

She was so used to the sound of the place, its rising and falling with the hour of the day, its clattering, its buzz, that a change in it was as keen as a clock striking. Now, amongst the lowered general noise at this time of illness, she caught a quickening – a mixture of calls and footsteps from the far end. Something was wrong. Minutes later Bridget came down the stair, her little white goblin face screwed up. 'That Lolly – she has *died*.' It was as though she was angered at an insult.

Flo started up the stair. What could she do? She had no right, she was not Lolly's sister, or her mother, hardly a friend, even. She must at least make sure that the dead woman was at peace. No good – the door through to the south wing had been locked. At the end of the afternoon Lolly was wheeled past the kitchen doorway on a canvas trolley. Her nightie might have had no body inside it, it lay so limp and slight. Her arms had been crossed on her breast and her fingers were rigid and separate, like the teeth of two ivory combs, as though she was still gesturing. The two men in charge were strangers in black coats. The sound of a motor came through the front door as some kind of vehicle drove off.

This became familiar. Johnny Downie died, too choked in the chest to utter a last 'Help me'. Ella died, the words of the Bible silenced in her mouth during her last four days. Tam the Strap died. And a dozen others who were just faces or names to Flo. She was reluctant to bring such news to Morag as she convalesced. She knew anyway. One night when Flo came in late in the evening and sat down on the bed without a word, Morag said, 'What is happening to the poor souls? Bad, is it? Flo, is it very bad?'

'Yes. Lolly. Ella. Tam.' That was all she had the energy to say.

'Poor souls. Poor souls.' Flo expected her to talk on, to crown it all with a fine old saying. No word came and they fell asleep exhausted.

Why am I so well, Flo found herself thinking, on many mornings as she came out of sleep unwillingly. Why did I not die of ship fever or scurvy on an emigrant boat? Or smallpox on Cape Breton? We pick our way through the waters, among the submarines – if nothing hits us, it is luck, just luck.

As Flo went past the door of MacQuarrie's suite, Bridget came flying out in a flush of glee. As Flo was thinking, Oh no, she is in the harem too, the girl hugged her and danced her round in a whirl of steps.

'It is all over! The Doctor said. There is an armistice.'

'What is an armistice?'

'They have stopped fighting! Why is your face so long?' The girl was pouting. 'The boys will all be coming home. There were be ceilidhing on the island. I have had no letters in a year. But now I will go across for a holiday, or maybe get out of this pigsty altogether and go down for a job in Glasgow when my brothers come back to the mills.'

'Is it true? How can we be sure?'

'The Doctor heard it on his set. But do not be going in there.' Her face took on its twisted look. 'He thinks that Nurse Wyllie is going to die.'

Murdina was found sitting in the kitchen with a basket of potatoes beside her, her knife dangling from her hand, unused. Dinner was late. When Flo went over to help with the work, the woman looked up with swollen eyes and seemed ready to use the blade on her. Hyde must have died. Murdina's sausage curls were hanging down like the unshorn hanks on a stray sheep. Suddenly she overturned the basket and the potatoes bounced wildly over the floor. The maids and patients who were standing about or busy at the stove started to crow and chatter and shriek.

MacQuarrie seemed unashamed that a woman, one of his staff, had died in his quarters – unashamed, and untouched by her death. He moved about the corridors as usual, taking pulses, checking temperatures with Jekyll, who seemed to be acting almost as matron, ensuring that codeine was still being given to new cases – he seemed as pleased as ever with his mastery of his domain.

When Flo told Morag about his eerie composure, she sniffed and said in her old spirited way, 'Ice, he is – hollow ice – he was born without a heart.' Her eyes were clearing day by day, her voice was strengthening, and she was sitting up and looking eagerly out of the window. A frosty calm had come over the season and the tall features of the castle rose among the foreign evergreens like a picture from Switzerland.

Before Flo went back to work Morag caught her by the arm and said, 'Flo, will you look at that awful place we are living in. Can we go away now? Now that the war is over and done with?'

'You know about that, then.'

'I head the horns braying from along Ardessie way, and then I caught a snatch of chat from the scullery. You were not hiding it from me, Flo? Of course you were not, pay no attention to me – my thoughts are sickening as well as the rest of me.'

'You are a wonder. Your ears are everywhere. If you are back in the world, you had best be up and about and along the shore for something we can eat.'

As Morag pretended to get out of bed, Flo pretended to struggle her back down, then said as she left the room, 'I was only waiting till you were yourself again. In a day or two we can make a plan.'

When Bertha died, the last root seemed to have snapped in the ground. Before the pneumonia overwhelmed her entirely, she lay on her back like a beached sea-creature, propped on pillows, drowsing, startling awake with her eyes huge and dark as though some terror had been creeping up on her. Each rustling breath seemed to tire her out. When Flo found her perfectly motionless, with her forehead still warm, she went along at once to the Superintendent's room, walked in without formality, and said, 'Kemp. Will you come?'

He looked up from his desk with a sharp face, as though minded to tell her off, then got up without a word and came upstairs with his stethoscope. After examining Bertha, he spoke a few words as though to himself, 'Dead. 3 o'clock precisely. Pulmonary oedema.'

'What is that?'

Without turning round, he said in a remote voice, 'Her lungs have filled with her own fluid.' He drew the sheet up over Bertha's chubby face, puckered and sallow with the weeks of illness. 'You will tell Nurse Goulding to make the usual arrangements.' He was still standing between Flo and the bed as though guarding it from her.

'I did nothing. Nothing at all.' Flo heard herself say this and glanced round, feeling a fool. Bridget, sorting laundry, was looking at her with a cross disgust. The other folk in the room seemed not to have heard. They would find her out of her wits one of these days, speaking to people who were not there. Would it be better to die before she came to that?

Fruitless worries. Fruitless guilt about Bertha, who had surely been doomed to suffer her own nature from the cradle up. The chief bully was dead. Her successors would be no worse and might be kinder. The thing was to get Morag on her feet and hale again. Then away, away, away to the West, the two of them, while they could still do for themselves.

Amazing stories were trickling through from town. The soldiers at the barracks had let off their rifles in the air, it had been like fireworks. Some of the officers had been frightened that the guns would be turned on themselves and had stayed in their quarters behind locked doors, blind drunk on brandy and French wine. People had gone off their heads with joy and strangers were lying on top of each other, like animals, in the park, in doorways, in the cattle market.

Flo found Bridget crying desperately in the scullery, dreadful howls, like cats at night. When she heard Flo's step, she looked up and screeched, 'Get out! Get out!' She held out a letter on white paper, in poorly schooled handwriting. Her mother in Eriskay had had word at last from the War Office – three brothers, Iain, James and Sorley, had been killed in Flanders, at a place called Mons. Seven weeks later the youngest, Angus, who was still living at home when he was not at sea, had gone down on a ship the Germans had torpedoed between England and Ireland, a month before the battles came to an end.

'Who will look after Mother now?' Bridget wailed in the terrible high voice. 'Me! Me! Me!' She tore at the breast of her apron, ripping the buttons, and Flo held her by main force, pinning her arms, smelling the salt odour of her face and the pink soap she used, until her throes died down and she curled up against her like a child.

The winter came in with heavy snows before Christmas and they knew they must sit tight, work quietly, and plan their leaving like a pair of soldiers who had been cut off from their comrades. They had to take a shovel back with them at night to dig themselves out again and back across to the castle in the morning. Rounded cakes of snow built up on the branches of the fir trees and sat there, motionless, except when a rook perched on an upper twig and a white lump fell straight down and landed silently on the layered ground beneath. Her bothy would be drifted up and her packages buried. Better that way. They would take little harm until the thaw came, they would be as dry and sheltered as sheep under a drift. If anybody went there, a poacher, a keeper (but most of them were still in the army), she would be able to tell by the tracks in the snow. She waded a few yards in that direction and stared into the bluish glimmer of the half-light under the trees. Neat, dog-like pads of a fox. Four-toed prints of many birds, one trail ending in a churned scuffle. No human traces of any kind.

In the mornings she and Morag lay as long as they could, watching the glittering greyish swathes of frost-fern on the window gradually sparkle into water as the sun came round. No hurry to go to work – the habit of the place had slackened, no new patients had seen sent to fill the places of the many dead and all tasks had become lighter. Surely they would be going back to Craigpatrick some day soon, once the limbless soldiers had been sent off south to some huge repository for the damaged in one of the cities.

'Nurse Goulding,' she said one morning, 'are we here for good?'

'Are you not happy in your work, Flora?' said the nurse in her lightly sarcy way.

Flo said nothing.

'You should make the best of it. There are worse places. And worse masters.' She smoothed down the bib of her uniform as though enjoying the feel of her body beneath it and looked coolly into Flo's eyes, her lips parted in a slight grin that outfaced any rejoinder.

She had written Peg as soon as the armistice had held for long enough to be trusted, saying they hoped to come over 'sometime soon' – not asking for hospitality, almost dreading that it would be offered and they would be beholden. Months passed and no reply came. Were Peg and her man still there? Or were they dead in the epidemic, their children gone into the charge of older neighbours who would not think of writing?

Chilblains grew on her knuckles, lumpy and rosy and itchier than fleas, maddening her until she wanted to throw her hands away. She could not have borne to hold a pencil or even a brush, even if there had been room in her mind for a picture or a part of one to form. Her toes too – she sat flexing and clenching her feet inside her shoes, hotching to rasp the skin off, to reach the heart of the affliction and tear it out.

The sky glared blue as the frost-fog parted – blinded over grey as the next snow came looming over from Norway and poured down like oatmeal, endlessly. For fifteen weeks in a row Morag failed to make the trudge to Ardessie for supplies of fish. She was well enough again but the track was barred by great white groynes of drifted snow.

'I know I am old at last,' she said one night, 'and I know that I will not live forever. Once I would have wished to, when Ranald and myself were in the prime of our lives and singing to each other in our bed. Ach well, the dead know not anything, neither have they any more a reward ... I always used to wonder when they read out that bit, which was not often – I wondered if it was not a sin, although it was in the Good Book.'

'It is too true a saying to be sinful.'

The air one morning smelt of juice – not any more the fuming, earthy bite of frost but the green odours of bark and shoots and moss. A mild breeze was flowing across the head of the firth from the western hills. Their Arctic whiteness disappeared into the greys and blaes of rain-showers. When sunlight shone through again, the snow had shrunk back from everything, tree-trunks, rocks, clumps of daffodil leaves, the tidal water lapping the shingle. The countryside was dappled brown and black with freshly ploughed land or last year's late ploughing laid bare again. Morag took up her creel straightaway and set off along the shore for Ardessie. On the way back she came in past the steading, put down her load, and came up to the bedroom where Flo was resting.

'What have I been hearing at Ardessie?' she began, as though setting out a catechism.

'Good news.'

'Good news on whose behalf?'

'On ours.'

'News of a wedding or news of a journey?'

'News of a journey.'

'A journey east or a journey west?'

'A journey west. Morag – tell me – you met a rich man at the port and he is carrying you away in his golden yacht.'

'Not a rich one but a good one. It is Betty Fraser's great-nephew Angie MacLeod I was speaking to. He had an ulcer so they would not take him for the army. And now – and now – Flora dear heart – it is all going right for us – Flora –' She was stammering and weeping, too full of the news to get it out. 'Angie – brought a boat round – from Barra – the first autumn of the war – and – he could never take it back – and now – he is taking it round to Castlebay –'

'Morag dear, have you booked our passages?'

'He said – I should have asked you first but I thought … I knew that we had one mind between us and one heart – he said there would be room for two old ones with little more of a burden to our backs than the fish in the sea.'

Chapter 52

She had packed her necessaries once again – the canvas bag with her clothes, the shawl, the pretty blouses, some underwear and stockings, the soft leather moccasins that gloved her feet so comfortably, most of her brushes and pencils, her patched purse with £147.10/9d. in tightly folded notes and a coin or two. Morag's treasures and life's savings came to little more. Between them they had carried the packages of paintings and drawings the three miles to Ardessie, two creelsful, burdens that made them breathe heavily. Morag had spoken not a word of complaint. But they had had to leave the board on the wall. Flo did not care – it was in her mind as clearly as the memories that were going into it.

They stood on the jetty beside the glassy spread of the water, high tide in the firth on a morning that stretched its long curve from coast to coast, and looked at each other without speaking. Had they been missed yet at the castle? Were the surviving gurrlses shambling down the corridors, muttering and girning their way into yet another day? Flo felt not a pang of regret now, or guilt or doubt, just a quickening of expectancy, with a cold undertow of misgiving.

To get out of herself she said to Morag, 'We will be going down the Canal, I suppose. I have always wanted to see it.'

'They have to go round by Pentland, to pick up a lad from Scrabster.'

As Flo felt colder still (might MacQuarrie or his minions not come hounding a missing patient?), a voice behind them said, 'Now are you fit and ready, girls?' They turned and saw Angie MacLeod the fisherman with his brother Willy, two men in their sixties, cured by sea-winds, the one with a reddened face and bleached eyebrows like oat stubble, the other with skin like faded mahogany. Willy looked away from them with a shut face. His brother was the talker, pawky and gallant, making a little ceremony of handing them down the slatted plank from the quayside onto the deck of the *Evening Star*. At the sight of the stacked packages Willy looked still less hospitable. Without a word he manhandled them aboard and passed them below. It smelt of aged fish down there, of low tide and creosote and coal-dust and the insides of crabs. It was a long cave with dirty wooden walls whose planks were as dark as the caulking between them.

As the women looked about in the half-dark, trying to find bedding or furnishings or whatever might make the passage bearable, they heard a laugh and saw Angie's face upside down above the combing of the hatch.

'It is a wee bit rough down there. We had to burn the most of the woodwork when we ran out of coal in the winter of '17. Never mind, never mind, there is any amount of sacks for your bed and maybe there is an old rug in the forward locker. And you will be eating with us in the howff. Do you like halibut?'

They dined on the best whitefish as they left the firths behind and beat up the long drag past the bleak lands of Easter Sutherland and Caithness. Black jaws opened in the rocks of the shore and the brothers exchanged looks, Angie sardonic, Willy grim.

'Whaligeo,' said Angie to the women. 'No' the place for me. If you missed your footing going down to the port, you would fall a hundred feet clear and burst when you hit the water. There was a blind man there, he could find his way from the house to the shore by three hundred steps and never go wrong by an inch.'

'They are all blind there,' said Willy. 'Blind or mad.'

'Ach well,' said his brother, 'it would be terrible if we were all the same. Now can we put a bit of good stuff in the furnace and get round Duncansby before we lose the day?'

The black plume bellied out of the funnel and wreathed away to seaward, lying down on the heaving water, whipping upward as a gust took it and thinned it out of sight.

'I never liked the sea,' said Morag, as they squatted in the lee of the deckhouse. 'It took away my Ranald and the twins and killed my joy. "Eternal Father strong to save" – he never bound the restless wave that ever I could see. It only made it worse when they sang that hymn – a surging thing with the sound of lost souls in it. But och, we will maybe get there before we drown.'

'Where?'

Morag looked puzzled.

'Where are we going?' Flo protested.

'The boat is bound for the far end of the Long Island. They are going to be fishing out of Castlebay until the herrings are travelling round to Shetland. Then they will follow them. And so it ever was.'

'So we are going past Uist.'

'And maybe we will be getting off there.'

'If they put in at Lochmaddy.'

They were daring each other to stop playing games and make a choice. In the end it was Morag who laughed first and turned away to find out if the land was still to be seen across the cold ridges of the sea. Soon it would be too harsh to bear out here. Neither of them could face the stink of that den below decks. Their chat was coming slowly now, it was dying out as they both felt full and weary with the seasickness rising in them. It was no use fighting against the weight of her eyelids, the swimming in her head. She heard Morag gag, then get to her feet and stagger. Willy growled through the deckhouse window, 'Not there, woman – over the side.' Morag leaned out and a shining yellow stream came from her mouth. As it floated away gulls swooped onto it and began to feed.

Flo drowsed, her head bowed onto a heap of nets. They reeked of mildew. How could they make a living, fishing with this rubbish? Something was wrong. Were the timbers sound … She woke and slept and woke to see a memory of thirty years ago, the wicked black fingers of Duncansby Stacks poking out of the surge. The boat pitched violently as it rounded the headland and felt the westerly. The sea was as disturbed as though invisible wild animals were trampling it. White water flowered at the bow and the swill of it soaked her feet.

Where was Morag? She dared to clutch her way back towards the stern and peered into the hatchway. Throaty snores – Morag was sleeping out her sickness. Flo joined her in a nest of sacks and coarse grey blankets, swaddling them over herself to send her brain to sleep and quell her thought, her certainty that they had embarked on a terrible mistake that they would never be able to undo. The shell of the boat lurched and creaked, she could not tell which way it would swing as it fell from wave to wave and the water seethed past so near it seemed to be running through her head …

They were perfectly still. She looked out through the hatch and saw a stone jetty above them with a light at the end of it. Yellow images squirmed on the shiny black skin of the water. A slim male figure dropped a canvas bag from the quayside onto the deck and jumped down after it. 'Angus Mòr,' he said and shook hands with Angie. 'Willy John.' A stocky figure on the quay was casting off their ropes. The boat shook as the engine chugged.

'What? Flora! What?' Morag's voice was gruff with sleep. Flo gave in again to the sinking inside her and stumbled through the night, hunted by frightening dreams ... A dog was barking – it was Calum, and he did not know her, just stared with baleful eyes ... Men with moustaches had gathered round her, saying nothing, eyeing her, lifting their hands ... She woke in a muck sweat, starved of air, and went up on deck into a cold blue gloaming, a dawn without colour or opening in the clouds. Astern the coast was leaving them in serried blunt headlands, the limbs of the land chopped off. It was the same ahead. The sea churned itself white against the feet of dark cliffs with broken gullies between them. As she stared at this foreign land, a horse appeared at a cleft in the skyline, galloping, its mane tossing. The gulf dipped steeply towards the water, the animal kept on headlong, stones crumbled under its hooves, it fell forwards, bouncing and flailing. On a flat ledge just above the surf it landed on its side and lay, then reared its head, shook it, struggled to its feet and stood with its forelegs straddling. After a minute it trotted off eastward along the reef below the cliff.

Had she seen that? Was she still asleep and dreaming, and had only dreamt she had wakened? Whoever was at the wheel must have seen it too. In the deckhouse Willy was looking down at his compass and up again at the way ahead. Angie and the youth were nowhere to be seen. She shuddered, as though she had looked through a gap into another world.

Willy could not be confided in, at this or any other time. As the hours passed, the other men too turned in on themselves and kept in a huddle, talking in low voices. Meals were quiet and they were sparse – no more halibut – porridge, hot in the morning, cold cakes of it in the middle of the day, salt herrings at night from a barrel of crusted, old-looking fish that stood in a corner of the galley. Morag tried to talk to the men, about the fishing, about the villages scattered along the coast, strung out on straight roads along the sides of narrow sea-lochs.

'Is that a good place there? Who is living there now?'

'Call it living ... The worst crofts in the country ... A poor, poor place ... Strath Naver people, what is left of them ... ' There was grievance and grudge in their voices – Flo and Morag could not tell who it was they blamed.

At the mouth of a river a tall headland was overwhelmed with sand a hundred feet above the sea. Two broad-winged birds were circling, mewing. An hour later they were steaming past a much broader estuary where sand-bars made a pale gold braiding at the meeting of the river and the sea. More clachans perched along the slope of the moor, then not a house or a croft for many hours until they saw the squat white tower of a lighthouse high up on a fastness of colossal red rocks with gorges between them where the sea jumped in bursts. Soon after, when they glanced back, they saw that the wake of the *Star* had curved – they had changed course. When the sun appeared as a circular yellow glow behind high haze, it was more or less ahead. Their hearts quickened as they realised they were heading south.

'The last stage of it,' said Morag, in a voice that pleaded for encouragement. 'We are just cruising homeward now, my dear. They used to say that on a calm day you could smell the smokes of the Island from fifteen miles away. Do you remember, Flo?'

Flo looked at the peaking and tilting waters of the North Minch, the cold, hard greenish-grey of it. She felt as small as a fly on a floor. The nearer they came to the islands, the less time they had to think some useful thoughts about how they would live. She said, 'Morag – what will we do?'

'I will be kissing the ground and thanking my stars that we have lived to see the day. Do you remember, Flo my darling, that song the Griminish emigrant brought back from Manitoba?' She hummed to recall the tune, then sang in a reedy voice –

'If I had two suits
And a pair of shoes
And the fare in my pocket,
I would return to – '

She broke down before she could sing the word 'Uist' and stood staring ahead of her, tears streaming, her lips laughing.

Flo hugged her and looked over her shoulder at the breadth of the blank horizon surrounding them. They must talk more soon – or else they could walk off into the next part of their lives and starve quietly to death if the necessary miracle failed to come about.

No food was offered that night. They waited and waited for a word from the men. When Morag at last went aft and approached the stern door of the deckhouse, it was shut in her face and she could hear the grunt of a laugh from the men inside. Even her spirits lowered at that and they huddled in the lee of the deckhouse, staring at a single blue monster of a mountain raising its head out of the moors.

When they woke after a cold, restless night with their stomachs griping, and looked out of the hatchway, a long body of land the colour of a faded mussel shell was rising and falling in the west.

'The Long Island,' said Morag in a disbelieving whisper, as though she was saying, The Promised Land.

Ahead of them a group of islets humped out of the water, piebald green and dun. A black bird flew past, neck outstretched, so low its wingtips nearly skimmed the crests of the waves.

'A cormorant. Do you remember, we ate them when it came to the worst.'

'Do not be tormenting me with food.'

This morning, however, the men had relented. Angie put his head out of the door and said, 'There is porridge in the pot.' As they sat supping at the table fixed to the wall, he addressed them with a touch of his pawky manner. 'Now, ladies, we had better be getting down to business. Would you say you had had a comfortable cruise?'

Was there any point in complaining? Morag said, 'We are still in one piece, Angus Mor, and you are a canny skipper right enough. Now, when will we be there?'

'It depends on yourselves entirely.'

'Where we are getting off, you mean?'

'Oh aye, that, and the kind of money you have in mind.'

'It has been a safe trip and we will pay our way.'

'A safe trip and fair treatment, would you agree?'

Flo spoke at last. 'We were hungry last night, although we were all right before.'

'Well now –' Angie was fixing an unwinking stare on them, still with his smile. 'It was a wee bit difficult last night, although I did my best for you. Because, you see, there is no great store of food on the boat – we are poor enough ourselves – and young Dougie there was not expecting to find womenfolk on board with a call on the victuals, which he had great need of himself, young strong fellow that he is. Never mind, never mind, we will not be falling out over a fried egg or a drink of tea if we can just agree the price. 2/6d the meal, each, and £10 a head for the passage – £21.5/-. What do you say?'

'I say,' Flo began, and Morag, hearing her tone, was about to interrupt but Flo would not be checked, 'I say that it would take two months to earn that and we have been two days on your boat.'

'Take it or leave it.' Angie was no longer smiling. 'Take it or leave it, and if we cannot agree, well then, you will just be staying aboard until we do.'

They heard a movement behind them and saw young Dougie blocking the doorway, a raw-boned silhouette.

Silently they counted out the exact money – they had kept their purses on them night and day. Neither could bring themselves to speak, or look at each other. In five minutes a kind of friendship had turned into this bitter brew of threat and enmity. How safe were they now? It was like being at the mercy of pirates. And the man was smiling once again!

'Now, where is it to be, ladies – Tarbert? Or Lochmaddy? Boisdale? Castlebay? We are at your disposal.'

They had passed the Sound of Harris with its islands like stepping stones barring out the everlasting spread of the ocean beyond. They had passed the watery maze of northern Uist with its glistening bogs and lochans. At the first sight of their island Morag clutched Flo's arm with numbing force and seemed about to speak. No words came from either of them. They were not seeing the houses of Hoe Beg or Cheese Bay, the drying-poles for the nets or the creel-buoys in the inlets or the black cattle on the croftland behind the clachans. They were seeing island faces that they knew, Allan and Mairi and Roderick and Alasdair and Alasdair's Flora – these people who might as well be here and there yet, among the low hills of the island, although if they had been they would have been more than a hundred years old.

Flo felt some part of herself fainting, or drowning in the floods of time that poured over her from its source in the long ages before her birth or the birth of anybody she had ever known. She was being carried away. She always had been. She seemed to have chosen nothing. She had made her ways east and north and south and north and west again urged as irresistibly as these geese that were passing over them now in a long, rippling arrowhead. This was nonsense. She had chosen to flee from her gutted home – chosen to dodge out of the hands of the young lord at the Castle – to follow Sandy MacSween to Balta – to leave Richard when he had turned indifferent and cruel. So she had known when a place had finished for her. What she had never found was a way of foreseeing whether there was a life for her at the other end of a journey.

They were leaning together at the base of the foremast, unable to find words for their brimming feelings and thoughts. Soon they were gliding between skerries and islets with green scalps of pasture growing on their crowns. For the last few hundred yards Willy John put the engine out of gear and the almost silent motion of the boat slid over them like a dream. He put it into reverse, the propeller threshed, and they were at the quayside. Dougie came past them, ignoring them. He tied up the boat and the two older men handed the women and their belongings onto the quay. Angie was smiling at them. 'Will we shake hands now, ladies, since we have all kept our bargains?'

They paid no attention to him – although some folk nearby were looking curious – and gave their minds to standing securely on the quay. Its granite setts were still quaking under them with the unsteady movements of the voyage.

Chapter 53

Panic was rising in her, making her swallow convulsively and drily. Morag was as bad, chattering and fussing like a clucking hen. 'We cannot stay here. We will maybe have to stay here for a wee while. Where should we go first? Flora, are you listening?'

Flo was thinking, I have £137 and that is all – how long will it last when we have bought a wee house of some kind and a few sticks of furniture?

Morag was saying in a frantic whisper, 'Do you see that one looking at us like strangers?'

'We are strangers.'

'Somebody must be kind. My Ranald used to say, if the first person who speaks to you is kind, then the place will be all right.'

When they had been sitting on the pile of packages for ten minutes, a middle-aged woman in a maroon coat and matching hat came up to them and said, 'Is somebody meeting you, ladies? Or can I help you at all?'

'We are just waiting,' Flora had begun to say when Morag blurted out, 'We do not know very well what we are doing – you are kind – are there any lodgings here, do you know?'

'You can lodge with me. We are in the old Courthouse – it is just a step.'

'Even a step is hard with the things we have.' Flo pointed to her packages, feeling a beggar again.

'My husband will pick them up in an hour or two. He has a lorry for delivering the coals …'

They sat in a gloomy, comfortable parlour waiting for Mrs Morrison to bring them a cup of tea. Stags looked out from large landscape paintings composed of brownish mists, greyish mists, and waterfalls amongst purplish heather. A photograph of a young man smiling above black robes stood on a well-filled bookcase with glass doors. Outside, in a garden with a high wall round it, the last of the kail crop stood in a bed of black earth, its fretted leaves gemmed with drops of fog. The sudden shelter and hospitality were muffling her thoughts and soothing her almost into a sleep which the landlady's probings could barely penetrate.

'Are you here on your holidays?' she asked them at once. Her eyes were flickering with curiosity.

'We have come back,' said Flo, then stopped. The whole of their story was weighing on her head in a great stack, stifling her. The vagueness of their plans – the sheer lack of them – made her feel a fool.

'Come back, is it? I thought you had the local voice. My husband is from the island – we met in Glasgow. He will want to hear all about you. Have you been away long?'

The weight on her head grew heavier. Morag was saying in her most sensible voice, 'For quite a number of years, Mrs Morrison. I married away. And my friend here went – she went off to work, when she was still a girl.'

'There was a lot of them went away at one time. But Iain will tell you about it in the evening.'

They sat on the sofa, under the looming brownish pictures, and Iain placed his armchair facing them and interrogated them like a judge, a just one who was on their side. 'From the north end, you say. Now was that Trumisgarry, or Grenetote? Skellor – you are Skellor folk! There are MacAulays from Skellor who used to write to my father from New South Wales. They left on the *Pict* in '55. We are not related, but my father had made himself the historian. You are not MacAulays, or McCuishes?'

'I was a Matheson. And she is a Campbell.'

'My father used to tell me about Alasdair Mor, he was said to be the only man who could lift the Great Stone – it is still there in the heather – I saw it when I was a boy.'

'My father.' Morag tapped her breastbone. She was rosy with pride and tearful with it. 'Alasdair Mor was my father.'

'And there was a Campbell – now what was the story? He was a carpenter, and a very clever man – that was the name he had. He was not island, he had come from somewhere on the mainland, and my father said they always wondered if there had been trouble long before. But he was clever. His wife was Mairi MacQueen from Malaclete and they had a daughter, but she disappeared. After the Battle.'

Iain Morrison had paused and was looking dark about the face, as though the evictions and the fighting ten or fifteen years before he was born still gave him difficulty.

'My father,' said Flo in her turn. She was having the extraordinary feeling that she was balancing down a long stone wall and must look neither down nor up for fear of toppling out of control. 'He died there. In the house. When they burned the roof over our heads.'

'It is difficult to understand the cruelty that is in man's heart. And it goes right down through the animal kingdom. Do you know where you are sitting? This was the prison where the four men from Skellor were incarcerated, in the cells at the back there, before they were taken to be tried in Inverness. And my father used to say, he lived nearby, that he *hated* to hear the sound of the prisoners hammering at the oakum when they were doing their labours in the yard out there.' He made a wincing face, remembering his father's disgust. 'Ach well' – he reprieved them all with a long, gruff sigh – 'there is a better spirit in the country today. And not before time. And maybe you will be able to look at the place of the Battle and think that there was something won there after all. I will be going up there on my round tomorrow – you can ride in the back if you will put up with a bit of dirt.'

They sat amongst the belongings and several tons of bagged coal. Iain Morrison had laid down clean sacks for them with a nice air of spreading a handsome rug. The lorry jounced as its wheels ground into each corrugation of the road and brown spray flew past them, driven out of the puddles. They had been arguing since long before the sun got up.

'Now Flo, be reasonable, please, my dear. If we take our things up there, and if we find nothing, then what do we do? There are no buses, you know, and we cannot be finding a grand man like this at every turn.'

'If we stay here we are paying out good money. And we are beholden.' She was surprising herself by the stubbornness of her pride. She had never been like this before. If people gave freely, she had taken. Some other creature had entered her, a thrawn old body with room in its head for one thing only.

'Oh my dear, see sense. We must agree, or – or – *Flo!*' She was almost weeping. 'I never thought that you – it was you that ran from the place and now you are hurrying back as though the devil was behind you.'

'Ran? I ran? You and yours went meekly off to the black moor at Locheport, from what you told me yourself.'

'We none of us had a choice. Had you a choice?'

'Then why are you blaming me for running, as you call it? I was alone and you never were that.'

'We kept ourselves together, by the hardest work of our hands and the bloody sweat of our brows, even when Mother died and Father was away in Glaschu, slaving like a black man.'

They were speaking like enemies, hissing across the space between their beds in the small, cold room with its pretty pink paper, pink roses on trellises, a bowl of wax fruit on the dressing table, more roses running round the jug on the washstand. Like enemies and the true enemy was somewhere else entirely. She should have reached out her hand from under the slippery pink quilt and given Morag's a squeeze. The stubborn creature inside her would not do it. Their breakfast was silent and it was hard to find replies for Mrs Morrison's cheery questionings.

For a time they could have been on any island at all. A fleece of white mist trailed over the ragged skylines on either side of the road. Sheets of water stretched away – they seemed to slope upwards under the fog – it cleared and they were only lochans fringed by banks of peat or little shingle beaches. They passed the fork to Hoe Beg and turned west without making a single call.

The day was beginning to glare, the grey of it was turning white. The stretches of moorland were eerie and luminous. A gleam on the right broadened and yellow sparkles appeared on its surface – the channel between the island and Berneray. At last they looked at each other and exchanged crestfallen smiles. Still Flo could not speak. A warmer current was flowing in her now, she felt less resentful and less afraid of what might be in wait for them.

The dunes were a shaggy crest between the shore and the first of the crofts. Had she drawn them right, at either Firtrees or Dunaldie, on those two boards that could be firewood by now? The ridge of heaped sand and marram grass was lit by sunrays, it was a frieze of ivory and jade. Richard could have painted that – he had, in that canvas he had chosen for the cover of their book. She felt herself swither between memories or pictures and actual places, and memories of memories, seventy years of remembering. Her head swam and pounded and she wondered if she was going to have another turn. She tried swallowing – her throat worked easily enough. We never died a winter yet. This had better be our watchword now – have faith in ourselves – believe that we can live.

The graves of her parents were coming near. Morag knew it as well as she and both of them looked across at the same moment, singling out the little topknot of bents, the dune that had been made into a graveyard, miles from any church, thin headstones leaning this way and that like people who knew each other too well to have need of speech. Morag was squeezing her hand. She did not want it. She wanted the whole of herself to melt into a great pouring of tears. The creature inside her was gripping her, stopping her from showing the least twinge of feeling.

Iain Morrison was reaching out of the window and waving his hand. He shouted to them, but they could not catch the words. A minute later he stopped at the first house of several and emptied four bags of coal onto a black patch at the roadside. A woman with a scarf over her head and a print overall on top of her dress came out to pay him while Flo and Morag sat tight in their nest and hoped they would not have to speak. When Iain came back he looked quizzically at them and said, 'I thought you might want to keep to yourselves for a wee while yet. They are new people here – they came in about forty years ago from Harris. But there will be people knowing who you are when we get further along.'

They drove on for about a mile, making two more calls. There were few people about, and several of the houses looked blind and dumb – no gear lying about, no washing line or stack of peats at the house end. On the inland side of the road, at the head of a field full of rushes, a larger house with dormer windows displayed a lettered board – 'A MACRAE. GENERAL MERCHANT.'

'Who is Macrae?' Morag whispered. Why was she whispering? 'The only Macrae was Slippery Finlay the minister.'

'There was a son.'

'A fine come-down, if he opened a shop.'

Iain Morrison had stopped and come round to unload their things. 'Folk generally wait here, to get a lift with the carrier, or just watch the world go by. Alex at the shop will do what he can for you, he has all the threads in his hands, or young Alex, he is very capable. If you are determined to stay …' He looked quizzical again, then said, 'Very well. Now mind, if you need a hand, just give us a ring on the telephone.'

To watch the world go by … On this space where the road grew wider by some yards and there was close-bitten turf on either side, Allan had defied the Sheriff, and somebody called 'the Procurator', when they came to clear the clachan. 'Our place is here.' His words were fresh in her mind after seventy years, his voice not loud but definite. Or had it been on that hummocky green beside two ruins? She shook her head, to clarify her memories. It was not the time for musing. They had nowhere to live.

Would they have to go and beg favours from Slippery Finlay's son, or his grandson? Her father's joke about the minister came back to her for the first time since she was a girl – 'If ever Mrs Macrae gives birth, it will surely have been an immaculate conception.' She had had to ask him what it meant.

They did not have to consult each other to be certain that they would avoid using Macrae's good offices if they possibly could. The day was fine and there was nobody about. They left their belongings at the side of the road and walked down the pasture towards the sea, beside the burn where the women had washed their wounds after the battle. So few houses still stood that the stony scatter among the grass and nettles and yellow flags looked like a burial ground. Would they be able to tell their own homes from the many shells and mere heaps?

'I cannot see it,' said Flo at last. 'I was born in it and my mother and then my father died in it and I cannot tell the place. You would think – you would think – that there would be its own atmosphere still there – a smell – a look …' She ran out of words. She still could not weep and the pressure of it was like killing fingers inside her chest.

'Morag –' They stopped, and sat on a low wall – part of a house or an old kailyard dyke? They looked at each other, and Flo was momentarily amazed that the old woman she was seeing, with her red eyelids and her bristling tussock of white hair, and herself, with her beaky face and her tangle of faded brown hair stained with iron-grey, were not, the both of them, as transparent as ghosts. 'Should we be here?' She had to bring the question out of her depth like a pail of water from the bottom of the well.

For once Morag did not speak readily. Flo looked away to give her time, and saw a long, low breaker rippling first black, then white across the bay as though a line had tightened under the sea and lifted the water like a cloth unfurling. It had been doing that for how many thousands of years? And for thirteen years of her own life here, and she had lived to see it once again …

Morag was speaking. 'Flora, however long we have left to us it will not be long, and I am not bringing bad luck onto our heads because what I am saying is as true as this stone.' She thumped the grey block beside her almost angrily. 'We cannot be trailing round the country like tinkers for ever and a day – my back is sore enough with sitting among the coals for an hour. I am tired, Flo my dear, and so are you if you are too proud to admit it. I believe I know what you are thinking, that there is a curse on this place of ours. Well, there is no such thing. The potatoes failed when we were little but that is all as past and done with as the seven plagues of Egypt. And the clearance was none of our doing. We *fought* with them, Flo, the constables and the drunken bully-boys from along the coast. We did not want to be banished then and no more do I now.' She had taken Flo by the arm and half-turned her, forcing her to attend. 'Look – will you look, my dear? Who was desperate to come here? It is not all ruins, and maybe there is room for us. I want that place.'

She sounded like a child choosing an apple. Her finger was pointing at a longer house than most of the old ones, with a kind of double byre built onto its end, not far above the high-tide mark.

'The MacPhails'.'

'I thought it was. Do you remember, Flo, you were sweet on young Roddy, and your mother sheltered him when his father tried to beat him like a beast? Between drink and religion they were a pair of demons, Roderick and Morag. How did Roddy spring from such a couple? I would have died for an hour with him. But he would only look at you.'

'The Sheriff's men tore out their roof. So why is it thatched? There must be somebody in it yet.'

They walked down to the house between the nettle-beds and the slim shoots and blades of the flags. It seemed to be deserted. The cobwebs inside the glass of the two small windows at the front were woven so thickly that they could not see in. No hens or tools or boots, let alone a washing-line or the barking of a dog. The thatch was rank with weeds, gaunt rusty sorrel that rattled in the breeze. Morag tried the sneck of the door and it grated open, the door budged and then jarred over the stones of the floor inside.

On the oilcloth of the living-room table stood a white cup with the scum of the drink dried and brown inside it. Beside it was a paraffin lamp, the glass shade streaked with soot. There were a few powdery ashes in the grate. On the mantelpiece with its fringe of fancy paper pinned on with rusty tacks there were two postcards. A man in a soldier's tunic and a hat with a flat brim and a pointed crown, smiling awkwardly at the photographer. A city at night, tall towers with rows of lit-up windows and fireworks filling the sky with curves and bursts of orange and yellow sparks, which had been tinted in with streaks of garish colour. On the one it said 'Royal Canadian Mounted Policeman Alexander MacLean', on the other 'Toronto Great Exhibition 1908'.

Morag looked quickly behind them, saw blue-black writing and Canadian stamps with the head of King Edward VII, and replaced them on the thick dust of the shelf.

'Why did they leave, I wonder?'

'Why have some of their family not come back and cleared the place out?'

They looked round eerily, as though the owner might be standing in the doorway or the clumping and lowing of a cow might sound from the other side of the wall.

'Whoever it is will have gone to the war, and his family will be staying with the old folk.'

Flo sat down on a stool, feeling spent, and looked round the room. She had never expected to see glass in a Skellor window, or a solid wall between the room and the animals, or an iron range in the fireplace. There was a long cushion on the bench against the back wall. It looked made for company. A faint smell of mouldering hay tinged the air, or was it mildew from the furniture? No stink that wild animals might have made, or a rotting carcase. The place clothed them like an accustomed garment.

They heard footfalls outside and had no time to get up before the door was pushed further in and a large, plump man entered the room, a white-faced man with a white apron and white hair oiled and combed in a parting. Alexander Macrae, the image of his father.

'Ladies,' he said with a small courteous movement of his head. 'It is quite pleasant out, is it not? Are you, er, on your holidays? Or, er, maybe you are some of the family come back to the auld hame?' He laughed, and in his hesitancy and his anxiety to manage the situation without offending, she was seeing his father again, the Church of Scotland minister she had never met close up until Allan haggled and clashed with him in the parleying before the clearance.

'We were born here.' Mr Macrae looked round him in a questioning way. 'In Skellor. We have been elsewhere for most of our lives.' She would not apologise for entering the house – what business was it of his? No doubt beneath his sleek white surface he was hotching with inquisitiveness or readiness to fault them.

'Well, well, you are Skellor folk! It is always grand when folk come back for a visit! I saw Iain Morrison drop you off. If you are, er, going back to Lochmaddy tonight, my son has a taxi. There is no, er, public house, of course, and it is early in the season, but Mrs Macrae would be willing to provide you with a sandwich.'

She would have said anything to get rid of the man but here was Morag making the best of the occasion once again.

'You are right, Mr Macrae, we would like to stay for a while. And there is some business you could maybe help us with.'

Up at the house behind the shop, as they ate ham sandwiches made with soft white bread and margarine, and Mrs Macrae lurked silently between the parlour and the kitchen, Morag said with a readiness that made Flo's wits reel, 'Mr Macrae, the empty harp down there – we were not prying – '

'No, no, no harm at all.' The man had raised a large white hand in a show of horror.

'You see, we need a place. We have a mind to live here. There is nothing to tie us to any other part of the world at all. Now, that house – no doubt the family will be keeping it for themselves.'

'The family have long since moved elsewhere. Alexander has been very successful in Canada, very successful – we have had news from time to time. His parents both died in the same week – very sad – that was ten, no, eleven years ago this summer and Alexander was, er, unable to make the journey back. And then the War … I believe he is quite the Canadian now – he has married there, of course. He, er, instructed me to keep an eye on the house until it could be, er, put on the market. There are not many strangers coming through here, as you can imagine, and the place is quite untouched, quite untouched.'

'Is it for rent?'

'Alexander would rather sell, or that was the case when I, er, last heard. I would need, or course, to be in touch with –'

'How much?'

Mr Macrae looked flabbergasted, as though it should have been another two hours at least before money was brought up. 'A hundred – and fifty – pounds.'

'One hundred and twenty-five. For cash.' Morag was speaking with eager confidence and Flo was thinking, all those years at the fish – they have made a merchant out of her.

'That is acceptable.'

So quickly? The man must be getting his cut, he must have despaired of making a sale in this neglected quarter. His white face was glowing now like a candle just below the wick. He went to a cupboard at the back of the room and spoke to them over his shoulder. 'Will you take something, ladies, to mark the agreement?'

Over their drams they arranged to move in right away. There was no complication over the croft because there was no croft. It had been 'detached and re-assigned' when the owner, 'a Lowland gentleman who spends much of the year in the South', had broken up the farms again, divided them into half-crofts, and welcomed applications 'from as far afield as Lewis.' The walled space at the rear had been a vegetable garden and belonged to the house. The contents of the house, 'such as they were,' were thrown in with the property.

'Morag, how can we sleep –'

'I believe that there are beds upstairs,' said Mr Macrae, who clearly knew the inventory down to the last saucer and the last mouse-trap. 'Of course the bedding would hardly be, er, adequate. However, I can supply winceyette sheets to your needs, and feather pillows and cotton pillow-cases – on credit, if necessary – and dish-cloths and dish-towels and dusters, anything of that kind, brushes for sweeping and scrubbing, certainly. The pots and pans should require just a good scour out – the old people were good housekeepers, were they not, Margaret?'

His wife had appeared from the back as though drawn by the magnetism of a deal being done, or perhaps by the rising and quickening of her husband's voice. 'They were good people,' she confirmed. 'Always at church on Sunday without fail. Until the end.'

'Yes, yes, good people indeed. Now, would you be requiring provisions at all, ladies? We have everything here, plain but fresh, and a large selection of tins.'

At night they sat on the long bench in a stupor of weariness. The fire burned low and red in the grate – a load of peats had been dumped outside and they would stack them in the morning if the weather held. Washed clothes hung on a line above the range. Perfectly clean dishes stood on the draining board in the scullery built out at the back. Through the windows, now free of cobwebs, they could see waves spreading under a full moon, their ridged surfaces glimmering like frosty pasture.

'We are not here,' said Morag out of the three-quarters dark.

'We are in Roddy's house,' said Flo in a voice of disbelief. 'He had a soft face – soft as a moth.'

'He will be into his eighties by now.'

'If he is still alive. And if he was, would I know him?'

The red of the fire pulsed a little brighter and they heard the breeze that had reached it, a long sough in the flue.

'When I think of heaven …,' said Morag a little later, ' when I used to think of it – I had a picture of all the folk I ever liked. My mother's mother and father – my father's died before I began to remember things – and yourselves, the three of you, and young Archie, he will always be young to me, daft gangling body that he was, and Roderick McCuish, that Irish-looking man, your father's friend …'

Her voice was running down, laden with sleep. The twilit air in the room, acrid and fragrant with peat reek as the wind rose and blew down the unswept chimney, was full of faces, distinct as anybody they had met that day. The people themselves had gone beyond the curve of the world. Or vanished into those towns which were like battlefields, or so she imagined, tramped through by thousands of foreign feet, bleared by smoke and fire and acid. If she had had children, she would be going forward in a company. This was not loneliness though. They knew the lives that had been lived here and they could summon them up again, cleansed of the pains and troubles that had racked them, the hateful people defeated and the beloved people happed in the contentment they deserved.

'Who would have believed' – her thoughts were speaking themselves – 'that a lord, an owner, would be welcoming the crofters back again? I suppose he has more than he can spend.'

Morag snored, the merest ruffle of a sound, little different from the breath of the wind at the corners of the house.

Chapter 54

Flo looked along the range of her paintings and drawings. Morag had agreed that she should have the byre to work in and she got a handyman from Balelone on the west side to break out two windows in the front hall. If she could save up some of her pension, she would have them glazed. In summer, at least, she would be warm enough. She had done the final job herself – fixing battens to the wall, on which she hung and pinned her pictures, too close together but it would have to do.

She had spent a day arranging the work from the earliest to the most recent. They could have suffered worse in the moves from place to place. Some of the pastels had smudged and the softer papers had grown spots of mildew. The oils were almost intact, the surfaces still glistening like the rinds of fruit. As she looked at her very first drawing, the bean vine, the stone-dust smell of warmed earth came into her nostrils. There was the beetroot plant and the other pastels bright with carmine – foxgloves, poppies, clover. Wally the eel-catcher in a frenzy of black spatters and hatchings. Richard naked – when Morag saw it she said, 'Ooh, Flora, no wonder you liked him!' The cartoons that had started as the bitterness grew in between them – Richard the spoilt god, the clowns and fishermen tormenting women, the giraffe with three legs. (Were Richard and Weston under one roof now, and stinging each other to death with the last of their energies?)

The paintings of cabbage and potato fields delighted her with their succulent colour, the paint set in the wrinkles and clots she had laid on with such relish. The likenesses of women – memorials – Mary and Bertha, their eyes looking out from the paper as though they were still watching her. Faces in the clouds, the womenfolk looking down on the battle, and fighting in it, hands scrabbling and flinging. There were more components for the big picture than she had thought. Reviewing the sheets, she understood for the first time that she had been seeing in her mind's vision both struggles mingled into one, Sgiach and Uist. People getting their blood up now here and now there, and long before their battles some big fight on the mainland, it almost sounded like a war, which Allan had told to her like a parable. Eight hundred people up in arms from twelve clachans, tricked and trapped in the end, their spokesmen, Allan among them, carted off to jail – not before they had made the lairds sign papers against the recruiting. She must find out more about that, she must save the story from dying into the ground.

She had ordered a fine broad length of plywood from Donald MacDonald in Balelone, roomier than she had had before to make space for the three-layered picture she had thought of at Craigpatrick. She would screw it to the end wall as an undertaking to herself that she would, at last, decide it and make it and bring it to a finish.

Smells came out of the walls and out of the beaten earth of the floor as the spring warmed them through and turned into a summer, then an autumn, of long sunlit spells – white sea-fogs – more blue and golden days when sheets of water seemed to glitter in the air above the strand and the little islands to the north appeared to be resting on panes of cracked glass. She could smell corn, bready and dry. The blood and milk of cattle. Their dung, so dried and old that it was faintly savoury, not filthy at all. These were the smells of home. She felt herself hanging in time, as much at the sources of her memory as in her present life. A barley husk caught on a thread of cobweb was spinning slowing in mid-air, blond and frail in the slice of sunlight from the open door. As she stared at it, feeling herself drawn out and away, the light was blocked and Donald MacDonald was leaning a length of board against the door-jamb.

'Now, Mrs Campbell' – he always called her that, as a title of respect, she presumed – 'what am I supposed to do with this?'

'I am not Missus.' Should she explain? Too much of a bother. 'I am Flora.' She smiled at him. He did not smile back, neither did he look away. His caustic, green-eyed look and his young-old, leathery hatchet-face made her feel that he was as sound as a tree or the stem of a seasoned boat. 'How much will it be?' she asked and was sorry at once that she had mentioned money so soon.

'Ach – it is only a bit of wood.'

'There is your time coming over.'

'Time. There is plenty of that. Enough and to spare. I got out of the regiment in the first lot but I might as well have stayed in, for all I am doing here.'

'Are you fishing at all?'

'The long boat is too heavy to get down into the water, or to row it once it was afloat, with the few men that we have.'

'Were they killed, the others?'

He looked at her for so long that she was ashamed to go on holding his gaze. 'There was one lost from Balmartin, one, no, two from Baleloch, four from Tigharry ... And there are still seven to come back. And when they do, they will not be liking what they see. Fine big fields at Balranald, at the *Captain's*' – his emphasis was biting – 'and ourselves living on strips that are a quarter bog and a quarter rock. You forget how poor they are when you are being clothed and fed at the expense of the government.'

Nothing was said for a time until Donald pushed his cap back on his head and said, 'Is the wood for a parti-wall?' He looked round and seemed to see the array of pictures for the first time. He let out a whistle, looked at Flo and again at the pictures, then walked over to the back wall and started examining them from six inches away as though to see what they were made of.

'Well,' he said at last, 'those are turnips right enough. You could eat the things if you had the stomach for it. Now – is she an African?' He had stopped beside the portrait of Bertha and pushed his cap still further back on his head. 'Tell me – Flora – where do you go to buy such things?'

'Oh, an art shop, I suppose. I have never tried. I made them myself.'

He turned, grinning in a puzzled way as though at a joke half understood, and saw that she was being straightforward. 'Well then, you are a very clever woman. Could you make a picture of me?' He pulled his cap down over his brows, scowled furiously, and held up his fists in the air as though he was being a warrior.

They worked for an hour or two hammering plugs into slots in the drystone wall and screwing her board into the plugs. She did not want to explain her plan for the picture – she hated the thought of pinning it to the one place or the one real history – and Donald was content that she was going to paint 'a very big view of the countryside'. He had sawn the board exactly to her specification and when she pinned up the sheets of the ideas she had drawn so far, they covered eleven squares of the grid. If her vision would only come clear, she would be able to fill in the remaining seven with things and figures, scraps winnowed from recollection, grimaces and signs that dogged her like images glimpsed in dreams.

Since they had settled into the house, she had taken to sleeping deeply for the first half of the night, then waking with the early light and lying for hours in perfect contentment, trying out phrases she would letter in near the heads of the figures: 'FORM A HUMAN CHAIN' (words of Allan's); 'WASH YOUR HANDS IN OUR BLOOD'; 'WILL

YOU GO OVERSEA?'; 'MURDERERS'; 'JUDAS WHAT ARE THEY PAYING YOU?'; 'NOTICE TO CLEAR'; 'WE WILL NOT BE MOVED'. She remembered shouting that out again and again, until her voice was ragged, while they poured the basins of milk into the fire and began to break up the loom with their lump-hammers.

Morag's bed was creaking beyond the flimsy attic partition. She called out, 'What was it that Agnes McCuish shouted at Cooper?' and Morag answered at once, as though she had been asked her name and address, 'May the devil come with his angels and sweep you out of here.'

That would be too long to fit in. And she must not be bound by the real happenings. Still, the words of that time quickened her like nothing else. And it was good to be working with Morag, on this as well as the house.

They should be doing more of the practical things. Donald had looked up at the overgrown thatch and said, 'Now is that a garden you have up there?' It would need to be renewed before the winter. In the meantime they were easing themselves into a kind of long relaxation from the whole of their lives. When Donald was mixing cement to make good the stonework round the new windows, Morag borrowed some of it and began fixing sea-shells to the wall. What was she up to? She was overlapping cockles in an oval. Shards of razor-shell fanned out at one end – it was a tail, a fish's tail. Toothed fragments made the fins on its belly and its back. She stood away from it, then came forward with a water-worn brick-red piece, like a flake from a flower-pot, and stuck it on to make the eye. There it swam, luminously pale against the dark-grey stones between the windows.

'You see, ' said Morag, enjoying the astonishment of the others, 'I can play as well as you.'

After a time Flo understood that her wakefulness in the middle of the night was because she was listening to sounds that were no longer there. Horses' hooves on the hard sand and pebbles of the road. Their whinnying to each other from croft to croft. Cocks crowing. The clash of pails dipped into the pool edged with mossy blocks. The rattle and grind of cart-wheels. Had it really been so dumb ever since the clearance?

She asked Donald about it late in the autumn while he was up on the roof replacing the thatch with sheets of crinkly tin. His answers came between the hammer-blows as he pounded galvanised nails and washers into the old joists, which would, he said, 'see us all out and generations to come'.

'Och aye, the place is very quiet. As dumb as a graveyard. The factor put in an English shepherd, so my grandfather used to tell us, and he had no use for cattle, or for much else except his bleating sheep. The word was, if you listened hard enough on a calm day, you could hear the creatures munching from here to Burrival. The goats had gone, of course, and the few pigs that there were. The geese. And there was quite a lack of the human sorts of animal.'

He had paused, his feet on the top rung of his ladder, his hand fishing for nails in the carpenter's bag at his waist.

'I liked the sound of the horses, and the heat that come off their flanks when you were putting them between the shafts or having a good look at their hooves. You could not tease me away from them when I was a nipper – Father would skelp me for it when I had been out at them in the evenings when I should have been doing my lessons. Well now, the year I went to the War, that fucking Captain …' he paused and swallowed – they had never heard him swear before – 'that fucker went round taking the horses from the old people, that was his job, commandeering the horses, and my grandfather says to him, "Why are you not in the army?" and he says, "Because of my bad eyesight they would not take me." "Well," says Donald Alick, "you recognised the horses half a mile down the machair." '

He was looking down at the women in a glare of rage. He raised his hammer and battered it down on the rim of the wall. Sparks flew out and flakes of stone showered round their heads. He was down the ladder in an instant, dusting their shoulders and saying, 'I am sorry. I am sorry. I had better not be thinking of that man. Before the War I thought he was just a drunken fool. When I came back and saw Father thinned away to nothing, with his cough and his wee sups of bread and tea and bread and tea, and looking forward to my return because he knew I would be bringing in the dole, I saw who was at the bottom of the whole jing-bang, and the other soldiers know it as well as me, and we *will have* the spare land that is there, if the bugger takes a gun to us.'

'Now tell me,' said Morag as they sat by the light of the embers at the end of the evening, 'how can it be that we are comfortable here, and the owner is easy-osey and the neighbours hardly know what he looks like because he is never here, and over on the west side the man is sitting in his place like a prince and the crofters would be letting the blood out of him if they ran into him on a dark night?'

'What are you saying, Morag?'

'I am saying, where is the Government in it? There should be an equality – they should make an equality.'

'There is a Board. Maybe the Board is full of Captains.'

The winter closed over them, blae in the daytime, as though all the rain in the skies had gathered into a bruise. Not much fell, only a spitting of cold drops from over the rise of the moors to the west. On some nights the wind rose, a wide opening of its lungs, a dry whistling in the chimney, and they looked at each other with pleasure, hearing no sounds from the tight new roof that Donald had painted ox-blood red.

Heavier squalls in November still got nowhere near her pictures, although she had to stuff sacks filled with old thatch into the windows to keep out the draught. On calm, cold days she took the sacking out by noon and spent the few hours till the sun set with her coat on and the blankets from her bed wrapped round her legs, drawing the remaining squares. Macrae had ordered two large pads for her which came in the carrier's lorry along with a buzz of questions – 'You must be writing a terrible lot of letters, Mrs Campbell!' and 'Are you papering the room, then, ladies? It must be quite the parlour!' Flo thought to herself, Your father was the man who advised us all to knuckle under and creep away like worms. She escaped back to the house with as little chat as possible.

The number of figures in the pictures was dwindling at each attempt. There was no difficulty with the faces in the clouds because they had not troublesome bodies to dangle downwards, taking up space and looking ridiculous. The houses in the middle layer had to be there, they were the heart and hearth of the life – they were what she had lacked for more than sixty years. She overcame the want of room by placing them one on top of the other, ignoring perspective, and when she saw that this was not silly but compactly patterned, she was set free to compose the whole scene with far less labour of getting it 'right'. On days when her head was at its clearest, she felt like a bird hovering, looking down – it must be like this on aeroplanes – the entire world laid out.

The crest of the dunes was now too 'near' the topmost house – no bother, everybody knew that the sea could not be falling straight down into the chimneys like a waterfall. As for the battle itself ... This was turning out to be the hardest thing. It loomed in her mind like the slope of a storm sea bearing down on you. The thought of it – of making five figures, seven at most, look like a crowd – it was too much for her brain, her hands, it haunted her so that she failed to hear Morag speaking to her at the table or when they were out putting a turf roof on the peat-stack. No, the fighting among the houses must stay as it was when she thought of it in the bothy at Dunaldie. A loom coming out through the doorway, its clumsy timbers jutting. Another doorway making a frame round the person (woman or man) clinging to the jamb, the clutching fingers impossibly large, knuckling the looker's eyes. Two roofs, not more, with pink and orange flames springing upwards like triangles cut from red-hot metal.

The six squares at the foot of the picture remained to be filled with figures, or limbs of them. Cooper, his beard black spikes, his arm ending in another black spike of a pen, writing down the names of the resisters. Morag, her hand flinging a dripping stone, balanced on her foremost foot like a dancer. A man whose head bulked straight down into his shoulders, his hair cropped like a convict, no visible eyes, a hen crushed in his hand – she would paint it in a splintering and gouting of pure crimson-lake.

This left Roddy and Allan. She knew she could not paint Roddy handcuffed, or Allan like a timber smashed to the ground, half-buried in wreckage, without collapsing in tears, whether for grief or in chagrin that she could not do justice to their faces. She remembered them. She thought she did. She went out and along to the room, where Morag was simmering barley and onions for their broth, and said to her, 'Roddy's eyebrows met above his nose, and he had plenty of hair and his mouth was wide and turned down at the corners. But was he tall? Was he broad-built?'

'Make him a hero.'

'And what do they look like?'

'Bonny. As bonny as you like. Show him *dragging* the villain who is chaining him.'

In February the coast was spellbound in a pale-blue haze. If it had not been for the pallor over all the country, the curving strand that lapped the headland to the north and west of them could have been one of the pleasure beaches on the mainland where people larked about in the summer and donkeys trotted along. It was sheer, with not a thing to break it except for the dark upright at the far end which looked like a person and was only a mooring post.

'Let us go for a bit of a walk,' said Morag.

'Where to?'

'Along the shore to the Great Stone. Big Alasdair's Burden.'

They picked their way along a thin trod in the heather. In the quietness they could hear the seaweed ticking as the tide flowed in amongst it.

'I have lost the way.' Morag looked ready to cry. Then she scolded herself. 'If I do not know this ground, I must be as daft as they said I was.'

They were among clumps of knee-deep ling and wiry sedges, threaded by little peat haggs thatched by the undergrowth and impossible to see. When they were ready to give up and save themselves wet feet or a broken ankle, Morag saw the brow of the boulder rising like a harvest moon, rough-faced, rounded, faintly pink.

'However did it come to be here?' said Flo. 'It is nothing like the other stones of the shore.'

She stooped and set her fingers beneath the cheeks of it and tugged. It was more rooted than the found of a house. She straightened again, fibres wincing in her back. 'Did you see your father lift it?'

'Fourteen times. Nine times that I can remember, on mid-summer's night each year when we could see by the afterglow.

'Did he get it clear of the ground?'

'He held it up in front of him.' She mimed the action with cupped hands. 'I wonder you were not there.'

'I was there a few times. Remember that Allan and Mairi kept to themselves. I think they thought folk held it against them that they were not married – not in the church.'

'There were bitter people in the clachan, although mine were not among them and would never cast a stone. And there were a fair few who did not enjoy being joined for life by Slippery Finlay.'

Chapter 55

Morag was knitting again – a jersey, taking shape in a steady flow of woven wool from her needles as she walked about the house, or sat at the fire or went to the door to look at the weather – at any time when her hands were free. As Flo looked up from the table and saw her busyness, she was reminded of twenty, thirty, forty women in the houses of the clachan long ago. She shrank herself from the confinement of it, the indoor labour – she was waiting impatiently for milder days when she, or the two of them, could get outside to turn over the garden patch and see if it was fit for cropping.

In the meantime she wrote to Peg at last, swallowing as best she could her qualm that she had betrayed her by not travelling to Sgiach before their final move.

14, Skellor,
March the 19th, 1921.

Dear friend Peggy,

Look at where we are. We have come home at last. We are in a house which is as sound as it will ever be. Glass windows, new tin roof. A Carron range in the fireplace. I look out at the hummocky green ground of our childhoods and I think of the many deaths that might have taken us, also of friendly faces, dear faces, and hating and despairing faces.

Savings nearly finished so we are relying on the pension. Are we reckless? Well, we are not starving. 'We never died a winter yet.' We will have potatoes planted in a little while, and kail. Carrots if the ground is light enough.

Are you both in good health? Have the children left the nest? I would like to see you all while we are 'spared', as they say. One fine day we will get on the boat and come over on a jaunt. Or maybe you will be doing that. You could lodge here and there would be ceilidhing in the night-time, while we can still mind the songs.

Your friend,
Flo.

When she took the letter to the Post Office counter at Macrae's, young Alex turned it round to see the address and said at once, 'I will take it myself, if you like, when I go over on the boat tomorrow.'

'A stamp will do.' She left the shop without looking at him and walked home thinking in a burst of rage, His grandfather stood by while we were burnt out and now he can come and go like a duke and make his bit on every necessary that we use … Useless, rankling thoughts – a bitter cud. Ignore such folk, if not forget them. At least she would keep Slippery Finlay out of her picture. She had laughed aloud as she thought this – cackled, more like. Perhaps there was something to be said for witches.

'Would they have called us witches in the good old times?' she said to Morag in the evening.

Morag looked startled, then her face lengthened. 'They called me that when I set fire to my house.'

'Who did? The bad lads?'

'Grown folk, men and women both, who should have known better. Never mind, never mind. Burning lips and a wicked heart are like a potsherd covered with dross.'

'Morag – if you become a real Christian again one day, then how shall we live together?'

Morag blushed. 'Och, it is only the fine words that I like. Those bards must have been as clever as our own, for all they were living in a howling desert.'

The gales at the end of March reminded them of the most surging days of their childhood when they had been forbidden to cross the threshold and hens had been blown clear away and never found again. They eyed each other as the wind tore over their heads with a scream. The door was shuddering against the latch and they were coughing as smoke belched down the chimney, the blue of it blackened by old soot.

'If the roof holds, we will have Donald to thank for it.'

'Flo, I think you are getting sweet on the man.'

The roof held and the yellow of a mild April shone round them, reminding Flo of the primroses beside her bothy at Dunaldie. They took the spade and the graip that had been left by the MacLeans and went into the vegetable yard to see if it could be tilled. No bracken had moved in. A few nettles and thistles were still standing, winter-starved. The dyke was breached in places and sheep had been in, grazing the grass close.

Morag struck the spade in with a will and it sliced into black soil which had kept the mealy goodness of being turned and dunged repeatedly. Long yellow skeins of nettle root twined through it and she chopped and dug under them again and again, saying between grunts, 'Take that, you devil, and that and that and *that*!'

After the first frenzy she saw sense and began to peel off the turf in squares and lay it along the top of the dyke.

'They will look bonny enough with the daisies springing out of them.'

Flo followed her, loosening the soil with the graip, finding new stones. Between hefts she had to pause. Thankfully, the ground was still quite free and untrampled. By nightfall, when they were too exhausted to speak, the little croft was fit for planting, as even-crumbed as gingerbread. When Donald came mooching over a few days later, Morag asked him outright, 'Have you a few potatoes to spare and we will give you back some good boilings before the autumn?'

He said nothing while moments passed. His sharp-cut face was looking more angular than ever. At last he said, 'You know I would do what I could. We are so hard-pressed we are saving the eyes when we peel the end of last year's crop and planting them instead of whole ones. Of course they may perish in the ground. It is all we have.'

'Have Macraes' got seed potatoes?'

'At a price.'

The women looked at each other, knowing that their store of cash was down to £22 and a few shillings. In the end they made with the eyes from the last half-stone they ate and set them tenderly into the ground as though they were precious jewels that might spoil. Before there had been time for the first leaves to break the ground, Donald visited them again, in his Sunday suit, his face alight. He had brought them kail seeds in a poke of newspaper and an old spade handle he had cut down and trimmed to make a dibber. He stuck it into the earth beside the potato drills as though he was planting a dagger in the enemy's breast.

'Great times, great times!' He smiled fully for the first time since they had known him, showing gaps between yellow stumps of teeth. 'Now what do you think we have been up to over there? Ach, it is better than whisky, that we have got off our backsides at last.'

He paused, waiting to be asked for his story. Morag was looking alarmed. Flo said, 'Donald, what have you done?'

'Made a start – we have made a start. Perhaps it will be a good year after all. We went to look at the seaweed, and it was very plentiful, so we knew the Captain's three old men would be at it, for bringing it up to his fields, so we marched down through the dunes, twelve of us in a wee platoon – we should have kept our rifles' – he gave a chuckle of glee – 'but anyway, they knew what we were after and they stuck their forks in the ground, as much as to say, "We surrender" ' – he chuckled again – 'and one of the lads said, "We hereby take possession of this abundance of tangle which the Lord hath cast ashore for the good of His people," and with that we took hold of one of the bloody carts and tipped it over and the old soul said, his lips was shaking, he said, "Good for you, boys, I am on your side." But Angus Alick had the right idea, he said, "Lads, we should not be wasting this fine stuff," so we *commandeered* the other handcarts and we began to run them from the shore to the old croftlands between the ruins and the Captain's horrible barrack of a place. So what does the fucker do?'

His eyes sparked at them, wanting their collusion.

'Not the police?' said Morag, looking fearful and old.

'Not at all,' he scoffed. 'That man at Lochmaddy will keep his head down and wait quietly for his pension. No, no – the Captain gets on his horse, that never went to the war, and he comes charging down at us but he pulls up when he sees how many we are. We should have kept hold of our guns right enough, and a few rounds to put into them. So wee Sorley, he would punch a tiger between the eyes, he whips a big tangle out of the heap he was forking, it was as hard as a whip, and he gives the bugger's horse a flick on the leg – the horse goes up into the sky and the Captain comes walloping down!'

Flo was thinking, How can this last? What next, Donald – what next? She said, 'He will never let you seaweed outside your own crofts, let alone plant it.'

'No – no, he will not, but he will have to fight us for it. And anyway, we have made a start, because the next day, that was Friday, we had taken all the old men's loads and spread them on the machair at our end – the old swine has let it go back, of course, he has more than he can use, but there is plenty white clover and red in it to keep it sweet, with a bit too much silverweed, although we would have liked it once, so we were at it all day, coming and going, and it is covered all over now, three acres and more, and once it has rotted down we will be digging it in and setting every potato we can scrape together. I hope.' He had come to a pause and was looking dark.

'What?'

'Ach – he came down himself at the end of the day, on foot, and looked out to sea, he would not look at us in the eye, and he said that if we came onto his land again we would be charged with breach of interdict. Now what does that mean?'

'It means they will twist you with their laws. Donald, please keep out of prison.' She was thinking, Seventy years have changed nothing, and the battle on Uist and on Sgiach, and others we have heard tell of in Lewis and Sutherland and Tiree, did no good at all.

'That is all their laws are good for. My father is bleating about the Crofter Act and how they cannot evict us any more. Fine for those who have a place of their own. We *fought* for this country and thousands of acres of it are lying idle when we would be working it by the light of the moon if it was our own.'

He was glaring at them as though they were enemies. 'Courage to you, Donald,' said Morag at last. 'And remember what the Book says – "Woe unto them that join house to house and field to field."' He looked at her as though she was speaking in tongues and left a little later.

The women stared at each other, then went out yet again to look at the vegetables. On the darkness of the turned earth, one – two – and another – a good five rosettes of leafage like green plush were showing, some with crumbs of soil on their surfaces. Contentment brimmed in them – here was the true springing of the year, and their own hands had made it happen. The sheep, or a few deer forced down from the hill by unseasonable snowfall, would have them in minutes unless they patched the wall. They laboured till sunset, fetching stones from the many tumbled cairns nearby – their own old homes, very likely – and piecing them into the gaps, then finishing them with turfs and gating the narrow entry with wooden fish-box lids from the shore.

As the fire sank and cooled, Morag was nodding in front of it. Flo could not keep her mind from racing and pestering. 'Interdict' – whatever it meant, it must be a shackle on the men who were struggling with the Captain. If they tried to ignore it, they would be arrested and taken away. In her picture Allan's words spoke out – 'FORM A HUMAN CHAIN.' It was up to them to weld themselves together. If they did, they would be harrowed under like clods in a field. She had been made to think this so often, it choked her gullet like heartburn.

'Morag!' she cried out in a burst of hopeless protest.

'Eh?' Her friend opened her eyes, aghast.

'Morag, what is to be done?'

'I thought there was a wild animal come in.'

'Morag – it is happening again – people have worked like slaves since they were weaned and now they hardly have enough to keep their health.'

" 'The wicked shall flourish –' "

'Oh aye, we are good at lamenting and girning, but we are as helpless as mice. Morag – I never told you – when I was up there, at the Castle, I had a friend called Mairi Bealista, from down the coast a way. We had fun …' She could still see the petal sheen on Mairi's cheeks, her legs. It would have been sweet to tell Morag about her. She could not do it. 'She was sent away, on a whim of a housekeeper's, back to her clachan. They were going to clear it, of course, and we were creeping about with black on our faces, like spies in a war. It was a war – they sent a battleship. Morag – why did they ever think they could stand up against a battleship? And yet, I wish I had been able to think like that.'

'Why do you? Why, Flo dear heart?'

'Because – och – because if enough of us could think a fiery thought, then maybe … then …' There was still no finish to the sentence.

Chapter 56

On the day the news came that Donald and eleven others had been arrested for 'breach of interdict' and had gone quietly to Lochmaddy, Flo and Morag had gone to Macraes' to buy seeds for carrots and beetroot – reluctantly, because their cash was shrinking as fast as the peat stack. Coals would have to be bought as well as tea and sugar and oatmeal and eggs and salt herrings, and the winter had told them that their pensions fell just short of what they were forced to spend on the most necessary things.

As they stood in the shop examining the plain brown packets stacked up near the spades and riddles and small bags of seed potatoes – whoever bought those? – a low pitched voice behind them said, 'The last carrots I saw in the clachan were planted by your father.'

They turned and saw a man as slight as Flo with deeply-furrowed cheeks and brow and his dark-brown eyes looking out under a thatch of black hair threaded with white ones. It was the crofter from the last house down the track towards the eastern headland. They had seen the black, slow-moving figure of him along the dunes, as though they were looking backwards down a telescope. His face was so like the one Flo had imagined belonging to the hand clutching the doorpost in the middle layer of her picture that her wits shuddered, memories and fancies and hearsay smelting together in her mind's centre. This man – he could not have been there ...

'I was Archie Boyd's eldest. You are Allan Campbell's daughter, and you are the daughter of Alasdair Mor.'

Morag's face was molten with feelings, as her own must be. She wanted them all to be embracing and stamping and dancing. The clothy white bulk of Macrae the elder was uncomfortably near. They bought their shilling's worth of seeds, and the son of Archie Boyd his packet of plain biscuits and his jar of strawberry jam, and the three of them went out into the keen sea breeze.

'I was Archie's Alex. I am just Alex now, because there are not so many who are knowing the ins and outs of the families any more.'

'Alex Boyd. Alex Boyd.' Morag was saying his name like a child's chant. 'How are you here, my dear? Your father will have come back from prison to a black ruin.'

'Och aye. But the Catechist was still in his house. My uncle, Blind McCuish. Because they were terribly kind, you know, and he was a man of God, with white, useless eyes in his head, so they did not put him out. He took us in – into his lair of a place. He looked after himself, you know, he grew his own potatoes, and when I went into the cupboard where he kept his store, there were stones and stones of them had shot and the long stalks of them were coming for me like the bottom of the sea.' He made a face. 'Well, we lived there, and he died, and my father died – he was not very old – and I lived for many a year with my mother, working on the new farm.' He made his face again, crumpling his features still more deeply. 'And then I thought that I might as well follow the money instead of growing thin in my own land, so I was a lot of years on the Clydeside, and I married at last and we came back when the owner lotted the crofts again.'

The bright jingle of a bell broke into his story and they saw that they had walked straight across the road in front of a bicycle ridden by a young woman in a mackintosh with flushed cheeks and a woolly cap on her shock of yellow hair. She barely missed them, wobbled desperately, and saved herself by jamming her foot onto the ground.

'I am sorry, I am sorry. Are you all right?' Morag was in a fluster of apologies.

'Sure. Are you all right?' The girl spoke from her nose in a twanging voice.

'No harm at all. We were far away. Are you on your holidays?'

'A busman's holiday. I thought I would take a trip round the island – I only ever heard of it in a book before – and then I ran clean out of cash so I called my Dad collect and he said there was a paper back home that could use a story about the old country? The High-lands? And this war you guys are fighting against the landlords? So here I am. So where is the war?'

Was it herself she was laughing at, or was it them? Alex Boyd had become his darkly shadowed self again and was looking out to sea. Morag seemed to be at a loss. Flo spoke up carefully. 'There is no blood being shed. Not now. They are just hanging onto a croft or a half-croft, or trying to win it back.'

Would this American person be disappointed that they had no dreadful deeds for her pen? She was giving them frank looks, both friendly and appraising.

'I sure would like to talk to you some more about what is going on here. Can we go some place?'

'I will be going home now,' said Alex, moving away. Flo and Morag looked at each other. While Flo was beginning to feel again the clammy exposure that had come over her more than once before – on Balta, in Yarmouth – Morag was saying, 'There is not a public house hereabouts – some of them are severe on the drink – and we have nothing in the house. But if you would be satisfied with a cup of tea …'

They talked for several hours. The American was Ella Mae Scott. She was not as young as they had thought. The brown of her face and neck was toughly seasoned and a line was scored from each wing of her nose to the corners of her mouth. And she was not a reporter. She studied what she called Folklore and she had been working for two years in Arizona, writing down the chanted stories of the Navajo Indians which told how the world made itself, the first animals, the first people.

'These songs, they are their Bible,' said Ella Mae, and seemed to wait for their disapproval. Sensing none, she went on, 'They are real musical but it's their own music – it would be hard to hum along with their tunes. I'm still trying to figure out ways of writing it down.' She became perfectly still and expressionless, then sang out the same note several times, ending with one that curled upwards and abruptly finished.

'And do they listen to that for a very long time?' said Morag.

'Depends on the ceremony. Yeah, it could take hours.'

'Och well, we used to have to be very patient in church. Do you think the Red Indians will be coming over the water to have a look at some of our worship?'

Ella Mae looked caught out, then amused. 'You are right, Morag.' She sighed. 'We think they're so special, hunters and warriors, with this amazing world-view. But we are all amazing!' She flung up her arms with her fingers stretched out wide. Her face looked nakedly young and zestful and Flo felt shabby in the face of so much confidence, then crabbed and mistrustful. Were the Macraes' 'amazing' in their piety and dogged money-getting? Or their own two selves, clinging to their lives like barnacles on a reef and hoping each year would not be their last? The day had passed easily, with a stir and a spring in it – maybe this was how to live, with your eyes lifted beyond yourself. She remembered, as keenly as a fresh green smell, those first bantering, dragon-fly conversations with Richard, in the studio room with its tall windows pouring their light …

'What do you want to know about the land war?' she asked abruptly, unknowing that she was interrupting.

'What*ever you* want to tell *me*.' Ella Mae emphasised half the words in every sentence.

'We only came back last year. We remember the start of it –'

She was stopped by a knock on the door. Alex Boyd came in and said, 'I thought I would bring you a wee load of tarry boards. To stop the fly from spoiling the carrots. My father would be telling Allan to do the same – well, he was always obstinate, and he lost his first crop.'

'Thank you, Alex. Will you have a drink while you are here?'

'I had better be getting back to the wife. And I see you are busy.'

'Alex,' said Ella Mae, 'can I come by and talk with you about the land problem? Would you do that? When might be a good time?'

'You will be wanting to look for accommodation.'

This was true. The hours had flowed away and here was a stranger without a roof. Morag was flustering again.

'Mercy me, there is nowhere, nowhere at all – unless she goes right round to the inn at Kirkibost, and it is just a drinking shop. And we have only our two rooms in the roof. Unless – could you be comfortable on the bench?'

Ella Mae shifted from buttock to buttock on the scanty cushions and said, 'It was harder in the desert.'

'We will find you a better place in the morning. Alex, will you be thinking of a place for this lass from oversea?'

They talked for hours again when they had eaten, as the fire dwindled from flame to ember. Ella Mae was full of herself and as she roved back through the Boston of her parents and grandparents, telling them how many 'High-land' folk there were out there, MacMillans and Curries and MacMasters and MacDonalds and MacCuishes and MacLeods, loggers from Nova Scotia, miners from Cape Breton looking for a better wage in the U.S. of A., their sisters and daughters working as maids in the grand houses of the fish merchants and lawyers, Flo gradually lost her uneasy sense of being a show or a curiosity and felt that the woman might even become their friend.

News came, with young Macrae and his parcel of newspapers from the boat, that the twelve from the west side had been tried and sentenced to a month's imprisonment in Inverness. They had gone in their regimental kilts and had been told to take them off at once, it was 'a disgrace to wear them when they were convicts'. The MacAulays from Balmore were going to take their arguments for crofts to the Land Court and were 'hoping for a decision before all concerned passed on to a better place'.

Old Macrae died suddenly and Alex Boyd got in a blaze for once when he said, 'I would not let her [his wife] go near the funeral of a man whose father stood by while the lord's men burnt our house down and the loom with the tweed in it.'

Ella Mae was to be seen all over the place, cycling or walking, her knapsack full of books and pens and notebooks. She had been lodged at the Boyds', in the closet between the room and the kitchen. Quite often she took her meal at night at Morag and Flo's, leaving money on the table when they refused to take it into their hands, and they told her what they could about the histories of the people she had been seeing during the day.

'That man!' she almost shouted. 'That madly military Captain! What war did he win his spurs in anyway? I went to his house to interview him – it is more a fort than a house and it smells like a distillery. He looked so fierce at first, like crazy? And he spat out, "What do you want?", like a bullet from one of his little guns? I was standing there on the doorstep and this shower of hail came on, it was turning his grass white, so he changed his tune and said, "Come in, come in," but he stayed stock-still in the doorway, like a bull in a pen? And he touched me *there* as I went past, so I thought, Time to get outta here, girl! So I said, "Maybe some other time, okay?" and I jumped onto my great little mount here and rode back into the real world.'

They would miss her when she went. She was blowing through them like an early-summer wind. She had 'mailed' one story to Boston already, covering the first seaweeding and the arrest. Now, she said, she was waiting for 'the big one' – the coming back of the twelve from their cells on the mainland. 'Gonna be a real big night,' she assured them – she was as much a bringer of news now as a getter of it.

As they walked north along the shore one night, flicking away the midges with young brackens and turning now and again to see whether Ella was coming along the road yet from the west side, Flo let her thoughts turn into words and said, 'If I had a daughter, would she be like that?'

'Granddaughter, my dear,' said Morag gently.

'You are right. But anyway, she could have gone to America, or her mother would have gone, and if they had survived the ship fever maybe she would have gone out west, the way we hear about, with her wits springing out of her like lightning, and taken her chances like a man.'

'We had our day.'

'Yes, we had. We had. Only – I would like to be knowing that there was part of me going on into the years to come, the time we cannot even think about but I hope there will be nobody going hungry, or holding their tongues because they are poor and frightened, or ...' There was something nearer the bone than this which she ached to find words for. She could not, so she turned back by herself and went through to her pictures, leaving the door open to make the most of the salmon-coloured sunset light.

Maybe she could never finish the big picture. Roddy and Allan – she would hate to show them beaten. They had lost, and Skellor had lost. On Sgiach she and Peg, and Maggie and Hugh and John and the hundreds of others, had given the strength of their arms and the skin of their scalps and they had got the grazings back. The Crofter Act had come to pass – the men speaking up for them in the Parliament – and the Land Court, to see fair play, but the lords and the captains would get round that soon enough. She and Morag had lived a little better than their forebears – no famines, and a pension at the end of their days – was this a victory? Maybe she should paint Allan and Roddy forced down to their knees, knees swollen like millstones, and at the same time stretching strongly upwards from the mire.

The room darkened like a fire quenched and she turned to see Ella Mae in the doorway.

'Flo, it's you! Can I come in? I thought for a moment it was a prowler in here and I was going to beat him up.'

'Yes, come in.' She should have kept to herself. Supposing Ella was so clever that she could make little niggles, like Richard – 'The arms, of course, are impossible', 'the humble vegetable' – she could still hear his sarcy drawl.

Ella was peering, giving up on the poorly lit end wall and concentrating on the pictures opposite the door. Midges came into the dusky silence and Flo brushed irritably at her hairline. The American voice sounded – 'Flora, I would never have thought ... I mean, I didn't know ... Sorry, sorry. These are wonderful things, wonderful. I never guessed ...'

'No more did I. I surprised myself when I made a drawing for the first time, and it looked like anything at all.'

'And when was that?'

'Oh, twenty years ago and more.'

'Is it here?'

'Yes. The beans.'

'Not an island crop, I guess, so …?'

Her questions were coming without a pause, the kind she must have asked a thousand times in this work that she did.

'That was England. I lived in England then.'

'You were going to classes?'

'No. Never. I was living in a studio.'

'Flora – can we talk again? And can I come when the light is good? I promised to meet some of the Balelone folk down at Alex's. They are fixing to meet the Twelve with one big welcome when they come over from the evening boat tomorrow. Okay? You'll both be there – okay?'

She cupped her hand under Flo's forearm, squeezed it, and went out with her usual springy stride.

Chapter 57

Flo left her-bed at first light and trod down the stair with her shoes in her hand, to let Morag sleep on. She had dreamed so much, hour after hour of it, that she still felt she was in the midst of some swarming other world. A stretched-out pack of white hunting dogs was flowing over the ground of a green field and across a broken wall, as smooth as sea-foam running into the head of a geo, pale deathly animals swallowed into the shadowy thickets of the wood and all in perfect silence, dogs without tongues ... She was on the outside ledge of a window, in a tower, she was facing outwards and the grey gravel on the ground was forty, fifty, sixty feet below, her stomach swirled, she would be sick before she fell ... She was curled up under the roots of a tree which arched like joists above her head, brown pots of food stood on shelves, in neuks, on the floor, it was water she needed, her mouth was dried out when she tried to swallow ...

She had woken up in a clammy sweat and thought at once of her picture. She had been backing away from it for weeks, as though waiting for some decision, and it was entirely up to her. She had more ideas than the one board could make room for. How to decide? Maybe you did not decide, maybe you just came at the board, the paper, the canvas with your brush loaded and whatever shape it made, that was the one.

She went outside and drank in the early-morning coolth like draughts of water. An ocean of yellow light was pouring out of the east. The pale-gold surface of the bay was ruled from side to side by incoming ripples, each one rising in a dark stripe, the hollowed front of it reflecting the sun in a quick gleam before it fell and curdled in blond froth like churned butter and died into the sand.

She felt perfectly alone, seeing everything happen into being for the first time. She opened the door and took the sacking out of the windows. Her pictures made squares and oblongs of white glimmer on the walls. Patchy pallor where the eleven sheets were pinned to the board. Should she leave them there as she drew the new ideas for the last spaces, Roddy and Allan stricken and defiant all at once? For that matter, did you remove all the sheets, then copy from each one until you had painted the whole surface? Or did you …? She was swimming out of her depth now, there was no ground under her feet, she could only keep breasting forward.

She left the sheets in place and started to paint the figures in the lowest layer directly onto the wood. Two colours, brown for their clothes (black would be kept for the two enemies, Cooper and the bully-boy), white for their hands and faces. The wood was nothing like canvas to work on, the brushful of paint almost skidded off it instead of clinging. When she looked closely at the Allan figure (leg buckling to the ground, arm brandishing upwards), she saw that, as the paint dried, the grain of the wood showed through the brown of the clothes, like the weave of the cloth, and through the white of the face, like lines of strain. It was good, she would not paint over it, she would leave it in its roughness.

Hours passed. She had heard Morag's footsteps – coming, no doubt, to say that the porridge was ready – and heard them go away again. She was aching so much at the base of her back that it was getting between her and the work. Supple, she wanted to be as supple as a dancer. If only she had come to all this when she was young … She made herself paint until the first three figures were solid and complete, Allan thrown down, Roddy shackled, Morag hurling her stone. A tingling was sounding from outside – a piper was playing somewhere, seemingly from over the moors to the west. When she went outside, she realised that the echo had confused her. The music was coming from along the Lochmaddy road.

Two pipers appeared, out of the hollow abreast of the graveyard, one with tartan war-pipes, the other with just a plain black bag under his arm. She recognised the one – Iain Morrison from the Old Courthouse. Behind them, three abreast and four deep, marched the Twelve, their kilts swinging in a dazzle of scarlet crossed with black. The pipers' cheeks were ballooning with their efforts and their music was skirling with that noise which had always stirred Flo and dismayed her – the sound of blacksmiths forging weapons was in it, and a mad iron din that scrambled her wits, and beneath these clamours that fateful drone, like a lament that could never have an end.

A gaggle of children were hurrying along beside them, trying to keep up. Three of the boys were marching, looking sideways at the tramping boots to keep in step. Two tall girls were standing where the path to their house joined the road. When Donald MacDonald came near them, he seized one of them by the hands, crossed arms with her, and twirled her in a few steps of a 'Dashing White Serjeant' before unhanding her and leaving her breathless and laughing by the roadside. At the broad place where people sometimes stood, the cavalcade halted in perfect unison and the pipers finished their music on a ringing chord.

They were at once surrounded by a little crowd, many of whom Flo and Morag had seen only in the distance. A bottle of whisky had appeared and the men were drinking drams from it and passing it round.

'We will be needing a cairn here,' said Donald MacDonald in a lordly way, looking round as though he expected stones to come winging out of the ground, and sure enough, some of the children began to ransack the old heaps and bring small boulders to the spot. Alex Boyd, an acknowledged walling expert, was eyeing the proceedings in his doubting way.

'It is not a funeral, Donald,' he said. 'In times to come you will have them thinking there was a coffin resting here.' He then began to pick out stones from the children's hoard and set them onto the turf in a circular found.

Ella Mae had laid her bike down on the turf with a final jubilant ringing of her bell and was snapping the scene with a little black camera. A short, paunchy man, who looked almost too old to have been in the War, had stepped forward out of the huddle. He posed briefly for the camera with a lift of his chin, took off his soldier's bonnet, baring a head of orange hair as stiff as a brush, and began to speak in a steely baritone.

'He looks like a MacVicar from Claddach,' Morag was whispering. 'I never heard that the MacVicars were bards.'

'A hundred salutes to the Skellor folk,'

the man was declaiming in throaty, drawn-out notes that made Flo's skin quicken from her scalp right down her back –

'From a bard of the people of Claddach.
It is a pity I was not with you
When the dogs were driving you over the ocean.

Twenty smokes rose from the clachan –
They were not from your hearths.
Your houses warm with kindness
Were left for the snipe and the crow.

I will not be happy
Until I see the Captain's windows
Empty and black as the night
And the corners of his house collapsing.

Folk of my heart, we are marching now
To the music of the chanter.
We will take the plough from the cross-beams
And turn the arable land again.

The low land will sprout with corn
For the growing generation
Now that Black Cooper and his ewes
Have been banished to the mainland.'

Everybody was clapping and calling out. There was a lull after that and Alex resumed his building. They must do something – dance, or sing, or storm the Captain's house. The pipers were blowing up their bags and tuning their chanters. To music that had more the snap of a reel in it than the tread of a march, the Twelve set off again, surrounded by nearly everybody in Skellor who could walk, and headed west towards the croftlands of Claddach, Paiblesgarry, and Balemore.

Before they had reached the watershed, Flo was stopped by a stitch that bit into her side and shortened her breath. With dread she remembered that Mairi her mother's last illness had come on like this. Morag would have turned back with her but she made her carry on and took refuge herself among her pictures. She must do as much to the big one as she could before … No need for panic fear – death was inconceivable – had Allan known, on the morning of the Battle, that before the sun set …

She steadied herself by tidying up, cleaning her brushes in turpentine, and looking over her paints to see what might contrast most vividly with those first figures. They made a turbulent, earth-coloured element all along the ground of the picture, the land arising in waves, throwing out limbs. Were they persons enough? Each face, the Roddy figure enraged, the Allan figure in agony and resistance, the Morag figure in a glare of accusation, consumed by effort, was a sharp-cut mask, with those lines grained down or across it. They looked themselves and more than themselves. It is what I meant, she thought, in a pulse of excitement.

By the time Morag came back, as the afterglow paled in the north, she had ruled squares of the exact size onto the board in the faintest pencil and brushed in the shapes of the uppermost layer, the heads above the dunes, with a brush barely dipped in grey. To have painted freehand would have been nice. As it was, she scale of what she was doing was like a great drowning medium overbearing her, which she must grapple down and steer through to a finish.

'Are you well, dear heart?' Morag was saying, seeing that her words were reaching Flo through some hindering veil.

'I am fine. Just fine.' They embraced and Flo smelt bonfire smoke and whisky.

Morag sat down heavily on a stool. 'What a night, Flo. What a night.'

She laughed, then sighed. 'I am far and away too old for it.'

'Morag, you were in your seventh heaven. Who was there?'

'Everybody. I did not know the most of them, although there were faces ... Flo –' Her head swung round as though on a hinge and for a moment she seemed to lose her thread. 'Flo – do you mind a tall young man who had a grand head for poetry? Iain ... Iain ...'

'Iain Alasdair MacDonald. From Boreray.'

'There was a man with a white beard, sitting on a chair they carried out for him. I think it was Iain Alasdair. I should have gone up and spoken. The noise – there were four more pipers came up from down by Clachan, and a Berneray man with a mouth-organ – Flo, he made it weep, and sing and lilt, and talk, nearabout. Then he played a slow air, one of the pipers joined him on the chanter and they set my heart crossways. Mostly it was jigs and reels, of course, and you should have seen Donald – he was like a devil, jumping up and down between two bonfires, and his feet going like – like ... The green eyes of him, glaring in his head. It will take a strong woman to get into bed with that one.'

'There are too many men unmarried.'

'Just what I thought when the wee bard talked about corn for the growing generation. He said his poem all over again, and they were all speechifying, and the more they were taking drams the longer they stood up there, saying everything seven times. There was one of the Twelve, one of the Balemore MacDonalds, and he was fit to fight the war all over again. "They promised us," he kept saying, "*they* promised us," and he was throwing his arm to the east, "*they* promised us that the land from which out forefathers were cleared would be placed in our hands again. And what has happened?" And we were all roaring "Nothing!", and an old man beside me says "Bugger all," and Sandy MacDonald booms out louder than ever, "While we were on the bloody fields of Flanders nothing was too good for us, we were going to be living in a bed of roses. There were one hundred and sixty-three went from this parish and there are not fifty have seen their homes again or ever will. They tell us we are heroes. Well, heroes need homes, and crofts to go with them, not a wage from a lord, dragging the deer out of the hill for him or mending his fences. *Fences*!" he says, as though he was spitting out an evil word. "I know what I would do with the Captain's fences," and he threw a stob into the bonfire like a spear. The sparks were tailing upward like the picture of a comet and the fog above us was as red as the end of the world.'

'I should have been there. Never mind – the men are home again. What will they do now, I wonder?'

'Wake up with sore heads. Ach, they will get potatoes in the autumn from the machair they have turned but they will still need the wage.'

'A wage and a piece of land on their own doorsteps. I think I have been a wanderer all my days.'

Morag had keeled further and further sideways until her head had come to rest against the painting of the new potatoes, pushing it sideways on its nail. 'I can still see the glow of it through my eyelids,' she said in the voice of a wondering child.

'Go to your bed now or your joints will be cracking in the morning.'

In the morning Flo was awake again not long after sunrise and wishing that the doorway of her studio faced east, or south, better, to give her a true sight of her work. At least she could finish the brushing in of the uppermost shapes and leave the full painting of that layer for the best light of the afternoon. She was not weary, she was not hungry, she was on her own between the present and the past, with not the least bother about whatever was to come. Painting time was like no other time, there were no hours in it, nothing but the shape that was about to grow out of the one you had just made.

When her back ached so much that it distracted her, she treated a noise outside as an excuse for putting down her brushes and palette and going into the fresh air for a long easing of her backbone and her ribs. Ella Mae was laying down her bike with care on the hard ground in front of the house.

'I was afraid you might still be asleep.'

'Morag is sleeping – sleeping it off – they had the ceilidh of their lives on the west side.'

'Flora, I was there. I danced so much. They are demons, those guys – I think they do it just to faze you? The more you try to keep up, the faster they play, and guess who wins! You missed yourself.'

'Well – I was never a dancer, although I like to hear the music.'

'You must have the one clear head on the island today. Are you busy right now?'

'I think I will be busy for a year. When I have made the picture, I think I will want to unmake it and do it again in a better way.'

'What will you do with it in the end?'

'Oh – it will be there. It will last a bittie longer than me.'

'I guess we should all leave something. I would just love to look after your work when –' She stopped, and blushed.

Flo smiled and said, 'That is all right. I know I am very old. I do not mind being old because if you are, then you know what has happened.'

'You must have so many stories …' Ella had sat down on one of the big stones that rounded out from the foot of the wall.

'You will get sore sitting there. Let us get the bench.'

Between the two of them they lifted out the bench from the room and set it facing the sun, or where the sun would have been if a haze had not come whitening over the day. Flo went back in to make tea and when she came out with it Ella had fetched a reporter's notebook from the saddlebag of her bike and placed it, open, at her side.

'Flora,' she said, 'when I came here, I thought I was on the trail of hot news. And sure it was hot last night. But what do I know? Land raids – court cases – headline stuff. Well, I love it here – Alex and Kirsty have been real hospitable – why, they seem to think I might stay on. Do you know what Alex said last night? He said, "It will be fine to have another pair of hands when we are bringing in the hay."' She laughed, between surprise and glee. 'So, nights, when we all get chatting and the lights are low, I sometimes ask him – ever the reporter – "Alex, how much do you remember about the Clearances?" But he was only a toddler at the time. And Kirsty does not like it – she gives him a look and says, "There are things they do not like thinking about too much." She still calls the islanders, "they", after how many years?'

'Some will talk about it and some will not. Some of them keep it gripped into themselves until it festers, and some of the fiery ones are almost proud of it.'

'And you?'

'I like to know things.'

'You must have known a lot – seen a lot?'

'Remember that I was not here. I went – away. Morag knows more – she was among the families who had to make their homes on the black moor beside Locheport.'

'You went away?'

So she was being interviewed. And why not? She would pretend nothing, mention nothing she had not seen for herself, and if it was not historical enough for this bright young woman, so be it – there would be history enough in her picture.

'After the burial of Allan my father,' she began, 'next to Mairi my mother's grave, in the sand of the dunes, I was fleeing eastward across the island from my burnt-out home. I was scooping raw meal into my mouth from a bag that I had, and washing it down with water from the burn, until I choked on the sour, dusty grains. And when it ran out, what would I do?'